SONIA OVERALL grew up in Ely and later moved to Canterbury, where she studied Literature and Philosophy. She lives in Kent with her husband, a fine artist. She is currently working on a second novel.

For automatic updates on Sonia Overall visit harperperennial.co.uk and register for AuthorTracker.

From the reviews of *A Likeness*:

'In terms of its visceral resonance, Sonia Overall's dazzlingly accomplished historical debut is likely to get under the skin. A vivid tale, part-political thriller, part-potent account of the perils of ambition and desire ... its plot is pacy [and] Overall's rich language intoxicates'   HEPHZIBAH ANDERSON, *Observer*

'Ripely written and unconventionally erotic ... stuffed with period atmosphere and court intrigue. This is a book that wants to ravish the daylights out of you'   *Daily Telegraph*

'Portraiture, courtiers and a courtesan called Kat Joyce all play their part in Overall's debut historical novel. Set in Elizabethan England and with a treasure-chest of detail (fashion, food and flirtation are threaded together like jewels on a glittering neck-lace), *A Likeness* is all about love and art'   *Elle*

'Overall's writing is a potent and rich brew ... *A Likeness* is an excellent, beautifully written and very entertaining novel'
Booktrust

A Likeness

SONIA OVERALL

HARPER PERENNIAL
London, New York, Toronto and Sydney

Harper Perennial
An imprint of HarperCollins*Publishers*
77–85 Fulham Palace Road
Hammersmith
London W6 8JB

www.harperperennial.co.uk

This edition published by Harper Perennial 2005
1

First published by Fourth Estate in 2004

A catalogue record for this book is available from the British Library

ISBN 0-00-716474-2

Set in Trump Mediaeval by
Palimpsest Book Production Ltd, Polmont, Stirlingshire

Printed and bound in Great Britain by Clays Ltd, St Ives plc

For the unsung heroes of English portraiture, past and present

ACKNOWLEDGEMENTS

So much has been written on Elizabeth I's life and times that it would be impossible for me to credit all those whose works I have drawn upon. Despite this, nothing on the art of the period could be attempted without the vast scholarship of Sir Roy Strong, whose meticulous research and infectious enthusiasm has been a goldmine of inspiration. I am likewise indebted to Karen Hearn of the Tate for her work on Tudor painting, and for gathering together the works of Marcus Gheeraerts exactly when I needed to see them. I have also plundered Judith Cox's book on Simon Forman, Mary Edmond's study of Hilliard and Oliver, and Alison Weir's comprehensive biography of Elizabeth. These writers have given me much food for thought: all errors, flaws and corruptions are entirely my own.

I would like to thank those who have supported me in the writing of this book; my family and friends; my energetic agent Simon Trewin and Claire Scott of PFD; my editors Philip Gwyn Jones and Nicola Barr for donning their armour; the community of Hengrave Hall for their kind hospitality, and the Greenwich Maritime Museum for their timely exhibition on Elizabeth. Special thanks must go to Chris and Pru Cherry, in the company of whose charming cats much of this book was written. My greatest debt goes to my husband James, who has been my unpaid research assistant, proof-reader, editor, artistic advisor and the provider of endless cups of tea and coffee. Thank you.

I must also acknowledge all those men and women of the past whose stories I have retold and whose histories I have ransacked. I hope they can forgive me for it.

A Likeness

Prologue

MY COURAGE HAS NOT straddled oceans, nor my arm wielded more weapon than pen or brush. I am no Sir Pip or Sir Walter. Though I know well enough my letters, I am neither scholar nor wordsmith. My eye does not bend to a book's verses; better do I strive to see the tracings of flowers and beasts in a margin. Spare me then my lines, and seek your explanation between them.

In labour as in life, a man must choose his methods. A man free from labour has no choice, for he is compelled to excel in all things. For this, I am grateful; never was my station so high that I should be all things to all men, or by their grace, to all princes. It was my lot to choose, and when I was breeched and schooled and had played my country part I set upon the tools of my trade. I did not grasp for the soldier's gauntlet or offer the weak handshake of a diplomat. I seized at what I knew as my only true merit, and with its possession in my sights I rounded, wooed and flattered it with the tenacity of any seasoned courtier.

I chose oil over ink and panel over paper, yet it may be that no image of mine remains in testimony. There were many whose eyes looked out from my painted boards upon great halls and parlours. Had I not put them there, none might later know them. Such is my trade and the custom that I have lost sight of them all; a number perhaps survive. Often I have thought how some lady in her silks or lord in his doublet might lie hidden in cloister or cellar, swathed in cloth or put to use against a draught. I hold to my hope of their later uncovering – the dust removed and the garments marvelled at. I see how Fortune might discover them, picture some gentleman's son who seeks again his family's toppled wealth. He prises out the loose bricks of his ancestry, removing piece by faded piece the ancient panels. He picks through vermined nests in search of a single seed pearl, he whose grandsire's grandsire was once, in favour, an Earl. That forebear, wanting discretion, fell face down into a basket; so all who shared his name fell further still. The young squire turns about a fireguard in some kitchen room and there he stands: the Earl, daubed with the smoke of chimneys, facing the fire in this world as in the next. Clean him of his dirt and ashes and set him to – for though he has long been licked by flames, yet by my hand is he immortal. I am the giver of eternal life – the Earl, resurrected, is triumphant and whole! His pupils dart forth and, as though still watching, take in all sights. Only in the tail of his eye might be seen the shadow of an axe-head. The thrust of the chin is certainty, the jaw resolve, the lips full-blooded lustiness. They may yet part to utter some treason or blasphemy. The doublet is slashed to show the crimson stuff beneath; the ruff is a stiff white circle, all intact. So might the youth of God's tomorrow look upon that Earl's neck and sigh – *that thou might have held thy tongue, thou might have held thy head* . . .

All that may be to come, God alone knows. 'Til then I will speak of these likenesses as best I might, words being a petty form of language on my tongue. I fall to words, for pictures have betrayed me. Lacking the substance of what I was and what I have done, may this record alone bear the scrutiny of posterity. It was ever so, that what lacked made up the most and greatest part of me. Absence has been to me of such import that I take it now as my motto: *semper absens*.

Pride unsated can be stilled as a child in the belly. A realm without an heir is a barren waste. The precious knots of an ornament, cast in the fire, unravel like twine. A lady dancing at the volte rises high; her partner turns aside and she, falling, shatters on the flags. In all things, as at the last, it is absences we count; for what is not done, not for merit, are we judged. From all great things, save my art, I was absented – now the very fruits of my art lie scattered.

Part the First

One

I WAS NOT THERE when it was done. I did not escort the cart from the drab watery fens to the sharp white frost of my country. I was at bay in my father's house, a coil of ambition pacing the boards in stout boots.

My mother paraded the garden and had the paths swept of snow, for we were to make a great show to our party. My father grew hearty and leered as a grotesque, clapping me on the shoulder and pronouncing me over-hasty to be wed, *there being time enough to repent of it after*. Mother saw to the covering of the dishes, the table having long been set in the great room – the fire had grown fierce, the pressed cheese bogged watery at the edges, and the sweet marchpane pieces gleaned with sweat. My mother strode from door to table, whipping her tongue in agitation at the kitchen girls. *The meats will dry within their crusts*, I heard her hiss. *See they are kept from the heat 'til she come.*

She appeared beside me and took gentle hold of my elbow to still me from my pacing. *It is the lady's modesty that keeps you waiting*, she whispered, preening the cuff of her frock. *It is only right that she demur a little.*

I shook her off. As the sun took to the trees on the near ridge I set off to find them.

I was not there when it happened, yet I picture it to the finest detail. There must have been little time between the event and my finding of it, halling hard over the ridge and sweeping down at speed towards what I feared to meet, training my eye on the scene for the first of many times.

The three wheels of the cart have ceased their airy spinning and the hocks and flanks of the mare have grown stiff and up-pointing. I ride down the ridge and from its height I see the stain of colour seeping out over the white field and the black bank, and it seems at first as though the Earth herself has met with some deep gash and is spilling out vermilion. I come close to the far edge of the field and see the cart in its crushed strips. Beside it, the mare, brown limbs and trunk lying amid the great wood splinters, like some clumsy piece of felling. Wet earth is ploughed up before and after it, and sad drapes of faded blue and yellow tapestry are wrapped and tucked thereabout. I slide from my horse and leap past the boxes spilling out their polished plate and 'broidered women's cloth, down past the carter with his grizzled face and white up-staring eyes, his neck all at curious angles from head and shoulder. My pace is unchecked 'til I come to the bank's edge, muddied and warped with sliding, and stumble down to that worst and yet brightest sight of all.

All is colour, all a vivified array of possibility. All shades and tones are there in their intimate glory, the very essences of life, human and natural, of things stitched and moulded, of the Earth's diversity. As I steep my eyes in this vision I see not the tragedy of a young girl's mortification, nor do I see the death of my beloved. I see the beauty and splendour of all things in their true colours, and in that sight my heart trembles and soars.

Bess lies with her pale face skywards, unchanged but for a deeper pallor. Her hair is of a copper gloss shadowed with darker strips as an early acorn. The spread hair casts a wild halo about her brow and ears, showing here and there the grey hood and fur trim. The staring eyes are still wet and of unbroken silver ash, floating as if on two pails of milk. Her lips are tinged with violet, yet there is still a little of the delicate blush to be seen showing in the parting of them, and about the fair small teeth. Her chalk hands, palms out and spread in open beckoning, lie far to either side of her.

Bess' back is raised with the bulk of that fourth cartwheel. She rests across the circle of wood and metal as though she has but tipped back in a chair fallen from table to floor. Yet she herself is the cushioning of the broken chair, the sharp spokes and splinters of its making poking out through belly and chest. All exposed is the lavender frock trimmed with cream lace where the cloak falls away, and beneath, the skin of breast traced with purple veins thin and thick. Torn apart, the flesh shows such striking shades of blue and red ne'er seen in any paint or flower garden; viscera more lustrous than lapis or ruby, of no gem the like. As the dye of mulberries is the deepest gash, and from it layers of all reds deep and pale, from garnet to gillyflower, darkening where it dries, the cream glaze of bone showing smooth through in part. Around it all – the dull dark metal of wheel, in places rusted; the gaudier yellow gold of ring and twisted locket – the brilliance of white snow, cleaner and purer than any ermine.

It was a sight most terrible and most lovely, that stirred me to a passion and a wonder. That Bess had died so sudden, I was wretched; that she had shown me so selflessly the inner world of her body as no wife might, that she had lain a bloody sacrifice to the revelation of my senses, that she had opened my eyes to the very core of truth, of sight and reflection, of depth and of colour, I was unboundingly grateful.

I took Bess' hand in mine and touched the ring of our betrothal. *For what you have shown me in place of marriage I shall be ever faithful.* So I stood, with my eyes wide upon her, 'til my father's party came with their cries and horses.

My father was strong and calm, his horror mixed with pity for my grief, his hand quick to my shoulder for steadiness. His man Clarke fell from the saddle with a cry and straightway vomited. Others had ridden with them from the farms about and stood agape, many finding their hands crossing, unthinking, over themselves and the party. Others muttered at the slope and wondered at the manner of the fall. Bess and the broke-necked carter were lifted onto broad horses in place of palls, and borne in slow process over the ridge to the house.

The men dallied in the courtyard with their horses and shameful burdens. I approached the house to find my mother in the doorway, smoothing her skirts and smiling. *I heard the horses,* she said quickly, *is she come?*

Bess was borne unwed and unshriven to the cold church, not to return from its sight.

My father stood with me in the great room, the table and walls stripped of all festival.

There is much time yet to find another wife, my son. Grieve and let it pass. You are young.

I'll not marry now, Father, I replied.

Do not think it some curse on you. What has befallen the lady touches you but slightly. You have no fault in it.

I beg you, do not speak of marriage again.

My father nodded, his dark brows meeting at the fork of his nose. *What for you then?* he urged. *What will you now?*

I am even clearer in my purpose than before.

To court? He spat, the word evil-tasting to his tongue.

Aye, Father, I said, *to court; and there to paint.*

Two

THE PURSUIT OF FORTUNE is a weakness in man and it might be said that I was prey to it. The notion of being at court ate at my brain, for I had been long infected.

It was not always so. For some years before I had nursed the image of a modest workshop, myself at my easel, a Prentice or a like-minded fellow for company and assistance at my elbow. Then came the notion of marrying, and with the thought of a comfortable home for wife and family I had settled on moving to the city. There, I reasoned, I would find a stable means of living; in their good time, Fame and Wealth would follow.

Men say that the vision of Wealth stirs the mind in many ways. To my mind She was a bright show of beauty, wrought of brazen colours; to see such a thing a man in my place was forced to travel – unless Wealth Herself chose to make a visit. This She did, and with Her came that disease of the brain that festered and bubbled as sure as hemlock in the ear. Her poison took hold in the heat of my nineteenth Summer.

Before She came Her missives dispatched a warning. First arrived papers, then single riders in tight black doublets, their padding bulging like the parted bodies of ants. Expeditions of men rode out among us bearing measuring sticks, tapestries and cases of silver plate. Houses were inspected, stables quartered, horses taken and put at posts along the roadside. Tempers were lost and honours promised. Nothing was our own, as all folk were reminded – possessions were lent by the grace of God, and could be recalled for His favourites.

She came on the road from Norwich. To see the train was to feel as a man invaded, the army of guards, carriers, courtiers and cooks stretching a mile and more along the route. From the flats of the fields we watched and wondered as this floodtide of greed and servitude swelled towards us. The roar of adulation and awe was great, but not great enough to stifle the whispers of fear. It would rob us of grain, this wave of wealth: swamp our villages, destroy our roads, drown us with demands. For some it brought power, order and preferment; for others it meant ruin, pox and a rough debauching.

Many cried out as She swept past us, our Ship of State. There were flowers thrown, of course, and the eyeing of clothes and jewellery. Folk were struck by fashions, banners, piled hair. We bobbed, bowed and knelt in the dust and ditches.

Never had I seen so many people, things and manners in one place. That Progress was the very city itself, condensed. I saw gentlemen with virile purses hanging heavy from belts and saddles. I saw grooms dripping in the heat, stinking of sweat and horses. I saw the cooks' boys, greasy lads who would turn the meat and feed the ovens. I saw the wealthiest woman in Christendom in the force of Her middle years, and the meanest serving girls in simple collars. I saw variety, and I ached to capture it.

That was my first epiphany, my vision on the road to Thetford. While my fellows dreamed of fine shoes and silver petticoats my nights were haunted by a crowd of faces. I filled sheets of paper with their proud mouths, fleshy noses, subtle eyes. I longed to follow the court to catch those features, to mould the chins and shoulders, the lips and ears. I began to believe that I might pursue my Fortune.

It was not wealth in silver I wanted, for the riches I sought would be cased in paint. To be recognized, approved, discussed by learned men – these things allured me. To make the very mirror of Nature, to capture the spirit in oils and pigments – this was the pinnacle of my desire. I knew then that I must take myself to London, for only there was the variety, the movement, the contrivance and tumult in which I could achieve my great ambition. There, in the flotsam of the court, was the diversity I needed. The ferment of hope, vigour and disdain that was my inspiration would also feed and clothe me, and in time, it would make me immortal.

That Summer passed and another took its place. The faces – their shapes and shadows – stayed strong within me. I could sketch a likeness in moments, pin a man to a page as sure as amber may fix down a fly. The fever of the court still raged in my head and my mother assuaged it with promises of a bride. So it was that Bess was chosen, approved and secured, my parents' final hope that I might stay. I had other plans, and they did not feature the breeding of bay horses.

Bess did please me, she was a handsome girl. I knew that as my wife she would be obedient and undemanding. I had no doubt that within the year I would take myself, my bride and belongings to the city. I was sure that Bess would not alter my course.

I have never been more certain of a matter than I was in those final days at home. Bess' sacrifice was no burden to me – rather, I was like a man who awakes in a state of grace. The revelation of my wedding day was proof enough: I was blessed, for the Heavens had marked me out. I had been given a gift that would swell my talent; I had seen Truth. That I must not err from my path, that I must record what I had seen – these were the only thoughts I entertained. I must be in the city that Spring, or prove unworthy of the gift; and I would not prove unworthy.

My actions were much against my father's wishes, yet he remained gracious, giving me a fine new suit that I may look well at court. A tailor came from Thetford bringing swathes of cloth in a wagon. My mother stroked these and sighed, her greatest *O!* sounding over a swatch of soft scarlet.

That is a rare piece of cloth, madam, said the tailor.

It is too fine, Mother, I said, *and costly.* I picked out less gorgeous stuff. *This grey is better,* I said, *or perhaps the brown.*

Grey! cried my mother. *Brown! Would you have us send you to court dressed like a beggar?*

It is fine enough, I said.

For shame. She turned to my father. *Thomas, would you have your son look so?*

My father grunted. *Black is a brave colour.*

Black? she screeched. *Like a Puritan? Never. Red. Red is a brave colour, and would mark him out.*

It is too costly, Mother, I repeated.
We will take that piece, she said to the tailor.
He smirked. *Madam*, he said, *this piece is a sample only.*
She did not twitch. *So then it will be cheaper. Work it into the shirt, right across the chest.* She pointed at my breastbone. *It will fill you out, dear*, she said, *and you will be noticed.*

With my clothes in order, my mother turned her fretting to my lodgings. She traced the address of a woman who was known to her cousin, who, that one believed, might give me a furnished room. I took the paper with her name upon it and put it to use as a marker for my books. The household was next to be packed into cases, that I might lack nothing in my travels – my mother's trick, to put me in mind of her comforts. I worked against her, taking only those things I had greatest need of: my journals of thoughts and idlings, bound books of sketches and all materials. The best of my wardrobe was bound into a trunk, my clothes for travelling aired, and the scarlet-breasted shirt, with grey jacket and hose, wrapped inside clean linens.

Though I was on fire to leave, my mother so contrived and parried that I was kept at home 'til Spring. Those days I spent in wandering and musing, thinking on my best course. I knew from some friends of my father, merchantmen with cousins and such at court, that the places where nobles gathered were walled and guarded. At first I had thought on slipping into some courtyard and finding a side room through which I might enter; there, I mused, I might sit down and fall to sketching some object in the place, 'til I be noticed and questioned. Then I would show my work and win over any who apprehended me, be taken to some gentleman who was seeking a man to paint him and, thus, win my patron.

As the skies began to clear I walked in the fields. I fell to thinking how the sun brought cheer to people, making them more inclined to give out favours. I contrived that, on reaching the city, I should get into the palace gardens – I would find a good aspect and begin drawing birds and flowers. I saw well how the plan would unfold: the sun burnishing my fine clothes, its light falling favourably across the shadows of my work. A party of nobles would take a turn in the gardens after dinner and happen across me, seated against a tree. They would send a boy to see what I was about, and he would gaze amazed at my pretty pieces. He would run to his masters and point with a trembling hand, telling them directly that here was *some master of art that truly must be seen*. The cluster of Earls and Barons would be led across and I, so entranced by the capturing of some delicate foliage, would be silent and transfixed. I would not hear them, would not see them as they approached; they would gather in reverence behind me and mutter praises. The most noble man there – a Garter Knight – would clear his throat and address me. *Why have I not seen your work before?* he would ask. *Pray, come inside, I must show this to the Queen.*

It was folly, and I knew it. When April came I kissed my father and mother, strode a horse and followed my trunk to Thetford through the rain.

Three

MY JOURNEY WAS MADE in stages. The weather was dismal and the road, all mired from March storms, broke apart beneath us. Two others travelled in the coach from Thetford: a man of wide girth and muddy boots, who smelt of roast meat and slept fitfully, and a widow of forty or more, silent and of sombre face.

We made slow progress. The rain made all about us murky and damp, and the water from seat and floor crept steadily upwards. The widow chafed her hands against the cold. I saw that her gown, though grave and black, was of good stuff, and her travelling cloak was stitched with fine silk threads. I wondered why such a one would ride the roads and studied her features closely. Her nose was pinched with cold, the bone of it raised and tinged with blue. It seemed more beak than nose and her mouth, drawn with long lines downwards, was grey with sorrow. As a woman little over my mother's age, her face seemed much tormented. Wondering at her sufferings, I resolved to cheer her.

'Tis a poor season for travelling, madam, I offered.

She looked hard at me. Her black eyes were wet and rigid as a sparrow's.

Do you venture to London, madam? I asked. She nodded slightly. *I go there also*, I said, brightly as I might. *May I enquire of your business there?*

In the muffled coach my voice seemed shrill as trumpets. The widow sighed.

As you might plainly see I have lost my husband, she said.

I am loath to hear it, madam.

What means it to you? she crabbed. Her voice was flat yet piercing; she clasped her hands fiercely before me. *May that good man sleep sweetly, his troubles past!*

Indeed, I muttered. I began to repent of my friendly feeling and looked to our fellow passenger for relief. He slumbered noisily, shifting against the panels.

My good husband was a slave to hardship, the widow cried, *and a proud man!* She moved insistently towards me. *He overstretched himself and brought us sorrow. Yet I shall endure it! I seek mercy at court. His ill-judged words will be forgiven through Her Grace!*

I sat up stiffly. *You go to court, my lady?*

O yes! she cried. Her eyes leapt with sudden violet flames. *O yes, I go! I will beg unto Her Grace, I will seek the forgiveness of Majesty—*

You know the court? I insisted. *You have been before?*

I knew it, she said. She sank back as one exhausted, her face collapsing into folds. *Ah yes*, she whispered, *I knew it.*

Tell me of the court, madam, I beg you! I have longed to hear about its ways.

I know not its ways, she snapped, *not as you would have them told.* She folded her hands pettishly. *All that is long past.*

Pray, tell me, madam, I tempered, softening my voice. I leaned towards her; the knot of her cloak gave off the scent of cloves. *I would learn of your experience*, I urged.

You would not, she barked, *I see well what you are! Full of youth and hope, a body of greed and lust!* Her voice mounted to raging, her stiff mouth snapping open and shut as she bit each word and tore it from her tongue. *Find a wife at court, would you, marry a courtier's daughter? Ruin her lot and strip her of honour? Spend her jewels and rot her fine estates? Put her people out and watch them hunger? Let her mother fester in a hoghouse? Fie! I know right well enough what you would learn!*

The widow's rage had brought her to her feet and she swayed back to her seat in a swoon. Stung, I waited 'til her breath grew stronger, her chest swelling and bucking with anger. The booted man grunted and shuffled in his sleep.

Madam, I whispered, softly as I might, *madam, you do me ill justice. I am a widowed man, a painter of likenesses; I seek work at the court, no more.*

Fie! the widow huffed again. Her eyes flicked across my clothes and cap, the simple brown stuff of my travelling cloak. Shame prickled me and she smiled, mocking my discomfort. *You'll cut a poor show at court*, she sneered.

I have finer clothes for court, I said hastily, then sensed the trap. *And yet*, I added, *meanness of clothing speaks of honesty.*

The widow scoffed. *Honesty has less room at court than you do.*

I made to protest but she held her hand up to silence me. She turned her face down and began toying with something underneath her cloak. Her eyes closed, and her wrinkled mouth grew tight and unforgiving as an oyster. I heard a clack, and saw the gleam of beads in her lap. It was a rosary.

The rest of the day passed without event. At the first inn where we broke our journey the widow removed her case and disappeared. She did not rejoin the coach as we moved on. The slothful man in boots did not much speak, and after my Thetford road sermon I was ill inclined to conversation. Short-stage travellers ascended and alighted: a serving woman and her girlchild, plainly dressed and ill at ease; a Prentice taking up a new place, fitful and skittish. I paid little heed, watching the tones of country change, willing the soft swells to gather into villages and towns.

I was little travelled. I knew that some craftsmen, securing patrons, would leave the land and take a tour of study overseas. Those were the few who might see the fashioned works of the French court, look on Italian scenes and learn new skills. There the vaulted buildings fostered brilliance: from that rich loam sprang the Masters of grand designs, men who could use all the fabrics of the arts. There every church was bathed with lustrous colour, a sprawl of rich ornament in glass and stone, in gold and gems, on painted walls. My eye, I knew, would relish such sights – yet I was wary of that hot girdle of the South, the cradle of popery.

If I might travel, I mused, I would go to the Flemish court; in that cooler clime men looked to the spirit, set down clear character. I had seen engravings of the Flemish works, and once had looked upon a book of German pieces. I knew of Holbean, a sober Master, who could trap a body's temperament with his pen. He could set a man fast in oils and hold him there for ever – his skill never waxed or waned, but was whole from the first and remained so until he died. As a youth I had wished him immortal, that he might be alive to teach me as he had nurtured others.

To travel would be good schooling, yet I needed a whit of patronage more than a whole world of studies. I lacked the advantages of many, those who had been Prenticed to a Master, or learned their skill from fathers or uncles in trade. My learning had come by myself, by wit and presumption. Only by the same methods would I prosper now.

I thought much, as I journeyed, on that creature Opportunity. I determined to put myself in the way of chance, knowing that when I did I could make much of it. I mused on how my father's line, though far removed as could be from my calling, had yet proved useful.

My father did good trade across our country, his horses being the finest for spirited riding thereabouts. Much hunting was done, for the deer stocks there were plenty. Fine houses with large estates spread out across the boundaries, and my father's bays, eager in a chase, were often called for. His dealings with gentlemen's grooms took him up to the coast towns and, quite often, down to our Suffolk neighbours. One visit of business took him near Saint Edmund's Bury, and into the Kytson home of Hengrave House.

Thomas Kytson of Hengrave had married a papist. When the head of his traitorous friend the Duke of Norfolk fell at the foot of the Tower, Kytson was one whose neck seemed very slender. A subtle man, he could write with marvellous zeal and talk himself out of prisons. When he came home to Hengrave, the best of his hunters had somehow galloped off.

My father's bays were called for. Knowing my fancy for collecting new sights, he offered to take me with him to the House. Mother feared my going to such a place, lest I catch a feeling for the Mass.

Let the boy come, ruled my father. *The Mass is not the Pox. That may be*, said she, *but 'tis as harmful.*

* * *

Hengrave House was locked from sight, as if a fortress. Barns and buildings were set about the walled edges, and Father's horse led us past these to the stables, where we were to meet and bargain with the groom.

In the turn of the stableyard stood great water butts, and beside them a man, splashing at his face. He turned at the sound of our horses and shook his hands at his sides. He wore a soiled apron about his waist, the dust of which ran with muddy channels from his splashing. I marvelled at his rusty hair, which stuck up like gilded straw. His face was hot and grimy.

Th' 'ossman, Master Thomas? he said, tipping his head.

Aye, said Father, *and my son with me.* He pointed to the horses we had led. *We bring the bays, Master Kytson ordered them.*

The man screwed his eyes up against the sun. Trenches of dirt fanned across his face. *Brave 'osses,* he said. *Them cud use sum' drink, n' doubt.*

So could we two, said my father.

Aye. I'll call th' grum, an' w'll blunt y'urn thust.

The man ducked out of sight behind a wall. We set down then and led the horses to the butts. The bays drank deep, nudging against the rim, our own mounts kicking up impatiently. I began to look about.

Where is the house, Father? I asked.

Beyond these walls.

Will we not see it?

That much depends upon the bays, he said. *The groom will choose.*

Was the red man not the groom? I asked. My father made to quiet me as the man came out again.

Nay, lad, the red man laughed, *naught b' a gard'n han'.*

The lashes of his eyes were pale and I saw how his pupils seemed small coral discs set in beds of yellow. He looked askance at me and winked.

Ne'er seen a red m'n afore, lad? he asked.

No, sir. I stared amazed and stupid.

Nay shame. Come gaper, I care n't. I hung my head. *Nay, lad!* he laughed. *Folk'll of'n stare. You's strange to me as I 'ee, n' doubt.* He turned to my father. *Grum's about sum'ere. H'll hie back. Come b'th in an th' gals'll get 'ee sum'at.*

He led us through a low building and unlatched the far door. As he opened it, a great light flooded in.

The house, son, said Father.

I stood amazed. Hengrave was a marvel; its white walls, dipping down into the moat, shone and quivered in the wide sun. Ornamental towers curled upwards from its corners and flanked the great door, the drawbridge lolling forward and resting on the stones. Panelled glass was shaped with diverse colours, and to one side of the door rose a set of pieces cut with scenes and figures. The red man led us about the courtyard edge towards another crossing, shaped from rough boards.

'Tis mos' used fo' th' church, he said, and pointed through a gate to a small round tower.

We crossed the moat and followed him about the stone walls. Set within the house were more glass windows, bearing painted shields. The water of the moat was close and flat, yet twitched with fishes; we kept near to it and passed behind a tower. Here was the servants' place, though grand enough, and we were shown into a parlour by the kitchen. The red man left us with a maid who filled a washbowl for our hands. Father took it and held it out for me. The water was cool and sweet.

Lavender, Father, I whispered.

He nodded. *'Tis a good place we've come to. Speak little, and then only to your credit.*

I understood. My father could speak to men of all places and seem as one of them. Today he would parley with a gardenhand, a groom and a gentleman. He would win over the kitchen girls and woo the housekeeper. His talent could buy us a supper with Kings if he wanted it – yet he would never abuse when bargaining.

When we had washed, another maid led us through the place. Doors and windows branched on every side and we passed into a cloister; here, at the heart of the glass and shining walls, stood an open square of courtyard. We stopped at a door in the panelled wall and were shown within.

The Summer Parlour, sirs, the maid said, bobbing in her skirts. *Ale will come directly. Pray seat yourselves.*

She rustled off. I staggered through the door, my eyes aswim.
Father, I gasped, *'tis a palace!*
Touch nothing, son, he warned.
May I not look?
Aye, look, he sighed, *and handle not.*

I had been in the houses of gentlefolk before but none had been
so rich and rare as this. The window glass was cut with crests
and fishes, and in place of heavy furs and tapestries were green
'broidered silks and gauzy hangings. The room was so light that
the very air seemed to sparkle.

'Tis warm, I said, *yet there is no fire lit.*

*'Tis the Summer room. They build these places by the sun.
'Tis fair enough weather yet for stopping here. The Winter room
will keep light longest in the cold days, and this one stay warm
without heat in the long days. The glass does help it.*

Cushioned stools, tall as my chest yet no span across, were
stood about the room. The table and sideboard, covered in
green cloth, sparkled with polished plate. Each surface held
some crafted object and I moved amongst them: here a lute
for music, there a casket or a jewelled book. On the far wall
hung a dark and heavy frame – within it, the painted figure of
a man, his face bulbous and eyes too small for his cheeks, in a
black cloak and white collar. I regarded him, but his eyes did not
meet mine.

'Tis an ill-looking man, Father, I said. *His face is oddly made,
and his eyes see nothing.*

My father stood behind me. Together we studied the man in his
heavy clothes, which were too hot for such a room, and his thick
thatch of hair, upon which his cap seemed to perch unsteadily.

See how poorly his hands are done? I asked, and pointed to the
fat, boneless fingers which bore no resemblance to any hands I
had seen on man.

A low laugh came from the doorway behind us. We turned
about in fright. A tall, fine-looking gentleman stood there, smiling through a black and handsomely oiled beard.

Sir Thomas! My father bowed, and nudged at me to do likewise.

I am no Lord yet. Our host smiled wryly, and winked at me.

No ale! I declare that these maids are grown slack. I have been much away, and they have had little cause to give service. We shall see to it.

No matter, sir, said my father, though his voice cracked with dust and thirst.

The gentleman addressed me. *We shall find you a drink, but first you must speak frankly to me. What think you of the room, young master?*

I think it a marvel, sir, I breathed.

It pleases me greatly. Sir Thomas – for he seemed as much Lord to me then as any might – stood before the high windows. *We yet have good fair weather, and I like to keep to this room as long as I might. We have other rooms for withdrawing, and the Winter Parlour serves us well enough. Yet I always feel quite sorry when we move there, for the day that the maids air that room, I know that the Summer is over.* He looked across at me. *Do you not feel so, when the nights draw in?*

I like the Winter, sir, I said.

You do? A young man like you, not mourning for the sun! And why is that?

I will be fourteen in December, sir, I said.

Ho! he laughed, and winked then at my father. *So, hasten to be a man then, is that it? And when you are full five and twenty, will you like the Winter less?*

I do not know, sir.

Ah, you will know. And when you are five and fifty, you will curse the damp and cold and your bones will ache. But enough of that! Let us find refreshment for you. Come.

He turned to the door and made to show us out. I glanced again at the ill-shaped man upon the wall. Sir Thomas paused and frowned.

My father is not to your liking? he asked, his voice grown stern.

Your father? I cried. *He looks not a whit like you, sir!*

Hush! my father started, but Sir Thomas laughed again. He came and stood before the picture, turned his head to match the man in the frame and held his hands aside. His chin a little up, and his eyes twinkling, he asked me, *Do you see no likeness now?*

Sir Thomas' handsome looks were dark and slight, and a mockery of the bloated creature on the wall.

I see none, sir, I said, *and little wonder!*

Sir Thomas broke his pose. *And why is that?*

Why, sir, I said, *this man cannot be real! Look how his face does seem to float above his body! And those fingers could not bend, they have no bones within them!*

Son! rapped out my father, his fists now clenching. *How dare you speak so—*

Peace, peace! bawled Sir Thomas, holding out his hands. He clasped my shoulders and spun us both about to face the picture. *Tell me, lad,* he said, *be not afraid. Tell me what you see.*

I studied the painting. It was so ill made I knew not where to start, and told him so.

'Tis hard to see, I went on, *how it was made so poor if a man were really there to paint it from. There is no neck,* I said, *and the collar of his shirt seems stuck on, not tucked in. Also, the cap is false, for if his hair was such, no cap could rest upon it.* I glanced at my father, whose own cap was now being wrung between his hands. *Then,* I said, *his ears are very small, too scarce to alter the fall of his hair, and his nose is flat and not in the middle of his face. See too –* I pointed *– his eyes cannot be that shape.*

Why so? asked Sir Thomas, his voice very soft and believing.

I looked at him askance. *Why, sir,* I said, *if your eyes were that shape, you would not see at all!*

Sir Thomas nodded, then looked at my father, whose cheeks were grown as pale as the painted man's.

Your son is very wise, and most observant.

Sir, bowed my father, his arm sweeping shakily. There was a rustle at the door and a maid appeared with jug and cups on a board.

Drink, at last! cried Sir Thomas. *Pour it here, would you,* he said, *and leave the jug.* He turned to me. *We'll walk with our ale, for I would talk more with you.*

We drank gladly. I refilled Sir Thomas' cup, then came to my father's. He cast me a warning look above the jug and I smiled back. He took the jug stiffly and poured more ale for me.

Sir Thomas led us from the room. *Walk with me, young master*, he said, *and I will show you something fine.*

We followed him about the cloister and into a long gallery, lined with pictures. Sir Thomas motioned for my father to be seated and walked to the furthest end of the gallery. I moved about one side and then the other, gazing at each painted face and form. The paintings here were finer by far than the man in the Summer room, and I stood long before a large and solemn gentleman in a gilded frame.

You show a great dislike again, Sir Thomas said.

O no, sir! I think this likeness very fine.

You do? In what way fine?

I studied the gentleman's fatly folding chins, his frowning brow. His eyes were moist, and his thumb, thrust into his clasped book, was flesh and bone.

He seems quite real, I said, *even to his eyes.*

Indeed. This is my father too, the very man you said could not be real. Do you concede?

I looked again. Both men wore the same gold chain and rings, the same fur trim. *This man has a real head for his hat to sit upon*, I said.

Sir Thomas nodded. *Holbean could take a fine likeness, and this is cunningly made. Have you seen any picture done so well?*

O yes, sir, I began, *nay better yet—*

O! cried Sir Thomas. *Have you now? Then tell me where this marvel can be found!*

I looked at my father, who by now was staring at his feet.

Well, sir, I said, *I have seen Master John.*

Sir Thomas breathed out loudly. *Indeed*, he said. *And who is he?*

The finest painter, sir, I gasped, *quite the best! Last year I saw a jewelled lady he had made. It was in Thetford, when Father took us to Traitor Howard's house.*

Sir Thomas' face grew hot – as did my own when I thought what I had said.

You went to Norfolk's house, Sir Thomas sighed, *when his estates were settled. He was a friend of mine, young horsemaster, and he died foolishly. I do not wish to hear of him again.*

No, sir, I said. The man became a blur within his frame.

Our host drank off his cup. *Well then*, he muttered, *well then. So your Master John is quite the best thing, eh? Well, look at these.* He held his hand up to the wall behind him. There were two fine pieces, one of a lady in a tall plumed hat, the other of a darkly bearded man with chain and ruff. *What think you of these? I have them newly done, with some other works.* He stood beneath the picture of the man and posed again. *Are we two not like as twins?*

I looked from the man to the frame and back again. Truly this work was a fair likeness, yet the painted man seemed sad and dark.

Sir Thomas grinned. *You disapprove?*

I shook my head. *I think it very fine, but somehow sad.*

Sad? How so?

Well, sir, I said, *you are a laughing man and kind, but this man is stern and looks much older.*

Well, so, said Sir Thomas, looking at the board. *It is a sad face. And the lady?*

She seems quite bored, sir.

Ha! the host laughed. *So she was! My poor Mistress thought it very dull to sit so long. And George is not a lady's man. O no!*

I frowned. Sir Thomas pointed to a plaque, beneath the frames, that told the painter's name. *Gower*, said Sir Thomas, *a rare painter of likenesses and well thought of at court. He'll prosper further yet, I'll wager. Will you challenge him?*

I should like to paint, I said.

My father yawned, his hand clapping too late over the great *O* of his mouth.

'Tis a fancy of my son's, he said, rising from the seat. *As yet, he makes only likenesses of bays.*

The two men laughed. Sir Thomas clapped my shoulder.

Perhaps you would draw me? he said. *A likeness of my laugh?*

My father shook his head. *Do not trouble, sir*, he said, *'tis just the lad's folly.*

No, I would have it! Will you draw my profile, if I find you chalks?

Gladly, sir, I said.

And so it happened. I drew Sir Thomas with his glossy beard, his full moist lips, his darkly smiling eyes. That day his dress, though fine, was loose and he wore his collar flat. His hair curled over onto his left cheek girlishly, and this I liked the best.

Well made, Sir Thomas said. *Well made indeed.*

My father's bays were sold and we rode home in silence. My father, much troubled by my eagerness, told all to my mother when we were back at home.

I'll wonder Sir Thomas bought the bays at all, she screamed, *when you put yourself so forward!* She made to strike me, but my father caught her hand.

Nay, wife, he said, and looked at me with heavy eyes. *He was forward, but he has a way that Sir Thomas liked. It all came good.*

It came better for me that Winter, for on the week of Nativity, and my own day of birth, a package came to my father from the Thetford coach. He opened it and cried out quite amazed.

See here! he called, holding up a wooden box. He set it on the table and we poked inside. Within were sables for paint, stoppered bottles, a bowl and grinding tool and phials of powder. Each piece was wrapped in swathes of clean waxed linen.

Here is a note, my father said. He held it out.

To the young horsemaster of Norfolk, from the workshop of George Gower, London. Master Thomas Kytson requests that you be sent these objects for the making of picture boards in pigment paint, in thanks and payment for the likeness you made of him in the Long Gallery of his house.

G. G. – 20 dec. an⁰ dni 1573.

And so I learned to paint.

Four

SOME FOLK, UNACCUSTOMED TO putting up in inns, find more delight in the stops of a journey than in getting to a place. Though I had stayed in Norwich taverns, and further yet, I relished stopping in some new town and listening to the talk.

Not so the night that broke my ride to London. I cursed the horses, cursed the need to sup and cursed the coachman, who, I swore, made the going slower than travelling on foot.

All out! he cried, dropping to the road. *We leave again at dawn.*

The sky, being dark all day, gave no signs of turning to night, and I marvelled how we could have come so little way before putting up.

How far to town? I asked him. His eyes rolled about and he began to throw our cases to the ground. *How many miles more?*

We leave at dawn, he said again.

And then? When do we see town?

Fear not, you'll pay city prices for tomorrow's dinner.

The inn was full of men back from a market, their boots wet with filth and stinking of cattle. The small fire in the corner smoked evilly and gave off little heat. I asked for a room on the road side of the inn, for I had seen how busy the courtyard would prove with the comings and goings of men, carts and horses. The hostess laughed and gestured to the boards, full already with travellers at their supper.

We have no empty rooms, she said, *but I'll wager you can share.*

I had no wish to bed down with such company, and I saw that the woman understood me.

There is no other inn, she said, *unless you hie to Chelmsford for the night.*

How far is that?

O, she laughed, *a matter of an hour or three, with stops for robbing.*

I paid for board in a room already hired by a merchant. The man was not at the inn, and the hostess assured me that bedfellow would be late to come in, if he came in at all that night.

I would like to sleep a little before supper, I said, *so please be good enough to warn him, if he returns. I've no wish to give him a fright.*

He's visiting, she said. *The lady is young, the gentleman old and not at home. Would you say he minds bedsharing? I'd guess he's grown used to it.*

There was much laughter about us, and I turned to see two men leaning against the post behind me, drinking. Their hands were raw and bloody, their faces all grime, and I guessed – and prayed – that they were local provisioners just finished at a slaughtering. The woman poured out ale for more travellers, who also asked about setting down for the night. She told them the same tale of shared rooms, rubbing her hands irritably across her apron. Her fingers were short and red with cold chafes, and I wondered how she had such weathered hands, working indoors as she did.

Could a maid see to the room then? I asked her as she came near. *I would have hot water for washing and the bed warmed.*

The woman raised an eyebrow. *Would you have brandy, sir, or perhaps the sweet Spanish wine?*

If you wish for water, bellowed one of the bloody men, *there's some in the pump in the yard. If you run about with it long enough it'll warm a little.*

Aye, bawled the other, snorting, *and while you're about it, there's some pullets out there an' all. P'raps you'd be good enough to pluck me one for me supper!*

I flushed hot. The woman looked with some pity and told me to take my supper now, if I wanted any.

The maid is run off, she explained, *and I am maid and tapster both until another girl is found.*

The maid was maid no more! chimed the voices behind me.

Pay no heed, said the woman, *but we're short here. If you would eat, eat now, and rest later.*

I took claret and beef for supper, thinking it might sustain me through a cold night in an unwarmed bed. The claret tasted more of blood than the meat did, that being dry and salty, and tough to chew. I warmed myself as well as I could by the thin and stinking fire, which was sodden with ill-dried wood and other matter that I could not and did not wish to discern. More cooling yet was the talk about me, made between locals in loud and practised voices and meant for the overhearing and frightening of the travellers amongst us. One set, on the right side of the room, brayed across to those on the left about their roadside meetings with a roving band of cutpurses, a violent group that had taken up stations between that very inn along all roads to London. The left side of the room, not to be outdone, told how the roads, treacherous as they were with robbers, were safer than the city itself, which was host to all manner of thieves, cutthroats and pox-ridden lunatics. One by one the travellers took to their beds, and when I had endured my fill of local talk and stringy meat I grasped a candle and went up to the room. Within it stood a small trunk, strapped tightly shut, a wine flask and a pair of sodden hose. I crept into the cold bed and drew the curtains about me. I lay long awake, thinking at every moment that I could hear the merchant return, his tread upon the stairs and his hand at the latch. I woke suddenly, amazed at finding that I had slept at all, to see that it was just approaching sunrise. The merchant had not returned, and as I stretched my cramped back and legs I cursed my nervousness and the fitful night.

Tonight, I told myself, *I will sleep in a fine city inn, with a full city belly.*

The coach into town was crammed with folk and their boxes, pressed firm together and each holding down to the sides or to their packages with whitened knuckles. All were silent, save for the soft and sickly moans that some gave forth as we jolted over ruts and troughs. The man to my left was much shaken of stomach and pallid of face, and I prayed that he might quit the coach before he fell against me in a fever. I was loath to find myself seated beside this wretched traveller, his lank hair falling moist against my cheek. I sat as if wedged on the inside of the row, unable to enjoy either the damp dawn air or the approaching views as the sky grew lighter. We would, I had been assured, reach London in time for dinner; I had a childish longing to see the city walls.

It was a long, irksome morning. When I had at last forgone all hope of a city meal, the coach pulled to a sudden halt. The coachman jumped down and, with a cry of *Spitals' fields!*, threw a basket from the pile to the ground. An old woman on the edge of the row stood unsteadily, tucked her skirts about her and set down from the coach.

Is it the city? I murmured, stretching my neck for a view.

Without the walls, said a man, swiftly reclaiming the old woman's space as more of his own.

We took up again, and as we went, so the roads became ever more broken and our pace more halting. I stretched to look above the heads of my fellow passengers, eager for signs of our approach. I could make out the different noises of the road: lightly stepping horses, heavy carts, our dragging coach and the slap and pull of mud and mire.

The coach slowed to a halt.

The Aldgate! Any for Aldgate without?

None moved, save to gather their bundles more tightly in their arms, or shape the hair about their faces. The sickly man beside me rolled his head, the bones in his neck grating and cracking unsoundly. He turned to me, his eyes fogged and watery.

Forgive me, brother traveller, he said thickly, *but I am ill accustomed to the road.* He licked his lips with a thick and sticky tongue, long and pale as a milch cow's. I felt my own stomach turn then and looked away. The man pressed closer, his body dropping with a heavy sigh. *We are nearly at an end*, he whispered. *I pray you forgive me, brother.*

The coachman's voice sounded above us and the horses jolted forward. The young woman seated nearest to the door let out a cry of delight. She caught my eye and smiled, her teeth a pretty row of white whose neatness altered her face entire.

London! she announced, her voice all contentment. *We have passed within the walls.*

Any might have known it by the clatter about us. I could discern nothing above the heads of my companions, though some muttered to themselves of what they could make out: *Such brave cloth, such fine attire – See there! The water pump – I'd not thought my first city sight'd be a bull standin' i' the street – That there's an old old cross, I'll warrant.*

The houses are tight, said the smiling girl to her neighbour.

Too many come here, said one, *and seldom leave. I'll be glad to make my journey back again.*

We jolted through the din, the exclamations of those within and without the coach growing ever louder. The chatter of passers-by and the cries of folk selling wares were marred by the slopping of wheels through filth. As the noise grew, so did the stench, heavy and sour, then sweet with smoking firewood, bread and boiled meats. My mouth loosened and dropped into a slaver.

We drew up.

All out! yelled the coachman. *East Cheape! All out, and so fare well!*

We swayed to our feet. The smiling girl was the first to step onto city ground.

'Tis all dirt, she said, looking in from the street. *Be mindful of where you tread as you come down.*

We crowded out. I thought to begin my new life with an act of kindness and gave the sickly man my arm. When all had gone I handed him down before me.

Take care here, brother, he said from the roadside. *Go by water when you can, 'tis safer than streets and coaches.*

I watched him stumble away from the step of the coach. The kennel of the street ran before me, beyond which rose the open door of a tavern. Holding in my breath, I leapt clear of the running channel, landing on a clean spot beneath the gilded sign of a Boar.

Your stuff, barked the coachman, flinging my trunk to the ground. *I go no further.*

Might you take me later, to the West? I asked.

Here I stop, he said, slapping the horses' necks. *Here I stay.*
How then might I get to Westminster?
On water. By car or cart through town.
Might I find one here to take me? I looked up at the inn. The parchment tangle of a broken wasp nest swung from the belly of the upper floor, which thrust into the street.
Aye. If you care naught for cost nor comfort. He turned the horses and led them into the yard.

I looked about me. My fellow travellers were gone, swallowed by the crowd. My trunk and case lay where the coachman had flung them, soaking up mire from the street.

East Cheape. London. I tried the sound of these words out loud. One seemed curiously sharp, the other bland, as if they were names for places as far apart as Gaul and Gethsemane. The tavern was pressed in by cookshops, and in every door and window folk were cramming their mouths with pies and puddings. Straddling trunk and case on either side, I pushed my way into the swarm of the Boar's Head Tavern.

London fare was not all I had hoped. A mutton chop in thin and brackish gravy, a dish of gritted greens and a sop of bread and wine was all the city found to greet me with. I slopped my way through it, wishing I had walked on to seek something better. I paid my shilling grudgingly. Come suppertime I would find a place where courtiers sat to eat.

I pressed through the streets, the smell of hot pasties hanging about me, my stomach a beast that growled with irritation. I knew that the court could be found at Westminster, in a palace beyond the walls but close at hand. I hailed a car; the cunning horseman listened to my voice then asked for twice the fare I'd paid from Thetford. I let him go and shouldered my trunk, irksome as it was. The crowd was thick with those come out from dinner, the taverns emptying and the cookshops spilling over. Elbows poked me, boots knocked at my heels. One fellow, pushed by the crowd upon his left, lost his balance and fell against my trunk. His skull rapped hard on a corner of it, and he gave me a sharp kick in the shin as like payment.

The palace was on the river – this I knew. If I walked by the water's edge I might find a way through quiet streets. I stopped where the road ahead crossed; before me was a block of stone and I set my trunk on the ground beside it. My shoulder ached and my hose were soiled from the kicking. The carts and horses passed by thickly; I leaned against the stone, and looked for a passage that might take me down the slope towards the water. Ahead, a loaded wood cart swayed to make room for another, its wheels churning up the flats of mud and foulness settled there.

Hie there! Come away! cried a voice. I felt a shove in my back and spun about to see a man's face close to mine, his brows arched in surprise. He pulled at me, then leapt across the road, his hand stretching out for me to follow. I reached for my trunk.

Leave it! he shouted. *Have done!*

I had seen London trickery enough. I bent down by the stone to gather up my things. As I straightened to shoulder my trunk, the shouting man was obscured by the shadow of the tall cart, its great bulk swinging to either side as it passed close by.

Down! he shouted. A woman screamed behind me. I kneeled by the stone, and as I did so a pile of logs rained from the sky and splintered at my feet. The passing cart, spilling its towering load, grated past – its wheels nipped my sleeve, spraying an arc of filth where I lay pinioned.

I cursed in torrents. I cursed with the foulest words I had ever heard men speak as I wiped at the stinking black slime on my mouth and cheeks. I cursed the city folk, more wretched than pigs, for throwing their shit into the streets and grubbing in it. I damned the souls of all carters, those charioteers of the Devil. I raged against the choppers of wood and the makers of axes, cried fury upon the forests of England and all the creatures creeping therein.

I stood and looked about me. None had stopped to listen to my rage; all those who had seen the fall of wood now stooped in the road to gather it for themselves. The man who had shoved me aside caught my eye. He shook his head, then turned limping into a narrow alley.

I lifted my trunk and case. Anger, quick and sharp in my mouth, grew stale and sour. I followed the man down the sloping lane; his shoulders were twisted to one side and his left foot dragged haltingly. I was soon beside him.

My thanks, I said. *You sought to help me.*

No more than the luck of the stone.

You warned me. I stepped before him but he pushed forward, brushing past me. *Will you not halt?* I said. *I would thank you, truly.*

No cause, said he, limping on.

I let him pass. His boots slid and fought against the slope of the alley as he went. The lane was glistening and wet, and through the filth on my clothes and hair I could make out the smell of fish guts.

Then will you not help me now, sir? I called.

The man stopped and waited for me. *What do you seek?* he said, his mouth twisting away as he spoke.

Westminster. I would get to Westminster today.

He grunted. *Through town*, he said, *you must take the fleet roads, past the homes of gentlemen. You will look well there, dressed and perfumed as you are.*

I need an inn, then, somewhere I might wash and dress again.

There are plenty. Here I stop, he said, halting before a doorway. *There is the river, at the bottom of these lanes. Keep the water at your left hand and you will come to Westminster. There are boats for hiring.* He opened the door, bowed and went within.

It would not be unfitting to say: when I came to the river I sat me down and wept. So bitterly I had come to hate my journey and the vanity that had brought me on so far; yet as I saw the city wall and the shimmering Thames itself, my heart was filled again. There were the fine barges tales told of; there rose the Great Bridge with its palaces and spires. Beyond was the South Gate, glorious and forbidding; noble heads, those baubles of men's folly, decorated the tall poles planted there. I was here – I had come to the city and I would seek my place within it, though I be daubed with the stink of a thousand streets ere I found it.

The riverside was bogged deep in places and I made my way as best I could. Ahead, a tarred platform was settled on the mud. I thought this must be a place for getting oars, so set my trunk and case down upon it. I wondered how a man might call for a boat to hire, but saw none near me crying out or rowing. On the far side, a clutch of folk dragged ropes about the water's edge, yet from what I could see they had no vessel with them.

I looked for a place on the boards to sit and rest. The edges, slippery with greenish slime, dipped in the mud; I took my seat upon my trunk instead. Perched thus, all smeared and stinking, I laughed aloud to think of the elegant clothes trussed up beneath me: white lawn, soft brown boots and the brave redbreasted shirt. I crouched and cackled, thinking how I must seem very like a lunatic myself, or as one of the monstrous creatures I had seen carved on the city houses. The river flowed on and on, curving away and out of view; so would my journey take me beyond that bend. Westminster must be there, with hours of laboured mud-walking ere I reach it. If I took to an inn now, put on my finer clothes and called for oars, I would be without the burden of my things and better fixed to travel. Yet then I might meet with some other accident of filth and ruin my suit on the way; better to dress near to the palace and so risk fewer roads.

Resolved, I stood and gathered my things again. As I stepped into the mud a splashing sounded behind me – the stroke of oars drawing closer. I turned to see a boat pulling to the platform; in it, two figures: a brisk and wiry rower and a blackbearded gentleman in a fine blue cloak. The oarsman set the boat against the boards and threw a rope to me.

Hold there! he cried. *Hold steady and give no length!*

I grasped the rope, all slimed and slippery, and held it fast about me. The gentleman stood uneasily and stepped onto the boards; he feigned to grasp my arm for help, then thought better of it, checking the state of my sleeve. The oarsman held out his hand for the blackbeard's coin, pressed the piece of silver within his shirt and beckoned for the rope.

Will you take me to the West? I asked. *To Westminster?*

I go on farther Eastward. I go not so far West.

Then on that way? I looked to the gentleman, who was picking at his cloak. *I have coin also.*

The oarsman looked me over doubtfully, then saw my trunk and case.

New come hither? said he. I nodded. *Aye, well then, I'll take you.*

My thanks, I said.

The cloaked gentleman stepped from the boards into the mud, his soft shoes sucking down beneath the swill. He hissed something that sounded a curse, though I could make out none of his words.

Foreigner, said the oarsman, nodding at the gentleman's back. *Feet's made o' silk an' han's o' lilyflowers.*

The oarsman rowed swiftly. His breath, coming in puffs, made him ill inclined to speech. I pressed him to tell me where I might stop near Westminster, needing an inn to change and wash in, and spend the night.

There's Charing Cross village, he gasped, *without the walls. Set between Strand an' the gates o' Whitehall.*

Set me down there then, if you may.

There's houses all along. I'll show you.

We passed by many fine places, beautifully fashioned and rising up from the water. Many times I thought this must be the palace, seeing the walls of gardens and river stairs.

Houses of gentlefolk an' courtiers, huffed the oarsman. *There's yet a way.*

The river curled then straightened out before us; at its crook the boat began to pull in.

See behin' me, said the man. I peered above his shoulder.

There it was, set amid great houses, stairs running down to the water and the barges there.

The great palace. I sighed.

'Tis but the trimmings, he puffed.

*   *   *

The boat pulled up and bumped against a plaform. *Out here*, said my guide, *an' up this lane. Keep the houses on your right an' you'll come to Charing Cross.*

I thanked him and paid him overmuch, glad to be close to the caresses of soft water and fresh linen.

The lane rose steeply and was much grown with thorns and ivy. As I came to the top I saw a wide road of rutted earth, piled stone and horsedung, from which sprang great tall houses, finer than any merchants'.

I had seen brave places in Norwich town and been much affected by their size and craft. Here though, I caught my breath, amazed to find such beauty growing out of filth and mud.

The houses, like bravo courtiers, fought for attention. They ranged along the far side of the street, their views from the top casements, I guessed, taking in the riverside. Each was solidly built, with the levels evenly placed one above the other, not nailed or piled on hastily like cheaper places. Many were of stone, with timbered porches and casements neatly added, and of the windows some showed designs and emblems wrought with coloured glass. The doorways, all arches and carved friezes, were set with great wood doors brightly polished, patterned and studded. I stood open-jawed, my country lumpishness nailing me to the spot.

I followed the curving road, a great walled place at my left and the houses at my right. Ere long I saw a spread of green like to a village common, and a lump of weathered stone, which I thought to be the cross. I sought the sign of an inn and soon found myself standing before the tapster of the Bear and Ragged Staff. The man saw my face, then looked down at my cases.

Travelling, sir? he said thickly.

An accident of the road. I have great want of water to wash with and a bed for the night.

I'll warrant, said he. *And ale for the dust of your throat?*

Most gladly.

I drank a pitcher of ale, not knowing how great my thirst was 'til it was named aloud. A manservant led me to a side room and opened a door upon a crowd of men, huddled about a table in tight talk. The servant bowed and the talking ceased. I was led through the room, feeling all eyes upon me and my things as I passed by. Another doorway led to a case of stairs, which the servant began to climb; uneasy, I pulled the door behind me. As it shut, the low buzzing of the men began again.

The room was small and dark, but the servant was swift with cloths and heated water. I peeled off the filth of my clothes and set them out for drying; much of the mud would come out with stiff brushing. I washed hurriedly, for though I relished the sweetness of clean water, I was urgent to make my way again.

The day seemed born of brightness as I pressed towards the gates of Whitehall. My mother had perfumed my grey suit as she wrapped it, and as I walked I could smell the crush of lavender within its folds. The scarlet front of my shirt caught the sun's rays, glistening proudly. Beneath my arm was my best carrying case; within it, rolled drawings, ink and chalks.

My horsemaster's nose made out the stink of stables, and I saw a great place for the housing of horses, set far from the palace wall itself. I had hoped the stableyard might prove my means of entry, yet now saw that it clearly would not serve. I pressed forward, the gates rising up grandly before me, and eyed the high stretch of wall ranged wide about. From my river progress I knew what folly were my dreams of slipping privily into a palace garden – even the nobles' dwellings were clapped close as towers. Here was a greater obstacle, and I might not pass but through the gates themselves. I readied myself for the quizzing of the guards, smoothed at my hair and straightened my scarlet cloth.

To my great surprise there were but a clutch of persons standing by the gate, and none vastly armoured or musketed. I bowed and cleared my throat; the gate swung open. Two men in servant gear came forth, one carrying buckets and another wheeling a handcart of soiled straw. They nodded to me and, seizing chance, I took their place for mine, passing within the gates as bold as may be. I nodded to the guards who looked not at me, but closed the gates behind; I made my way roundly about the palace walls, seeking the place the servants might have quit.

I tripped with glee at getting myself thus far – and would have stood in gaping wonder at the fine halls and houses had I not feared closer-watching guardsmen. About one side I saw a great park enclosed, and a raised and covered causeway linking to it. Many stirred about there and I made past swiftly, seeking some entrance to the servants' place. There, I thought, I might pass undetected to the courtyards beyond, and those walls that looked to house fair Whitehall itself.

More servants with household burdens came from a passage-way; I crossed to the shade of a tree and feigned great interest in the sole of my shoe, the better to watch them pass. They rounded a corner and swiftly I bobbed into the passage, slipped along it, and found myself at the mouth of a broad and bustling yard.

I looked on in amazement. An army of folk swarmed about with brooms and bundles of cloth, pans and water butts, while four men, raising their hands above their heads, carried a length of rich carpet through the place.

Whose man are you?

A hand clapped on my shoulder. Its owner, a broad and ruddy man, was decked in regal livery. He kept his heavy grip upon me; his right hand clasped the hilt of a sheathed sword.

I might parry and dodge, or I might speak plain truth. The man's eyes, small and piggish, told of malice and snapped bones.

I am newly come to court, I said, quite gravely. *I am a painter of likenesses.*

New to court? How long since?

I pulled myself up, dignified as I may. *A matter of a week or so*, I said. *I have not been shown this part of the palace and mean to look about here.* I shrugged with contempt beneath his tightened grip. *If you please?*

Nay, sir, if you please.

The man laughed and turned me rigidly about. Walking me before him, he steered us towards a water pump.

Make way! he bawled. *Make way for the brave new courtier!*

The bustling folk stopped and parted for us. Murmuring, they closed about the pump.

What ails, Will? said one of the carpet bearers. *Not the pump again?*

This gentleman is newly come to court! jeered the liveried man. *I thought to show him a fine Westminster welcome.*

He marched me to the pump and held me there, pushing my head beneath the waterspout. Struggling, I fell to kicking at his knees, which brought me no more gain than fresh bruises on the neck.

Stay, Will, said a woman's voice. *He is made fool enough.*

We will jest more! yelled my captor.

Peace, Will. I beg of you.

I twisted about to see my saviour, a sweetly spoken angel of a maidservant, and one such as Sunday dreams are made of. Her hair was brightly fair enough as to be yellow, and her pleading look finally loosened the brutish grip upon me.

Well, have done then, said Will gruffly, kicking me soundly. I stood up and watched him skulk away, head down as a hound abased.

The bustle about me began again. The carpet bearers hoisted up their load. One winked at me. *Rare luck for you that Sarah's here*, he said.

She's the only one can tame him, laughed another. They walked on, carrying the carpet like a litter.

No heed, said the girl. *Now, what of you?*

I looked to see if Will stood near, but he had gone.

In truth, I said, though much of it had been true, *I came to chance my luck at court. I paint men's likenesses.*

And women's too?

Aye; women, flowers, beasts.

The girl laughed. *And are we three alike?*

Some folk are more like to flowers. Others, beasts.

Her cheeks glowed and she smiled merrily. *You would do well at court. But you're amiss.*

How so?

The court is gone.

Gone?

Gone to Greenwich. The Queen left yesterday.

But all these people?

Stayed for the sweetening.

I hung my head. *It cannot be*, I said. *I cannot bear it.*

Shame! laughed the girl.

You cannot know, I said, *how I have travelled! Such a foul journey, such an evil day! Twice to get a kicking in the shins, to be near broken by jolting coaches, river-sodden, soaked in filth, rough-handed and laughed at!*

Stay, she said. *There are none here laughing, and you look dry enough.*

Aye, well I might do now. I sighed. *Is there none left here that want a painter?*

There are yet some gentlefolk left. Come, I will find you a place to talk.

Sarah was much respected, it would seem, for she brought me without hindrance to a parlour by the servants' quarters. She left me there to pace and fret, and returned soon after with two gentlemen, richly dressed: one grey and dignified of manner, the other close to my years, with a thrusting lip and rash, distrustful eyes.

I bowed low, and glanced thanks to the maid as she left.

Well, what sport is this! cried the younger gentleman, pulling at his feathery moustache. His lips quivered upwards in a sneer as he touched the hairs. *Look you at his shirt!*

Well met, young man, said the grey fellow pleasantly. *What is your will?*

I opened my mouth to speak.

Fie on his will! crowed the moustache.

Good sir, I put in hotly, *if I might speak?*

St Peter's wretched bones, he snapped, *how like you that! Pox on his country manners! You are a rare cockrobin, with your proud eyes and scarlet breast. They say that bird does likewise force his way, so pleased is he with his drab grey wings and vain frontage!*

By your leave, sir, bowed the grey gentleman to the moustache, *if this young man does so offend your sight, might you not be gone that I may speak to him?*

Gladly! yelled he, thrusting his face at mine and spitting out venom. *If you would lend your ear to such a knave I'll not be privy to it!* He turned about sharply, the tall heel of his jewelled shoe rasping on the flags; I held my peace 'til the rap of his feet grew faint in the corridor beyond.

Gracious sir, I humbled, bowing even lower than before. *If I did speak hastily—*

Mark not a whit what that young man might say. None others do. Now, to your purpose?

I relayed to the gentleman the tale of my travels, of how I sought a position at the court and came in hope of patronage. He nodded soberly.

Very well, he said. *I know of Thetford and likewise Norwich town. Your Master there, tell me of his name.*

I have no Master, sir. I teach myself.

What, are you not of some workshop?

No, sir, save for the home I left.

You have some papers then? Some letters of introduction to the court?

I opened my carrying case. *I have no letter*, I said quickly, *but I have these drawings—*

Drawings, indeed! Drawings you may have, and talent you may have, but without a letter, no doors will open.

My spirit sank as a bucket in a well. *It cannot be done? There is no other way?*

It cannot be done. Without assurances, you may not come to court.

This is the worst, I sighed, my strength all fled.

You are courageous, eased the gentleman, *and you have come far on youthful hope alone. Be not dispirited. Your chances now lie with a Master's school. There are those that take on painting Prentices for courtly works. You must venture that.*

I am far in age to be taken for Prenticeship, I groaned.

He looked me over and nodded. *That may well be: yet there is doubtless a school to be found for you. Some Master will be glad of such a dogged pupil.*

Kind sir, I said, offering another bow. *Do you know of any such schools hereabouts?*

I know of a Master Swift, he muttered, *though I like him not. He is ill-tempered, I have heard, yet many at court set great worth at him. He keeps a school, which lies near to the old Black Friars' Priory.*

I put out on the road again, towards the city, my best boots pinching me as raw as pride.

Five

MY LONG ROAD TO the Black Friars unwound with little care and I paid no heed to what I walked beside. Instead, I found myself thinking on Sarah, the maiden with the yolkish yellow hair. She was comely enough, and had wit, and I knew that she was such a one as men would court and praise and try to tumble. I hoped these thoughts would warm me as they might others, yet felt no stir in either breast or hose.

Had I so soon forgotten my dead Bess? No, not a whit; yet all my thoughts of her were shrouded by her death, as if a living Bess were some dark mystery, or a riddle that confounded. I had never lain with her as husbands do, in part as I was saving up my lust, and more because I had no chance to do so. We had few meetings and, if left alone, would be ever listening out for creaking boards or a lifting door-latch. The day when Bess agreed to be my wife we had sat ourselves by her mother's parlour window. The sun was cool and fading. Bess' hands rested in mine; she kissed me then, her mouth reaching up and parting softly. That kiss did warm me, as it rose in her; she arched towards me with a sweet, deep moan. The window seat was velvet-clad and we crushed ourselves into it, fighting Nature. Bess' fingers scratched the cloth and caught the threads.

Stay, stay, I said, *your mother is without.*

I care not. She pressed me greedily, seeking out the lacing of my points. I shook my head, yet so sweet was her touch I could not stop her, nor would dare speak more. *I care not,* said she, *I would know what I marry.*

Why did I think of this? Before, that memory had heated me and made me eager for my wedding night, yet now it brought no rush of blood. Was this grief I felt? Or had my oath to Bess removed all thoughts of pleasure?

I felt little loss. Such play as I'd enjoyed was limited, and knowing not what I missed made missing easy. With Bess' death I had seen the wealth of womanhood exposed; what greater riches could follow? I had seen the rutting of beasts and heard the braying that they made. I had seen, when yet a child, a farmhand chase a maid across a field and thrust himself in brutish force upon her. Those couplings, born of violence, slaked naught but violent needs. I felt no such needs, and was glad of it.

I came to the old Priory and walked about its walls. Narrow streets spread out about it and these I took to, looking at each house or shop for a sign that painters schooled there. Beyond was the great shadow of Paul's, in whose churchyard I knew I might find the stalls of booksellers. I would take myself there another day, when I had the time and purse for pamphlet buying.

I came to a place where the lanes ran steeply down towards the river. Many folk cried out wares and pushed their handcarts; one man was selling roast meats on a spit. I looked long at the joints all crisply dripping, and thought of the tear of flesh between the teeth. The man grinned blackly and I stepped up beside him.

What would you, sir? he asked.

No meat, though it looks well enough. I seek a Master Swift.

'Tis finely cut, this meat, said he.

As is my cloth, and I might greasen it. Do you know the man?

I do. The man looked at my shirt. *He's sharp on Addle Hill, just here a way.*

I followed his pointing arm and found the place. The door seemed dwarfish, set amid the great length of the house, though its upper levels seemed to spill and range to either side. I knocked hard, my guts rumbling from the sight of meat and wretched nervousness.

A woman opened. Huge, she seemed, her head bent down to reach through the shortened doorway.

What do you lack, sir? She looked me over covetously, as if to see rather what I might possess. Her eyes bulged grossly.

Is Master Swift at home, madam? I would speak with him.

Do you buy, sir?

No, madam, I seek a place.

Fie, she said, her face falling. *Well, come on then.*

I stepped in. The woman uncurled herself, her head so high as to almost kiss the ceiling. *He's upstairs*, she said. *I s'pose you'll want taking up?*

If you might be so good, I flattered.

O, aye. She led me through the place and up the stairs, her hips all swinging, looking back to be sure I noticed them. As with an ox, they could not well be missed.

The workshop rooms upstairs were light and ran together, without doors. My spirits rose to see what ranged about them: easels bare and furnished, boards and frames, grinding stones and great jars of dyes and pigments. Unfinished likenesses stood all about, with arms and hands uncoloured and naked faces. Pieces of rare cloth and fine hangings were hung across the corners, draped and framed as for plays or pageants, and a chest lay on the floor, spilling out garments. The woman led me towards what sounded a sermon; I saw the backs of men gathered about and a voice raging. We paused; a young man pushed from the group and passed us. He winked at me and bowed.

Papists, roared the voice within, *are the putrid bawds of Satan, yet they have one thing aright. What do we see in their falling down to idols? We see the power of images. Well it might be that these vile sloths worship lumps of wood and golden calves, yet from their folly we learn what sway can be held over those with greedy eyes. What am I about? I am about setting up new idols, yea, setting up the idols that men would have us raise, and pay well for to be raised. I am about the worship of men with purses, I am—*

Master Swift! whined my guide. The raging voice halted; I could not see its owner. *Master Swift*, she called again, *a word.*

Pox on you, Popham! yelled the voice. *What will you now? It's not time to sup. And where's Petty gone, the pisspot again? I will remove his bladder.*

Visitor, Master Swift, she said, jerking her head at me. *Well, here 'tis.* She sniffed and stalked away, her skirts swinging overmuch.

The raging man was slighter than his voice. He stood of middling height, with middle girth, and seemed to be living out his middle years. His features, taken together and placed on a more pleasing face, might have been handsome; his nose was straight enough, his lips fairly full, his eyes, save for a glint of cruel intelligence, light and green. His head hair would have been curling and of a ruddy brown, had it not already begun to flee. What was left clustered boyishly around the nape of his neck or stuck up in strands on top. Beardless, his face was scarcely framed at all. I disliked him at once.

God in his Heavens, he sputtered, *what is this?*

I met the gazes of the group. Some looked amazed, others more abashed. They ranged in age and face; the eldest stooping and simpering like an ape, the youngest gaping wide and empty at me. They seemed a troupe of players, gathered round their fool.

Give you good day, Master Swift, I bowed.

A swarthy man, his long nose quivering with a haughty indignation, stepped up beside the Master. *This is no buyer*, he said lowly. *This is no man come with a purse of gold.*

I can see that, Swift bellowed, *as any fool might do. Have you naught else to say?*

I remark the bib of scarlet.

And? What think you of it? It puts me in mind of some garden bird, though I cannot name it.

Cockrobin, Master? he sneered.

Ha! Yes, Lovett, yes, that's it, that's it!

I had endured this before, and bowed again.

I have come from Westminster this afternoon, I put in grandly. *A gentleman there informed me of this school, and so I come to seek a place with you.*

There was a sudden murmur. Swift brought his hand down sharply on a table.

Enough! he bawled. *Back to work, all of you.* He flicked his hand at me. *You! Come this way.*

I would sooner have laid myself upon a rack than sit through the talk that followed.

I relayed to Swift my tale. As I came to the point of my

arrival he yawned noisily. His teeth, all black and wretched, were oversized and more fitted to a horse's mouth.

What do I care for this? he barked. *Do you paint or not?*

I do. I have some drawings here.

Well then, show me, show me.

I offered him my favourite pieces; he snatched them from me and spread them on the table. A stain from the dampness there seeped across the papers.

And you admire—?

Holbean, sir, and King Henry's Master John—

Dead; dead and forgotten. Any living?

Not that I could name.

Name is everything. Title tells of rank. I am Master Swift, and what are you? A country bird, a cocksure Robin.

As you will. I went to take my papers, but he held them down.

Promise, yes, you have that, you see lines.

I would learn more, I said. *I have such a love of colour that I—*

Love is pointless and it wearies me. You are scarce old enough to know the word.

I have been widowed.

That's well; a Prentice cannot wive. This is no pleasure house for colling in.

All here are bachelors?

All but myself. I am a man of needs.

I nodded, thinking here was one for braying, especially with that ass' mouth.

Then will you take me? I said.

I may, he snapped, *I may.* He leaned back in his chair and tipped his head. *Lovett!* he screamed. *Get your stinking arse in here, you whoreson!*

Lovett straightway appeared and bowed to him. *Shall I show him out now, Master?* he smirked.

Sit down and try him. What think you of these? Swift shoved my drawings at him. *Ill or fair?*

Lovett looked at a piece I had made in chalks, a likeness of my father's face. *This is a man,* he said. *You can draw a man,*

Cockrobin, and seem pleased about it. Pity the man is so ill made. Is that your hand, or Nature's?

Swift barked a laugh. *Well said!* he sputtered. *Answer him, then!*

That is my father, I said. *His face is straight and clean, far better formed than yours will be when my hand has worked upon it.*

Swift barked again. *That's better said!* he cried. *Come, Lovett, answer that!*

Lovett's lips and nostrils tensed, as though he breathed in something sour. *Vanity and violence, both,* he said. *You are a country clout.*

That is easy talk, I answered, *and safer for you than venturing my talents.*

Ha! said Swift. *You are undone, Lovett, and the Robin wins his place.*

Lovett scowled and rose to leave the room. As he quit the table he paused and, smiling, wrung my father's likeness in his hands. He dropped the ruined paper to the floor. *Welcome to the workshops of Master Swift,* he said, and laughed.

Swift waved him off. Turning to me, he rocked back in his chair and placed his boots upon the table. I gathered up my things.

Come back tomorrow, early, he said. *There are rules and such but they bore me. Ask one of the others.* I nodded. *Well, go on now, go away.*

The rooms were bustling with the student artists, wiping off their brushes and their hands. Lovett stood in a corner with the stooping man, hissing in whispers. They broke off when they saw me. Lovett sneered.

I looked round for the door. By it stood the first man I had seen, the winking one. He smiled roundly at me and began pulling on a cloak. I went up to him.

Is your name Petty? I said.

I am he. And are you in?

I fear so.

Ha! laughed he, and clapped me on the shoulder.

Is he ever thus? I asked. *My ears are ringing.*

O, he is like to thunder; much noise but no real harm in it.

And what of lightning?

Ah! She will be back later.

Popham, the one who showed me in?

*Nay, not her, though she is fell enough. But Mistress Swift –
she strikes.*

I see.

You will do. Well, I guess he told you naught? I shook my head.
Just so, he said. *Well, here –* he waved his arms about him – *is
where we work. And there –* he gestured to the floor – *or rather
under there, we eat.* He leaned close to my ear. *In truth, I do not
eat there. The food is swill, and Popham's company a hag-ride
for the stomach. Still,* he said, brightly, *keep by me and I will
show you sumptuous fare. London is a ripe plum for the eating,
is it not?*

I have not eaten well here yet.

Not well? Where did you dine today?

The Boar's Head, East Cheape.

Fugh! he snorted. *Little wonder then. I'll show you better; I
live beside the Mermaid, close at hand. Have you thirst? We'll
sup. Where are your lodgings?*

*I put up at an inn, in Charing Cross. The Bear and Ragged
Staff.*

The Staff! God's Soul, he cried, *we'll get you out at once!*

Why so? Is it not good?

Not good! It is a barbarous place.

It was the first I found. The ale was good.

*Aye, and overstrong, betimes. Did you arrive today? They
must have smelled you coming.*

I laughed. *You are more in the right than you know.*

Well, said Petty, ushering me out and down the stairs. *There
you must not stay. They slit the throats of travellers in their
beds.* He opened the door and we stepped onto the street. *Come,
let us fetch your things, if there be any left. And then we'll sup.
You can lodge with me.*

You are all kindness, yet I would not put you out—

Be not so mannerly, he said, his eyes clear and very blue upon
me. *Truly, I would wish you to. I've more room than is civil for
London.*

I thanked him. He smiled handsomely and grasped my hand. *I'm hungry*, he declared. *Shall we sup first?* My stomach growled an answer. *I hear your thoughts!* he said. *We shall do well together. My belly is a tyrant. What would you eat?*

All things, but better hot and savoury.

That's my good fellow. We'll sup at the Swan and then take oars out to Charing. They make a handsome stew of peppered veal there, though they serve the Rheinish. Rheinish is like to water mixed with straw, do you not think? We'll quench later, at the Mermaid. There they keep a bold and hearty claret, good as monks would drink.

I know little of drink or monks, I said.

Fear not, said Petty. *We'll soon alter that.*

Part the Second

Six

LITTLE CAN BE SAID of mud miring the surface of a plank. So might little be said of the work of Master Swift, there being less of Nature in it than a mired plank, and smaller cunning still.

The panels that Swift himself produced were the very essences of flatness and of dearth. Had Famine himself taken up the brush He might produce the same. Not a single thrust of light or life played upon them; not in all the flaccid strokes of his hand could be found one single beam – nay, less still – not a *mote* of truth.

It was such a piece that, one grey unwholesome Friday, Swift set upon an easel and gathered us about. Lovett fell straightway into rapturous postulations.

See here! he exalted, pointing at the dislocation of the painted noble's wrist. *The angle of the hand suggests movement ere it happens. The sitter is not at his ease but ripe for movement, poised to spring forward with rapier or pen. This is finely wrought indeed!*

A scholar, said Swift, puffing out his middling chest. *Council ambitions, wanted to look the figure of service and duty. It is all there, in the wrist.* He flicked his own contemptuously. *This you must learn, those few of you that have the skill.*

There was a deal of murmuring and crowing of approval. John Benson bent his golden head and peered at the painted wrist as if to discover some mystery writ upon it, showing that he understood nothing of Lovett's praises.

Petty leaned towards me and hissed, *There is as much life in that wrist as in the flounder I supped on last evening.*

The recollection was apt. The fishy wrist of the courtier flopped and flapped from the cuff of his sleeve, a greyish piece of flesh with little show of rigid bone or muscle.

Fishes were much on our minds, for the air about us stank

of some poor sea creature fast-boiling in the kitchen rooms below. The hour of dinner approached us, slow, solemn and threatening.

Another sole flounders now in Popham's fires, I murmured.

Petty rolled his eyes. *Heathen flames, those*, he said. *Ah, we grow lyrical. It is the humour we have been put in, staring at that hapless courtier. We should be gone, to commune with some good Christian piglet. I could rhapsodise until Judgement over such a subject. I could wreathe a hamhock sermon of it.*

Amen to that, I whispered, *though it would make a poor sermon for a fish day.*

Aye, Petty sighed. *'Tis a fish day altogether, alas.*

We turned back to the painted noble. Swift was discoursing on the importance of a man's ears – they must be neat and slight, the better to flatter a beard. Lovett and the simian Falconbridge simpered and brayed in his wake. Neither men had beards, though their ears were vast enough, and strongly vaulted.

On this day of fish I had been four full weeks in London, and settled comfortably in Petty's ample lodgings. He and I grew thick together, keeping ever in the other's company. Petty was not much liked within the school, though I could see no reason for it: a man of great discernment and ideals, he made a fine companion and knew the best taverns in the town. To one of these we made our way as soon as the fishy noble was laid against a wall and Popham appeared to cry all down for dinner.

God's Soul, swore Petty, as soon as we were settled with our cups, *how long must I endure this torment?*

What torment is that? I said. *Hunger?*

Of a kind. He sighed. *Do you not rail within, as I do?*

Against what, I laughed, *the World? Youth, Nature, Fortune?*

Come, do not jape. We are something in the nature of friends now, are we not?

You have ever been friendly to me.

Petty sighed again, quelling the outward breath with a deep draught. He wiped the lather of ale from his lips absently.

Rob, he said, for so he called me now, *Swift is a man without a soul. How can such a one paint another?*

That is plainly said. I joined his sighing with my own. *This is not what I had in mind for a painter's life.*

Petty raised a brow. *What did you have?*

O, I muttered, *something of truth, something of beauty, something of capturing essences.*

And the noble wrist that flounders?

Is nothing of nothing.

We agree then. He sighed afresh. *That, at least, is a benison – I am no longer alone in my troubles.*

Benisons aside, I said, *Benson is of our mind.* I noted his eyes upon the nothing.

His eye is an eye of logic.

There is room for that in painting, is there not? The logical mind can see where bones should be.

I fear he does not understand the craft, Petty said. *He would have all things correctly wrought, but that counts for little in itself. So would a wheelwright, or a gardener.*

Yet both are craftsmen's trades. He is enquiring, I said.

Aye, as a child: ever asking – why? – yet quickly satisfied.

I think you are hard upon him, I said. *He renders well.*

Well enough. Yet there is something lacking, some intelligence.

He has instinct, then – that has merit, for a painter.

Petty shook his head impatiently. *An artist must have both. Benson is a fine enough young man, save for his limping speech. But he will not make a Master.*

The girl brought bowls and hornspoons and set them on the table. We drank deeply and renewed our sighing.

Ambrose Leggatt is the one to watch, Petty said. *Leggatt is a good name for an Inquisitor.*

Do you so dislike him? I asked. *I thought him quiet, and gentle.*

He is quiet, and reveals nothing. I do not trust a man who will not trust another.

That is a puzzle! I laughed, wishing to lighten him, yet it rang emptily. *Ambrose once spoke against Lovett*, I added, *when I first arrived.*

Petty's eyes grew wide. *And did he so? Do tell me of it.*

There is little in the telling, I said. *Lovett was his cruel self, baiting me. Ambrose bid him halt.*

I wonder at that, said Petty frankly. He rubbed his chin. *I have never seen Ambrose speak for any. There must have been something in it.*

Nothing I could discern, I said, somewhat offended. *He spoke out honestly. I believe he dislikes Lovett as much as any.*

Petty shrugged. His cheeks were drawn in as if with fever, his eyes raw about the edges.

Ambrose will make his fortune, he said, *for Fortune's favourites are all diplomacy. Ambrose is an ambassador for the even word. There is nothing vital in him, he is like to ice. He will prosper, surely.*

That he would prosper, I too was certain. Ambrose's London features were as even as his voice – all smooth and pleasant, yet unyielding as marble. I began to understand my friend: Petty was for plain and outright speaking, Leggatt disliked confrontation and dispute. He was more peacemaker than defender, yet I saw no wrong in that.

Apes that daub at art! Petty lamented. *Soulless vessels vainly preening and posturing! What is to be done? You have seen my work, Rob. None would pay for such a thing upon their walls.*

I had seen those of Petty's works which had no place in Swift's shallow school rooms; voluptuous and rich, a brew peppered with idolatry. They lay within his chamber, covered with cloths against the landlady's eyes.

The Italians would have them, I offered.

Aye, the Italians. Fifty years ago I need not have looked so far.

To reform is not always to refine.

That, Petty whispered, *is a truth not to be spoken loudly.*

We sampled soup and herrings. The savour of both was strong and heartening, yet Petty seemed to get little pleasure from them.

You are unwell, I said kindly.

Aye, sick of heart. There is much we have not spoken of.
You pine for a lady?
I bear a love that cannot be spoken of freely. I feared some proclamation, but Petty laughed roundly. *Nay, fear not*, he said, *I see your look. I do not forget where my chamber ends and yours begins! I am not given to that manner of night wandering, though I would never speak against it. It was valued by the Greeks – it has its place.*
What then? I asked, and much relieved. *Do you court someone unwilling?*
My lady is known to many, yet all chastity, he said sourly. *Let us speak no more of her here. Come, eat my herring, I have no stomach for it.*
We fell to silence again. I picked over the herring bones with little zeal.
Have you remarked Falconbridge? Petty said suddenly. *I sense a danger in him.*
He does not seem dangerous.
I know a little of him. He acts the fawning dog, but he may bite.
He cringes, I said, *he is a simpering ape. When the Master speaks, Falconbridge falls to licking his boots.*
Petty nodded. *His work is tedious but his spending is not so. Every Friday evening he visits the trullhouses in Southwark and gifts his coin to Venus.*
There is nothing new in that, I answered. *You disapprove?*
Petty shrugged. *Each to his pleasure, if it harm none. Yet I hear that Falconbridge takes great pleasure in harming.*
The stooping man seemed a harmless creature, and I told my friend so.
On every holiday, Petty intoned, his voice high with revulsion, *Falconbridge visits the bear ring. He goes from there to a house of very tender flesh whose owner keeps a back parlour, close as a prison. For sufficient silver a man may purchase untouched girls there, very young. I do not speak of practised whores, for whom one man is much as another and all is business. I speak of the selling of children, and for whatever end one will. Falconbridge's end is vile.*

I pushed away my plate. *How do you know of this?*

O, Petty grimaced, *the ape has no head for wine, though he seems keen to drown in it at times. When he drinks, he brags.*

We might have him put from the school, I said.

Petty shook his head. *I am in no place for tale-telling. And Swift will hear no word against Falconbridge.*

Why so?

There is something close between them, though I know not what. Swift is a man of murky thoughts himself. Petty shuddered. *It would not amaze me if they share some unpleasant history.*

I would not think of it.

That is the way of most. Petty was deep in his ill humour and angrily pulled on his jerkin. *We must return*, he snapped at once. *Come.*

I was loath to be in the workshop again, with all that Petty had told me of our fellows. I looked about me. Falconbridge could not be seen, and for that I was grateful. Benson and Lovett were at work on a vast mythic piece, with a tottering armoured knight astride a monstrous horse. Swift's voice bellowed *whoreson!* from the side parlour, and Lovett straightway answered. I took the moment to test Benson for myself.

Your work is vast, I offered, standing beside him.

Benson bowed. *I am – not –* he faltered – *not altogether is it my work.*

You work alongside Lovett, yes. Which part is of your hand? Did you shape the horse?

We regarded the creature, its grossly muscled hocks all ill-proportioned. Benson regarded me in turn, with the corner of a soft brown eye.

Not mine, he breathed. *It is – well – is it not? I mean – rather – that it is well made? The horse?*

I smiled slyly. *Do you ask me, John, or do you tell me and so convince yourself?*

His smooth cheeks reddened like a girl's. *I, I—*

I spoke lowly. *It is no horse of God's creation, is it, John? Nor is it yours. You would not make a horse that could not stand.*

Benson shook his head and looked about. *Speak softly, Robin,* he said. *Do not loudly dissemble.*

I marvelled at the straightness of his speech, which sounded so often like a chipping away at words. *You speak boldly,* I whispered. *Why not speak so aloud?*

I cannot, Benson answered. He hung his head.

You loathe this work, I said, *you hate the falsehood. Am I in the right?*

Benson inclined his head, nodding slightly. He caught my eyes a moment then moved away.

Do not hesitate! I urged him. *We must speak, and speak together soon. It is treason against art that we learn and practise here. Come to the tavern when we sup, speak with me and Petty.*

His eyes turned up to me, wide and fearful. *Petty?* he whispered.

Yes, I implored, *I and Petty both. We feel alike. We have spoken of it, we spoke of you today.*

You – spoke – of me? Benson piped. *To Petty?*

I nodded in earnest. *We must speak against Lovett and his like. Swift is in the wrong, this is no artistry. You feel the same, you told me so—*

O! he cried, his mouth atremble. *I said nothing, nothing! I have nothing to say – to you – or Petty. Petty! O, I – I beg you – say nothing – nothing more.*

Benson bounded like a hare across the workshop. I turned to see Swift as he burst through the doorway with Lovett, the hound ever at his heels.

So! Lovett snarled. *Studying my work? I'm glad indeed that proud Robin would make such a pilgrimage across the room, to marvel at my brushstrokes.*

If you refer to the carcass, I said, pointing at his horse, *I surely came to marvel. Never has such a creature been seen in Christendom.*

Swift roared, the black teeth parting. Lovett's jaw struck out angrily.

I am mighty glad I took you on! Swift barked. *You two make better sport than a cockfight.*

I thought much on Petty and his mysterious love as we worked that afternoon, the taste of herring lingering amid the scents of oil and pigment. Benson was frightened, more by the sound of Petty's name than anything I had said about the Master. I knew Benson to be timorous, but of a mind, and thought I might win him to me yet. He worked through the lengthening afternoon in silent solicitude, watchful of me and keeping close by Lovett. In turn, I watched my ill-tempered friend, and resolved to do what I might to comfort him and win his confidence.

The day grew languorous and all fell to yawning. Toby, our simple-minded grinder of paints, dozed standing in the corner, his head resting on the hand that held pestle to mortar. Swift saw him waver where he stood and fetched him a sharp clap on the ear. Toby started, yowling, and in his alarm spread vermilion paste on the wrists of Swift's worn doublet.

Idle wretch! Jibbing dribbling fool! Swift rang blows with his curses upon Toby's head 'til the boy lay whimpering on the floor, his lips all bloody.

Let be! I shouted, a fury in my throat. *He has enough.*

Swift straightened and looked about in great amazement. *Who dares to speak?* he bawled. *Who dares direct me?*

I stepped forward. *You may bravo with me if you will*, I said. *I can match blows and curses.*

Swift looked down at his wrists, all besmirched and red with blood and paint. He shook his head.

Fortunate for you I little like this cloth, he snapped. He turned to leave the room then, kicking Toby like a hearthdog as he did so.

The boy scrambled to his feet and fell again to grinding. I dabbed a cloth at his mouth.

Leave the paint now, I said, *we will not need it. The day is late.*

Ambrose was at my elbow. *Have a care*, he warned.

This is my care, I said. *Does he often use Toby thus?*

The delicate nostrils quivered. *I have seen it before,* said Ambrose smoothly. *I would not say how often.*

Would you say the boy deserves it?

I would not take it upon myself to measure his deserving.

Jesu, Ambrose! Would you speak so if Swift broke his neck? The boy mumbles strange words when he falls to dreaming. Perhaps he should be burned for heresy?

Ambrose was unmoved, his downy cheeks unflushed. *Have a care,* he said again.

Enough! Petty? Petty was a statue in the doorway. He stared from me to Ambrose and shook his head. *Let us be gone, my friend,* I said. *I would not bear this company a moment more.*

Aye, said Petty thickly. *Let's be gone.*

We walked about the streets in silent fury. Petty strode briskly, ever a step before me. We rounded the corner of Paul's. I caught his doublet.

Peace, Petty, I said. *I did what you would. You are enraged with me and I know not why. Let us take a draught and talk.*

Petty's shoulders heaved. *Fetch us some wine, then, and we'll drink. We'll talk when we are home, and not before.*

He walked on and I followed, mute and obedient.

I wondered as we walked. My Prenticeship had proved a poor and foreign country to that opulent land of my imaginings. I had dreamed wealth and achievement; I had gained abuse and a surly companion. In my Norfolk mind I had conjured up the stink and noise of London, yet the swarming crowds about me still astounded. Over Cheape a cloud of kites, ominous creatures, swooped darkly above us and landed in the street. They hovered and stalked in such numbers as to seem like rooks in a cornfield. The filthy birds put me in mind of Lovett. I kicked at one as I passed.

In this place the courtesy of the country was forgot. Villainy was so familiar that few men would reach out to help a fellow

– even when he fell facedown in the kennels – for fear of some trickery from cutpurses. So too ran the common law of Swift's – none defended any that faltered and gained abuse, so quick was the company to pass on the disease of derision.

At the lodgings I fetched a jug and took it to the Mermaid. Petty would not come with me to the inn but waited in his chamber, chewing sourly on a rind of cheese. I returned with the best Burgundian my purse could cover, an offering for peace. My frowning friend had set out goblets.

I poured the wine, splashing a little on Petty's foot. He wiped at it.

A libation, I said. His face cracked with a smile. *Do this in remembrance.*

We raised and drank. Petty's knit brows turned to arched surprise. *This is good*, he said.

As you are to me. Yet there is a sour note.

He wiped his mouth. *Our talk today. The flounder.*

There is more.

I meant it as a warning. You did not heed.

I would not see poor Toby struck so, I said.

You were in the right. But not with Ambrose. What was it he said?

To have a care.

And you had none, said Petty. *You spoke of heresy.*

To furnish an example only.

Ambrose, I told you, would make a good Inquisitor. You know the word Recusant?

I come from Norfolk, I met with Kytson once. I told you of this.

We spoke of pictures only. Now I speak of men.

The wine was fast in my throat and I poured again. *I see not where you lead*, I said.

Petty smiled sadly. *You are of Norfolk, but not of Norfolk's mind.*

You mean the traitor Duke?

I mean the Duke. I am of Oxford.

I nodded. *You say little of your family there.*

I see them little. I hear a little more. He drank hard and came up gasping. *Petty may seem a little name, come from a little word. In Brittany my forebears were noble.*

Petty is a Frenchish name. What do you hear of them?

Of a wool trade gone stale, of lands removed. Of fines.

The cause of his worries at last. *Has there been some crime?*

He laughed bitterly. *The crime of Kings. We are Catholic.*

My friend a papist? My breath fled in an outward rush. Petty's eyes grew small.

Now you're afeared, he said. *Would you leave here?*

Nay, I said. *We are friendly still.*

I am a heretic, am I not? My Romish tendencies.

I should have guessed at it; your Italianate boards. The mysterious lady?

Our Lady, full of grace. Fair of face. Not fit for tavern talk.

I understood him now, though misunderstanding suddenly seemed safer. *Do any know at Swift's?*

Aye, Benson only. His family are of my country.

Of course there was Benson, with his eyes brown wells of worry, startled by Petty's name. *And what would Swift say?*

O, you were greeted with it, were you not? Foul wretches, the Pope wears skirts for he's hell's harlot, putrid bawds of Satan. Do I miss anything? I must often leave Swift's sermonising. There is naught wrong with my bladder.

Nor with mine, I said. *Come, let us drink.*

Seven

IF I FRETTED FOR my friend and raged at Swift's injustice, I need not have done so long. Nor should I have thought too much on my Prentice life. These are the comfits of experience, sweetening thoughts when bitterness is past. When the world tastes ill, sweetness is forgot: in those days, life gnawed like toothache.

My work was ever the same. Swift would tame me as a shepherd trains a dog, and I must begin with crawling. So I worked on flat planes of paint alone: the mixing of colours and the filling-in of boards. Swift worked on mauling hands and faces, Lovett was prized and might reshape anatomy. Ambrose did as he was bid and so stayed safest. Falconbridge seemed never to finish a piece, but daubed a little at a time, and sparingly. For this, Swift gave him precious leaf to sprinkle. Benson, being silent, seemed best fitted to underdrawing and all things inanimate. He would breathe life into chairs, though Swift's bodies might heap dead as wood upon them. Petty was jewel and cloth, his drapes all rare and classical.

The weeks that followed Toby's grazing were thick and still. The air was thunderous, the stink high in the streets. The Summer neared, its heat an angry mob that approached with Plague and Pox. Our work was languorous, for we were too lame to fight and bravo. I felt a storm approach, and feared when it might break.

The pieces bored me, so I worked quickly that I might have them done. I did as Swift bid me: *the ochre here; full out that curtain; here's a floor for thee, Robin.* I filled, floored and ochred, and then I rendered. I had my own chalks for the purpose and got more than I needed from Petty. I marked vast papers with squared lines and within each square I worked a visage. I passed the days thus, each day marking another square. Petty I drew the most, being familiar with his face. His cheeks were gaunt and I strove to catch those hollows, more noble than any perfumed beard. Lovett appeared often: I caught opposing natures. His great hook of a nose was simple stuff, his sharp malicious eyes easily wrought. Benson was pretty to draw, Ambrose disappeared. Falconbridge I would not look on long enough.

My Maying had been a silent one – we were not green and merry. Likewise the passing of the month went by unmarked. As June warmed, so Swift became uneasy.

The court will progress, he barked. *Which of you will come?*

I looked about me. None moved, save for Lovett, who crossed his hands with maiden modesty.

I'm looking, Swift said, his eyes all fiery. *I watch you all. Be mindful. Visitors are coming.*

And come they did: two nobles, in patterned cloth and golden braid, silk slippers for shoes, one sporting peacock plumes. Popham made a slatternly siren, though she tried with eyes and hands to draw them closer. Petty rounded his mouth in mock astonishment – I choked on laughter.

The nobles were soon closeted with Swift. We regarded the closed door.

Well, well, gasped Falconbridge, *a very fine pair of gentlemen, very fine, hahahaha! I wonder that they would come all this way from Greenwich, that is supposing that is where they have come from, expressly to see Master Swift – though I have no doubt, no doubt indeed, that Master Swift is very well thought of at court, and that they come here expressly on the word of his reputation.*

You burble like the tide, said Petty, *but to less purpose.*

You would prefer he mumble like a Latin priest? That came, of course, from Lovett's mouth.

They place commissions, I said quickly. *They are preened and finely feathered.*

You would know of feathers, Robin, Lovett sneered.

I am of the country, I said. *I know how to snap a neck or break a wing.*

Enough, said Petty. *Wait 'til they be gone.*

We went back to our painting. I had done my final background piece and turned again to my drawings. Here was a square unfilled and I began with two peacocks, then fashioned them into men.

The door opened and Swift, obsequious, bowed the nobles out. *Allow me the honour*, he flattered, his speech slow and slavish, *to show your lordships over my students' work.*

Petty pursed his lips at the *students' work*. I turned back to my page.

The nobles walked about, nodding at the boards. Swift steered them to Lovett's work, showing them his lately made travesty of two young girls holding hands. Falconbridge followed them.

Two sisters, my lordships, he prattled. I caught Petty's eye and my flesh crept coldly. *They are prettily made these maidens and young Master Lovett here has them done all quite intact in their youthful loveliness, see, has he not? hahahaha! and they are quite modest yet altogether lively-looking, and quite a pretty piece for admiring, haha! they are two sisters, of a noble family, perhaps you know them, sirs? There is no son, alas, but time for that and with two such pretty daughters—*

That's so, Falconbridge, Swift snapped. Outside the nobles' sight he dealt a sharp stamp on the toes. Falconbridge yelped.

I am of noble family, he rattled on, though his voice had grown higher. *My forebears go beyond Conquering William's time and we fought for Harold, yes, haha! though he be not in the right but we were loyal and so noble that William himself invested us as knights and one of my father's line also fought at Agincourt, he was well bethought by King Harry Fifth that was—*

Is this man your fool? asked the plumed noble. *He prateth overmuch.*

Ah, yes indeed, your lordship! Swift said, laughing, stamping again, and harder. *He gives us great mirth with his tales of old, he lightens our hearts so!* He punched Falconbridge's arm merrily.

He makes my head heavy, said the second noble. *Bid him retire.*

Petty suppressed a snort and covered it by banging at his easel. The nobles turned then and made towards him.

Good my lordships, cried Swift, *would you not see Lovett's brave work?*

What do you here? asked the plumed noble.

Petty turned and bowed. *The cloth for a portrait piece, sirs*, he said. *I hang the fabric and copy the folds and shadows. It sits so on the gentleman, and so I paint it on.*

This is fine good work, said the unplumed one. *I would have you work my wardrobe thus.*

And I, said the plumes. *It is bravely done.* He turned to Swift. *This man works on my likeness!*

And on mine. The plumeless man nodded and enquired of the painter's name. Petty made a bow and answered him.

I look to see more of you, Master Petty, said the plumes. They moved along to view Benson's boards.

Petty raised me a grin and Swift glowered. He strode up to the nobles.

This here, my lordships, is simple underdrawing. It is base measuring. Pray do not trouble yourselves upon it.

And who are you? the plumed one asked quivering Benson.

He is no one, your lordships, Swift put in, *a Johnson only, Ben Johnson.*

John Benson, I corrected.

It is all one, no matter, Swift hissed, his narrowed eyes on me. The nobles turned my way.

This youth, Swift put in quickly, *is our meanest painter. He works on flat pieces, fills in backgrounds. His work need not be viewed.*

I would see it, said the plumes. I made to hide my paper. *What is that?* he asked.

A practice paper only, my lord, I said.

The peacock feathers neared and brushed my easel. *I would see that paper.*

It is unworthy, sir.

I will judge, he said. He took it from me and handed it to his friend. The unplumed man laughed roundly.

This is marvellous well! said he. *See you the painter of the sickly girls? His nose is wondrous large and quite the image of it.*

This one is the clothman, said the plumes. *And this pair of peacocks have our faces.*

I reddened. The plumed noble held my gaze, then broke into high laughter. *You have me well!* he said. *You will work my face, and the clothman there* – this said to Petty – *will make my silks.*

It was a short triumph, but enough to fire us both. Petty and I made our own peacock struts that morning and ordered veal for dinner, so pleased were we with our prowess. We returned with bellies full, our tongues and heads wine-emboldened.

You both, snapped Swift, as we climbed the stairs. *Here, now!*

We followed him into his closeted parlour. Swift dropped scowling into a chair.

You may stand, he said. *You come from the tavern?*

We do, said Petty. *We dined well there.*

Too well for your purses, I'll warrant.

We have commissions, Petty remarked, and smiled scoffingly.

What commissions? Swift sneered. *I know of none.*

Petty regarded him quizzically and turned to me. I shrugged.

Lovett will paint their lordships, Swift said. *You go on as before.*

We do not! bawled Petty. *That work is ours, all saw so.*

You are mistaken, said Swift, smiling blackly. *The only commissions I know of are Lovett's. I have it here, set down in my ledger.* He read from his book, bescrawled with spidery ink. *Item: two painted boards, rendered by the hand of Master Benjamin Lovett for delivery of the pair no later than Lammas.* He looked up, brows arched. *I see nothing else, do you?*

Petty blenched with anger. He threw the ledger to the floor then burst from the room, fist-clenched and raging. Swift barked triumphantly.

Did you truly think I'd let you have them? he laughed. *You, a green lad, a nobody! Lovett paints the lords. Falconbridge may do the gold and so on. If you play your part deservingly, I may see to it that you fill in the floorboards. Ha!*

A screeching issued from the workshop and I ran without to

see Petty, his face all bunched and writhing, pressed close against Lovett's. His hands clasped about the vile neck. Lovett was ill balanced against the wall, his heels kicking high with Petty's lifting. I had not thought my friend so strong.

Damnable whoreson! Petty screamed. *Thieving pox-ridden sot, I'll flay your crooked carcass now and give me one sound word against it or I swear—*

Petty! I called. *Be not hasty.*

I'll hold him, Rob, cried Petty, his lips all foamed with fury. *I hold, you break his nose!*

Come near, Robin, and I'll pluck your feathers, Lovett hissed, though his voice was much choked with strangling.

Drop him! bawled Swift from the doorway. *Do it or starve, I'll not have you here again.*

Petty shook Lovett hard. Teeth rattled and cheeks danced about them. Lovett fell to gasping.

Drop him, Petty, Swift called again.

Beat him outside if you will, I urged, *but do not harm him here.*

I'll kill him, I'll eat his wretched blackened heart cased in pastry!

Petty, let be, I said. *See how his cheeks are purpling.*

Purple? Petty screamed. *How dare you to wear purple, you base ignorant—* He dropped Lovett to the floor and commenced kicking at his belly.

I wrestled my friend from Lovett, though there was more landing of blows in the process, and some of them my own. Lovett rubbed at his throat while Petty lunged and bristled furiously like the boar at the hound. Swift stood between them, smiling.

That's an end, he said. *Lovett begins his rendering of the lords tomorrow. Petty, you will finish the clothes on Lovett's lady here. She is a lord's wife, and close as you will get to noble-painting. Robin here will assist you. You wished to work together, did you not?*

Petty made to fall upon Swift then, but I reined him back. Swift waved a hand, his final judgement, and left us for his parlour.

Lovett sneered, though wheezingly. *So Cockrobin, your ugly*

71

likenesses are o'erlooked again, he said. *Little wonder. You draw like a Netherlander, all warts and wrinkles. Think you that is artistry, showing a man's faults and pustilloes?*

There is not paper and chalk enough in the world to record your faults, I snarled back. *'Tis a wonder I found such a vast territory to fit your nose.*

Benson laughed, but cowed away at Lovett's stare. Ambrose went back to his easel and picked up brushes. Falconbridge stayed, twitching and hopping from one foot to the other.

I think you should not speak so to Master Lovett, he began, *haha! No indeed, for he is a most senior painter and skilful, and he is much prized—*

Peace, fool! Petty bawled. *I shall cut out your tongue.*

I shall cut out yours, and cure it, Lovett said. *You think yourself well favoured now, do you not? Petty has a friend at last, Petty has a companion. Fitting that you choose that drab bird, that country jape, a Netherman from the arse-end of nowhere, bred to crawl through the godforsaken Low Countries of England!*

Falconbridge commenced dancing and whining anew. *O! Master Lovett, that is most wittily said, most wittily, haha! haha! indeed, most prettily, wittily—*

Petty prettily and wittily split Lovett's lip with his fist. Falconbridge broke into a donkey trot and fled the room, arms flying. Lovett dabbed his mouth.

I'll see you out of here yet, Petty, he menaced, spittling scarlet. *And your darling too.*

Eight

PETTY AND I BROODED long over our lost commission, while Lovett took all pains to have us see him at the work. The nobles' faces were thinly spread across their boards, flat and shapeless as the poverty of wit that stretched to capture them.

The lady that Lovett abandoned to us was a cone of cloth with head and hands pieced on. Petty and I sighed over it, fighting to find some form within the dress. I knew the fault – the lady had no backbone.

Have you ever remarked a woman's back? I asked Petty. We stood away, regarding the board.

I see more the front, he answered, winking.

Jest not, I said, *this is no matter for jesting.*

Petty shook his head. *There is naught to be done, let be.*

He dabbed at the lady's ruff. I stared and, staring, I saw Bess. Her back was an arch across the cartwheel, her trunk a bridge from shoulder to hip. The sight was stretched, heaped and rounded.

I pushed Petty aside and grasped his brush. White lead was on the sable.

A back is no straight rod, mattered of metal, I said. I put the sable at the lady's breast and sliced the crimson velvet from her. *A back will bend, will curve.*

Petty gasped. *My cloth!* he said. *I had that velvet well.*

I stroked the white from breast to waist, and out across the hip. *Here is a woman,* I said. *Here, 'neath the fabric. This we must paint first, then the cloth above it.*

You undo the work, said Petty.

That is well, this is a manikin. Here, I will round the shoulders.

It was all we were given, Rob. You are too serious.

You would not have Lovett's hand in our work, I reasoned. *Let us have a hand in his. These are clothes we paint, not people.*

73

None would have themselves look as they are, said Petty. *We must make ideal that which is base.*

We must show that truth is ideal, and Nature perfect, though it might seem base. This woman is a puppet. Let us give her life! See, I said, cutting through again with the white, shaping ankles and fingers. *See, this must have life, it must have blood and gristle, bone and flesh. That back would break ere it made an arch, but now—*

Petty grasped my wrist and stayed me from the slicing. *Have it, then*, he said, though frowningly. *Rework her, Rob, make her a shape – I will have the cloth when you are done.*

So we agreed. I took the stuffed and stitched lady and cut from her rounded limbs, smooth thighs, full high breasts, arched feet and a graceful, bending neck. I snipped away the stiff bodice of Lovett's work, untrussed her farthingale and petticoats. I stripped her and started her anew; then I gave my prize to Petty. As a tender waiting-maid he worked, stepping her into soft lawn, bright silk and, again, the rich velvet; laying on her skin the gentle white cloth, vigorous scarlet skirts and jewelled bodice. Gold we set on her, and pearls about her neck, still wet as from the oysters. Garnets and opals clustered her slim fingers, fingers that worked and pulsed, that left oiled traces from skin on plate and pewter. Her hair we piled high with pins, the locks curling the thick brown of Petty's own hue. The ears were small and pale. The face we worked from Lovett's sketches, meagre though they were: the shape squarish, the jaw pointed at the extremes and meeting in a shallow chin. The nose, being made by Lovett, we made much larger than he wrote it: the wide nostrils stirred with breath. The haughty lips yet quivered with mirth; the cheeks were stained with the modesty of one undressed by painters. The brow showed fashionable plucking and perfumed pastes.

She is good as Master John, Benson breathed, a low aside. *Swift will not have it.*

And yet he must.

God's death! he roared when we presented her. *What trull is this?*

Lovett's lady, sir, said Petty modestly. *We have her finished.*

74

Finished? he screamed. *She is utterly destroyed!*

We worked from Lovett's own hand, Petty said.

We'll see, Swift threatened. *We'll see what he's about.*

Petty and I dined and laughed the hollow laughter of revenge. We knew that Lovett would appear that afternoon, flourishing his sketches of the peacock noble. That morning had been appointed for rendering the plumed one at his court lodgings. Lovett had made the announcement loudly the day before, repeating the details with a malicious savour.

He will come in with his papers and vile scribblings and crow at us, Petty said over dinner. He was now spent of all laughter. *He will see his lady and we will lose our places.*

He will be taught to keep his place, I said. *For him we lost our commissions.*

We returned to the workshop with less fire than we had left it. Lovett and Swift stood before the painted lady. Swift's arms were contentedly folded, happy to witness a brawl. Lovett was greenish and trembling.

What insult is this? he hissed at me. *This is your hand, Robin, I know it – you are writ in all things base and loathsome.*

You do not like your work? I said. *I painted from your hand.*

You painted o'er my hand! he screamed. *You had no right to do it! This was my work, and you have undone it—*

As you undid ours, said Petty calmly.

You think you could paint my nobles? You! Dribbling school-boy, you are scarce big enough to wear breeches. What know you of the court, of its wants and manners? And your groom's boy from Thetford paints a horse's arse for a lady's face. Are you so in love with the mares still, Cockrobin? You are beset with unclean thoughts of hippomanic nethers, Netherman.

Liked you your lip when it resembled a swollen bladder? Petty said. *You speak as if you would have it so again.*

I'll crack your head like an egg, Lovett scowled.

'Twill be hard when you have no fingers to make a fist of.

Enough, Swift yawned. *You bark but do not bite. Who unmade Lovett's figure?*

We both did, said Petty.

Forgive me the intrusion, Master Lovett, Master Swift. Falconbridge appeared, horribly scraping. *Hahaha!* he piped. *I have something to offer you in your argument, that is rather, some matter to bring conclusion to the matter of your circumlocution, haha! in a manner of speaking.*

To the point, Swift snapped.

Well, Master Swift, and Master Lovett likewise, as this does most concern you and will indeed give you the most concern – I do, by most fortunate Chance, or chancing Fortune, happen to know the manner in which your painting of the lady standing here, or rather, as she was before she is now, and is standing as she is now in place of how she did stand when you had devised and rendered her with your hand, Master Lovett – how she did come to be altered in the face and body and furthermore who did do the altering and when.

Lovett scratched his head. Falconbridge continued and, with more directness than he was wont, said: *Robin of Thetford did it.*

It all? said Lovett. His nose twitched eagerly.

He painted it o'er with the white lead and Master Petty was forced to withstand it, and did try most faithfully from your sketches, Master Lovett, to rebuild the face when the Robin had completed his butchery.

My butchery is far from complete, I warned him.

The lady is better for it, said Petty, *and the face is none of mine.* He clapped my shoulder. *I would never have it so well.*

What answer? Swift asked of Lovett. The words seemed practised, as did the mocking manner in which Lovett appeared to consider, rubbing his chin.

Think not too hard, Lovett, I said. *I see thought clouding your brow. Does it know the way thither?*

Wretch. He mewed to Swift, all supplication. *His insult is great, Master. Could he not be put from here?* His eyes were hard and narrowed. *And his accomplice likewise?*

Swift's black smile broadened. *Not so. Petty has been here awhile. Petty, you are warned. No further horseplay.* Lovett snorted, though he tried to look abused. *As for the Robin*, he *went on, you try my patience. One month's suspension. After that, you grind paints with Toby for a week.*

My fists clenched. Petty was once more raging.

Suspended! he cried. *For painting true? This is a travesty.*

'Tis all a travesty here, Petty, I said. *What does the dog Lovett know of truth? You should be grateful, Lovett, that I gave your daubing some grace.*

Lovett smiled unpleasantly. *Farewell, bonny sweet Robin. Find some other trade. Go clean a stable.*

I will find a school that knows its craft, I said. *This is naught but a bawdy house for pedants and pederasts.*

Enough, said Swift again.

Not so! I answered. *You do not have enough – not enough wit, nor talent, nor sight, nor Nature, nor understanding of the craft—*

Puppy! snapped Swift. *Do not speak to me of talent. You lack the training even to fashion yourself a bare Prentice.*

I have an eye! I bawled. *'Tis more than you have. Looked you at Lovett's board? No woman is made as that was! How can you paint if you do not look? How can you know how to show what is there if you know not what lies beneath?*

Ba! sneered Lovett. *And what would you have?*

Anatomy, fool, I said. *You might learn how a body is made – 'tis not wrought of stuffing. And rendering from life. Know you what that means?*

We know it well, said Swift. *You are a baser dog than you seemed. Do you think I'll have trulls in here, stripped for your pleasure and prying looks?* He smacked his lips. *And you call this a bawdy house! Get out, filth, and come not back until September.*

September? cried Petty.

Aye, and not a day before. Let the dog keep away 'til the dog days are spent. Go find yourself a whore to paint, Robin.

Lovett laughed. *He prefers horses, Master.*

Master yourself, Lovett, I growled. *We are not finished.*

I am not, he smiled, *but methinks you are.*

Nine

THE FLOOR OF PETTY'S chamber was ill made for reclining yet I passed many hours there, sprawling. The Summer had waxed to fullness and the streets stank highly; Plague was on the city. The court and Her followers fled to the country, where death and dearth parted before them as Biblical waters. The waters of London itself lowered and the Thames spread out like a mud flat. I too was parched, and so drank an ocean of claret.

What do you there? asked Petty one evening, as I rested my cheek on the unwashed boards.

'Tis cool, I answered. *'Tis a fit place.*

'Tis a fit place for a dog. Get up, man.

I am a dog, I said, and bared my teeth.

You have been taverning. I will bring food.

Petty banged the door and ere long banged in again. This bang brought with it the savour of heated pastry and gravies.

Come, dog, called Petty. *Meat.*

We ate in silence, I with a dribbling fury and he with an unnatural calm. I licked my fingers clumsily.

Rob, he said, *I worry for you.*

Why so? I have a Prentice holiday.

Swift closes the school soon, he went on. *He and Ambrose follow the court Progress.*

I soon awoke. *Not Lovett then?*

No. The plumed one likes not his likeness. He smiled. *God has some mercy. Lovett must deliver the boards by Lammas, remember? He cannot leave the workshop 'til they are done.*

May the Plague knock merrily at his door each morning.

Petty shook his head. *That is evil wishing. He is already made a fool.*

He was born a fool.

My friend sighed. *I will be forced to make good the cloth again.*

Will you use the white lead?

That is your practice, and I wish you were at it now.

I have no boards to whitewash, I remarked. The *whitewash* was messily spoken.

You understand me better than you show. Drink less, Rob, and paint more. I can bring materials from the school once Swift is gone. Lovett is idle, he will not be there every day.

There are others.

Falconbridge will be off, hunting young coneys. Benson visits home. Petty sighed afresh. *Would that I may do so. Why do you not pay a visit, Rob? Thetford is a better place than this for the Summer.*

You do not know it as I do. I thought on my father, and his look that would say *and so you failed then?*

You are proud, said my friend. *Put your pride to better use.*

I did as I was bid. For the days that followed I took myself into the streets and drew the faces there. I had on paper scraps the sellers of silks, the carter boys, the lads that shouted wares from the open doorways, the book men of Paul's. That was a fine place for sitting and rendering, for the holy walls were tall and cool and there was shade, though no breath of air stirring. Now I had the leisure for reading I had no purse for buying, and after the first three days of watching and lingering, the book Prentices saw me off. *An' you buy naught, you copy naught!* one yelled, thinking me a scrivener taking notes from the pamphlets there.

My fourth day without direction gave birth to a great, sore thirst.

I walked to the river and idled across the bridge to Southwark. I had spent little time there, having no cause to visit entertainments, and thought to see some new faces amongst the sporting and trugging folk. No baits were on, it being too high in the season, so I took myself into the first tavern I saw to wet my throat.

I drank Rheinish, for there was naught else better. I smiled at the chaffish taste, which Petty had rightly spoken ill of. Despite myself I drank the jug and then another, my legs growing heavy beneath the table, the quality of the wine growing with the drinking of it. I pulled out my papers and set to work at rendering the tapster, who would not keep still for long.

Three Southwark wenches came in and looked about. A shout went up near the barrels and they walked across to make their banter with the landlord and his tapster. They were ill-looking trulls, these three: one short with greasy black hair, her chest hauled up high on view; the second with lighter hair, though no less matted; the third with her head trussed up in a dirty cloth and one leg dragging as she walked. Their faces were heavily lined with trade and the black-haired one was pox-faced. I set to rendering at once.

See him there? the poxed one squawked to her fellows. *Scribbling?*

They nodded and made towards me. I regarded them over the Rheinish.

You're a fine gen'lem'n, said the wench with the head-cloth. Her mouth was a vast wetness as it opened, the teeth broken upon the shore of her lips. *What's y'r pleasure?*

Perfection, I answered. I copied the line of her snarl and the shipwreck within it.

A perfect gentleman then, said the light brown one. *And would you prove gentle to three ladies?*

To such a three as you, I would prove nothing but gentlemanly.

They simpered foolishly. The black-haired wench with the highly fortressed bosom leaned forward, the sweatiness of her pox-scarred flesh close to my face. *You copy us. You have not asked if we will it or not. That is not gentle.*

Is it your pleasure, I said, drawing back from her rankness, *that I draw you three together?*

How much'll you give us? said the head-cloth.

Let us call for more wine and so decide.

A third jug of Rheinish came to the table. My head was beyond the tallying of costs.

Our time costs, the poxed trull said, hearing my thoughts. She poured quickly. *If we sit here with you we make no coin.*

Drink, drink! I cried, rendering feverishly. I now had the bound head of the drab well drawn and turned back quickly to the brown one. She grinned apishly.

I see no purse on the table, the poxed one continued. *What measure for our time, I said?*

I smiled at the wench I was drawing and she tossed her matted head like a colt. *Let us think on the matter a little more,* I said.

P'rhaps you'd like more than just thinkin', said the head-cloth.

Perhaps we could take you to a little place near here, said my sitter. She stuck her chest out towards me. *Perhaps you'd like to see more than you copy now.*

Perhaps so, I said. The idea struck me as wondrous and quite unexpected. *Perhaps that is the very thing that we should do.*

I followed the vile trio out into the heat and along the lanes. They pressed me into a trugging house in Rose Lane and up some stairs into a tiny, stinking room. The room was dark but for the sun coming through a piece of torn sacking. I pulled the cloth back to let in air and met with the stench of the streets below.

The brown trull pushed me and we fell onto the narrow, greasy bed. *Me first,* she said, and commenced pulling at my points.

Not so, I said hastily, putting her aside. *I would have you all together. As a group.*

The poxed one laughed at that and lifted her skirts. *Even the Devil has only one tool for ploughing,* she said.

Take off your gown, I declared. *Take off everything, all of you.*

The drab in the head-cloth was quick to oblige, stripping off her skirts and filthy bodice. Her skin beneath was patched with grime and sore places, red and wealed, but her shape was high and comely, save for the one withered leg. The poxed trull was unwilling. *Your purse,* she said, and I waved my moneybag. It sounded with the clink of coin. She nodded and began unlacing.

You do not unlace, remarked the brown one. She seemed much offended. *You do nothing but look.*

That is my pleasure, I said, and took out my papers again.
Come, unclothe yourself.

She looked from my papers to her companions: one standing
and stripped to the waist, the other sitting naked on the edge of
the bed.

He's going to draw us! she screeched, horrified.

That's not mannerly, said the poxed one, her scarred breasts
swinging. She set her hands on her hips. *That's not our agreement.*

What's wrong with us? whined the naked one, still wearing
her head-cloth. She leaned back and arched her belly. *Don't you
like me?*

Stay like that a moment, I urged. I traced the curve of her
stomach as it blended into hip and thigh: a medley of hard and
soft, bone and flesh, pulling solidly and seamlessly together.

The brown trull let out a screech and tore at my hands, pulling
the chalk across the page and clawing at me. *It's what's wrong
with him!* she screamed. *It's him that's vile!*

The poxed one swore and threw open the door, crying, *George!
Trouble!* I struggled to sit up, yet the wench was in a fury and
set upon me, pinning me down to the bed. I twisted as her nails
scratched at my cheeks – the naked drab leapt up and pulled her
skirts about her and a red-faced man towered over me, threw the
wench aside and with a cry of *Sodomite! Bastard!* beat at my
eyes with his fists 'til all was dark and bloody.

Ten

PETTY WORE A CIRCLET of gold as he bent above me; of this I remain certain. My saintly Samaritan helped me to my knees and then swung me to my feet. He swore angelically.

Christ's bloody wounds, Rob! What has become of you?

The wounds are all my own, I mumbled. *I am Saul. See how I lie in the road! The light has struck me down.*

Drink has struck you, and some gang of cutpurses. He looked about him. *This is a foul street, how came you here?*

I was tendering some Magdalenes. How came you here?

In search of you, though God curse me for the folly. He shook his head. *You are unworthy of pity, Rob. I feared you lost and find you here sodden and sottish. Now you'll be poxed as well as robbed.*

Nay, I gurgled. I spat and a tooth fell ragged and bloody onto my palm. *I was not tender. I merely rendered.* My head seemed ringed with iron, my ears began to fill with an angry roaring. *Did you truly seek me?*

Aye, all over town. What of your face? He held a hand up to my eyes. *You are black and crimson.*

Brave colours. I pulled back from his hand. *And still wet from the palette.*

How came it, Rob? He spoke coldly. *Do you brawl in taverns now?*

Nay, only in trugging houses. I shrugged, though my arms hung loose already. *Be not enraged. They set their George upon me – they thought me some unnatural kind of monster, that I would sit and draw them arse naked, yet never deign to fuck them.*

Petty laughed then. He put his arm about my waist and limped me along the street. My feet dragged, my bones ached, my purse hung empty at my belt. Worse yet, my chalks and papers were gone – all had been for nothing.

We sat in Petty's chamber. Though the day had scorched, the night seemed chill and damp. Petty lit a small fire and seated me before it.

You suffer and shiver, he said. *'Tis the beating; you may grow feverish. Wash, then I will fetch some salep.*

Petty regarded me as I dabbed a wet cloth at my face, dipping and darkly staining the basin water. I patted and winced, and my friend gave me an ointment that stung and soothed together. I shed torn hose and a shirt all blood-encrusted, bathed and dressed again achingly. Petty left me and came back with a welcome jug of frothing sweetness.

You think yourself altogether beaten, my friend, he said. *Yet it is not so.*

I have not even the drawings that cost me this, I sighed. *I gain nothing.*

What would you do? What do you seek, Rob?

We sipped our salep and I unburdened all: the glorious loss of sweet Bess; the treasure of her many oils and pigments, spilled before me; my pledge to make paint live as brightly and purely as she had died. Petty sat attentive to my tale, his clustered brows the affinity of one likewise tormented, one who has endured the very same rack and wheel of frustration.

I need a patron, I cried, *a man wealthy in both purse and intellect. Swift will destroy me, I need a workshop of my own!*

Petty laughed. *You ask for so little! What else would you have, Master Rob – a golden litter to transport you thither? Liveried men to clear the way, or eunuchs to grind your paint?*

I need a model also, I said, *one who will unclothe herself with neither shame nor expectation. Yet how can it be? This is no Florence.*

Petty rose and went to the great hangings that obscured his own work from view. He pulled aside the heavy cloth and bent into the alcove from which, with many muffled sighs, he removed a large board, covered in rags. He dragged the board across the room and set it before me.

This, he declared, unravelling the rags, *is mine own Florentine.*

He stepped aside. At first the board seemed but a mass of limbs, a fleshly contortion, yet as I looked there appeared a woman's face, repeated above those limbs – a comely face, lit with wit and excitement. The nose was small between wide dark eyes, the mouth parted with amusement. Across the vast panel were writhing, tangled shapes, as in some frieze: breasts and buttocks arched; fingers pointed and curled; feet delicately raised or slyly curving, beckoning arms and thighs.

What is this thing! I choked, incredulous. *You said nothing of it before!*

Petty smiled. *This – this is my longing. You would have the truth, as your eyes see it. Yet man has but two eyes! The truth cannot be grasped from one side alone, even with such eyes as ours.*

We regarded the figures that sprawled and danced before us. *What do you aim for!* I asked. *I cannot grasp it.*

Have you ever thought of how light is shaped! Have you wondered how we may set down a form that is round on a page that is flat! How can such things be rendered as a whole! We must set down every angle, every possibility. Petty commenced pacing, his hands thrown up in wild, describing circles. *You would encase a form in a paint that lives, yet I would capture the very forms themselves: they change and shift, and so I must grasp each moment of their changing and shifting. That cannot be done with paint alone, even with a paint that has the very warmth or pallor of flesh, the very thread of a hair or moisture of an eye. It must be done by capturing the form itself from every side, over and over again!*

How! I cried, peering at this many-figured Venus. *And who is she!*

He sank into his chair. *She is Mistress Katharine Joyce, the best-read whore in Christendom – and not of Florence. She would sit for you.* He leaned forward and gazed at me in earnest eagerness. *If we had eyes like flies*, he whispered, *we would see every angle. Would that not look fine on a painted board!*

Aye, if you think it, I said. I studied Mistress Joyce's myriad faces. *Would she really sit for me?*

If I arrange it, she will, said Petty. He shuddered. *She would do much that others would not; she is Master Swift's mistress.*

Eleven

IT SOON CAME ABOUT. Swift set off to sniff at the heels of the court Progress, hoping to beg a patron's scraps. With him went Ambrose, and soon the workshops stood deserted. As Petty had guessed, Falconbridge took off at once to hunt female quarry in the country. Benson followed soon after, hiring horse to Oxford. Lovett, raging at the demands of his nobles, grew too ill of temper to work beside Petty alone. In his turn my friend swept in, trumpeting triumph, a week after his ministrations with the salep.

'Tis done! he cried. *She meets us in the morning.*

We cannot use his school, I straightway answered. *It is not right.*

Fie, said Petty, *a delicate conscience! Mistress Swift is gone to visit her mother; Popham is released for there's none left to feed. The workshops are empty! Toby can be easily persuaded.*

I scowled, but Petty nipped and prodded at me. *Frown not*, he said, *it is set.* He tugged my doublet, winking. *Wait 'til you see her, Rob.*

I awoke early that day, an ache in my bladder. I drew back the bedcurtains and felt for the pot. The light in the room was dim and I knocked my toe on the bedstead as I clattered about. I pissed, thinking what relief could come by such an act; I thought then of the relief that comes by a similar way, and how much stock some people set by it – but the notion was hazy and sleepborn and, as before, my mind confounded.

I readied hot water and cloths. Petty's scratch of a knock came at the door. He bounded in and swung himself up on the end of the bed to watch me.

Mind you wash behind your ears, he pecked.

Aye, Mother, I'll do that.

She'll be glad of it. He sniffed. *Camomile?*

Would you have me stink like an ox?

An ox? You are often as stubborn. Now you bark like a fox.

I slept little. I wetted my hair and scrubbed at the back of my neck.

Camomile is a meek fragrance. You will readily submit. Are you anxious?

Aye, a little.

There is no need. He swung his legs like a child. *She is most open.*

So you tell me, but I have no need of that.

He snorted. *Why do you pomade then? Surely you are courting her: when she scents you, ere she sees you, she will be won entirely!* He gave a lovelorn mew.

Poet. I flicked my washcloth at him. *Why do you come to torment me?*

I come only to give you heart and prepare you for adventure. I wiped my razor and set to sharpening the edge. Petty watched me, his brows drawing in a frown. *Do you mean to shave?* he said.

Nay, I mean only to cut your throat. I soaked a cloth in the scented water and pressed it to my cheeks. The hair was unmannishly soft and the curls unfurled with the dampness.

Why shave today? he asked, stepping over to the basin. *The lady might be partial to your whiskers.*

I turned him round to face me. For a soft-skinned man, his chin and cheeks were swarthy and I felt the sad want of his fine growth on my face.

Look at you, man, I said, showing him my handglass. *You could brave a full set of whiskers and they would be black and glossed as a Spaniard's. Mine is sparse stuff. See? It grows red and gauzy as a tomcat's. How can I show it to advantage? It must come off.*

I whetted the razor and stroked my right cheek. The whiskers did not resist but swept off cleanly as with a scythe through seedgrass. Petty inspected the blade and nodded. He went back to the bed and flicked his eyes from the haired to the smooth cheek and back.

'*Tis true*, he said, *I've seen more hair on a cat's arse*. I brandished the razor, but he laughed. *Do not give me your wicked looks. I might have named worse places.*

I scarce know how it came to be this colour, I declared mournfully. I stroked my left cheek with the blade. *My head hair does not have such a hue.*

It is your youth. You might work on it a little, and sprout a beard as full and red as old Harry's.

I would have a fine way with women then, I said. *They would see me and tremble.*

Aye, laughed Petty, *and hold on to their necks. They say that his daughter is also partial to a redbeard.*

I thought her partial to Frenchmen, I said, *so long as they grow girlish locks and wear gold petticoats.*

He snorted. *She'll never marry a papist like Anjou, however she fawns on him. Nay, he could be manly as a Dudley with a yard of codpiece and still she would not wed him. The sheets would reek of incense.*

Would you have her do so? I put down the razor. *We have never spoken of this.*

What's to be said?

The Queen and a Catholic Prince of France.

Petty nodded slowly. *You think I would wish a Catholic King upon us? Perhaps. But she will not wed, Rob. Where is the profit? She's past childbearing. It would be Philip and Mary again.*

I waved my cloth. *That is unwise speech*, I said. *Do not speak so beyond this room. Yet you give no answer. Would you not wish Anjou upon us, child or no? He is young, he might produce an heir.*

On her? I cannot think so. He shrugged. *She is not the youthful goddess any more.*

She would not have that believed. I think she may wed him yet.

She blows East and West daily. She mourns and weeps, then scolds and blazes. Petty pulled dolefully at his lip. *She is her father's daughter, she might do anything.*

I sighed and sickened. *I cannot think of Anjou here, it wrenches at me. She raged at Bartholomew's Day, yet it was his family's doing—*

And proved a bloodbath. Petty gasped in exasperation and leapt to his feet. *I know it! And I know of none here that approved it. What sane man would? Such a business is naught to do with faith. Do not dip us all in Huguenot blood.*

I mean no such thing, my friend, I said, *I know you a peaceable man.* I saw again how Petty had lifted the squealing Lovett by the neck, and split his lip with a fist. Already he was afire from speech alone. How would he have fared when they massacred the black Puritans?

It took a Medici woman to have it done, Petty railed. *What sane man would approve of Mary's Smithfield bonfires? What sane man would have put her sister on the throne to follow her?*

This was a jolt. *You cannot think so, truly?* I said. *Do you think the fault to be women?*

Ba! he barked. *Women, men, what difference? All with crowns are equally corrupt.*

Have a care, I warned, *you might hang for less.*

Under a Tudor, yes. After Harry, anything may happen. A man may denounce the Pope to marry a whore and rob a holy house to feed her brat. A man may print God's word for any to read, and so call his own judgements God's will. Such a man may climb high enough to pull God off his throne and sit in it himself. Forbid that one may speak a mind against him.

The blood had risen to Petty's face and he strode about to calm himself.

You do not speak like yourself, I said. *You would not have us as Rome, ruled by priests?*

What difference the tyranny of priests to the tyranny of Princes? he cried. *Better to throw all sovereignty aside and govern through wisdom, as the ancients did. Men must not be left to the rule of despots –* no, he said, catching my eye, *nor by schoolboys who believe themselves well enough equipped for justice after reading a prayerbook.*

Aye, I said. *Well, there is much to think on.*

He was in great earnest and I had no wish to argue with him. I wiped my cheeks and studied them in the handglass. They were boyish once more, showing a little pale where the sun had been barred from the skin by whiskers. I put up the cloths to dry. Petty paced about behind me, his irritation unabated. I washed, then opened the casement and threw the water into the street. As I did so, his feet ceased their drumming on the floor and I heard him groan slightly.

He had slumped upon the bed again. His face was drawn and his very spirit seemed to crumple in the fold of his lap. He shrugged and straightened, as if our talk, and his ire, had tipped from the room with the washwater.

What is the clock? I asked.

I agreed that we would meet her at eleven, he sighed, *in the chophouse.*

Is that a fit place? I said. He snorted, and his face raised up with a smile. *Why scoff?*

You will see, he said. *You will see.*

Excitation, sleeplessness and fear invaded my innards, which turned over profoundly when we stepped inside the chophouse. It was now not the closeness of the hour that troubled my guts, or the dangerous talk of my friend, but the stench of mutton and boiled greens that hung in the air. Petty was, as ever, a furnace of appetite and he ordered a stew of oysters and a jug of canary. I took a cup of strong beer, hoping for comfort from the hops, which, my mother had told me, were an ease for courage. The drink was unwholesomely weak and had the tang of rust about it. We sat at a wide, well-scrubbed table and watched the merchants and such weave in and out, scarcely ceasing their bustle to spoon, chew and swallow. It was not an unmannerly chophouse, save for the poverty of the beer; yet I wondered if it were truly a good place to meet a lady of the court to ask – would she strip herself naked and spread out before me?

Petty poured his wine and rubbed his hands together at the thought of oysters. He drank, smacking his lips clownishly. At that moment a scuffle sounded outside the door; the chophouse fell still and silent, the landlord stuck his head into the street, barked a few sharp words and hastened back within. As he did so he held the door open, allowing another to enter. This one wore a thin grey cloak, which was speedily brushed at with small, busy hands, and a hood, which shook from side to side and then swept back to reveal a woman's face, surrounded by fine black curls.

With a slight gasp, all turned back to their talk and chewing.

'Tis she! hissed Petty, and shoved me firmly with his elbow. We rose from our seats.

The woman looked about the tables 'til she spied us. She nodded at Petty and we bowed stiffly; she made her way across the room like a housekeeper with some distasteful estate matter to settle and stood before us. Petty made to offer his hand, but she shook her head.

Forgive me if I do not take it, she said, *I have need of a kerchief.* Her voice was deep and languid, her words seemed practised. She fell again to picking at her cloak, which I saw was splashed with something foul-looking.

I felt about and produced a square of linen, which, I saw gladly, was one of the few I possessed with no paint upon it. She took it with an *O!* of surprise and wiped with it at her cloak and fingers. Petty commenced an embarrassed foot shuffle 'til, at last, she threw off the cloak and seated herself at the table.

Damn these filthy streets! she snapped, clapping her hands in the air. A boy ran up. *Beer!* she exclaimed, then looked into my pot. Her nose wrinkled. *Nay, not beer*, she corrected, *I'll take some of this canary. Bring another cup. God knows what is in that fetid mixture.*

So it was that Mistress Joyce entered my acquaintance. She sat across the table, smiling as Petty declaimed and made flirtations, and she seemed all oblivious of my being. Her voice and laugh were deep and mannish. There was altogether something masculine about her: her hips were slight and straight, and by the rise of her ribs I saw that her chest was not so buxom as her tight lacing supposed it. I judged by the narrow slope of her shoulders that, were she to lie flat upon her back, unaided by her bodice, she would be almost as smooth and breastless as a boy.

Her face had an angular form, as if her jaw might continue to grow with the years and begin to jut, manly and stony, beneath her woman's lips. The lips were, in truth, the most feminine thing about her, although her brows, softened by plucking, and her ears, lengthened by drops of opal, were very comely. The slow slyness of her eyes, long and cinnamon, promised prowess; I could scarce draw my own away from them.

When Petty's dish of oysters arrived he fell silent, save for the slurping and scraping of his spoon. The oysters bobbed grey and jellied in their spiced gravy, giving them the look of bloated bodies in a ditch. Mistress Joyce turned her eyes instantly upon me; she met my gaze with a look of disgust, which I feared as much for me as for the oysters.

So, you desire me naked? she said. Petty snorted.

That is baldly put, madam, I wheezed.

As you would have me, she returned.

I wish to study anatomy, I said, my tongue tripping about. *I am certain that, without studying the human form, as the Italians have shown us, there is no hope of us ever capturing Nature.* I heard the piped notes of my voice and cursed myself a boorish fool.

And that is your task, she said, *to capture Nature?*

To capture the essence of things, yes.

I thought you a painter of likenesses. The boy appeared with her cup and she inspected the rim with suspicion. *This is not clean,* she said, and made to hand it back, then withdrew and filled it from Petty's jug. *No matter,* she told the boy, *you may go. I have a thirst.*

I am, I pressed, seeking her eyes again. *To capture a true likeness one must capture the essence of the sitter. It is the only way to show us as we are.*

She raised her cup and drank it down like a farmhand, wiping her sleeve against her mouth. *Tell me,* she said, reaching for the jug again, *how many of your male sitters pose without clothing?*

You misunderstand me, madam.

I think not, she retorted. She filled her cup again and passed the jug to Petty. *I think you wish to draw a naked woman and not a naked man. That is the way of artists, is it not?*

I looked to Petty, who was scraping at the base of his dish. *Madam*, I said, evenly as I might, *Petty has drawn you, has he not? I think you may trust from his manner towards you that I wish to take no advantage.*

She squealed with laughter then, a shrill trumpet against her speaking bass. Petty's face was shining and crimson.

If you can promise me that you will behave exactly as James did you are welcome indeed! she cried. *Few could make such a boast.*

Petty flushed a deeper red above his spoon. *Truly, Kat*, he said smilingly, *you deal with me too kindly.*

Come, she laughed, leaning across the board, *you were not one to complain of my kindnesses before.*

They giggled together a while. I grew prickly and felt myself redundant.

I seem to have chosen an ill-suited subject, I said, breaking back into their mirth. *I did not know how your business together had concluded.*

Mistress Joyce let out another squeal. *God's blood!* she cried. *You are altogether too serious! Nay, I am quite sure you would not deal with me as James did.* She winked at Petty.

My cheeks burned, yet I began again. *I wish to draw a form*, I insisted, *a human form. I wish to capture the spirit of a human form by seeing what is ordinarily unseen.*

The spirit can be seen through the skin, then? She raised a brow. *Not in the face, or behind the eyes, but in the buttocks and the belly?*

I tired of her mockery. *The spirit does not reside in the clothes of a man*, I snapped, *that is certain. It is not made of mere cloth and drapery.* I looked at the bodice of her gown, which was richly stitched and very vainly 'broidered. *I see*, I sniffed, *that I cannot be so certain about the spirit of a woman.*

She held my look sternly. A hush descended on Petty's eating, which could only prove the nearness of my mark. The flesh about Mistress Joyce's neck blushed delicately. She put a hand upon it, and for a moment I thought she might rise and sweep out of the chophouse, knocking over my beer or abusing me as she left. Without lowering her eyes, she very gently shook her head and leaned across the board towards me.

You have much to learn about women, she whispered. *What lies beneath my cloth and drapery is more gorgeous than silk and pearls. And I do not speak of spirits.* She leaned back again and picked up her wine. *You will learn*, she said, raising her cup. *I will teach you.*

Bravo! said Petty, pushing his bowl aside.

I understand, she said, *that the workshop is closed and you are banned?*

I swallowed hard. *I am obliged to keep away 'til September; others still use the place.*

No matter. She shrugged. *James has the key?*

Indeed, Petty said, *or as good as. Toby sleeps there – he is Swift's guard dog.*

I think it unwise, I said. *Lovett may appear, or Mistress Popham—*

You lack courage, Mistress Joyce said shrewdly. *Perhaps we should forgo the venture?*

Not at all, Kat, said Petty. *Simply name the hour.*

She smiled and picked up her cloak. *At seven this evening.*

We will be there, said Petty.

She nodded. *Come alone*, she said to me.

I looked to Petty, who bowed gracefully.

I will see that the key is in place, he said.

We stood together. Mistress Joyce looked with dismay at her cloak.

It is irksome, I said foolishly, *riding in the city.*

O, said she, *I had no trouble riding. This was from the boys who saw me coming in. They often throw soils at me if I am alone.* She gestured with my kerchief. *I will have your cloth laundered*, she said, *and return it to you.*

No need, I replied, much dismayed, for it seemed a sorry rag. *Do with it as you will.*

She tucked the cloth into her bodice and pulled her cloak about her. *There. It will save my spirit from soiling*, she said, her lips twitching with amusement.

Twelve

PETTY WALKED WITH ME to the workshop. The hour was six and many were at supper, yet still I had no stomach, though I had not dined that day. Petty planned to await me at the Mermaid, where he said he would sup and save me some claret. I had taken a cup on the way to still myself.

You will have greater need of it when you return, he winked. We rounded the corner and paused before Swift's door. *I have bid Toby unlock to us and then receive none but the lady. He thinks her some new sitter come from court.* He rapped the door.

How does it feel to act the apple-squire? I said.

He smiled. *You are green-gilled, my friend*, he said. *Do not fight it so.*

There is naught to fight, I snapped, though my belly was churned and waterish.

Toby opened and clumsily made his bow. Petty drew him aside and repeated the plan like a lesson. The boy nodded carefully and Petty slipped him coin.

We climbed the stairs to the workshops. The first room stood bare, but for a few washed pots and some new-primed boards. We walked through to the second, where Toby's grinders stood amidst jars and slabs. Petty strode across to Lovett's space and turned his heavy easel to the wall. *I would not have you see the nobles*, he said, *for fear they make you weep. This room is best for the task.*

The other is cleaner, I said.

Aye, yet dark and unlovely. This room has better windows for the light.

We might be seen.

You will not. Who will look? And if you do not take her by the wall there's none to know it. He rubbed his chin. *We must make a bed.*

A bed? I piped.

Aye. Would you have her on the floor?
I will have her nowhere, I spat.
Then our journey is wasted. She must lie or sit. She must have comfort.
A stool suffices.
Fie! cried Petty. *What do you fear so?*
I fear her craft, I sighed, *in truth, I do*. I shook my head. *I only wish to draw her.*
He smiled. *You are subtle, my friend*, he said. *You will have your pictures.*

I paced and waited. The bells of Paul's sounded the hour, followed by lesser chimes and distant peals. I set out chalks and paper, and readied a board, though I little thought to use it. Petty had fetched cushions and spread them with cloth for a bed. Another cushion rested on the stool and I picked it up to follow its threaded patterns with my thumb. The house creaked about me. Toby stirred below. A cart scraped in the street and I went to the casement to view it. I threw the cushion at the stool. I walked to the staircase and back. At length I went down and called to Toby for wine.
I do believe the lady will not come, I said. *Kindly take this coin to the ordinary and bring me a flask of claret.*
Toby hopped from foot to foot, shaking his head at the coin. *Masher Petty done it*, he said. *Masher Petty brung thee Bargandy.*
Burgundy? I said. *When was this?*
Masher Petty give me coin and I brung thee Bargandy. He hopped again, then jolted from the room, coming back with a corked flask and two goblets. *Masher Petty sed brung thee Bargandy soon as lady come.*
Let us uncork it now, I offered.
Toby shook his head fiercely. *Masher Petty sed soon as lady come. Lady come soon.*
I made to wrest the flask from the lad when the door rattled behind us. Toby jumped merrily towards it and handed me the flask. *Lady come*, he said, smiling, *now take thee Bargandy.*

*　　*　　*

Mistress Joyce stepped within and passed her cloak to Toby. She had changed her gown, and the new bodice was lowly cut and very tightly laced. She flicked her glance upon me as I stood by, clutching flask and goblets, and let out a low laugh.

You look the footman, she said, *even to the wandering of your eye. Put that flask down and pour it, would you? You lack the livery to act the part.*

I had thought you might not come, I answered shakily.

Burgundy, is it? I nodded. *Good*, she said, *you offer a fine French welcome.*

I thought that more of your manner, I retorted.

Dieu! she mocked. *That is not mannerly. Yet as you have such a low view of me, shall we go to it, monsieur?*

I quailed and stepped aside. *The workshops are above*, I said. *Permit me to show you.*

She nodded, seized a goblet and drank deeply. *Bring the flask*, she said. *I know where I am going.*

I followed her. At the stair top she turned sharply to the left and opened the door into the household quarters.

Those are Master Swift's rooms, I called out. She nodded and strode into the passage.

At the third door along she halted and looked about. *I cannot recall*, she said, *which is his and which belongs to the harpy.*

The workshops are readied, I insisted. *The rooms are set for your comfort.*

She raised an eyebrow and drank again. *Do you truly think*, she said, holding out her cup, *that I wish to sit in the stink of your vile workshops?*

They are freshly cleaned, I said, pouring more wine. *You will have every comfort.*

I think not, she said slyly. *I spent an evening on the floor in there before. It gave little comfort. Would you treat me so?*

No, indeed, I submitted, *and yet—*

Aha! she cried. *I recall it now. This is his chamber.*

Mistress Joyce flung open the opposite door and strode within. She turned about, her gown brushing the boards. The room was low and dark, though the bed itself was hung with cloth deeply red and rich enough to have been stained by the wine I carried.

God's Soul, what a drab little room it is, she said, and sank sighing onto the bed. *A drab little room for a drab little man. Is it not as poorly appointed as your Master?*

Her manner irked. *You would better know that, madam*, I retorted. *He is your Master too.*

Ha! She waved her goblet at me. *Come, more wine, Master Footman.*

You have a thirst.

Aye, and a hunger likewise. Peter Swift is not my Master.

You are his mistress, I countered. *Does that not make it so?*

Mistress, mistress. She laughed again. *What a word is that! It signifies nothing. I am Mistress Joyce. Master Swift has his Mistress Swift, and you, no doubt, have a Mistress – what is your family?*

I am a widower, I said.

Indeed? Then a free man. I am glad of it. She drank off her wine and held out her hand. *Would you deny me?* she said, smiling.

You may take more wine if you will, I said firmly, setting down the flask. *If you wish to sit for me here I will fetch my chalks.*

You are an angry man, she said quietly. *Be not so quick to judge me. You care little for your Master Swift, and believe me truly, I care even less.* She beckoned to me. *Come, you are free, are you not? You told me so just now. And I am also free. You think me a creature of pleasure. Well then, how should such a creature deal with an artist, in an empty house, in a broad and red-hung bed?*

An artist such as I would fetch his chalks, I answered flatly, readying my retreat.

Mistress Joyce rose quickly, came towards me and, setting down her goblet, held up her hands. *You are a very proper man*, she whispered. She touched my cheek artfully. *Almost beautiful, like a woman. See your hands? They are very soft.* She turned my palms over, then, stepping forward, cupped them to her breasts. Her bodice twitched; I cried out and, though I sought to wrench away, she held me fast. *I am glad you came,* she said. She breathed quickly, the wine from her mouth strong as she spoke. *I liked you greatly for your spirit*, she murmured, *but I already thought you very handsome.*

I pulled from her but she thrust herself against me, pressing me to the wall. She raised her mouth to mine and crushed it, parting my lips: I gaspingly tasted the Burgundy of her tongue as it slithered between my teeth. As suddenly, she drew back again, her eyes regarding me with glittering triumph. My lower lip pulsed achingly and I pressed my fingers to it.

I have stolen your breath, she said, *as you have stolen my heart.*

I laughed, though shudderingly. *That is a practised line. Where did you learn it – in the playhouse or the whorehouse?*

You are not hospitable, she said, wagging a finger with mock severity. *I must teach you better manners.* She thrust at me again, her mouth wet and eager.

I twisted away in alarm. *Do not handle me so*, I begged, *you are in error!*

Why did you ask this of me if you did not desire it also? You saw very well how I looked upon you in the chophouse.

You did not look at me at all! I cried. *And when you did you grew vexed.*

Truly, she laughed, *you know nothing at all of women! Would you have me make moon faces at you like a serving girl? But you are from the country, are you not? Perhaps*, she said, grasping at my points, *you are accustomed to rougher courtship.*

My legs weakened and I could scarce think beyond her pressings. *I am accustomed to none*, I cried weakly and, pushing her aside, freed myself from her pawing. *Truly, madam*, I gasped, *I am not as you think.*

Pfu! she exclaimed, staggering slightly. She turned from me and poured more wine. *You do not desire me then? And yet you are flushed and eager!* Her mouth twisted angrily, her eyes blazed with accusation. *Did you treat your dead wife so?*

I straightened myself and pressed my hands together, moist-palmed and atremble. Looking upon her then, fierce and demanding, I truly wondered at the workings of my unmannish body. *I am sorry for the hurt of it, madam*, I said gently, *but I wish only to paint your likeness.*

She breathed rapidly and drank swiftly. As she drained the cup again she wiped her mouth as she had done earlier, in the chophouse. I smiled and she threw the goblet at me. It bounced and rattled cheaply on the boards.

Whoreson, she spat. She stood up stiffly. *Very well then, let us to the workshop. If you will not fuck me I trust you will at least have the courtesy to draw me well.*

I will not relate the whole of that evening, though it is burned upon my memory and, after all that has since passed, its meaning grows clearer with time. Yet, for all my shame in it, I must recall the greater part of what happened.

Mistress Joyce sat for me, unhooking and unlacing herself with ire and lying in exquisite wrath upon the bed of Petty's making. Truly there was never such beauty in woman as in the white limbs of Katharine Joyce that evening, limbs that beckoned with desire and pulsed with fury. Her body was smooth as I had thought it, her feet small, her calves narrow, her thighs slight. Her belly was a gentle slope that led to the childish roundness of her breasts, her arms spread with generous abandon. Her slender fingers curled with passion, yet pointed with a rigid indignation. She was indeed a siren of the fairest shape, and her dark eyes burned with such an intense hatred for me that – sweet Bess forgive me! – I craved with all my being that I might satisfy her as she so willed me to.

She watched me as I rendered her. My hands jolted much as I glanced up to her and down again, tracing her form upon the page. She was terrible and lovely, and none knew it better than she.

I see you, she said. *I see your desire. Are you an unwhole man? You quiver like a schoolboy.* Her look pierced me. *Do you grieve still for your wife?*

I sensed an escape. *You are in the right*, I answered, my cheeks scalding. *My grief is fresh.*

Then you should seek solace. Such a man as you should not deny his nature. She sat up then, breaking the pose. *Come to me, Master Painter*, she whispered, her fury gone. *Do you not miss the sweet comforts of your wife! Do you not ache for the marriage bed!* She patted the cloth beside her. *This bed is a makeshift, but it suffices. Would you not try it, and me, for comfort!*

Kindly desist, I muttered. *A man cannot miss what he has not had.*

How so! she said. *You told me you had wived.*

I did not tell you all. I paused to warn her off but, discomfited by her stare, relinquished. *My bride died on the day,* I conceded. *We were never brought to bed.*

O! she gasped. *Then I understand your fear!*

Mistress Joyce rose from the bed and bent before me, her face above mine; she held my chin and tipped back my head with expert grace. Her black curls fell prickling upon my cheeks, smelling thickly of pomade. Again she pressed her mouth to mine and I, unmade by my secret, did not fight. I yielded my chalks and paper and wrapped my arms about her waist; she laughed and, unwrapping them, straddled the chair, resting lightly upon my knees. Her skin was finely powdered and wondrous soft; fearfully I followed its lines with chalked fingers, besmearing the surface. She moaned and giggled; I tested the shadows of her flesh with my thumbs. *You know not how well I like a painter,* she sighed, leaning back and smiling slyly. She arched her back and thrust her breasts towards me; I marked the curves of her chest and ran a finger along each rib.

She laughed. *What do you seek!*

How differently made is a woman, I marvelled. I took hold of her elbow and raised her arm: the breast lifted, the nipple pointed.

In diverse ways, she whispered. *I will show you.* She stood and pulled me to the cushioned bed; I followed and she lay back eagerly, lowering me upon her. Smilingly she untucked the cloth of my shirt; her practised hand traced the hairs on my chest and belly, and sought between the lacing of my points.

She froze. Her fingers felt wildly, her smile fell into scorn. She pushed and pulled at me, frowning; she grasped and tugged as the dairymaid at the udder. I broke from her arms and sat back, smiling sadly upon her. *It is no use,* I said. *I cannot.* And alas I spoke true, for in the face of this, my greatest temptation, my manhood was little more than a button loosely sewn to the lining of my breeches.

Bastard! she screamed, clawing at me. *Get out of my sight, you filthy sodomite! Get out!* She flung her clothes at me, and then her shoes. *Get out, or I'll have you hanged for this, you wretched dog!*

Reeling and rueful, I made straight to the Mermaid.

God's teeth, Rob, what did you say to her? Petty was not yet deep in his cups and he sat me gently beside him. *George!* he called. *Get my friend here some hot brandy.*

Petty dabbed at my brow while the tapster hurriedly fetched me brandy and citrons in a mug. *Drink, by Jesu,* Petty urged. *You are paler than the grave, and you bleed again.* I felt where Mistress Joyce had scratched at me, a gouge that ran above both eyes. *Truly, Rob, you have a poor way with women.*

I knew it a foolish notion, I said sadly. *I feared she would work upon me thus.*

You refused her then? I nodded, and drank quickly. *For pity's sake, man,* Petty cried, *why did you not have her and have done? You might know she would take it ill.*

I shook my head. *I could not. Now she is in a fury.*

Little wonder, my friend said. *She is the finest piece in town or country. I am amazed she did not unman you there and then.*

She would have little joy of it, I said. Petty laughed.

The brandy scorched my tongue. Though the night was still and hot I badly felt the need of the liquor's warmth. Petty shook his head at me and shrugged.

What do I now? I said. *I have lost my model.*

Wait, he said. *Wait 'til September, and pray that Swift will give you back your place.*

I would sooner back to Thetford than cow to him, I said.

Then to Thetford with you, answered Petty mildly, *where you will keep safe and silent. You would fare better there. You have too quick a way of making enemies, my friend.*

Thirteen

IT WAS BUT A day before she came again.

Scribblers and players are ever meting out revenge and justice, thinking it the matter of our time and the proper course of Nature. Woman, they remind us, is an inconstant creature; roused in her fury, she is but a temptress beckoning us to damnation – she dances man to destruction as she first drove him from bliss. What poor lot befalls he who crosses both paths, the subject of a wrathful woman, bent on revenge!

Such players' yarns are heresies, for Woman is Nature, and Nature, though cruel, can be moved to fostering pity. Kat Joyce was no penitent Magdalene, nor did she think herself anything but wronged – yet she sought me out, and with no thought of my destruction.

Petty came to my room, his hands wringing. It was early, the sun not yet grown hot and the streets slowly stirring with business. I had lain long and wakeful on my bed, wondering at the days that would follow this one, and if they might ever yet serve some good purpose. I sat up when the door sounded below and pulled on breeches and boots. Petty found me at the basin, smoothing the hair that stood all at angles from my brow and ears.

Good morrow, Petty, I said. *You wring your hands like a laundress.*

Rob, be calm. He hemmed and shuffled his feet. *Katharine Joyce is below and asks to speak with you.*

I felt at the ridge on my brow, still raw and angry. *What business does she have?* I laughed and dabbled water on the scratch. *Does she bring rope and a warrant?*

Do not jest, Rob. She would speak with you, she has come alone.

How does she seem?

He shrugged. *I know not, but she seems unlike herself. If it were any other, I would say she seemed abashed.*

I will come down, I said.

Put on a shirt, then. If she sees you thus the plot will begin again.

Mistress Joyce stood at the foot of the stairs and watched as I descended. Her hands rested modestly together, her mouth was a tight line. I looked for some trickery in the fold of her skirts, some hidden flash of blade or iron bar, for I had heard of scorned bawds and women brawlers who caught men thus. I lingered on the stair for her to move aside, yet she stood determined. Petty was behind me and called out jovially to make way, but still she resisted. Her eyes, hard and brittle, settled on my brow, and her straight mouth twitched.

I should have killed you, she said evenly.

Madam, I began, *please do not think—*

I made good work on your face, she said. *Would I had done so lower. Yet who would suffer the difference?* She smiled bitterly. *There is nothing to be lost.*

Petty was on the stair beside me. He nudged my back and smiled briskly. *Well, Kat,* he said, *you caught Rob here still abed and without his breakfast.* He stepped forward and moved her aside with a graceful bow. *Would you eat something with us? Or perhaps you would care to sit—*

God's Soul, James! she snapped. *Hold your peace and let us speak alone.*

Petty looked to me and raised his brows: I nodded, for she seemed no more dangerous then than she ever had before. *Very good, Kat,* Petty said, his voice all honeyed, *I will take the sweet city air and return with bread and milk.* He skipped to the door. *Or eggs – you like a brace of soft eggs, do you not, Kat?*

The door closed behind him and Mistress Joyce's shoulders sank. She turned aside and studied the room afresh, as though she knew not where she stood.

Another drab little room, I said.

She picked at the cheap hangings. *Very drab, yet not so*

apt. She sighed. *Do not stand on the stair, I will not claw you now.*

I stepped down and straightway she came and leaned against me, pressing her face to my shoulder. I feared her still and stiffened, yet she laughed and held my hands to her waist.

Fear not, she said. She looked sadly at my face and, lifting a hand, traced the angry scar with her finger. *A Kat scratch*, she whispered, and smiled.

It is raw, I said, *yet you believe that I deserve it.*

She nodded. *It is true, for you were brutish. But now you must have pity, Master Painter. You have much affected me, and this is all a new matter for me to reckon.*

You will have known far better men, I said warily. *There is nothing new or of merit in me.*

Not so, she said gently, *not so.* She leaned harder upon me.

Madam, I ventured, gently prising her away, *I cannot give you what you crave.*

You might, she said. *You have what I would ask of you.*

It is not my part, I said, *truly.*

Aye, she laughed, *you lack the part, that much is certain. Yet you have something else you might give me. What was it you said you wanted from our meeting?*

Nothing but to paint you, madam. I would not—

Paint me, she said. *That is the very thing I would have you do.* She took my hands from her waist and held them before her. *There is skill in these hands, is there not? You wish to profit by them?*

I nodded. *It is my hope to do so. But I do not understand you.*

Paint me, she murmured, pressing my hands to her face. *Paint me, and I will see you prosper.*

I shook my head. *You now wish to sit for me? Madam, I am confused.*

Kat, she said. *I am Kat. I will sit for you, if you will paint me. I am proffering a bargain: my body for your brushes, my services of procurement for these subtle fingers.* She kissed my thumbs and gently bit the knuckles. *I will find you patrons and you, in return, will pleasure me with paint.*

So it was that Mistress Joyce and I bargained our futures together. Our pact was one to rival those revengers of stage and curtain, and we sealed it, that evening, with scarlet and sable in the hasty and ill-lit theatre of Swift's workshop. The time, as I would later learn, was short and eager; but Kat was much the keenest of we two and I left her neither maddened nor thwarted. I rendered her on a panel with deep hues of reds, fresh and vivid; she watched me keenly and beckoned me from my work. I quit the easel and took my palette to her skin, mixing upon her pallor the dark stains of sienna. I wrote upon her thighs the names of diverse colours; I played upon her with thick bristles and flattened sables. I sought for her all sundry textures, of smoothest oils and rough-ground pigments, colouring her skin with boldness and brilliance. I daubed her with broadly sweeping strokes and she cried out greatly; with better patience I filled in her shadows, working my sables finely. Kat was quick to school me, steering the fine hairs of my brushes with a trembling delight.

At length she desisted and stretched out, bruised and burnished, upon the workshop floor.

You have scratched me, she murmured.

We are equal then, I said. I raised myself achingly from the cushions. *I had no thought to.*

It did not hurt me. It was the sharper bristles. She sat up and regarded the earthen tones on her stomach. *What paint is this? I am not such colours.*

Umber. You are both raw and burnt, I said, wiping at her belly with the floorsheet.

Where was this cloth from? she asked lazily. *It is not a painter's rag.*

We keep a chest of cloths for draping and covering the floors. It will not be missed. I rubbed at the crimson line that stretched up from her hip to her navel. *This red is a fine foil for your skin.*

I have a gown that colour. She laughed. *It is also in your hair.*

I rubbed my head on the sheet. *I am now thankful that I have no beard.*

It is a pity. She stroked my chin. *You would make a fine, broad-bristled brush.*

As Petty does? She smiled and my gorge rose sourly. *I knew that you would have used him thus,* I barbed.

I told you how well I like a painter.

Swift likewise?

Aye, what else would I have him for? It is the paint I want of him, not the painter. She sighed and stretched. *He is a practised artist.*

He is a feeble artist, I crabbed. I pulled my shirt about me and made to rise.

Stay, Kat whispered, holding fast my arm. *You fared wondrous well.*

Then you will need no other painter, I baited. *Yet I wonder at that.*

You are young and proper, she said, *for what more might I ask?*

I took comfort from that, though it be but a gilded truth. *We are agreed then?*

She pressed my hands, much besmirched with oils, upon her hips. *You are skilled in your art,* she said slyly, *you seem no Prentice.* She leaned back on the cushions, moving her thighs apart. *Tell me, Master Painter,* she sighed, *what shade is this? I cannot see it thus.*

A subtle blue, I said, smearing some onto the tip of my finger. She gasped sharply. *See?* I held it up. *A rare and precious tone, and very costly.*

Preciously placed.

A fine setting for such a jewel. I dabbed gently with the cloth. *For our next sitting I will find some silver grounds; we use them often, they are but stored away.* I stroked her circle of ultramarine. *This would make elegant silver,* I said, *worthy of attentive polishing.*

You will make a fine courtier, Rob, she sighed. Her thighs twitched. *But you must be mindful of how you clean the silver – the blue paint stings.*

Fourteen

THE SUMMER, WHICH ONCE had threatened long, proved of few days indeed. September approached, heralding the return of the court and, with it, Master Swift. I had learned to dread the date of this homecoming; not solely for the shame of my forfeit and humbled return to the school, but for the now more urgent issue of where I might meet Kat.

Kat was unworried. We spoke of it throughout August, for I grew to fear the end of our evening sittings more than she. At the last I grew bitter, fretting at something I could not place. I tried a new panel, which I thought to overpaint for some commission – yet while all my early renderings were fair, this board took very ill. I strove vainly for an hour or more and then surrendered. Kat broke the pose and I sat on the boards beside her.

Swift will be here come Sunday, I said. *Mistress Popham arrives tomorrow, tending house again.*

Let them come, Kat said, studying my palette. *What does it signify?*

It signifies the end of our meetings. Do you wish it so?

It signifies no such thing. We cannot meet here, but that makes no end of it. She pointed daintily to a puddle of verdigris. *I would like this green, and thickly.*

Where then? You will not let me to your lodgings.

They would not suit, as I have said. She stretched out on her front and raised her shoulders. *Just between, and to the base.*

You have some secret there? You do not trust me.

It might seem, she said darkly, *that it is not I who lack the trust.*

I swept her spine with broad strokes, first with fingers, then with squirrel hair. Her back arched in delight. *We cannot be thus at Petty's*, I insisted.

He would not disapprove. Indeed, she teased, *he might well wish to join us.*

I rose and picked up the brushes. I was easily baited, though I knew it for no harm.

Do not desist! she wailed. *I do not mean it.*

I care not, I said, brutish. *'Tis but a whore's trick.*

You are uncivil.

I sat at the easel and commenced cleaning the brushes. *Let Swift come back, then*, I crabbed. *He can replace the painter and finish the man's task as well. He could install you here for all his students to practise on.*

It is not Swift I want, she said.

Nor one of his students, I'll warrant.

Kat rose and wrapped the sheet about her. She came to the easel to study my poor, angry panel. *You paint badly today*, she said.

I know it, I snapped.

You are jealous.

I gripped her waist, turning my face to the floorsheet. Bundled about her belly, it smelt warmly of dust and oil. Beneath the white cloth her whiter skin was streaked with verdigris; I turned her about to trace the paint with my fingers. The pale hue, meek and yellowish as new hay uncut, sallowed her flesh. A sharper tone would become her better; I set to mixing one. She leaned against me as I worked, dabbling a range of greens along her spine. *I will not share this*, I determined. I drew a swift arc of paint up to her neck, the skin between her shoulders rippling tautly. I flicked the tip of my brush against her ear, daubing it as with an ear-jewel. She shuddered, the fine hair on the flesh of her neck rising with pleasure. *What I do not enjoy you may share out as you will*, I said. My brush fell and traced a line to her hip. *Never this.*

The eve of Swift's arrival saw much industry. Petty took himself to the workshops to finish some trifle he had been assigned with, and there found Lovett and Benson both, speedily completing.

Lovett's nobles had been rejected anew, the date for their delivery a month past. His face, my friend recorded, was sour with fear and his brow thunderous; for the morning's length he strove over the nose and lips of his honoured patron.

I was near weeping, Rob, Petty reported. *Truly, I felt almost moved to pity.*

A worthy emotion, I said, *too valuable to spend on such a dog.*

Lovett had, it transpired, received an admonition, written in Swift's hand and delivered to his lodgings. Petty had heard this from Benson who, being waked by Lovett early that morning, had been obliged to make straight to the workshops and spend this last day assisting him. So fearful had Lovett grown of Swift's displeasure that he even approached Petty for some aid. Petty gleefully obliged.

Would you had been there, he crowed. *O! – says Lovett,* (here Petty's voice pinched whining through his nose) *O! kind Petty – I jest not, Rob,* he said *kind Petty – would you oblige me very greatly and advise me on the bridge of this man's nose? I see not where the fault lies, and yet I fear there is one. – Well,* I replied, *had it been a bird of some kind, or a likeness of yourself, there would have been no fault, for that is a masterful beak.* Petty laughed.

I nodded at the tale. He eyed me soberly. *What is it?* he asked. *You take his part now?*

Nay, I assured, *you were gentle with him. Did he not steal outright?*

He did. And yet you seem in doubt.

I shrugged. *Naught but a wish that things were not as they are.*

My friend knew well that I hoped never to go back – neither to cow to Swift, nor to face Lovett again, however shamed he might be. My Summer had seen a great shift in circumstance: I had learned such skills as I had never thought to use, and found a fond helpmate in my search for patronage. There was more yet, though I knew not how to name it. Without the court come back, no patrons might be found; with their return, other doors would lock.

*   *   *

Fortune showed her guileful hand elsewhere. Swift returned, red from much riding in the sun and standing about in court gardens, and grew redder with barely concealed ire at Lovett. Petty relayed all that evening, and announced that Ambrose, mightily swelled and in ascent, had garnered interest on the Progress.

He has some patronage, Petty said, *some new figures at court. Puritans, of course, but moneyed. They took to his icy manner, no doubt.*

And Lovett?

Lovett is in exile, while Ambrose basks in Swift's glory.

Until he sets up alone, I noted.

Aye, nor will it be long ere that happen. Ambrose is no fool. He grimaced. *Popham was vile as ever, you will delight to know, forcing us to dine all together. She dealt us some hideous flesh in a salted sauce, only God may know what ditch she found it in. Benson is grown more friendly. He spoke twice this day without his being spoken to first.*

He forgives your hideous papistry?

It is the Oxford air, he laughed. *It breathes confidence in a man.*

And Falconbridge?

He clapped a hand over his mouth. *God's Soul, I forgot! This is the most seasoned news of all! He was caught with a girl, a blameless young creature he found crossing a field somewhere. The townsfolk put him in the stocks! The maid – as she still is, it seems – was none other than the local JP's daughter. Marvellous ill fortune for the simian one. She had been visiting an ailing tenant's wife, or some such charitable thing, and Falconbridge took her and forced her in a ditch. The poor girl set up such a screaming that all came running to lynch him there and then.*

A pity they did not.

Aye, and a miracle that they did not hang him after. But she was of age, it turned out, though small for it. Old for Falconbridge. It seems he desisted when he saw the truth of it. No harm was done.

No harm? And if she had been broken?

Well, there's the matter of it. She was not. He shrugged.

Be sure he will want to relate all to you. He likes to tell his tales.

My gorge rose. Such were the men I must face at Swift's again. Petty gripped queasily at his stomach in retort.

Come, he reproached, *you did not dine as I was made to do. You have no cause to choke.* He cleared his throat with dramatic affectation. *Let us sup and sip to the Summer we have lost; we missed the Plague, though you dallied with the Pox.*

Rhymester, I sneered.

Petty grinned. *He wants you back, Rob. He asked for you. Will you go?*

Aye, I'll go, but I wish the company were better.

Petty's face was dour, but mockingly. *You scorn your fellow students now. You fall from leisured lover of courtesans back to mere Prentice!* He sniffed. *I recall plucking you from the kennels of Southwark but this season gone. Do not grow haughty.*

Fifteen

TRUTH IS SELDOM SPOKEN at first meeting, yet Mistress Joyce did not care for pleasantries. She had warned me in the clamour of the chophouse that I had much to learn of women: there too she had pledged to teach me well. I had not reckoned that my return to Swift's workshops, disgraced as I was, would prove the setting for another of her lessons – yet so it did, to the bemusement of us all.

I knocked on Swift's door in sombre mood. Petty had walked with me, buoying me with mirth, yet I dreaded sneering Lovett's face and, worse yet, Swift's refusal. Popham opened, her eyes agog as ever.

Good morrow, Mistress Popham! Petty cried heartily. *A fine Autumn morning, is it not? Most wondrous air for the complexion.*

She stared at me. *You're back then*, she huffed.

Good morrow, madam, I said.

She stood stubbornly on the threshold, her great length filling the space. She reached for the handle again, as if to slam the door upon us should we move.

Fine as the morning be, said Petty bluffly, *it ages quickly. Master Swift awaits us.*

Popham licked her lips thickly, her great eyes yet upon me. I felt as the hare before the wolf, and shivered as weakly. She huffed again and slowly turned her back, swinging away from us and leaving the door agape. Petty sighed.

She had thought herself cured of you, he laughed, *and you confound her. You are a breaker of hearts, my friend.*

That is evil talk, I hissed, *do not threaten so.*

I followed Petty up the stair and through the rooms. My eye took straightway on the spot where Kat had lain, the place of many meetings. I had scrubbed hard at the boards where we had stained them with favoured colours, the floorsheets rucked beneath or falling short of the cushions. A streak of crimson had taken hold and needed sanding; that board now showed as clean as if new shaven. Petty followed my look and smiled broadly.

Toby, stirring varnish, grinned a welcome. Benson appeared and blushed his surprise.

Well met, he said. *I am – glad – glad indeed, to see you returned here.* He held out his hand in welcome. *I hope, that is, I would much like to see, more of the manner of – your –* he whispered *– Master John.*

The sun has strengthened you, I said. We shook hands; his grip was staunch and sturdy. Petty raised a brow. *What has befallen you, Benson?* I remarked. *You seem much altered.*

Benson blushed again. Petty laughed.

I think it is wenching, Petty said. Benson's crimson deepened. *I hit the mark!* He clapped Benson's shoulder.

I – I made an offer, this month past. I think she may accept me.

A betrothal? I said. *Brave news indeed – but what says Swift of this?*

Benson shrugged. *He knows not.* He smiled thinly. *And I care not.*

The very spirit! cried Petty. *I am heartily glad for you, it will be your making.*

My unmaking – here – perhaps.

It seems the fashion, said Petty, winking. *One need only look about.*

Have no fear, I assured Benson, *there are far better places.*

A cry rose from behind us. I turned to see Falconbridge, gleefully stepping, and behind him Lovett, his mouth wide in exclamation.

Why, 'tis Robin the Netherman! he scoffed.

Benson stepped away.

Haha! squeaked Falconbridge, *I thought him gone, truly, I little thought to see him more, and yet there he be and bold as ever, as if—*

The magistrate did not cut your tongue out then, I snapped.

How are the horses, Netherman? Lovett sneered. *They say you have been riding much this Summer.*

They say you have been painting a commission, I answered sweetly. *How goes your work?*

Ask not Lovett how the work goes, Petty said. *Ambrose is the one with works to paint.*

Lovett strained towards us. Petty laughed and knocked at Swift's parlour. Swift's voice bellowed within and Petty opened.

I have brought him, Master Swift, he announced.

I heard Swift's grunt. Ambrose appeared in the doorway, bowing smoothly. *Master Swift will see you now*, he murmured.

He turned within and I made to follow, catching Lovett's eye.

The Master chooses a better-mannered dog, I said, stepping into the parlour. Lovett lunged as Petty closed the door; I heard their muffled kicks landing behind me.

Swift was indeed redder and shorter of temper. He eyed me with a furious look and leaned back heavily in his chair.

Well, Leggatt, he snapped, *think you the Robin has served his penance?*

I would not presume to judge, Master Swift, Ambrose said. *Your opinion will be well considered, doubtlessly.* He pressed his lips together.

Swift snorted at me. *Lovett still hates you, then?*

He is the same as ever, I answered mildly.

Ha! He opened a book on his desk and flicked the page impatiently. *That's good enough for me. If your presence irks him, you are welcome back.* He waved us away. *Get to your place. Leggatt will find you some task.*

The remainder of the morning passed evenly. I set up easel again and Ambrose bade me fill some blocks of background. Little seemed changed these many days, though the light was much altered in the rooms and I might no longer make free with costly pigments, nor lie upon the floor.

Shortly after dinner a visitor arrived. Popham came in with a deeply scoring frown, calling for the Master as though he be her naughty child. Ambrose, swanlike, moved across the room and effortlessly soothed her; he spoke to the visitor in the passageway and bid them enter. His steps were followed by the thud of Popham's descent on the stairs, and the delicate tread of a woman in soft shoes.

I knew the tread, of course, for I had heard it many times upon those boards. Petty saw my faltering and looked to the doorway, just as Kat Joyce entered, gauzily dressed.

Well, said she, brightly looking round, *so this is the workshop.*

I felt with my teeth for the inner swell of my lips and gently clamped them close. Petty frowned and shook his head at me.

My fellow students halted in their work and stared at her abashed. Toby began to murmur recollection; Petty grasped the lad and took him from the room.

This way, madam, said Ambrose smoothly. Kat put her arm on his and, smiling pointedly about her to all save myself, was led into Swift's parlour.

Benson beamed. Lovett let out a whistle and began to laugh; Falconbridge commenced his prattle. My blood had thinned to water and I sank heavily upon my chair.

Ambrose reappeared and called for Toby. Petty had taken the lad below, I guessed, and Benson was duly sent to fetch some wine. Footsteps sounded up and down the stairs, doors opened and closed, boards creaked. I could not follow all. Ere long I heard her laughter and looked up to see Lovett's eyes, hard and intent upon me. I stood to my easel and feigned attention to my board. Lovett nodded slyly; when I looked again Petty was at the doorway, beckoning. I followed him to the corridor.

What is she doing, Rob? he hissed.

I shrugged. *She is a whore, he a customer.*

Petty swore and struck me in the chest. I reeled – the blow was hard, yet I was so benumbed I scarcely felt it.

Fool! he snapped. *Whatever her purpose, it is for your good. How dare you speak so?*

I shook my head. *I speak as I see. I know nothing of this.*

A door slammed hard behind us. Petty froze, his eyes widening. *I could not keep Toby from her sight*, he whispered. *Now she has dragged him aside. She will ask him who Kat is, and he will prattle.*

She? I piped. I stared stupidly.

Mistress Swift! Petty urged. He looked behind him.

A querulous voice, sharp and spiteful, rose from the household quarters. I strained to listen and caught the sound of Toby's babble – *lady come oft*, he sobbed, *Masher sed to sey naught but she come oft an' now I ha' tell thee an' hil be raw wi' me.*

Petty rolled his eyes. *Let us be out of the path when the lightning strikes*, he said. He held my elbow and steered us back to our places.

The storm broke hard behind us. Mistress Swift raged into the room, a blaze of righteous fury.

I had heard of her often, yet I had never seen her. No tales could have prepared me for the sight. Her eyes, black-rimmed and staring, glared Medusa-like upon us. She was broad and heavy-boned, her frame ludicrously widened with a Spanish farthingale. Ropes of beading swung across her chest that, hoisted high, swelled forth from her bodice. She seemed a padded bolster sewn into the velvet of her dress, her stuffing bulging at the looser seams. Her hair was a frenzy of unpinned curls, false shaped and dyed with saffron, flying above her face like burning thatch. The face itself bore signs of a lost beauty, battered thin by cares and jealousies. Her ribs rose and fell in shallow, painful breaths.

Where is she? she bawled.

Lovett and Falconbridge turned back to their easels. Petty touched my sleeve and looked away. Even Benson knew how to escape, his bowing head aquiver. She looked to each in turn, and fixed on me.

She strode towards me – then, catlike, she froze. A sound had caught her ear, the sound of female laughter. She paused, head cocked towards the parlour, legs astride. Her skirts swung about her like a slowly tolling bell. Her eyes, still wide upon me, shone with tears.

I tasted the bitter share of this humiliation. I could not even curse myself a cuckold, having but held the fruit ere I had dropped it. Mistress Swift, in her anger, waxed magnificent; indignant, she ran upon her rival.

Her scream was short but piercing.

Drinking! she cried. *Drinking with her, a court whore!*

I looked to Petty. All were clustering before the door and he signalled that I join them.

Ambrose was already by Mistress Swift's side, speaking soft words of pardon. Swift himself was half unbreeched and fell to furiously re-tucking and re-lacing. Lovett snorted loudly. Kat remained languorous in her seat, her flimsy dress unrucked, her features all at ease. Mistress Swift made to strike her, but Kat held up her hand.

Do not upset yourself, madam, Ambrose soothed.

Mistress Swift lunged at him. *You!* she screamed. *I would have thought better of you, Ambrose Leggatt! To think it would be you, procuring whores and brandy!*

Claret, Kat corrected.

Ambrose smiled. *Come, ladies, let us make less of this scene, shall we not?* He gestured towards us, standing by and staring.

Swift, his hasty garb complete, raised a fist. *Get back to work, you idlers!* he bawled. He made to close the parlour door.

Kat held up her hand again. *I will leave you now,* she said, *you have much to speak of.* She rose, curtseyed demurely and stepped away. She paused to close the door gently behind her, shutting out Swift's astonished face and further ribald screamings.

Kat smoothed her dress and walked towards us, her head high, her eyes bright with amusement. We moved aside to let her pass. She brushed my sleeve and smiled. *I am free,* she whispered. She paused in the workshop door and turned back to us. *I am free,* she said aloud, *I am at liberty with the whole afternoon to come. And what an afternoon!* She smiled roundly at us, then turned and descended the stairs. All held their breath 'til the door below sounded and she went into the street.

Ambrose appeared behind us and cleared his throat. *Master Swift has granted us all a half-holiday,* he said softly. *Clean up quickly and come not back 'til morning.*

As any might guess, Petty and I repaired to the Mermaid. There we were hailed by George the tapster who, his hands busy about some brimming jugs, gestured to the table beside him.

A note, said he, *brought this half hour past for the hand of Master James Petty*.

We looked to the folded paper, sealed and titled. Petty took it up.

Woman's hand, said George, setting down the jugs. *Boy brought it, said he'd been told you'd come hither*.

I am a man of habits, smiled Petty. *All may know I would come*. He turned the paper in his hands. *We are released, so let us drink. Claret is the choice of the day, is it not?*

We took to a bench by the barrels. Petty waved the note at me and grinned.

I think this more meant for you, he said. *Yet, it has my name. I will open it*. He broke the seal and made a great show of reading the page, while keeping it hid from me.

I care not for your love missives, I said. *I will leave you if you have some assignation*.

He widened his eyes in mock astonishment, nodding at the paper. *Humm*, he said. *Humm! Hum-hum-hum*.

'Tis worse than the theatre, I said. *Shall I fetch you a bladder of pig's blood?* He ignored me and feigned reading the page anew. *Where is that claret?* I sighed.

George came with the flask and cups. He set them down and hovered at Petty's elbow; Petty drew the page away from his sight. George laughed.

No fear of that, he said, *I can scarce read a ledger*. He nodded at me and shuffled off. *I hope it be a woman*, he called, *with such concealings*.

I doubt it not, I said. I poured and drank.

Well, said Petty at last, raising his cup. *Well, well*.

Come, enough clowning. What does she say?

Petty huffed. *Very well, as you know all. Shall I let you see it or read it to you?* He offered the paper and then withdrew it. *I will read aloud*, he said. *There are passages I might omit*. I sat back. Petty cleared his throat as if to begin, then shrugged. *Aye! Enough indeed*, he cried, *read it for yourself*.

I took the page. Kat's writing was neat, yet long looped and slanting much forward. The paper was scattered with hesitant blots of ink beside great forceful letters. It was a halting page; I looked long ere I heard the words themselves.

Dearest James, she wrote, *it has come that I must act stridently and to good effect for the advancement of our professions and for the better hopes of your dear friend Rob, wherewith, as you doubtless understand, I have agreement. As my liaison with Peter Swift has proved of small advantage I deem to break with him in the shortest manner. This not least for the pleasure it gives me to throw him off, wretch that he is. For that end, I will seek him at your school this afternoon. I am informed that his wife will be at leisure to intrude upon us.*

I write of this for fear that your friend's pride may confound his reasoning. I freely admit that I do not indulge in that fashionable vanity, Shame – as you have cause to know – yet I would urge you speak with him and advance some understanding on my part. He is greatly skilled and I would see his merits answered. Tell him this.

You will delight with me that my efforts move apace. I am expected in the Strand tonight, where some well-placed gentlemen have arranged for entertainments. I will adventure some patronage for your ambitious friend. Kindly assure him that I enquire constantly of suitable lodgings for our continuation, even unto the irritation of my acquaintance.

My gratitude is as ever openly expressed; be confident that any visit to my lodgings will find me
Your Kind Kat.

I laid the paper in my lap.

So, said Petty roundly. *She works for your favour, Rob.*

Indeed! I took up the page frowningly. *Do not misplace your confidence – she is Your Kind Kat.* I threw the letter to him. *Do not keep the lady waiting, Petty, she is expected elsewhere this evening.*

God's blood! Petty bawled. *Must you ever deny what is before you? She has thrown Swift aside. She did so even before your very eyes, that you might know the why of it.* He poured and drank angrily. *I am confounded if I understand her love of thee, truly.*

You have mistook, I said. *Her heart opens as often as her legs. Now she offers you her favours.*

She procures for you! he snapped. *Who then is the whore?*

Though he irked me, Petty was in the right. Ever did he see Kat clearly, while I would but squint and strive toward her likeness. After a silent, scourging sevennight she penned a further note, sent straight to my hand; she had wooed and won me a patron, a gentleman usher in the circle of My Lord Leicester.

My directions were brief, for my nameless notable had no liking to discuss the trifles of art with some painter. *He wishes for something allegorical,* Kat wrote – that is, some classical piece that might easily excuse a lack of garments. *Be not too concerned with the merit of it,* Kat assured me; *he cares not a fig for art, but he likes to look on a fine thigh.*

Kat as Hebe? Hastily I composed and calculated. Better the nymph Galatea – aye, or Circe. Kat, the enchantress abandoned, seawater lapping her feet, breast bared in grief. And who Odysseus, who the man that could sail from her comforts and leave her thus dissatisfied?

Kat's bargaining had also procured some rooms, clean and well lit, near to Paul's Churchyard. *My gentleman would have us work on the board in some small house of his,* she wrote. *I assured him you would be keen to paint me, in your good time, somewhere* (I saw her sly smile) *discrete. Come,* she invited, *oblige me this evening with our first of many pleasant sittings.*

I feared – and it proved, rightly – that this board would be long in the finishing. Circe could never be more insistent, nor her shores more beguiling or arduous to leave.

Part the Third

Sixteen

THE CIRCLE ABOUT A nobleman is like to the halo of Michael: a close crescent of protection, the reflected glory of a fêted head. Many a man may prosper, if he but step from the shadow to catch some other's radiance on his brow.

With Kat's severing of Swift, she and I grew close of purpose, our talents coupled. Though we used the simple snares of bed and brush, yet we could cozen lords and brazen out our fortunes. For the fond use of my sables, Kat posed willingly; from these sittings I crafted many tempting panels of her likeness. These gallant pieces we sold to her many suitors, who gladly paid for tokens of her charms. The greater the man, the heavier his purse, and the better chance he have some space about his walls to hang my pictures. To that end, Kat's lovers grew yet nobler by the season; ere long she was admired in the best Long Galleries and bedchambers of England. Success is the bedfellow of Compliance; to succeed, so we adapted. We were all acquiescence.

Kat was Beguiling Woman from the very beginning of time; she was Virtue Corrupted, she was a Saint in her glory, she was a Martyr in her fleshly agonies. I made of her an Eve, subtle and sensuous; a Susanna, coy and trembling; a Helen, rapturous and ravished. Kat was the willing, unwilling, wilful yet ever-yielding woman of temptation that her suitors – and so my patrons – longed for her to be. Triumphantly she played her parts, while I moulded her limbs and features to suit each pose. We waxed magnificent and, in so doing, we waxed wealthier.

Pleasured by Kat, and pleased by my renderings of her, the gentlemen of Fair Eliza's court grew beneficent. They praised my use of shadow to round Kat's breasts; they spoke of the ease with which I expressed her wit along with her beauty, be it only in the sly tail of her eye or the graceful tips of her fingers.

Some bethought themselves a dark part of the composition, as a lover lurking beyond the panel's edge; others fancied a likeness of themselves in a figured Paris or a Solomon. So they came, by our foils of stealthy flatterings and subtle encouragements, to commission likenesses of themselves in chalks – and then, in time, in oils.

How did I render them? With honesty, aye; and yet with discretion. How better to know a man than through his chamber habits? How better to close on his likeness than through a knowledge of his urges, his desires, his whispered hopes and fevered exclamations? I captured my sitters, for I showed them as they were. My panels held up a glass to their very selves, for I knew what made them men. Kat saw to this, and delivered to me the shades and tones of their most vulnerable facets, the choice and subtle elements of temperament that only ardour discloses. I traced the love-lies of a man in the channel of cheek and chin, his cruelties in the grip of his hands, his weaknesses in the folds and slopes about his brow. If he were forceful, the ridge of his nose would speak of it. Were he a feeble lover, his glance evaded. If he cried out, I set the words in the parting of his lips; if his touch fevered, the mouth curled in erotic triumph. Ever in the mirrored shine of the pupil did I render a show of animal acquaintance gained, of intimacies shared.

What of jealousy? I had never loved my mistress as these men might, I knew no lover's hurts. My passion for Kat Joyce was the love of a painter for his works. We each formed the other, learning together the uses of pigment and brush. When languid, Kat begged for the lapping of white lead on finest, swan-soft sable. Regal, she demanded ultramarine, applied with a limner's deftness. Brazen, she cried for crimson and boars' hair bristles. It was this, and my art, that best delighted Kat, and with her I took my pleasure through my brushes. I alone painted her – so I alone had true contentment of her. I captured her in all her forms and graces, and many were those who sought, and bought, that beauty. Yet none saw her passion sated, as I did; they possessed but the painted likeness of it. Our triumph was twofold, for we would sell her twice.

All this long while, though I had painted lords with their

devices and great figured gallantries, yet I remained but a student of Peter Swift, Master Painter of Black Friars. This truth chafed cruelly. At first I had little minded it, using the school and workshops for my own end. While there, I might work in new pigments and varnishes, practising and bettering my craft without expense. With sleight of hand and calculation I procured bladders of paint and a grinding table, cracked and forgotten, that I made whole again. I braced my boots with knives and brushes, filled phials and gathered lengths for silverpoint. I learnt much from Benson's deft rendering of objects and instruments; I examined with Petty the varied merits of cloths and drapery. I honeyed my manner, looking to the mildness of Ambrose and seeing preferment. Now advantage had come, and my palette and brush neither dried nor rested; yet ever must I rein in my commissions, and my matters with Kat, to take myself to Swift's school and idle precious hours on childish tasks and futile foolishness. My purse had swelled that I might purchase my own stuff from the apothecary; I dealt terms with Swift's carpenter and took up his supply of woods for panels. Though I was a Prentice I had the favour and work of a Master, yet my life was thwarted, divided by the close green cloth of secrecy. I must restore the whole, I determined – I must break with my Prenticeship and quit the school.

Opportunity and Prosperity are like to joined twins, the one ever dependent on the other. With wealth I might establish my own place, and with prospects brightened, win brighter prospects yet. Kat earned much favour and gleaned handsome gifts, and, with higher prizes in her sights, took grand new lodgings by the Strand.

The house was vast and Kat, with her manner of living, had no wish to lodge a housekeeper; better were married servants who lived and slept elsewhere. She showed me the unused servant quarters – wide rooms, well appointed for the light and plainly kept.

Kat swept us through the chambers. *There* – she waved behind us – *you might sleep and lodge in better comfort than with Petty*. She pressed forward, her fine new skirts rippling. *This space* – she waved again – *would do well for a workshop*. She stopped at the room's end, pressing her hand against the furthest wall. *Beyond is my bedchamber*, she whispered, smiling slyly. *I would have your workshop close at hand, the better for our practices. Do you understand me?*

I had long grasped her thoughts. *You mean me to listen to your conquests now?*

The better to understand your subjects, Rob.

She gestured me towards her, took my hand and pressed it to the wall. I felt along it to the arras hanging there; the wall, seeming solid, melted with the cloth. Kat pulled back the arras.

You told me once that the spirit of a man lies not in clothes and finery, she murmured. *You said that to capture the soul you must see what is ever unseen. Now, you might see all.*

The arras covered a wooden hatch, finely carved and worked into a grille. The hatch opened to the bedchamber beyond; by stooping I could see the ornate hangings of Kat's bed, the heavy counterpane. I shook my head.

This is too far, I said. *A man must keep some dignity, even when he beds a whore.*

Be not hasty, she said. *The grille is handsome and seems but an ornament from within. I will keep it closed thus; you may use it if you will.* She drew the arras back across the hatch. *You need not move the cloth*, she said, stroking the threads. *It is a fine hunting scene, is it not? See where the quarry may be spied, hidden in the forest?*

Kat smiled as I studied the arras: a cheaply managed piece, the hounds at the fore, more like to rats than dogs, the horses monstrous beneath elegant riders. The forest rose dense and dark from a flat river, the water ill-woven in grey and yellow silks. In the centre of the trees a white hart crouched, a feeble creature beneath vast golden antlers. Between the branching horns a dark spot showed in the weave; I put my finger to it and felt a hole.

Kat laughed. *See*, she said, *how quick you are to find a flaw? You may wish to see more closely later.* Her voice grew low and mirthful. *Though you be broad of vision, Rob, you will find a mere moth-hole suffices.*

A spy-hole, rather. I put my eye to the flaw; through the broken weave I could see the bed entire. I straightened and covered the hole with my hand. *I think this no accident of moths*, I piped.

A propitious nibbling. She laughed. *You act the chaste maid, but I know well that you will look to it.* I shook my head again, my colour rising. She nodded, and, smiling, kissed my cheeks. *You will look, certain*, she declared. *Your scarlet thoughts stain your skin, Master Painter.*

For too many days had Petty gone alone to Swift's school, bearing some tale of sickness to cover me from censure. I had thought my friend would take my moving well, knowing long of my wish to quit the company.

Leave the school, he pouted, *if that truly is your wish. Do not lodge with Kat.*

She has rooms for a workshop, I countered, *and you are ever welcome there.*

She is known to all, he sighed. *No man of family or reputation will visit you. How will you prosper?*

I prosper now, I answered. *You little know who visits Kat.*

Nor would I, he barked. He shook his head. *Nay*, he said more softly, *I will not be angered with you. But if you go, you leave honour behind. What of your family, Rob? Leaving the school is but one matter. Yet to live with a court whore? What of your father's pride?*

I will send money, I reasoned. *They know nothing of courtesans in Thetford. Keep any letters they send for me, and they will think me here.*

I would wish you so, my friend said. *'Tis none of it as I hoped. I will miss you, Rob.*

Taking leave of Petty was an easy matter for my part, for I was in a fever of excitement for the new. At length I had my workshop – now came the reaching of my hand towards ambition, and the feel of gold on the fingertips. My few possessions were quick to carry, my leave of Swift's school a sweet shrugging off of distaste and drudgery.

Petty would not attend the workshops that day, awaiting my return in the Mermaid with a mournful morning jug. I reached the school late, that I might announce my enterprise to all at once. I spoke as though to the walls, for all stood unmoved and silent. My few words uttered, I rolled my papers and cleared about my easel. At the last, Benson crossed to wish me a quiet but hearty farewell, shaking my hand before Swift and smiling much. Ambrose was a silent equilibrium, save for his careful count of what I took and what I left behind. Falconbridge, stunned into a lapse of twittering, watched me leave with a trembling, twitching ire. Lovett struggled for some parting curse but found none to match his envy. Swift himself barked that he was better rid of me; Popham wept into her apron seams. Toby stared at all, insensible. I descended the stair, closed Swift's door behind me and, as I turned towards Cheapside, capered for joy in the street.

I drank hard with Petty that afternoon, then took myself to Kat. There we breached a flask of brandy and a phial of Toby's best ultramarine, Kat's fondest hue, secreted in my boot and meetly purloined for our celebration. Drunken though I was, yet I could paint Kat with sober skill; I traced her all o'er with blue beasts and foliage, 'til naught but the circles of nipple and navel stood bare.

I am your arras, Kat laughed, *all forested.*

Better figured, I said, *and with no stag.*

O, she giggled, *there is yet space for the hidden quarry.* She drew up her thighs and arched her back. *You are keen of sight, Master Painter. You need but search a little.*

Thus, through the seasons, Kat and I continued – she in her gaining of suitors and I in my rendering of them. We enjoyed much privilege, for Kat was a costly prize, though easily won. Aside from gifts of plate and jewel, the price of her time was paid in paint, be it on her, of her or about her in the likeness of her lovers. Few visited Kat that did not visit me, to press me with coin for my panels and my discretion. Though I lacked papers from the Painters-Stainers, those I figured thought me to be a Master. Little matter of this quiet patronage reached beyond our circle; Petty knew some of it, and I had none others to tell.

Many were the suitors that Kat passed on to me – none, save one, did she keep from my workshop. He came but once, and Kat announced him with much playful furtiveness.

I would you were not at home this evening, she said frankly. *I expect a visitor.*

I had meant to visit Petty, I said. *Now I will not go.*

If you stay you must be discreet, she warned.

As I ever am. Who is he?

That – she shrugged – *I may not tell, even to you, dear Rob.*

Then I must guess at it. He is high?

Too high.

Aged, I asked, *privileged?*

Young yet, and handsome, they say. She sighed. *He has ever stood close to power.*

He is of some great house, then?

Very great.

Close to the Queen? I goaded.

Kat put her hand to my lips. *Dangerously so*, she whispered.

Well caught, Kat, I said. *He will sit for me?*

Never.

And yet you invite him. For what prize are you aiming then, madam?

Kat laughed. *Do not madam me, jealous one*, she said. *He holds a golden key, he will open doors.*

Including your chamber, I rejoined. *How long should I give you?*

Very long, I would say. I bowed and made to leave, but she held me back. *I must entertain him well*, she added, *I had hoped for your assistance.* She drew out a purse of heavy coin and pressed it in my hands. She frowned, her brows drawing into two dainty creases. *This is a great enterprise*, she whispered, *it will aid us both.* She laughed again. *Petty knows his vintners and epicures. Perhaps you might take him with you?*

While Kat readied herself, throwing aside dresses and jewels in turn and snapping at her maid, Petty and I made free with her gold in the best houses of the city. Petty would not have us purchase anything untested; so we had no need for dining or supping, but sampled in the parlours of confectioners, the stalls of vintners and the kitchens of the East Cheape bakehouses. *No pies or puddings*, Petty warned, *nor heavy ales. No wine too strong, either.* He belched roundly. *We cannot have Kat's noble leaden in his chair, or full of the bladder all night.*

Kat was well pleased with my purchases, though the choosing had cost her dear: sweetmeats, citrons, small pastries of minced veal and saffron, honeyed figs, a shaped jelly of sole and turbot, artichokes in cold sauce and a basket of oysters, fresh caught and brought in at Billingsgate. We laid out the table in her chamber, close by the bed, yet with space for cushioned seats. Kat tasted from the two flasks of Petty's choosing: one lightly spiced French wine, clear and golden of colour; one ruddy claret, bright as new-drawn blood yet fresh and sharp as brambles. I gazed at the fare and the plate Kat had set out, the dressing of her hair, her gems and lacings.

Best to become accustomed to this, Rob, she said, much amused at my gaping. *Tonight, we are on the rise.*

I stayed safe in my quarters when he came. His carriage drew up thunderous below, shouting of wealth and title. I looked from the casement and saw the horses, plumed and haltered, and the carriage close-hung with cloths. The horseman dropped to the road and opened, sweeping his bow. A page knocked at the door; in the light of the house-lanterns I saw much velvet cloth, telling of rank, yet no livery. The lad's doublet was a costly blue, dark as to seem almost black against the night. The horseman wore no badge in his cap, nor did the carriage show painted arms. Kat opened below, the page swept low before her, and the visitor stooped from the carriage. His cloak showed the same blue shade, his hair curled long from his cap, dark upon his collar. His face seemed in shadow. As he straightened, a silver pommel showed at his side; he paused at the door, turning his head up to survey the house. His face was not in shadow – he was masked.

I listened laughingly for a while, thinking this show at mumming and masking a vain piece of theatre. Kat's voice sounded in the chamber beyond, but I heard no word from her suitor. I could settle at nothing, and ere long I grew weary of pacing. I took the servants' door to the road and walked awhile, taking the lighted ways through the streets. I took a beaker of brandy at a new tavern by the West wall; it stung dry and cheap in the throat after Petty's liquors.

The carriage was yet in the street when I returned, the horses snorting. I trod quietly within and stole straightway to my chamber where I lay long abed, wrestling my wakefulness. Sleep refused me, though I had tempted her with brandy fumes; I mused on some boards I might make, plotting figures on the bedcurtains. I thought on Kat and the spending of her coin, on how much she might hope to gain in recompense. I wondered at the masked face of the noble, and whether he be handsome or hideous beneath. At length I succumbed and, flinging off the bedclothes, crept into the workshop.

I could hear much from the doorway. Kat's voice was low, yet her breath drew loud and gasping. I made out the clink of plate, of liquid pouring. Kat gasped sharply, then laughed; the man laughed with her. *'Tis cold*, she breathed. *'Tis sweet*, he murmured. I pressed forward softly, levelling my ear to the chamber wall. Kat commenced a gentle moaning. *Drink*, she pleaded, *drink all*. I heard the clink of metal again. *'Tis empty*, the man said. *No matter*, Kat urged, *there is some yet here*. Something fell and rattled on the boards – the wine-flask, I thought. The man cried out suddenly, the bed-frame sounded. *Sweet angel!* he called out. *Sweetly seasoned angel!* My hand strayed to the arras, my finger followed the river's threads. *More*, Kat urged, *there is yet more*. I felt the forest closing about the stag, traced the flaw between the golden antlers. *See!* Kat cried. *See!* I bent my head to the spy-hole and peered within.

Kat was astride her lover, her face towards me; her body seemed glazed, and I saw that her skin dripped in places. The man's feet pushed at the bolster, his hair hung over the sheets at the foot of the bed. His hands reached up to Kat then retreated to his mouth; he raised his head as if to suckle at her, and I saw that, through all, he had yet kept in his mask. The wine-flask lay empty on the boards behind his head, plate and oyster shells scattered all about him.

See! Kat cried again. She held the man's head to her chest and looked sharply up; her eyes locked fast with mine. I wrenched my head away and closed my eyes. *No!* Kat cried. *See! See!*

Wavering, I looked again. Kat pushed her lover's head away; he had ceased his writhing and froze beneath her. *What ails, my angel!* he cried. *Do I cause some hurt!*

No, my lord, she breathed, stroking his hair. Her fingers strayed to the ribbon fastening his mask. She bent over him, her back arched highly, her hips swinging rhythmically, her breasts keeping pendulous time. *My sweet lord,* she murmured, artfully untying, her stroke unaltered by the knots. *I would see more.*

See more? he whispered.

Aye, my lord, Kat urged. She loosened the mask and threw it to the floor. He thrust his face against her, and she smiled to me above his head. *See!* she said, pushing him gently back upon the bed. She gazed at his face: it was young indeed, very pale and proudly shaped. A handsome face: a courtier's face.

He smiled timidly. *Do you see more than you would, madam?* he said.

O no! Kat cried hoarsely. She leaned far back upon him, her hips and thighs working him hard; he cried out for his angel again and grasped ecstatically at the bedposts. She held my eye and grinned, brazen in her pride. *I would ever see more, my lord,* she urged. She tightened the rack of his pleasure and, straining, he clenched and tore at the bedcurtains, his arms flung wide. *More, my lord,* Kat urged, *more, My Lord Seymour—*

Kat leaned in the doorway of my chamber, a cloak about her shift, her smile triumphant.

Seymour? I said. *It cannot be.*

She nodded shrewdly. *Did I not say it was a high prize?*

But Hertford is old, I said, *this man was scarce my age.*

This was not Hertford, she laughed. *It was his son.*

I shook my head; she laughed again and sat on the edge of the bed. *I ache like I've ridden the Devil*, she said, *may I not lie down?*

'Tis little wonder you ache, I answered, *and you have lain long enough.*

I scarce lay down at all, she moaned. *You have no compassion, Rob.* She pulled at my covers. *It is cold.*

Go back to bed then.

I cannot, she said, *it is wine-sodden.*

We laughed together then. Kat threw off her cloak. *Are you not soaked also?* I said.

I have washed, said she, climbing beside me. *I would not come to you had I not.*

I sniffed at her shift. *You smell like to a tavern*, I said. *French wine is a lasting scent.*

I would I had saved you some, she sighed, *but, alas!*

O, Kat, desist. I wrapped my arms about her, for she seemed cold indeed. *I wonder you do not get with child*, I said.

There are ways to prevent it. She yawned widely, settling her head against me.

Half Seymour and half Grey, I mused. *What a face not to have painted.*

A pity indeed, she baited, *when you took such trouble to study it.*

As you hoped I would. He has ever been the centre of intrigue, has he not? What fears he must have seen, closed in the Tower for naught but his parentage. I sat up then. *God's Soul, Kat, what if he has got a child on you? This is dangerous coupling.*

He has not, she snapped. *Not all coupling leads to breeding.* She sighed her irritation. *Some women are made that way, Rob. I am one of them.*

You cannot breed? I urged.

No, indeed. I cannot. She shook her head. *And there's an end.* She lay heavily against me and commenced chafing her hands.

What now for My Lady Joyce? I asked. *What family heir do you aim for? A Carey*, I teased, *a Sidney?*

I thought a Dudley, she said, and not altogether laughingly. *'Tis long since the time you should have been at court.*

I shrugged. *And My Lord Seymour? What of him now?*

No more for Seymour, she laughed. *He is to wed, he came for a last schooling.*

You are sorry for it? He is most handsome.

She turned sharply to me. *Did you wish him ill-looking?*

I wondered at the bad theatre of his masking. I am glad he was not vile, for your sake.

Well, he was not, she said bluntly. *He is handsome, and most amorous. He will make his wife happy in the bedchamber, have no doubt; he is a proper man. O!* she gasped, and looked to me wincingly. *I meant no hurt, Rob.*

No matter. I shrugged again. *I have seen more than I would know how to perform.*

Kat smiled and kissed my brow. *I would gladly teach you, if you would but let me.*

I am content with the schooling you already give, I assured. *It is far sweeter than Swift's.*

She laughed. *And you are likewise content with watching?*

To look upon fine things is the painter's pleasure, I mused. *Yet what of you, Kat? I wonder what might make Kat the angel happy. Where will you find pleasure in wedding and bedding both?* She eyed me angrily and pulled away, slipping from the bed; she took up her cloak and shivered into it. *Do not be angered, Kat*, I sighed. *How do I offend?*

She strode to the door and glared back at me. *You know right well*, she said, her mouth atremble. *Why taunt me for it?*

For what?

She flung the door open. *You of all might know*, she cried, and slammed it shut.

Seventeen

AS THE QUEEN IS to the Divine, so was Leicester beloved to the Queen, be he grown a man of broad girth, fat in the cheeks and much purpled with age and fond living. My Lord Robert Dudley, Earl of Leicester; of all the stars in Gloriana's firmament, he shineth yet the brightest. The Queen's fond favourite, our unacknowledged King, purchased – for a moderate purse of gold – a panel of my devising. So it was that Kat danced ever closer to the circle of brilliance, and brought within it her own Bonny Sweet Robin.

Leicester loved to look on a pretty woman, and he added Kat to his vast collection. He had heard word of her and coveted her; he had spied her at work in some grand entertainment, a sireless siren amid the harried waves of coupling, feasting and dancing. He had sought her in the chambers of her suitors, he had played his fingers lightly upon her open palms. He had purchased a likeness of her, a gallantry of mine acquired from a lover, long since spurned. He had given all the signs of pursuit and favour.

Yet Leicester would never be Kat's lover; this was a prize too high. Though he be balding and near to fifty, he must ever look to nobility for his play. His wife, the third as known of, was still a great beauty and of excellent marriage stock. The fury of that she-wolf would be hot indeed – and should the Queen hear of her Robin's whoring, there would be far greater forfeits. Yet, after Seymour, Kat could not but aspire.

She returned from another of her gentlemen's entertainments, hot and exhausted, yet skittish as a foal. It was late in the season, the court restless at Greenwich and preparing for the long Summer Progress. Soon the nobles would be exiled to some rustic weald, with naught to exercise them but dining and hunting, and the listless riding from one great country house to another. They would play at seducing each other's wives, or tripping up a maid of honour, then spend all on a kitchen girl in some cobwebbed corner, staining their new-dyed breeches. They would long for the city's entertainments; for those creatures, like Kat, who did not play, daintily gloved, at butts or bowls in scented gardens, but who drank and swore and wiped their mouths on their sleeves, and who rode them harder and longer than they themselves might ride their big-boned hunters. In this spirit of foreboding a courtier might wax wistful and desirous; for Kat, this was a plump golden season for early harvesting. A purse and a promise of more would sustain us through the Summer, buy us a month or greater beyond the Plague, and a country lodging to work in. I might finish a commission in good time, were it to be well placed by the hour of their leaving. Yet Kat still looked to Leicester.

He will not bed me, she sighed. *He is hot for me, of that I am certain. His eyes were upon me all evening.* She unlaced the sleeves of her gown and turned her back towards me. I played the waiting-maid's part and helped undress her; she arched and stretched with the removal of each piece. *I have danced too hard again*, she muttered.

We must aim lower, I said, untying her petticoats. *There must be some other way.*

O, he will commission, Kat cried, yawning widely. *He wants to try you for some court matter, with the Queen.*

I ceased unlacing. *You jest, surely.*

Indeed not. He spoke of it this evening. He means to find some new style to delight the Great One, and would have some new young man to do it.

How came this?

Untie me, for Pity's sake, she lamented. *I will die of this farthingale.*

I untied, and Kat stepped from her layers. *The ever-youthful virgin waxes ripe*, she barbed. *The Queen will be fifty come next Autumn, and Dudley plans to honour her Gracious Majesty with a new series of paintings, and a new painter to produce them.* She yawned afresh and stretched. *It is to be a great commission, as a pageant in scale, if he can but find the man to do it. He seeks someone eager and of good wit, unseasoned and unseen. Someone who will make her feel young as Spring again.* Kat turned and held my face between her hands. *Someone young and pretty, Rob, like you.*

Leicester had long been known as a lover of liberal arts. His attainment of my piece had showed how liberal he liked his art to be, for Kat's drapes left little to discovery. A panel of the Queen was by far a different matter; my Mistress' power was grown manifest. Fair Eliza's likenesses had ever been trusted to painters with courtly patrons. Was I now to be counted such a one? I could scarce think so. To the collectors of gallantries – such as My Lord L. and his circle – I was the discreet originator of erotic panels, sole renderer of Mistress Katharine Joyce. Should the World choose to look closely, I was but a failed Prentice without his Mastership, a man with naught but an eye for likeness and rooms by a courtesan's chamber.

Yet the World proved careless and short of sight. Soon after, My Lord Leicester came openly to Kat's house, unannounced and in some company. There, he claimed, he and his followers would pause awhile to wash the dust from their throats. They rode that morning from Greenwich to complete some matters of business in the West; they would make some farewells and conclusions ere the Progress, so shortly, departed. The day was hot and damp, the horses thirsted; they would take a jug, for here was a hostess more charming than a Baroness, and a welcome more pleasing than that of his own great Leicester House. The Earl's men cooled in the shaded yard, while he declared his will to look about the house.

He nodded at the Summer hangings, then offered new woven silks to replace them, should Kat but acquiesce. He marvelled at the likeness of Kat that hung upon the stair; yet, though the painter's skill be great, Nature's brush was ever lovelier. He goaded and flattered, and, Kat told me, pressed her to the banister, the better to feel her skirts. He spoke puffingly of his admiration, while my cunning Kat, knowing how a hasty submission would lead to naught, spoke only of the admired likeness. He urged; she triumphed. Kat led him from the banister to the furthest rooms, and into my workshop.

My lord was handsome yet, his whiskers neat and curling, his smile strong and disarming. Kat led him to me and then abandoned us; my lord's dashing manner swept from him with the courteous bow that waved her from the room. His eyes darted about the workshop, seeking some evidence that I might yet meet his needs. Standing in the clutter of my unfinished boards, the greatest Earl in England spoke of his desire: he would have me come to Greenwich and draw the Queen.

My lord explained frankly how a man might win advancement by looks and manner, as much as by his talent. His speech grew yapping; he was dour and ruddy, sore of the gout and waxing barrel-like, yet his eyes shone with the striking arrogance of one who enjoyed and possessed the best in all things. *Come to court at my behest*, he commanded, *on Thursday next. Dress well – the finest you might lay hand on. Show plenty of leg. And smile more with eyes than with lips.* He flashed me a look of mirthful adoration; were I a maid I would have swooned. *Thus.* He flicked at his bejewelled cloak, a garment worth the price of a hundred painted panels. *She hates a sour face but worse is a man that grins like an ape. And be mindful: Her Majesty is the fairest woman that ever graced the Earth. Do not forget this.*

So it came that I went, announced, to court. I dressed as well as I might for one of my means, Kat acquiring a rich scarlet doublet for me through some cunning bedchamber deception. I thought much on my change of garb as I made to Greenwich, taking Eastward oars. It was but two years since my first approach to court, and my humbling arrival at Westminster. The redbreasted shirt of my mother's pride was now greatened to a doublet of stitched, slashed and padded silks. I wondered, did the same servants attend the court at every city place? Would I glimpse at Greenwich the yellow-haired maiden who had saved me from the water pump, or the brute that forced me to it? I might now stand to him proudly, speaking a most powerful name as my surety. I attended the court as a painter of likenesses, by invitation of the Earl of Leicester. My pages and chalks were sealed in a scroll, tied with linen and wrapped about with leather. I would take these chalks and render with this hand the likeness of the Queen herself; I might yet sit in the gardens of the river palace, the regal sun of admiration radiant upon my face. The doors of the court would open to me ever after; I would render the Queen before her limner, I would even take precedence over the great George Gower himself.

Pride and Vanity make for heavy falls. My youthful head, full of foolish hopes and affectations, rang with eagerness; I pressed forth, and my haste proved precipitous.

Majesty is the garment of the absolute, and the court dazzled with determined finery. Though I had seen riches, I was yet a Norfolk man of two-and-twenty Summers. Though I had blustered my way to the halls of grand houses, and bowed before Lords and Earls, I had never seen Greenwich from within, had never been granted audience by the Supreme Head of our State – nor had I felt her eyes upon me alone.

We waited in the Presence Chamber. Leicester was secreted beyond the doors, with the Queen and her Privy Councillors. All attended in restless boredom without: ladies leaning against pillars and cushioned settles, aching in stiff dresses, gentlemen flirting discreetly while the Hawk's eyes were diverted. I stood apart, skulking beside a group of men in Leicester's livery – the easier for him to spot me without pains. The men talked of hunting and wenching. All eyes flicked to and from the guarded doors in weary anticipation.

And then they opened. Amidst much clatter and carillons, lords and ladies surged forward, forming a corridor of cloth and ornament. They bobbed and bowed as if greeting in a dance; I lingered by Leicester's men, behind the noble ranks, and looked above the sweeping heads – into Her eyes.

Would that the stone had gaped and let me pass; I had seen the Queen, and She saw me. I fumbled my cap like a farmhand before the squire and shuffled foolishly. I bowed low, too low. She froze, and watched me suffer.

The Thetford painter I spoke of, Your Majesty, Leicester confided.

The tide of bowing heads and curtseyed cloth parted before me. I fixed my eyes upon the flags, which I saw were skilfully cut and arranged in varied patterns. The hush of slippered silk sounded against them, drawing closer.

Look up, She said.

Your Majesty, I rasped, looking down and dipping further.

Look to us! She barked.

I raised my head; my eyes were slow to follow. She was magnificent: terrifying, thin-cheeked and ludicrously painted. Beautiful as the slip of the New Moon, so Her youth had been spoken of – now She had waxed past fullness and begun to wane, Her pallor not that poetry of youth's silver light softly shining, but of leaded paste thickly applied and settling in the shallows. The bone of Her brow and nose stood forth, cold as Italian marble, worn and wind-polished. Her sharp eyes were dark and dryly probing. My own were aswim; this was a face deserving of honest rendering. *Your Majesty*, I stupidly repeated.

You forget all courtesy, She said.

Forgive me, I hastily contrived, *what man would not forget all before such – majesty?*

She looked me over as I had seen my father look to a horse he would broker. Leicester glared beside Her; I thought on his advice and softened my painter's look, though I feared to seem a hapless dog fixed on a butcher's stall. Her jaw, stiff and pointed, seemed to soften; She smiled thinly. *Indeed*, She murmured to Leicester. *We will see more of you, Master Painter. We will take to the gardens*, She announced to all, then looked to me. *Ready your chalks.*

It was as a dream, for the ground beneath my feet could not be felt, nor would the light upon the leaves about me sharpen into stillness. All was as a haze, a fen fog: the Queen seated upon a stool in a sunlit close, the thick scent of warm grass and camomile, the air close with the perfumes and Plague pomanders of the court. I could scarce see my page, my fingertips numbed at the touch of chalk, my eyes were awash. This, greatest of mild mornings, was not real, and I could feel nothing of it.

I rendered Her, the Queen of England, with honesty and splendour. As I looked to Her features all mist was cleared aside, and Her face seemed as if closer, larger than in Nature. So clearly could I see each line, each stroke of paint, each fleck of whitened powder, I felt as if I were but a fly that buzzed and lit beside Her. I copied the angles of Her cheeks where once soft curves had been; I captured the hollows of impending age and careworn creases. Her nose spoke of pride and vanity, Her chin of duties borne, Her sinking eyes of maiden disappointments. Her brow, still smooth, was regal; here the weight of crowns had rested. I drew all that I saw there: avarice and awe, bitterness and mirth, a woman's desire and a longing for simple pleasures.

She stood and walked again, a page taking up Her stool. The sun waxed hot and the hour of dinner approached. The court pressed forward and I followed with my image, my chalks in one hand, Her likeness in the other. The Queen stood and shielded Her face from the sun.

We will dine, She declared. The court, obedient, followed Her within.

As the Queen reached the door of Her Privy Chamber She turned to take Her leave; Her eye rested upon the paper in my hand and She flicked Her wrist at me. I bowed and held the likeness out to Her. She took it. I held my breath.

Her silence rang on endlessly. The court, wanting for dinner, restlessly hemmed and shifted. Feet shuffled softly on the flags, skirts stirred and rustled. Leicester stood beside the Queen, his brows drawn sharp together.

What is this? She said at last.

I bowed again and offered with my eyes the treacherous Dudley smile. *A likeness of the wide World's fairest Queen*, I flattered. *It is a fair likeness, is it not, Your Majesty?*

She glowered: my breathing ceased. She held Her hand out before Her, the paper pinched between thumb and finger as though it be but some diseased and soiled rag. Deliberately, cruelly, the long white finger lifted; my drawing sailed to the floor. It skimmed aside and lay flat upon the flags, the likeness of the Queen pressed facedown against the stone.

This is no likeness of a Queen, She thundered. *It is neither fair nor liked. Get thee gone.*

I scraped my bow as lowly as I might, the better to still myself. About me the court began to move; the Queen retreated, My Lord Leicester striding with Her. The chorus of mutterings, the stirrings of cloth and leather, the heavy swing of doors – all sounds seemed carried from some great distance, drowned by the roaring tide of blood in my ears. My stomach soured and my tongue swelled thickly in the desert of my mouth. I knew not which was worse: the Queen's disgust, my deep humiliation, or the sudden death of my great courtly ambitions. My Lord Leicester's trap was sprung, and he was lost to Kat and me for ever. The sickness of shock rose in my gorge and my head reeled.

The paper lay upon the flags near to my foot. My bow was set, my body would not stir. I kept my eye upon the piece, hating it for so destroying me, yet fearing that some noble might cast it up and rend it. The Queen's circle moved away and the body of the court closed behind Her, showing me their swaggering silken backs. A black boot, small and silver-buckled, appeared at my side – a second landed squarely upon the back of Her Majesty's likeness.

The legs above the boots were thin and clad in sober black hose; above these, a doublet, also of black, though artfully worked with silver. I made to rise. A graceful hand, long-fingered and stained about the nails, reached towards the boot and retrieved my paper. I offered my hand tremblingly for it.

Well met, said the man in the black and silver. *I have heard much of you.*

I stood, seeming tall against him. His voice was gentle yet precise, and his face, long of chin and nose, seemed foxish. This was no Queen's guard, at least: his hair and beard were neat and short-shorn, the brow square where the hair began quitting it through age, the whiskers squared to match. His eyes were quick and small, the pupils vast within them; they stared hard, as if, by looking, they might make a print of me. I had not seen this face before, I was certain of it: it was an inquiring face, one not readily forgot.

Do I know you, sir? I stumbled.

In a manner, he replied. He looked down at my rendering of the Queen and frowned. *You were of Swift's school; I know this.* He shook his head. *Yet your rendering does not show it. I have heard ill tales of you.* He smiled thinly. *They say you are a brawler.*

Though my pride had been far worse pricked, yet still I bridled. *I might guess who would say so,* I growled. *They would also call me Netherman, yet I take no shame from that.*

Why so? the man asked calmly. His brows arched high upon the squared forehead. *Do you admire those foreign painters? Do they not come hither to take your work, these strangers? Do they not come hither to steal your place at court?*

They come hither with eyes for truth, I snapped. *I am not of Peter Swift's mind, I do not support the guild. Had King Henry been thus, we would have no Holbean.*

So, so. The man chuckled and nodded. *Such a loss would have been great,* he said. *Yet there were others of fine sight, also from other lands. Have you seen the great works of Master Eworth? He has ever affected my manner of rendering.*

Your manner? I exclaimed.

Mine, indeed so. He looked again at the paper, then handed it to me. *You are welcome to visit my workshops, young Master Netherman of Thetford – I have many boards for your viewing, the likenesses of which you might admire. Some are of my hand, others but of my collection. You are at liberty now?*

I hung my head. *It would seem so,* I groaned. *Alas, the Queen has no use of me.*

Though your vanity may smart, you might think but little of it, he said smoothly. *Yours is a fine likeness, but it is too sharp for this court.* We looked to the doors through which the courtiers were thronging. *I fear the nobles of this land are a herd,* the man said, *and where she leads, so they must ever follow. The Queen would have flattery, thus all men look for flatterers. I strive to flatter, but the Queen, in her wisdom, knows me too well to mind me. She forgives my weaknesses.* His pupils widened on me again. *You seem amazed, young man,* he said mildly. *You do not know me.*

I am unsure, I answered.

I am George Gower, the Serjeant Painter, he said. *I know you, for I saw your likeness of Sir Thomas of Hengrave, many years ago. Since that day I have ever looked for your coming here. So, here I find you. You were long in coming.*

Master Gower proved a man of excellent faith and hospitality. Aside from the weighty matter of my court humiliation, and the abrupt dispensing of all my careful plans, that day might have seemed wondrous. We talked long on the craft of rendering, on the uses of paint, on the wonders of the Flemish schools. Master Gower made of me an honoured guest, leading me through his many-roomed workshop, far greater and more handsomely appointed than Swift's drab school. All about the walls were boards new primed or drying, pinned drawings from life in chalks and metalpoint, and scaled figures of men standing, their bodies divided into squares. Brass bookstands stood in the corners, bearing bound volumes of engravings; of these were some taken from Italian works, and some in German. Two boys toiled in a side room, stirring foul vats of varnish and preparing pigment.

Do you work alone? I enquired, for the rooms seemed too vast for one painter's use.

I have a student, the Master explained. *He is at leisure today. I am too busy to tutor any but the best; he will soon be gone, he looks to travel in France. He thinks the French will prove well disposed to his somewhat mannered style.* I nodded, so as to seem knowing. The Master's clear eyes were wide upon me. *How goes your living now?* he asked. *You have your Master's papers?*

I have much— I faltered. The pupils widened further. *In truth,* I went on, *I did not finish my Prenticeship. Yet I have proved well placed.*

Master Gower smiled patiently. *I know of your position,* he said. *You are too old for Prenticing, yet as a Master's student you might prosper. Have you thought of taking up another place?*

To begin again? I shook my head. *No, sir,* I determined, *I have my own workshop, and good patronage, for all that I have no seal from a guild, and ill favour of the Queen.*

I am sorry for it. You were on the rise, he said, *now I fear you fall again. Your manner is not of the fashion, as was meetly proved this morning.*

I will make the fashion, I boasted.

Master Gower laughed indulgently. *Come,* he said, *let me show you something.*

I followed him to a room hung with finished panels. Here were many excellent renderings, some so darkly painted as to seem ancient. Master Gower stood before a board that showed himself, soberly and finely dressed, a palette of paints in his hand, a pair of balances beside him. A verse floated at the panel's edge.

I was born a gentleman, he said, *and my good family took my love of painting very ill.* He pointed at the balances; on one side rose a coat of arms, on the other, a heavier pair of brass dividers. *My art outweighs my lineage,* he said. *I would sooner be a poorman, whipped from the parish, than ever lose my skill. It is the only matter of import to me.* He sighed. *Few think we are worthy of merit, young man,* he continued. *They think us craftsmen, yes, and it is so, but there is more to our practices than craft. Painting is a liberal art; I would have all know it. Yet the fashion is not for liberality. I cannot steer fashion, I cannot tell the Queen what it is that she must merit. She waxes older, and she does not care for the harsh lines of truth to be painted on her likeness. So, truth is out of fashion; where then does that leave us?*

Poor, I answered, *yet honest.*

Master Gower laughed sadly. *A young man's words,* he said. *I would not be ragged in my age, thus I must follow fashion. I fear you must do the same. The Queen has come to favour limning and the craft has grown much these last years. Limning is an English skill, the Master of it is well known to me.*

I know of Hillyarde, I said, *the jeweller.*

That is he, a rare goldsmith and limner. Gower nodded. *You are young, your eyes are strong. You might look to limning; it is the art of the future.*

It is all tiny faces in gems and dainty lockets, I scoffed. *I am a painter in large; I will not make such works as can only be squinted at.*

It is not always so, he countered, *and even your Holbean practised it. A finely wrought likeness is such on any scale. I would have you meet with my friend Hillyarde; he has much skill, and he is widely travelled.*

Sir, I bowed. I looked away.

Master Gower gently clapped his hands. *So, so. Well, young man,* he said pleasantly, *I am most glad that we have met at last, though I be sorry indeed for the manner of our meeting. Now you have seen my rooms, I trust you will feel able, and well inclined, to call on me again!*

Eighteen

FOR ANOTHER CITY SUMMER, bitterness assailed me. I wrestled long with my humiliation, my schemes for future greatness sacked, my prospects plundered. Certainty, blossoming sweet in May, had withered, drooped and rotted with the sun. Our Dudley hopes were lost, the court fled far on Progress, and the Queen had turned her narrow back on London, her shadow long upon us. Denounced and dejected, Kat haunted the house, her face grown sour with swallowed fury. Her suitors were gone, for she too had fallen far from fashion. My Greenwich disgrace tucked silent, stifling folds about us. We grieved unheard. We were all obscurity.

The city suffered the torments of the season. Sun and rain came in cruel union, swelling the sickness that rose up in the streets. Many were lost, many more stayed away. News spread as hasty as the marching Plague and Sweat, and we learned how Kat's Beauchamp Seymour made his match that June, wiving in secret when the court departed. A lesser marriage bed was made in Oxford, for Petty sent word from his visit home that Benson had also wed.

My tasks grew slighter as the Summer heat waxed higher. I thought much on my interview with Gower and that Master's words, and worked my talents hard to sharpen them. I had striven from the first for truthfulness; I had pledged to Bess to make all painted tones as real and clear as her bright, fatal shades. I had failed her. Now I would recompense my vanity. Little wonder, I thought, that my chance at court had foundered. How could I, with my little show of work, think to have exacted my sworn duty? I was not worthy to receive acclaim, I was not worthy to paint great courtiers. I had captured majesty and frailty, this was true, but I had only shown its shape. I had traced the lines and likenesses of men, but my panels did not breathe. I had not yet made their colours live.

I had altogether broken with my plans. I had resisted Kat's embraces, this was true, yet it was naught but fleshly resistance. My hopes were linked with hers, my cares spent in her favour. Though she played the whore and I the eunuch's part, yet she housed, fed and tended me as a wife would to a husband. In my unmannish way I pleasured her as though she were my wife; or wife, at least, to my brushes. We shared our fortune as two spouses might, save that she had the greater hand in wealth. How then had I stayed faithful to my bride?

Had I forgot my Bess? Did I now scorn the riches she had shown me? Her wedding gift was wasted on idle gallantries and joyless poses. I had seen and taken all, giving nothing in return. Scholar-like, I must turn back to my books, and learn my trade again.

I would work the art of colour all afresh. I set at first to the over-grinding of my pigments, crushing them ruthlessly towards some faultless state. I pounded my powders 'til their touch was light and soft as Bess' cheeks. I burned ochre and burnished a copper mix, my aim to equal the adornments of her hair. I weakened my oils to washes, moist and supple as her lips, yet they slid and seeped languid and colourless with my use. I bruised and boiled plants for their rich juices, seeking the secret dyes of Nature; ever they faded on the page or melted in the sunlight. I could not match her hues and humours. My painter's experiments all proved fruitless.

I kept to my workshop. Kat grew piqued and complained often, lacking any to distract her and make practice of her art. I suffered also, though my suffering was the anguish of failed application. Despairing, I chanced the methods of new art and bound clean, fragile brushes, using but three squirrel hairs apiece. I thinned my paint and shaved a piece of vellum, brushing the surface smooth with scouring sand. I gathered my insipid tints and set them out; and then, in spite of all my disbelief, I tried my hand at limning of Kat's face.

I loathed the act: I loathed the outcome more. The

slight and meagre likeness I had made was naught but a round and dollish blot, the face a flattened ball of flesh beneath dull scratches for hair, lips but a wisp and eyes mere dots of darkness. Kat held her hand to take and look at it; I held it in a candle 'til it flamed.

When the heat had a little abated I took to Goldsmith's Row and looked about the shops there. Many were boarded against sickness, those open all cluttered with limners' lockets and painted pendants. Much of this work showed great poverty of skill, save in the jewelled settings. The failure was not mine alone, for on such a scale the eye could see so little of a man's features that any face might be writ there. Likeness of shape was all that a sitter might look for; likeness of Nature could not be worked so small. A pale and pressed-down face, floating upon a lozenge of ultramarine scarce the width of two thumbs across – such a piece might fetch a limner twice the worth of a full panel of mine, and more yet for a Master Limner's hand. I cursed Gower's Hillyarde for fuelling of this fashion. No courtier was now complete without some love-knot of the Queen, a trinket for his wife and a pendant for his mistress. How then might he pay for a three-quarter piece of any? All business for painters was now spent upon silversmiths and motto-mongers.

I walked South from Cheapside and went home riverwards. Many were the places I must keep from if I willed to live 'til Autumn. The houses seemed leaning close together, sweating the one against the other the better to deal disease. The kennels were flushed against sickness, the thin crowd nimbling about them, herbed cloths pressed at mouths and noses. I pummelled the pomander Kat had bid me carry, sour with the bitter fever-cure of rue, and kept watchful for marked doorways. Some burned lanterns and lit fires for the cleansing smoke, though the sky yet shone a furnace of heat and light.

With so many dead and sickening, what mattered these littlest things of courtly lives? What merited the meanness of things miniature, the novel slightness of images hinged and gilded? One plagued soul is a small matter in a city of suffering thousands. What import then this fashion of tiny faces? I paced the city, and as I strode I waxed from wondering to wrathful. What wealth could the over-lean limner's brush reveal? What strengths could such feeble delicacy speak of? Man is a bulksome creature, his tale must be told with large words, his image drawn of bold strokes and brave colours. A life in itself is small enough indeed: to shrink it to the width of a playing-card spoke violence.

I had made my error once; I had done with limning for all. I pressed further in my search for purer colours, for the light that illumined a body, that I may mix that sacred essence in my mortar. I toyed in my workshop and, rarely, painted Kat. She much lacked the spirit for our former sports, and lately she had seldom called for sittings.

Kat was ill humoured; of this any brute might tell. Petty had claimed her well read, and indeed she proved a great lover of the theatre and its men. Some players she knew were abroad with a comedy and in August she bound a trunk and followed them on their little country Progress. Alone and lacking comfort, I took Petty's advice and hired horse to Thetford. I had hoped to seek some familial solace, yet I was certain I would find no peace in that place. I rode beyond the city walls and, with greater foreboding than when first I passed under Aldgate, set my mare's head to the Essex roads beyond.

My father was much as ever, though not so straight, his fingers twisting roots that curled out from his hands. He claimed that the Winter winds had made them so, for they were ever set in reins or wrapped in ropes, and that Summer warmth made them not so gnawing. He clapped a swollen fist upon my shoulder and declared me well fed, filling out in manly fashion, and a fool for choosing such an ill-looking mare for my journey. My mother fussed about me, staring long upon my neatly hemmed shirt and fine breeches, and my London leather shoes, wiped and cleansed of their city stink on the roadside.

I fancy you will think us peasants now, she said. She kissed my brow and straightened my forelock, just as she had ever done when I was young, and as she still did to my father's favoured horses. *I fancy also that there be some woman*, she added, voice and brows arching.

I shook my head but she smiled a pinched smile, lips pressing tightly.

Mother had let the kitchen girls go and had now but one help-maid from the town. This one was a greasy girl called Sally, but thirteen and with a round face shiny and sluttish. She eyed me hard and said nothing, yet answered shortly to my mother. I had thought to better this, 'til Mother told of how hard girls were to get, many folk of the trade having gone away of late, and clean girls thus scant in Thetford. I saw a dearth in my mother's look and made amends with tales of Greenwich, though they be not altogether truthful. Her eyes grew round and proud. I spoke much of Leicester and his visit, though I said little indeed of where and why he found me. I said nothing of Kat, nothing of the workshop by the courtesan's chamber, nothing of my shameful presence with the Queen. My father, yet a sharp broker of his horses, knew the taste of a lie upon the air. His tongue flicked about his teeth when I spoke of painting gentlefolk and courtiers, warning me to measure my tales with truths.

I knew I would not stay long, for my work grew laboured. I made a likeness of my mother and one of Shiny Sal, who bobbed her thanks, then asked me for a limning in a locket. I rode the bays and wandered the fields with a length for silverpoint and a notebook in my shirt. I studied the faces and skinny forms of groom-boys. I rode to the place of Bess' fall that I might glimpse some shred of her, but the ditch had been filled, the field ploughed and planted. Nothing was as it had been. Ere the meagre Thetford crop was cut and gathered I rode back to London, eager again for Kat and paint.

Nineteen

THAT SEASON, THE CITY was a wrack. Drake's hulk of a ship, much over-picked and hacked by souvenirers, sat the lesser ruin in its dock. I had seen folk chipping at the hull for briny splinters and thought it a harmless trade, wondering at how those very boards had ploughed unknown seas and carried back strange riches. The Hind, stinking and rotting where she stood, sang a sad lay for glory. Where was her bold Drake now, the pirate lord with his unfathomed eyes? He strutted other boards, praising and tending a weathered figurehead. What wonders had this man seen, to come back to a sickening isle and fawn at the regal petticoats? How had Hillyarde trapped such a man in a tiny, bejewelled likeness? A venturer as Drake, I thought, needed vaster panels; and yet they said that Drake was a little man.

Kat had returned from her jaunt with the players, smiling much and bejewelled with sonnets to the softness of her manner and the firmness of her thighs. She bade me sit that she might tell me all and feed me peppered pastries. We breached a flask of canary and drank to reunion, to prevailing health and to a better hope of catching the court favour. Kat had news of the Progress, which she had seen somewhat about the country towns, and had heard somewhat more through its host of travelling servants.

There is gossip as ever, she nodded. *Seymour's marriage is as yet unknown, for the Queen would have clapped them both in the Tower were it out. One of the maids of honour is maid no more, and swells apace. There was some new musician at court, composing airs to the Queen's unailing beauty. I looked much for Leicester but did not spy him; they say he is much abed with his wife and so the Queen will not have him near. What of you?*

I went to Thetford, I longed to return at once. I'll not willingly play the countryman again – and yet I thrive not here. I thought much on you. I groaned. *I am yet sorry for it, Kat; for Dudley, and all you lost with him. Did any speak of it?*

You mean of Greenwich? She shrugged. *Nay, none mentioned you, though be certain that your performance is not forgot. The men of court grow wary, they barely noticed me.*

You were with players, I said, *I doubt they knew you.*

Kat laughed. *They knew me well enough before, whatever company I kept. Now all eyes pass through me. I am a shade.*

I clasped her hands and whimpered – *Sweet mistress, your pallor is as first light upon roses; you shine radiant as the dawn!* Kat giggled and withdrew her hand. I sighed demonstrably. *I cannot compare, alas,* I piped. *I cannot woo you as your scribblers would.*

She smiled and shrugged again. *You mock, you are uncivil. You may have no time for the Theatre, yet there is merit in play at times. My little troupe gave me much diversion.*

Did you break many hearts? I teased.

Alas, she sighed, *none costly enough, nor none that will not mend.*

Ere long I learned how Kat's own heart stood in some danger. She had seen more of the court circle than she allowed, and where courtiers went, so court limners followed. While I had been cursing his name, Kat had been swooning at his person; she spoke of it that evening as I tended her feet with indigo.

Are you yet set against limning? she asked suddenly.

I am. It cannot be done fair.

There is one that can do it, is there not?

You speak of Hillyarde. I picked out a narrow brush, very slight, and dampened it with white lead. The soles of Kat's feet were now wreathed with violets; I commenced picking out points of light between the petals.

Have you ever seen the man? she asked.

No, nor do I wish to. Gower would have me go to his workshop, but I have no wish to see him crow success. Kat shifted slightly and I held fast to her ankles. *Do I tickle?*

No, it is well. She sighed. *Rob, there is something I have not said about the Summer.*

And what is that? I rubbed her heels. *Come, let me put brambles on your calves.*

She sat up then, crushing the violets on my palms. *I saw him, Rob. I met Hillyarde.*

Indeed? Her look was fond, overfond. I set down the paint. Violet seeped between Kat's toes and onto my breeches. *You have spoiled the meadow of your soles*, I said sourly. *I hope he is worth it.*

He is beautiful, Rob, she breathed. *God's Soul! A truly beautiful man.* She smiled and leaned towards me. *He is not as you think*, she burbled, *he is very fine and gentle, not proud or vain but demure, graceful, very proper and pleasing to look at, and young yet.*

I stood up, my head awash and roaring. *'Tis well*, I said flatly. *He is a proper man, he is wived and has children.*

I like a married man, Kat sighed. She lay back and held her smeared feet in the air. *His eye is keen and clear, his work is so fine and delicate. His touch must be deft, do you not think? How attentive he must be with his sable.* She laughed slyly.

I was never so delicate, I said. I wiped off my brushes and stoppered the bladders. *Why do you not marry?*

Kat snorted and rolled over to face me. *I said I like men to be married, not that I wished to marry one. What would be the purpose? I enjoy the sport of the chase too much. I am like one of these new venturers, an explorer; I long to discover unknown terrains and learn strange tongues. I have no wish to arrive and dock my ship in one place.*

You are too metaphorical, I sneered. *You lack imagination, that is all, yet you dress it finely and make it seem adventure. It is not adventure that drives you from bed to bed, Kat; it is fear that you will be held to account for being so dull and feeble.*

Kat blenched, her mouth dropping wide and atremble. Her eyes narrowed and shone watery. *Why do you hurt me thus?* she whispered.

Where is your strength, Kat? I scoffed. *Will you weep all soft and womanish now? You sicken me. You are a whore, yet you think yourself an Amazon, conquering with your eyes and breasts. Argh!* I threw the palette to the floor. Kat darted away, astonished, and I rounded laughing on her. *O, I won't hit you,* I sneered, *I am not mannish enough for that, am I?* She cowered, a pattern of violet footprints about her. *Go, little whore, go and swive the limner if you think it will make you happy.*

Kat shook her head and seemed to sob. I turned away and picked up my palette, scraping the paint from it as foul scraps from a plate. Kat's dry sobbing softened behind me, and I realised that she did not weep, but laughed.

I felt her hand heavy upon my arm, and knew that it was I that stood atremble. *Rob,* she said softly, *you are too jealous.*

I? I snapped. *Jealous of what?*

She held her arms out and laced them about my waist, laid her head against my shoulder and pulled me to her. *Hillyarde is a handsome man,* she sighed into my shirt. *I wish I might care for him as I do for you.*

The Summer was long over, yet its will remained. Petty stayed at Oxford overlong and wrote that many there had also sickened. He feared for his family, for the Sweat had taken their neighbours – and another that he now called friend. Benson, scarce waked from his youthful stumbling to the marriage bed, had taken quickly and left his bride a widow. Benson's father sent the ill news to Petty, urging him to send word on to Swift. Petty's message was also an engagement: I was to seek the school again and tell the Master that my friend was detained, and pretty Benson lost.

I little wished to look on Swift again, and yet I could not fail my friend in this. Petty urged me to speak, begging me to stay mindful of Benson's wish for discretion in his marriage. Some little money and belongings of his remained within the school, and Petty considered them some comfort to the widow. I resolved to have them parcelled on to Oxford, and no questions raised that might give Swift weak excuse for deferment.

The lanes about Black Friars had been struck hard by the season. None sold wares there, and few cried trade or moved about the streets. The kennels stank, for as the heat had gone, so the city now swam with steady rains. The river had broken in places and set the banks awash; many doors between the Thames and Paul's Churchyard were yet boarded, the houses sealed from without, caging sickness. I wondered how ill the school had fared, sited as it was amid the Plague, for folk – and sitters – would surely keep away. I turned sharp into Addle Hill and saw it then; not with the leaden dread of one returning to their shame, but with the quick dart of fearful concern. The door was clearly marked, the casements boarded, the doorstep grimed with filth. I held where I stood and dared not near the place, fearing not contagion alone but how many, and who, might yet lie sick within.

At length I crossed the lane and watched from a clean doorway. My mother had gifted me a fine silver pomander, filled with a physick she had made against disease. I held it before my nose, a cloth against my mouth, and waited. The rain grew steadily and the sky darkened. I pressed against the wall behind me, for I could not move from the place, thinking that some sign might come, or that one would appear to make enquiry of.

As evening approached, so too did my answer. A man rounded the corner and walked towards me; he carried no lantern and did not seem to see me. He wore his cap far over his eyes and his head hung low, rain running hard upon shoulders and neck. His gait was unsteady, for beneath one arm he carried a vast bundle wrapped in cloth. He made straight for Swift's door and set the bundle against his hip. I stepped forward and called out a greeting.

The man swung round to face me; his free hand reached to his waist, then flashed with metal. I held up my hands.

I mean no hurt! I cried, pressing the cloth to my mouth again. *I wish to know of the Master of this place, and his painters.*

The man laughed and pulled his cap back. His laughter chilled, and I saw that his nose was exceeding large; a channel of rain commenced to pour from the fleshy tip.

Lovett?

He nodded. *Robin the Netherman. Come to gloat, dog?*

Nay, I come with tidings. I knew nothing of what had passed here.

Nay, you would not, for you are grown a gentleman of the Strand. He flashed his hand again and I glimpsed the bare point of a dagger.

Put up your blade, Lovett, I entreated. *I mean no harm.*

Indeed? He pulled his bundle close to him and stepped forward. *I might kill you at last.* His speech was cold and even, and he made unswervingly towards me. *I might cut you here, before the school; cut your throat and none would hear that could help you. Or I could forgo the knife.* He drew closer. *I could take you with a kiss.*

I stumbled away from the house and into the lane, backing from him. *What raving is this? Be civil, Lovett, tell me of Swift.*

Swift has what I must surely bear, though I have no signs as yet. He leered before me and I saw grimy kennels as of rain streaming his cheeks. *Come, Robin, might you not test me for buboes?*

Stay back! I piped, flailing.

Lovett laughed again. *I will not take you,* he said. *Your life is miserable enough – I know of it.*

I saw that his eyes knew much. *How sickened is the Master?* I asked, covering my mouth again. *I have word for him from Petty.*

Petty? he rasped. *Pity he was not here. He took leave, as they all did, rode out in the Summer and left him to lick his wounds alone.* Lovett waved his bundle. *Only I stayed for him, only I am here for him at the last!*

I know of Petty. But the others? What of Ambrose, Falconbridge?

Lovett roared. *You hear nothing, do you, dog?* he bawled. *Ambrose is gone, he tends only himself and cares for none. He too is grown gentleman now, for he panders to lords – though not in your manner. Falconbridge is in the Fleet for swiving, Benson fled, sniffing after some Oxford wench—*

Benson is dead! I cried. *The Sweat took him.*

The Sweat? Lovett shook his head. *A hasty sickness. He was ever fortunate.*

He was scarce eighteen Summers, I snapped. *I think that little Fortune.*

And I? Lovett yelled. I am not worthy of life? What of Mistress Swift, Mistress Popham, the idiot Toby? Did they warrant their deaths? They were not your golden-haired Ganymede; you spare them no thought!

I stood amazed. *All dead?*

All! Then the Master, and I to follow. I can do naught now but stay with him, ease his end. None others will remember him.

I nodded, shivering. The rain began to seep within my boots. *You did ever serve him best, I do allow it.*

The faithful dog. Lovett sneered, his mouth a snarl. *Go, your gentle feet grow wet. I will not tell the Master of Benson. He was fonder than he showed.* He turned away from me and went back to Swift's door. *Go*, he said, *he waits for me. Go back to the Strand, Netherman. Go back to your whore.*

Twenty

NATIVITY WAXED CLOSER AND the city was much frosted. Snow lay cleanly on the fields without the walls; the streets were grimed and over-muddied with carts and frozen filth. Petty rode the coach down from Oxford while his family made Northwards, there to celebrate a popish Christmas.

Petty made straight to us, for he had given up his lodgings and so lacked rooms in the city. He had thinned much, his eyes dulled orbs within their darkened, weary settings. Yet he ate heartily as ever, Kat sending for a vast supper of stuffed goose, which Petty seemed to consume entire. We drank deeply of claret and talked loosely on that sixmonth: of young Benson and his shortened wedlock, of Swift's death, of Lovett's loyal doggedness. We talked of the Spanish threat and Petty's brush with recusant-hunters. We spoke of Thetford, of Leicester, of the Queen. We swore expansively and later wept womanish in our cups, bemoaning the loss of art and the conquest of the limner, while Kat murmured softly of Hillyarde's brave looks and fine, pointed fingers. We laid our boots steamingly at the fire and slumbered fitfully: the drunken, slobbering slumber of tavernkeepers. We waked full-clothed and shivering at the grate with the morning yet dark, Kat a heap in her skirts, curled and tucked about our legs, and Petty's boots scorched and blistering in the embers.

When we had washed and rinsed the claret from our mouths I took Petty to meet Master Gower. I had told him of our Greenwich meeting, and that gentleman's invitation to visit again. We set out in the chill air, Petty in a borrowed cloak and pin, our backs and breath smoking damply as we walked, our heads and stomachs sour.

We came to the place and knocked gently, though the sound cracked stingingly about the cold street. We were met by a handsome girl with hair as golden as Benson's, her pale eyes lowered, her arms red and chafed to the elbows with work. I explained our business to her; the eyes lifted and narrowed.

Nay, good sirs, she said curtly, *Master Gower is about to leave on business.*

He is yet within? I urged, peering beyond her to the darkness.

He is certain gone, she rapped out.

Come, sweet mistress, smoothed Petty, his smile flashing. *Might you not announce us? We will not detain him.*

He is late already! she wailed, though her arms shifted yieldingly.

Petty held his hand to hers and she slumped in the doorway. Beyond, a figure strode into view, tugging at a cloak. He looked to the door and halted.

Pray shut the door, Lucy, a voice called, *we have no need of hawkers.*

Master Gower! I called. *We are not yet brought to selling panels for firewood.*

The Thetford painter! cried the Master. *You are very well met indeed. Come within, I beg you; Lucy, kindly show this fellow some courtesy.*

The girl sighed heartily and stepped aside, bobbing to Petty as he passed her. Master Gower trotted forth to greet us, heaving at his cloak and fastening the cuff of his doublet. He blinked into the white light of the street and turned smilingly to Petty.

My dear friend, James Petty of Oxford, I explained. *He is lately returned to the city.*

So! Gower exclaimed, clapping Petty on the elbow. *You are well met. You were also of Swift's school?*

I was, sir, Petty answered, *yet not of his mind. You have heard the news?*

Aye, aye, muttered Gower. *Though it be of little import to the craft, yet I am sorry for his pains, and his family's. So.* He blinked between us again. *Your arrival is providential; I am about to leave and shall take you with me. If you will come?*

Gladly, I nodded, *if you will say where.*

Why, Gower declared, *to my friend Nicholas, of course, the limner.*

*   *   *

We followed Master Gower about the streets. For a little man his stride was brisk and we puffed our speech in smoking bursts, boots sliding. Master Gower made apology for his haste; he was late indeed, for he had sworn to meet with his friend before a morning sitter arrived. We slipped and skated through Cheape to Goldsmith's Row, my gorge rising as we went with the taste of stale claret and the bitter jealousy of what might yet be to come. I had heard overmuch of Hillyarde's looks; soon I would see his fabled talents and his wealthy workshop.

How fares your trade of late? Master Gower enquired. *You thought to make the fashion when last we spoke. You have practised it well?*

I shrugged, my walk ill balanced. *My Greenwich interview did me ill service*, I allowed. *I have little work.*

Master Gower halted, his brow clouding. *What of your friend, Mistress Joyce?* he asked. *I understand that it is she who merits your commissions.*

My legs buckled on a stone – Petty grasped my elbow. We all faced within, each clasping the next as a circle of conspiracy. I breathed hard. *I did not know it so well published*, I said meekly.

Master Gower nodded to Petty. *Forgive me, good sir*, he humbled, *I believe you to be of no secrets?*

Indeed not, Petty murmured.

I huffed, much baited. *It would seem that no secrets are kept in this city.*

Master Gower laughed gently. *Take no offence*, he said softly, grasping my sleeve. *There are no secrets at court, save for those kept from the Queen, and men call that diplomacy.*

We pressed on our way, my cheeks grown unseasonably hot in the frozen air. Master Gower persisted, seeking some answer to my current state.

Mistress Joyce fell from favour, I explained, *yet now enjoys some court company again.*

Gentleman ushers, in the main? Gower suggested.

Aye. I have had some work from them, yet they do not inspire.

They aspire, Petty noted. Gower chuckled.

They want only limners' likenesses, I complained. *That is the fashion, as you warned me, sir.* Gower nodded. *Yet I have had some decorative works*, I went on, *some shields and suchlike, and patterns for glass. Also some copy work.*

Copy work! Petty squawked. *God's Soul, Rob, surely not!*

'Tis the work, Petty, I cried, *it cannot be helped!*

'Tis the time, Master Petty, said Gower. He chewed the words solemnly, his square beard awag. *'Tis a poor time for our art, my friends.* He halted and gestured to a doorway inscribed The Maidenhead; we had reached the Goldsmith's, unseeing. *Let us greet one who yet prospers*, Gower declared, *even so.*

The Goldsmith's house was marvellous well appointed, set with shop and workshop ranged below the living quarters. A nursemaid of a servant, babe on hip, bid us enter. She waved Master Gower through, scarce noting we two that followed. Gower made straightway to a heavy door, much carved with crests and devices, rapped hard and announced himself. A moment later the door was flung open by a dark and scowling youth, raggedly attired in over-washed black hose and a smeared shirt rolled back to the elbows.

Master Gower, he bowed. He looked enquiringly to us, his eyes as dark and over-used as his clothing.

Well met, Isaac, Master Gower replied, clapping the youth's sharp shoulder. *Your Master is within?*

He awaited you, Isaac pouted. *Now he readies for a sitter.*

I know it well, Gower laughed, *you need not scold me so. He will see me and my friends here.* He turned back to us. *Young Isaac is of French stock, and so naturally suspicious – is that not so, Isaac?* Isaac glowered. Master Gower pressed through into the room. *Nicholas?* he cried. *Isaac keeps watch in your doorway again.*

The youth let us pass, his cheeks pinched and crimsoned. Within lay a vast room set with two high tables: Prentice desks with lanterns lit, though the day be light enough. Upon the desks were boxish easels scarce two hands in size; another youth bent his head above one, turning to smile at Gower who hailed him as *young Rowland*. Shelves of phials, shells and bladders, and an array of tiny mortars and grinding stones were ranged about the place. A youthful panelled likeness of the Queen hung proudly by the fire, which swelled forth great heat yet gave out neither smoke nor stench. White light poured in through many casements, and mirrored glass spread the brightness throughout the space. All was clean as to be a palace, the floorboards newly sanded and strewn, the air sweet save for the wonted scent of washes and pigments. At the far end of the room a man patted about a grand chair with plump cushions, smoothing the cloth and tugging at a short blue curtain behind. Beside this lay a vast desk, set out as for painting but more neatly done, a boxed easel with an enlarging glass reaching above it on a metal arm.

The man turned at last. He was proper as Kat had told, very bravely dressed for workshop work, with a neatly turned beard and finely curling hair. He held up his hands to Master Gower. *My friend*, he said, his voice thick and soft, *you have no notion of promptness*.

Forgive me, Nicholas, Gower chuckled. *I was baited by Lucy this morning, could scarce manage the fastening of my own cloak and was met in the doorway by this pair of cozeners professing to be painters*. He turned to us and beckoned us forward. *This is the Thetford Robin we spoke of, and here James Petty, also lately of Swift's*.

Hillyarde came forward and clasped our hands in greeting. *I am glad indeed to meet you*, he said warmly, his lips curling with mirth. His manner of speaking was strange to me, and I knew it must be the sound of his country, far and low in the West. His eyes sparked as all charming men's eyes do, and I felt Kat's swoon in his look. He turned to Petty. *I am sorry for your recent loss*, he said, his mouth now straightened with concern. *I trust you are not hit too sorely by the blow*.

Petty smiled and bowed his head. *The loss is slight, as well you might know, Master Hillyarde. Pray do not concern yourself for me. I am well rid of the school*.

Hillyarde blinked amazement, then smiled again. *You take ill fortune bravely, Master Petty*, he said. Petty shrugged.

Gower grasped my elbow stoutly. *This young man is a finely gifted painter of likenesses, yet in the street he told me a sorry tale indeed.* He smiled encouragingly.

I heard of your misfortune with the Queen, Hillyarde said, nodding sagely. *I am sorry for it.*

The news seems stale and far reaching, I grumbled.

Gower's grip tightened. *So,* he said softly, *yet we will remedy it, and your patroness Mistress Joyce soon bring you better favour.*

I looked to Hillyarde, thinking to see his eyes shine cold and mocking. I sought to hate him, knowing it healthier thus to range my rival, as I had with Lovett and Falconbridge. Yet his look was all placid concern and interest, his eyes intelligent. I urged his contempt. *You have heard of this also, Master Hillyarde?*

I have heard tell of Mistress Joyce, he said politely, *a fine woman of much learning and great beauty.*

She is a whore, I brazened, *and I am in her keep.*

Hillyarde coughed gently; Petty shook his head and rolled his eyes. Gower's other hand found the first and seized violently upon my elbow. *I beg you, Master Robin,* he urged, *have a thought for the Prentices.*

No matter, George, said Hillyarde calmly, *they are of an age and know discretion.* He smiled thinly at me, his lips veiled by curling whiskers. *You are angered, Master Robin. It is the law of our time that we be yoked by women; so are we all in this nation, for God has willed it so. We are all subjects, are we not? Be it of the Heart or of the State.* His smile grew merry. *We must learn obeisance; I am wed, and I strive that Alice will have joy of me and our children. Your patroness is no burdensome matter, for the lady is generous and gracious, and she loves you well. Would that I had such a one at your tender age! I would have learned much from her.* He winked knavishly.

Gower released my elbow and rubbed his hands. *So,* he muttered, *so. We spoke on the way of copy work, Nicholas, for Master Robin has been forced much to it. Master Petty disapproves.*

He wastes his talent thus, Petty declared.

There is little to argue, I said, *yet I have had some other work.*

That is well, said Hillyarde. *What manner of work?*

Decorations, devices and such things, I grudged. *Trifles, yet fairly paid.*

Copies of the Queen fetch handsomely, Gower said. *I like it little though; fine works are made base by ill copying.* He sighed. *It is a sorry matter.*

I have made fair copies of fouler likenesses, I retorted. *Yet few wish for the ill works to be improved. It is my duty to paint true, I cannot do otherwise.*

Gower smiled indulgently. *You will make the fashion yet, as you say. Nicholas*, he added, *you must show these gentlemen some works.*

Hillyarde nodded. *I would do so, gladly, yet the hour of my sitting grows near. You might look to the shop, for I have some new pieces there. Have you tried your hand at limning, Master Robin?*

I nodded. *I fared ill at it. I do not care for such small work.*

It is taxing on the eye, Hillyarde assented, his face all modesty.

Indeed so, Gower muttered. *Well, we must leave you to ready yourself. What time does he come?*

A firm hammering sounded at the door and a page entered. *Sir Francis!* he bellowed, bowing low. The Prentices stood and hung their heads in deference.

He comes now, Hillyarde whispered. *He is one who knows the importance of timing, my friend.* He pressed forward, urging us to the door.

A Devonian concern, I'll warrant, Gower hissed, his bow scraping low as the page.

A short and ruddy man, lapped from head to foot in 'broidered green and white, swaggered to the door. Petty and I fell to bowing also; Hillyarde laughed and nodded.

You make a grand impression on us, sir, he said.

The man laughed back, the noise huge for his frame and vulgar for his silks. *Well met, Nick*, he cried thunderously, his voice thick with Hillyarde's strange burr. *Who are these? New Prentices?*

You know George Gower, Serjeant Painter, Hillyarde said. *These two are his friends and fellow painters.*

We bowed again and made our introductions. Sir Francis Drake, hero of court and city, took me by the hand.

Well met, he bawled. *I must be about my business. Have you met Alice yet?* He winked. *How is she, Nick? And young Francis?*

My thanks, smiled Hillyarde, *Alice and the children are well. Shall we begin?*

Arr, aye, Drake mumbled. He punched my arm with a brawny fist. *My godson, Francis*, he said. *Fine sturdy body*. He laughed again. *Alice too, and I a free man again*. He nodded to Hillyarde. *We'd no thought to see me so fine when the babe was born. Did we Nick?* Hillyarde assented and bade us farewell, handing us through the door. Drake puffed his cheeks and caught my wrist as I passed. *Nick likes not my talk*, he announced bluffly. *He thinks I would steal his wife*.

You might think to do so, Hillyarde said smoothly, *yet you would not, being friend and nobleman both*.

Drake's round face shone with glee. *Arr*, he said again. *'Tis so, alas. Strangest truth there be*.

We walked on apace to Gower's next interview, for he was to meet with another jeweller on a matter of business. He had long considered the making of a clock, he breathlessly informed us, being most interested in mechanical contrivances.

I would make it in the manner of a pageant piece, he explained, *as the Italian Masters did; yet I would have it most accurate, giving the hours and astronomical movements*. He waved his arms with excited agitation. *It would be a thing of great beauty and an instrument of knowledge. I have devised some schemes for it, yet I lack the complete knowledge for the construction. I hope to repair my ignorance shortly*. He paused and pressed into a doorway. *Well, here is the place, so*, he said. *Come and see me again, gentlemen, please*.

Petty and I made our slipping way back through the streets, the snow driving down again as we neared the walls. By Fleet we took refuge in a tavern, Petty's appetite welling up and in need of taming, his claret fog having cleared. He chewed resolutely on bread and sausage, complaining much about the lack of a hot broth or stew for the cold. We took a jug that was also little spiced or mulled, kicking our boots of snow and shivering by the grate. The fall was fast and in such pieces as seemed the size of a hand, yet turned quickly to a frozen rain that soon thinned and abated. We raced wetly back to the Strand and there thawed and dried, slumbering the afternoon beside fatly crackling logs.

Kat returned bright and brisk, for she had been given carriage back from her daily court adventure and had been at Whitehall when the Queen appeared. She yawned and stretched before the fire with us, arching her silken toes towards the logs.

How went the hunting? Petty enquired, stirring from sleep. He sat up, his stomach growling a salute.

You are hungry as ever, Kat remarked.

I did not have a courtier's dinner, he said, rubbing his belly. *I ate lean sausage in a ha'penny tavern.*

There was no need, Kat said, *the larder is not bare.*

I am glad of it, Petty chirped. *Shall we sup as well as you dined?*

I did not dine, Kat said, *I had no stomach.*

You are unwell? I asked.

She chafed her hands. *Nay, naught but over-weary and wine-sickened. We will sup expansively enough even for you, Petty, though first I must put off this velvet.*

We are too low to sup with court fashions, Petty groaned.

I have no wish to greasen my skirts, Kat said. *Let us send for pies.*

Kat's maid went out for pies and brought back a tart of cheese and a joint of mutton crisply roasted. She bobbed her apology, pies being, she said, hard to find on a cold evening in the Strand. Kat laughed and let her go, sending her home with a piece of the meat and some onions in a basin. We unwrapped the fare and ate before the fire, knives and platters ill balanced in our hands. Kat's drabber skirts were much smeared with mutton grease ere we had finished, and she shruggingly wiped her fingers on the hem. Petty picked at the mutton bones suckingly and then devoured two apples. The tart was rich and heavy, and we sat about awhile in silence, leaden in our gluttony.

You told us nothing of your hunting, Kat, Petty declared. *Did you make a kill?*

I fish, I do not hunt, she replied. *It was a better day, though the men of the court grow chaste.*

It is a cold season for courtship, I reminded.

I must have some surety by Twelfth Night, she said, *or we will not eat so well next season.*

I have some work yet, I assured. She shrugged. *We met with Gower today*, I went on, pausing to be sure of her. *He took us to Hillyarde.*

Indeed? she said, sitting up. *What do you think of him? Is he not gentle as I said?*

He seemed pleasing enough.

What did you speak of?

Painting, limning, nothing you would care for. We did not stay long.

Petty raised a brow at me; I warned him with a look.

'Tis a pity he said nothing of the court, Kat remarked sullenly. *He is well placed.*

He had a visitor, Petty declared, *as we were leaving. Sir Francis Drake.*

Drake? Kat smiled. *He has a pirate's eye.*

He seemed much interested in Mistress Hillyarde, Petty teased.

Pfu! Kat snorted. *She is a yellow mouse. She would know nothing of what to do with such a man.*

She caught Hillyarde, and he seems mannish enough, Petty said.

Drake is knighted and rich, Kat persisted.

And widowed, I added.

Aye, said Petty, *and stout, and past his youth.*

Kat sighed. *I would have the two men made one; a man with brave looks, gorgeous apparel, fine fingers and a venturer's stomach.*

Venturers and pirates like to roam, Petty warned.

I know it, Kat said slyly. *Would they would roam in my*

direction! She yawned again and waved at the mutton carcass. *That mutton puts me in mind of Old Hatton*, She said. *The Queen calls him her Sheep; never was a name so apt.*

You tried for him? I asked.

She shrugged. *He is marvellous well appointed and weak of spirit. I thought to try him, but he is too much the lamb.*

So there are none at court to tempt you? asked Petty.

Nay, she laughed, *we are in a lovers' drought. Only the bold Water could quench me, and it is for him all women are turned sirens.* She raised a brow. *Especially the Queen.*

Raleigh? I said.

Aye, Raleigh. He is the proper pirate for me.

Would you could net him, Petty declared. *We would all grow rich, selling his face in lockets.*

I would keep him hid, Kat sighed, *and never let him out.*

The Queen will never let him out, I offered. *Let us await what Advent brings.*

Twenty-one

KAT MADE SOME MANNER of a conquest, receiving a jewelled rope in exchange for her Twelfth Night duties. The rope was prettily woven of gold and set about with yellow stones, though it proved of less worth than she had hoped when she sold it to a broker in Gutter Lane. On Innocents' Day I passed into my twenty-fourth year and we drank deeply to our continuance. Petty stayed long with us, sharpening his rendering in silverpoint and developing a fine hand at shadowing Kat's features. Come Lent he announced that he wished to travel and planned to make ship to France, then venture South to his longed-for Italy. Kat was much pleased, being now given to the spirit of venturing. I feared for my friend, a mild recusant in that most papist world, and warned him that it might be long ere he return. Passports and papers were oft forbidden the Seal, and an English recusant, studying awhile with Catholics, was seldom given peace from Walsingham's men. Petty shrugged, waxed rapturous of French eating and Italian frescos, and swore to return as good a man as Titian, and fattened too. I offered him a place in my workshop but he declined, claiming he would give me room in his own come a twelvemonth.

With Petty gone, I saw much of Masters Gower and Hillyarde. I called often at the Maidenhead, later regaling Kat with tales of her hero and his yellow mouse. Alice Brandon was a softly featured woman with a cream complexion, there being something buttery and golden about her that made Kat's looks seem violent. She had many babes, with ever a child swinging from her hem or clutching at her from the nurse's arms. She wore a piped cap high upon her hair, yet seemed always looking down, modest as a milkmaid. Her father had not raised her on country manners, however, he being a city man of some income, likewise a Goldsmith, Prime Warden of the company, and Hillyarde's own Master when he Prenticed. Hillyarde was, as any man might be, inclined to seem wealthy and well-appointed to his Master's eyes. Yet ever was his complaint one of poverty and ill Fortune.

None think us gentlemen, that is the fault, he declared. *The court think limners to be craftsmen, as carvers and masons are. They will not pay fairly for what is given.*

Yet, my friend, Gower reasoned, *painters in large are but mural makers to them. You have the gold to your title at least.*

Yet not to my purse. Hillyarde shrugged. *I believe our arts a noble following, yet we are paid as paupers.*

You are paid far more than I, I put in. *You are the fashion, are you not?*

Hillyarde laughed. *Aye, the picture of fashion, borrowing funds from courtiers to buy court clothes, that I may limn their likenesses in fine style. And then they pay me naught for my work, that I must stand ever in their debt!* He shook his head. *I would have some men listen, yet my words seem wasted at court.*

I fear they be, Gower gloomily agreed. *We need tracts of persuasion that might be read by many, showing the truth of it. A scholarly argument for our inclusion in the liberal arts; that is our need.*

You run on the same course again, George, Hillyarde said. *One day I will write your tract. As yet I must bend above another Knollys work to pay off my debts to Leicester. I must needs work.*

You have much work, I put in. *It is not so for one of my standing; no guild, a failed Prentice come hither without training.*

Gower shook his head sadly. Hillyarde clapped my shoulder. *You think overmuch on this*, he said kindly. *Not all my lads have been bound by papers, yet lacking a guild seal will be little worry to them. Isaac least of all, with his keen eye.*

We looked to where the youth worked, his shoulders sharply stooped, his jaw sullen and resentful. *Isaac's keen temper is the greater worry*, Gower noted gravely.

*   *   *

Master Gower was in the right. Isaac's talent was sober and pleasing, for he did not delight in the filigree fineness of his Master's limning, but trained his eye to capturing likeness that showed much of a man. From this I believed him to be of my mind in matters of art. I had mistook.

One morning a gentlewoman, large and voluminously dressed, came to the Maidenhead to make complaint. She brandished a locket work she had lately commissioned, and stated with much determination that *it would not do*. Hillyarde enquired politely for the fault.

It will not do! she exclaimed again, slamming the locket hard upon the table. *What manner of limning is this?*

The best manner, madam, I assure you, Hillyarde smoothed.

It is foul! the woman roared, her cheeks mottling. *My daughter is to wed. What manner of love gift is this to give to her betrothed?*

Hillyarde nodded with compassion. *I am sorry that it is not to your taste, my lady*, he offered, *but I do not understand you.*

To my taste! she squawked. *Do not understand me! What is to be understood? The piece is base and ugly.*

It seems right fair work to me, Hillyarde said, *yet I am sorry it so displeases you. My Prentice Isaac rendered somewhat of this piece, and he is my finest pupil.*

I wanted a Master's piece for my daughter, the woman puffed, *not some base Prentice work!*

My lady, Hillyarde softened, *you did not furnish a Master's price.*

I did not expect a schoolboy's work for a marriage gift, and I will not have it!

Hillyarde beckoned to Isaac, who left his desk and stood sullenly before them. He picked up the locket and scowled at the limning. *Isaac is a fine limner, my lady*, Hillyarde assured. *Isaac, what say you of this?*

'*Tis a likeness of the lady I did limn*, he drawled.

The woman took fire, her height and girth waxing with her ire. *My daughter does not look thus! My daughter is beautiful!* She snatched the locket from Isaac's hand and thrust it at Hillyarde. *Regard, Master Goldsmith, the ugly chin he gave her! The boy mocks her beauty!*

Madam, said Isaac quietly, *your d…*
wrought.

Impertinent youth! the woman screamed. *…*
thus!

Isaac bowed his head. *I do not insult you, madam,*
his pitch rising. *I do not insult your daughter. I limn …*
and I saw that chin.

The lady screamed again, made as if to swoon, then stru…
cracking blow at Isaac's face. He stood still, white with rage, his
fists hard clenching.

Madam, said Hillyarde, his voice now atremble, *kindly leave*
this place at once.

The woman looked from Isaac to his Master and across the
room to me. *I will leave indeed*, she stormed; *such ill company*
brings shame upon me. She turned swirlingly and, tucking the
locket safe into her girdle, left the room.

All sighed loudly, Isaac shook his head. Hillyarde embraced
his Prentice roughly and made to the shop door. *You did well*
to keep your fists, he called back to Isaac. *I will see she be truly*
gone, then we'll take a cup.

I crossed to where Isaac stood and clapped him on the shoulder.
Well spoken, young man, I declared. *You answered well.*

He looked to my hand as though it be unclean and I hastily
withdrew. He bowed coldly and sat to his work again, though he
did not pick up his brush. Hillyarde returned with Master Gower
– newly arrived and much puzzled – in his wake. The Goldsmith huffed loudly between us, calling to the youth Rowland
to fetch some wine. I stood by Isaac and studied him; his
lip curled crossly beneath thin boyish whiskers, his eyelids
low and drooping. The limning he had set before him was
the shape and size of a hen's egg, the figure within outlined
in dry brushing, a wide ruff lumpish as a hunchback at the
neck.

I like well your manner, Isaac, I persisted. *You look to render*
honestly. The lad did not move, but set to cleaning of his fingers.
I was once called a Netherman for looking to the truth, I laughed.
You do not follow your Master's ideals; nor then did I. You have
a keen eye, Isaac; I wish only to hearten you. I bent towards him.

...ese little images, I whispered. *Try for a larger likeness, work at full panels.*

Isaac stood suddenly, toppling his chair. He looked up to me, his cheeks drawn, his eyes ablaze. *I know your work*, he hissed, lips atremble. *I am not like you – your pictures are dead as the past is dead. You have used your time.* He swallowed hard, the sharp ball of his gorge rising and falling.

What do you know of this? I exclaimed. *Limning is but a fancy of the age.*

Isaac pouted like a babe. *Men will look to my works when yours are long forgot.*

I recoiled; I might have felt it less had he boxed my ears. Isaac's brows pinched together and he shook his head as a cow shakes off flies. He swore quietly in French and, picking up his doublet from the toppled chair, stalked from the room.

Hillyarde drew near and smilingly offered a cup. I took it and drank gaspingly.

You are unwell? he asked mildly.

I am sickened indeed, I spat. *He is an arrogant youth.*

Come, Robin, he urged, *and you were never so? Isaac will learn to hold his tongue and show esteem.*

Look to yourself, Master Hillyarde, I warned, *he will outstrip you. You nurse a cuckoo there.*

Hillyarde shook his head and waved to Isaac's desk. *He is a fine student, yet he has much to learn.*

He has the Huguenot pride, I scoffed.

'Tis so, Gower called, crossing to where we stood, *and there are far worse than he. A great number of strangers are in the city*, he muttered lowly. *I own it, we have had much to learn from the Puritan lands; yet now we are overrun with immigrants. We must protect our interests, as the merchants and tradesmen do.*

The guilds see to that, put in Hillyarde.

Nay, my friend, Gower sighed. *A stranger needs to but call himself an Englishman and so he becomes one. We must keep our hands set firm upon the wealthy commissioners.*

Yet how might that be done? I asked. *The court is awash with foreign painters.*

I have a notion that it might be done by law, Gower answered. *Were we to have a paper drawn out, and royally sealed, we might have power over the likenesses of the court.*

Come, said Hillyarde gently. *It is not right to tell a man he might not be painted by another.*

Indeed, I agreed, *and how would those fare who yet struggle for acknowledgement? There is a scarcity of work for Englishmen alone.*

I do not mean to control all likenesses, Gower explained. *Only the image of the Queen.*

The Queen? Hillyarde arched his brows.

So. I am Serjeant Painter; you, my friend, are the finest limner in the country. We might have it writ that only we two may take likenesses of the Queen; all copiers and decorators to pay us a fee for the use of her image.

As the monopoly of wines? I asked.

Gower smiled. *In some wise, aye, it would be like that in law.*

Hillyarde raised his cup. *A steady means of money*, he said; *no more the tying of loans and bonds.* He drank and smacked his lips. *We should look to it.*

Though their talk of monopoly irked me, I was much indebted to both those Masters of craft. Master Gower paid me handsomely to complete some works of his that he had little time for: small panels, for little men, yet I was grateful. Hillyarde also sent me work, for he persuaded a gentleman merchant that his wife, far younger than her husband and of some dark beauty, might make a pretty likeness on a board. So I passed from Winter and beyond Lent with wood enough for fires and a bladder of ultramarine for Kat's bejewelling.

The Spring had proved irksome, yet when the May dawned I shared with Kat the rising hope of a sweet new season. Kat's favoured players performed that afternoon; in her absence I worked long on a hue of green to dress her with.

Kat returned from the playhouse and danced into my workshop, well pleased with herself and springing in the feet.

You were content with the play, I see. She nodded, and I gestured that she unlace herself. *Was it a comedy? Your eyes are merry.*

I met a man today, she said, throwing back her head.

Should I be surprised? I replied. *It is May, the buds swell forth, as do all willing knaves and playhouse wenches.* I circled the white lead with my knife and wiped it into the green, thickening and fattening the colour. It seemed a lush waterish green now, not still and brackish but teeming and brothy; a marsh green, a fen green, swampish as a soup of ferns and fishes.

You care not, she said.

Come, I care very well. Take off your bodice.

I have not washed.

It will sit well with my paste. I offered her the green. *Is it not full of life?*

It is ugly.

It is the green of well-water and chickweed. There are tadpoles in it, and small fishes. Come fish in it, Kat, dip in your paw.

She pulled off her gloves. *I am loath to feed your wants,* she said, holding out her right hand. *Here are my fingers only.*

You were never loath, I answered. I pressed her fingertips to my palette and stroked them through the paste. She sighed and offered her shoulder. I unlaced her left sleeve and drew it from her bodice, widened the neck of her shift and found the roundness of her arm. She nodded and commenced circling green patterns on her skin.

He is an unusual fellow, she said, stroking her neck. *He would seem to understand something of me.*

Indeed, I answered. *He is handsome?*

No. Ugly, almost goatish, in fact. He is quite a creature, hairy as to seem furred, his face particularly so.

I offered her the palette. *And you bedded him? You disappoint.*

Swift was not pretty, she said, her chin rolling languidly. *You are pretty, but you do not bed me. There is more to such things than a soft look and a firm resolve.*

That I lack the latter, I know well. What then does he offer you?

Kat sat up. *Mystery*, she said. She kneeled before me and laid her cheek upon the palette. *He is a strange being*, she whispered, *quite other than most men.*

He cannot be so different. He was mannish with you, was he not?

She shook her head, her face besmirched with my greenery. *I do not mean in his body. He knows secrets, Rob. You must meet with him.*

You mean me to look to the arras again? Come, Kat—

Nay, she said, *I mean you to speak together.*

Kat's goatish lover was a man of dark learning, yet bold as one of her venturers. He had spied her at the playhouse and watched her exit; in the crushing crowd without, he steered himself to press against her and whisper declarations. She had followed him to an inn and bedded him that very afternoon, yet she owned that there was little reason to it. Later they took a bottle and she told him of my work, which he answered with some riddled mumblings and whispers on the art of alchemistry. He was an astrologer of Salisbury, a man of repute, he claimed, a tutor and physician. He came often to the city, and Kat agreed to meet him when next he travelled.

Kat returned from their second meeting with a phial of strong ointment. Her Salisbury Goat had prepared this physick to ease some ache that pained her, a suffering which, she claimed, gnawed much at her joints.

You did not tell me you were in pain, I grumbled.

You did not ask.

And your creature did?

She nodded. *He noticed it. He saw some stiffness in me, some swellings about my bones.*

You told him that you suffered, I said, much piqued. *You said naught to me.*

What does it matter? You are not the physician, you did not give me balm for it. Simon did.

Simon? I scoffed. *Is that the creature's name? And he is an apothecary too?*

He is a man of learning, and healing. He has knowledge of

the workings of the body. His knowledge should appeal to you, Rob.

I am not for butchery and poisons, I piped.

He wishes to meet you, she said calmly. *Please say that you will bear him company.*

Twenty-two

KAT BLOSSOMED THAT SUMMER, her eyes aglow and her face rosy with sun. In her new manner I saw that she had indeed suffered in her body; after the flight of harsh Winter and the damper chill of Spring, she had straightened and skipped with such renewed grace and vigour that her former self seemed an ancient garment, cast off with her heavy petticoats. She applied her Goat's ointment with ritual care and her swellings smoothed to their girlish slenderness. She made much merriment at court and bedded a brace of minor lords, a young scholar and his less bookish brother-in-law, and a gallant who declared kin with the errant Percys of the North. I had little good of her conquests, making only some copy work for the Percy pretender, and an over-paid image of the scholar's hapless wife.

Though coin waxed more plentiful, my pursuit of perfected colour yet evaded. I struggled on in my experiments, engaging substances of a mineral base to corrupt, and so distil, my coloured essences. I took many Summer walks through the Finsbury fields, gathering plants and clay from the cleaner stream banks. Kat showed a willing subject again and I played many new paints upon her skin, finding that they sat more truly upon warm flesh than upon the cool of vellum, or the smooth unyielding surface of a board.

I thus saw out the heat, and though the season waxed high, the sickness soon abated, taking but few about us, and none that we knew well. The harvest was fair and the markets prospered. Word came via ship from Petty, for he was far into his season of French learning and had eaten better, he declared, than he thought man might ever do in a Protestant State. *The art of France is over-mannered*, he wrote, *too tumbling and false for the eye. But the tables! They are truly a glimpse of the sublime, and I am in my Spirit's own heaven. Flesh made holy indeed –*

you should sample the sacrificial lamb they sell in Paris. I will leave you Englishmen to mumble and choke on your daily bread, for I now mop up a good spoon of rich heretical sauce with mine. I hope to find the Italian fare as well suited to my soul and my stomach. Even the Pope cannot dine as well as have I tonight! I laughed when reading: I feared the dangerous savour of Petty's writing for a good while after.

Kat corresponded also, keeping a casket of Salisbury letters from her Goat. I cursed this idle fascination, wondering how the strange creature had thrown his cloak of affection about my Kat. I knew little of his worth and trusted less of his boasting. I learned that he would pay visit to us soon, and when his Lammas arrival was announced, it sounded an ill omen to my ears.

The Goat put up in East Cheape lodgings, and for this act, at least, I gave him merit. Kat had hoped he might lodge with us, for she wished me to make his likeness and to talk with him of my experiments. He declined, thinking a stay in the Strand over-familiar for their acquaintance; Kat grew formal also, setting out sweetmeats and wine. I stayed hid in my rooms 'til called upon, hoping I might not be brought to another candlelit study of the arras.

He arrived alone and without horse, rapping firmly upon the door and taking to the house much as a visiting physician. He was below stairs for a few moments only when Kat came to the door and bid me down to meet him.

Simon is here, she said briskly.

Sup with him then, I said, *and bring him here when you show him about the house.*

He is in some haste to meet you, she barbed. *I think it you he came hither for, not me.*

I followed her below. The Goat stood with his back to the door, a cup already in his hand. His small frame was thickly set and clad in cheap brown cloth, the colour of dry horse-dung and very poorly cut. A vulgar cap of the same hue rested on a chair beside him, limp and worn as a scabied dog in a collar of russet silk. The hair it had covered was of a paler reddish tone, yet thick as thatch and unruly. Kat followed my look, her eyes resting with shame on the table-rug and plates of dainties.

Well met, I said to the Goat's back. He turned hastily about and stared at me.

Well met, sir, he growled. His voice came deep and gruff from beneath the great yellowish mass of his beard; his lips were scarce to be seen. His huge eyes, vast and shadowed by the thick arbour of his brows, blinked rapidly. He dipped a bow. *Simon Forman of Quidhampton, and at your service. I may see your workshop?*

I learned swiftly that the Goat was straight to his purpose in all things. We left Kat for my rooms, she filling a cup and sinking upon a chair, part in disgust and part in relief for shame. The Goat showed no interest in the rooms we passed, nor did he speak as we walked, but set his brow stiffly, his hands clenched behind his back. I opened the workshop doors and bade him look about within.

He peered at some renderings I had about the table and looked briskly at the boards. Then he seated himself upon my carved sitter's chair and folded his arms abruptly.

Well, Master Forman, I said, somewhat bemused. *Do you wish me to render you now?*

Nay, unless you care to, he said. *Have no fear of me.*

I have none, I said. *I had no thought to bear any.*

Mistress Joyce has told you of my work? he asked. I nodded assent. *Good*, he continued, *then you know why I am here.*

I do not, sir, I answered, much confused, *save for the pleasure of seeing Mistress Joyce.*

He nodded curtly. *That is a pleasure, I am a man. I am here to talk of our work. You make experiments with colour. I would aid you.*

I laughed. *You practise alchemistry, I understand. Do you think to conjure gold from my base paintings?*

Gold can be used as paint already, he grunted. *The substance seems real in an image, for it is the substance itself that is used. Not so with all matter. Fleshly colour is not rendered with a paint made of flesh. Such paint fails Nature. You look for pure colour, true in paint as in life. As with gold.*

I stood amazed. The little Goat had spoken my very will, though I had not seen the method of it so clear as he. His eyes shone with the fervour of a zealot and he rubbed his hands together.

Colour is vital, he went on. *For you it is as the very breath of the man you render. The line defines the man, the colour gives him being. You would create him as God created Adam. You make his shape, then you strive to give him will. But you cannot.*

I felt for a chair and sat beside him. *I am a painter of likenesses*, I said flatly.

You are not God. Perhaps you are his messenger.

I swallowed hard. *I wish only to show men as they truly are*, I urged.

The Goat smiled thinly, the whiskers about his lips sweeping apart. *You wish to make your creatures live. You might learn of the act of creation through God's own creatures. I know a man can conjure and question Angels.*

I laughed, waking from his thoughts as if pinched. *That is madness and heresy both*, I said, rising. *I will not be trapped into such talk.*

Sit, Forman commanded. His eyes burned into me and I found myself sinking down again. *You lack faith, so be it. I am physician and astrologer. I deal with the human and the Divine. You think the language of colour to be sacred?*

I nodded. *It is a cipher*, I said, *writ for simple reading. Few care for it now; it is perished to naught but the matching of liveries and devices.*

It is, he agreed. *Matter and figure are coloured in images to represent their natures. Why the Virgin robed in blue? For so it is, and must be. It is thus in life, though we scarce consider it. Why the black cloth of the Huguenots? The yellow mourning of the Spanish Kings? The purple Robe Imperial?* I looked to the drab speaker and his earthen cloth. He nodded. *I have little care for the dressing of my body. I look thus and it serves me no ill. I have much good of the women that love me. When I have better purse I might dress in silks.*

I care little for fashion also, I humbled. *I leave that concern to gentlemen and courtiers, though they would have me copy it well in my work.*

Forman barked a laugh. *Men reveal nothing of themselves in apparel. Pigs might be made to dress in jewels. I look to what lies beneath such things.*

My very thoughts, I whispered.

Naming words have power, he said cryptically. *Musical chords contain the sublime and demonic. Yet God is not in the mouths of priests or the sheets in the printing press. Nor does He hide in song. The Divine is ever about us. Angels and Demons walk among us. Spirits reside in the walls of our bedchambers.* He leaned towards me. *God lies within the World Material, clothed in many colours. I can see Him.* Forman nodded to my brushes. *I will dip those in the well of the Holy Spirit. Then you can daub the essence of men on your panels.*

The sun was setting lowly; amber light blistered upon the boards and walls about us. God shone magnificent in every mote and speck. I gazed upon the strange man before me and felt, gaspingly, that I was drowning and he the only soul alive to save me.

How can this be? I murmured.

He answered with his history. He wished to come hither to London to set up practice, having been much hounded in his home country for selling physick without licence. He had passed a twelvemonth and more in close cells for his pains and was now tutoring the children of a Salisbury lord. Yet his true hope was in the practice of healing and the raising of spirits, for he had conjured with the necromancer Francis Cox and learned much of his secret arts. Physick and alchemistry were like to my work, he declared, for they were the studies of Man and Nature, the mortal body and the immortal soul. *We both strive to understand them*, he said, his growling voice swelling with conviction. *We both wish to contain and control them. Our practice is the sphere of the few. We must be secretive.*

I nodded eagerly. *Yet how might you help me?* I persisted.

I will prepare a substance for you. With it you might dissolve all matter into its finest state. Liquids thus made you may thin or thicken with oils. Solids you will desiccate and grind as though pigments.

And your fee?

He laughed. *The woman's pleasure when I am in the city. A purse of money delivered to me – for each of your first score of commissions.* I made to protest but he held up a hand. *And absolute silence on this, and all, of our matters.*

Twenty purses of money, I mused. How small would the coin be? I shook my head, for I might never be well placed enough for such payment.

The cost is slight, Forman said calmly. *You will make your fortune from me.* He rubbed his hands together again and stood abruptly. *Now*, he growled, *I will take an advance from our Mistress.* He bowed and left the room.

I listened in amazement as Forman trod down the stair, thinking to hear his goatish cloven hoofs scraping the boards. Yet I saw he was man indeed, though thick-furred as a satyr. I sat long in simple disbelief, yet stood longer that night at the arras, watching the little man bucking and writhing against Kat. They were joined together as two coupling dogs upon the counterpane; his body, short and ugly though it be, seemed strong and brutish. Kat struggled against him, and howled many times in her great pleasure.

She came to my bed at dawn, bruised and shivering. Her eyes showed round with fright and I wrapped about her beneath the covers.

That was no Seymour bedding, I said gently.

She shook her head. *You made agreement?* she asked.

He offers to help me, I said, *yet I will not bargain with him if you suffer for it.*

She sobbed her laughter. *O! I think he took some virile potion to be thus persistent! I am afeared, I have ever been the one empowered; here I have no control.* I kissed her gently on the brow and she sighed sadly. *Ever but once*, she corrected.

Cast him off, I urged, *I would not see you thus again.*

Nay, Kat said, *it is too late. We must keep your pact.* She sat up and leaned above me, her mouth hanging over mine. *I will not thwart you.* She smiled. *We are the same, you and I*, she said softly. *We are both out to trap men's souls.*

Scarce a twomonth later, a Salisbury parcel arrived. Within was a note and a purse of blue silk, fastened with ribbon. I unwrapped and took from the purse a small phial of clear yet foully stinking liquid. The note was writ with such a tiny, scrawling hand that it looked as a beetle dipped in ink had run across the paper. I read long before I understood its meaning.

> Do as I bid with this & you will succeed. Ask not of its
> content. Care must be taken to neither touch nor spill it.
> This purse to be filled with coin not smaller than shillings.
> I will direct where to send it for I soon cease tutoring.
> To be sent a score of times, filled as agreed. I come for
> other payment when free to travel. For you I have bottled
> Nature. S.F.

Part the Fourth

Twenty-three

MEN HAVE SPENT MANY grave words in considering the thirtieth year regnant of Our Dread Sovereign. That fabled twelvemonth saw dire and fêted happenings: accidents of Nature, threats and plots, and the fall of proud heads, bejewelled and helmeted. Though this Dark Year seemed evil to many, yet to my eyes it was one long season of vast benevolence. My hard bargain with the Goat of Salisbury had been settled – all twenty purses – yet I had more coin than many great gentlemen, and the sweeter promise of further wealth to come.

How had this turn of Fortune come about? The secret of it lay within Forman's phials, and the doors of possibility that liquor opened. Long had I used pigments of the mineral world as any painter might: lead both red and white, yellow tin, smooth gesso chalk, mercurial cinnabar for vermilion, infernal stinking sulphur. Now I might shake drops from my phial upon any matter and make it molten, grind it or bind it in gypsum and fix it, forever stoppered in bottles and bladders. I bled colour from stones and wrung the juice from sodden clay. I lay plants in shallow dishes and covered them with the essence: they lay, sweating and weeping out their dyes, 'til all colour was drained from each leaf and every stalk seemed a hollow, sapless reed. I thus distilled the life of each flower and herb; the very stain of its being, the purest hue without flaw or fleck. Juices bright as gems and clear as Venetian glass I pressed and drained from vast and varied sources. Beetles, berries, bone and ash – all became grist for my grinding stone and palette. I snipped a lock of Kat's hair; I pricked my thumbs into cups of preserving liquid. I gathered fur and shell and feather. I hovered with the flies at the dripping stalls of Smithfield gore. I seized and captured the essence of every shade my eye chanced to fall upon, I did as Forman had only claimed to do: I bottled Nature.

I had such a range of paints as could be used upon any needed surface, be it the lightest lake for smooth primed panel, the thickened pastes for trunks and armoires or the hardened colours used on plastered walls. I might have made wealth from the sale of these substances, yet I stayed true to my design, and kept my prized paints for purer purpose. No longer did I humble myself with the lacquering of devices or the mean task of copy work. No more would I trace liveries upon chests and hangings. I began my large likenesses anew, and all who saw my work begged for their own. Fortune nodded at the humbling of nobles, but to me she smiled and urged, *Up! Up!*

Up, so, I went. Some three years before the Dark one I rendered my first panelled likeness in perfected paints. I primed my board as I had ever done, smoothing off the chalk with a fleshy base wrought with lead pigments. All was as any other; then I spread upon the central piece a far more precious, subtle skin.

Kat sat with great excitement for the work, dressing as I bid her in lavender silks, a new trimming of cream lace at the cuffs and bodice. Though the day was mild within, Spring rain fell damp and chill into the Strand. I flung the casements open, propped wide the doors and cast water on the workshop fire to still it. The logs hissed, belching smoke into the room as Kat danced in. She halted and braced her arms shiveringly.

What madness is this? she complained. *It is not yet Summer and I have no wish for a fever.*

I must have you cold, I said. I passed her the cloak and hood. *These will keep you well enough.*

Kat shrugged into the cloak. She took up the hood and stroked the fur trim, making some idle speech on the wearing of brown against her face, it being a poor foil for her dark hair. I set white cloth upon the workshop floor and readied my easel.

Do I look well? Kat asked, smoothing her hair into the hood.

I pushed the cloak away from her shoulders. *Take off those gems*, I said, *and the ear pearls. Keep the gold ring.* She nodded and made back to her chamber. *And wear your locket*, I called, *the round golden one.*

*　　*　　*

Kat lay upon the white cloth of the workshop floor, her head tipped proudly back, her eyes fixed, yet all unseeing, upon her audience. I see her now as she seemed then, and as she was to lie within my panel. Her dark features are soft against the pale grey hood, the rabbit fur gentle at the angles of her jaw. The chill air plays on her face, showing a cool violet about the subtle parting of her lips and blenching her cheeks with a Wintry pallor. Her hands are also cold, the spread palms that lie far from the warmth of her cloak pale and stiff in the draught from the workshop door. The swell of her breast is white and chill, traced with blue veins and lacing. Her back arches over the bulk of the bolster, artfully draped; the wheel I paint beneath her is the cartwheel of my imagining for I would have no wood or metal bruise her flesh.

I scarce saw Kat as I worked, though I must gaze ceaselessly upon her. My manner of rendering grew blurred and feverish; though I knew well enough my task, my eye yielded to the will of the panel and its restless, daubing colours. My fingers would not quiet, my hands tirelessly seeking fresh paints and brushes – all actions were unpatterned and unthinking.

Of a sudden I stopped. The sunlight had shifted and retreated from the casements, creasing the floorcloth with shadows. I had scarce noticed the darkening of the room, nor heard the rainfall that now drummed steady on the boards. Kat leapt from her place and ran to the casement shutters; I turned from the easel and slowly wiped my brushes.

God's Soul, Rob, Kat exclaimed, *I am like to ice! This room is chill as a barn*. She stretched and shivered, then commenced chafing her hands beneath the cloak. *Is it done?*

We will see. I turned to look at the panel.

I will make some small defence for what would come – the common policy of Remembrance. Though I was no stranger to Pride, I had little thought of the heights or depths of his acquaintance. In ill-judged moments a man will find Pride's words swelling in his throat. To swallow then is the custom of the wise; I was not wise, nor had I outgrown folly, for though I was ripe in years I was very tender of ambition.

To look upon my panel was to gaze out from some great height or distance. So fixed is the image to my mind that it remains sharp and clear as fresh-painted, as if I had gazed overlong at a candle and the sight had scarred my eyes. To those who enquired I called her my Martyr Triumphant – here was Saint Catherine broken on her wheel – yet I had no word for those who asked why she lay in a snowy Norfolk field. I knew at once she was my Master Piece, the end to laboured experiments and the seal on my guildless Prenticeship.

The whiteness of this panel ached the eye, the gaudy crimson sprayed a harsh relief. Here was the true test of my new colours, bright in life as Bess in death, the tones so like to Nature that they swelled and shifted with the light. The lavender skirts of my saint were creased and tumbled, the fur trim rippled gently in the wind. Her skin was chill and moist as newly slain, her pale throat an empty funnel, her eyes, though set and staring, wet and dark.

I cut no lurid folds into the flesh. In place of Bess's viscera I heaped a vital garland of Spring flowers: torn spikes of rosemary poked the belly, thorny stalks and stems of blossom tangled at the neck. From her chest splayed Summer roses, eglantine and gillyflowers; her waist was a girdle of violent Autumn berries speared with thistle heads. Broken yet whole, she was flawless and majestic, her grey hood a pale halo in the snow.

You make me saintly as a virgin, Kat said. *It is a marvel, Rob.*

My Master Piece at last, I said. *I have you well.* Pride kindled his fire in my lungs and I breathed him deep. *Now I will have commissions*, I puffed. *Soon Hillyarde will come begging coin from me.*

Hillyarde came, but not for a purse of money. He had been pressed by Gower to offer me piecework, for he had commissions to paint in large and needed helpers. On any day before the painting of Kat's wheel his offer would have been cherished. Now I had another mind.

I cannot accept, I told him. *I have my own work now.*

He smiled. *I am glad for you, yet this is fine work I offer. I will pay you well, and I can also promise wealthy introductions.*

I shook my head. *I will fare well enough without aid.*

Do not feel abused, Hillyarde said softly. *I do not ask this out of charity, for I have seen your work and it is very fine. Likewise, George has much faith in you.*

Master Gower again, I snapped. *He asks you to help me, he thinks I can do nothing for myself.*

Do not misjudge our friend, Hillyarde rejoined. His face clouded as I had never seen it, his chest swelled and collapsed with deep-drawn breath. *George saw your poor acquittal with the Queen,* he said firmly. *He fears your Norfolk manners work against you.*

I barked a laugh. *Gower thinks me yet a horsemaster. He is mistook.*

He is a gentleman, Hillyarde snapped. *Painting is a gentleman's profession. Your manner now does little to convince me that you are meet for it.*

My hands twitched into fists; Hillyarde's bold eyes followed them. *Will you brawl with me now,* he said smiling, *to prove yourself well-born? I had heard this of you.*

I swallowed and steadied my voice. *Come and see my new work,* I said, *I would value your true word upon it.*

Hillyarde followed me to the easel where my new panel stood, turned to the casement for drying. I took the board and held it to the light. The Goldsmith stepped back, his head tilted as a garden bird at a dish of earthworms.

This is fine good work, he said at last. He peered at the panel. *I do not altogether see its meaning.*

Saint Catherine Martyred, I said flatly.

Is that not papist work? Who commissioned it?

None, I said. *I rendered for myself. I have new paints and I wished to work them thus to try them.*

Indeed. He nodded slowly. *It is an exercise in colour, then, as fruits or a lady in jewels. Thus the many flowers.* He peered again. *The snow is crisp,* he said, his voice betraying a growing wonderment. *It is a sharper white than lead. What paint is this?*

A substance of my own, I answered bluffly.

He raised a brow and bent to see Kat's flesh. *What hue is on the skin?* he asked. *This is no common carnation.*

Another of my paints.

You have it well. He straightened stiffly, his backbone crackling. *I am growing aged,* he said, smiling thinly.

Not so. You like the work?

It is very well, Hillyarde said, *but there are many that might see it who should not. Treat another theme, or better yet, keep to formal likenesses.* He shook my hand. *I am sorry that you choose to refuse my offer; such work, however fine, will not win you court commissions.*

I had hoped all would see my panel as I did: the brushstrokes pulsed and shimmered, the snow breathed a chill into the room and the flowers held strong perfumes. Yet I knew that the Goldsmith, for his faults, had told me true; it seemed a papist piece, and I must render safer likenesses.

Kat sat for me again, this time in silks and pearls, her eyes modest and seemly. She yawned much as she posed, as did I in the rendering of her. The finished panel was bland but artful, a bright show of talent but a blank page, void of character. Her black skirts rippled, her stiffened cuffs and collar were airily spun in lace, flawlessly patterned. Pearls shone, lips stretched, eyelashes trembled; it bored me just to look upon the thing.

I primed a second board and rendered Kat at speed, seated in the garden in a simple frock. She smiled and held an apple in her lap. The likeness was herself indeed; the smile beckoning, the teeth within her lips small and sharp, the quick tongue caged behind them. The apple was ripe and cool as to bring water to the mouth; the apple-maid herself won like attention.

Ambition beat and drove me on as it had ever done, leading me to wealthy patronage. Kat aided the work, as was her custom; she bedded her way through ranks of knights and gentlemen, her spirit never tiring, her manner sure. I rendered many persons of the court and also merchantmen, a breed of patrons wealthier than earls. These merchants did not find their way through Kat, but rather by dint of my growing reputation; sighting my panels in noble houses, they desired to see themselves lapped in my paints. I caught their greed and coloured their astuteness, fixed wealth in their eyes and meanness in their mouths. They sat surrounded by tokens of their skill: ledgers, oaken desks, balances and spoils of bounty. They thought themselves bold venturers in trade – a rank of gentry hewn from work and wit, not birth – yet they married off their daughters to aged rivals and built grand houses to seem as gentlemen. They bartered prices for my work and wished to bargain. I spent their coin with glee.

Two years passed thus. My wealth and my renown waxed greatly. Kat had many new jewels and silken slippers; I furnished my workshop with gauzy hangings, replacing all furnishings save for Kat's fond arras. I spent my evenings there, studying her quarry, and my days rendering the lies beneath their skins. When Kat tired or sickened I made likenesses of merchants' wives and daughters, swollen bellies heavy with dynastic sons and girlish cheeks pale with virgin worries. Forman the Goat, now a man of name in his own country, sent me further phials and came for his city payments. After his visits I made amends to Kat and gifted her panels for her favoured players. Her chosen sport was now with the scribblers and theatre men, and she drank hard jugs with them in Southwark taverns.

In the space of the next twelvemonth I made three fated panels; each merits attention and the spending of some words. This trinity of images was the true twist in my fortune, for they set me amongst the most luminous men at court, and those who Fame would later range against me. Each was complete by the dawning of the Dark Year, as though their weight had tipped the world's wheel round a place: those seated highest fell, and unwittingly I rose up close behind them.

Twenty-four

THE FIRST WORK IN my trinity was for a sitter of Kat's catch, and such a one as would grow very high indeed. Already he was a long-limbed youth, finely turned and coltish in his hose. In time he would shape himself rival to the Queen; when first I saw him he was naught but her new lapdog.

Leicester, broken by the burden of the Queen's hard favour, had long since lost his lustre. Like an aged cockerel he vainly puffed his plumage, watching as others battled for his place atop the dunghill. Raleigh, finely feathered, strutted fiercely and seemed the meetest man to take the prize. Who may Leicester preen for his replacement? His Dudley blood, though quick to take, had failed to sustain any legitimate fruit – yet he had a prodigy, the boy of his wife Lettice. This Robert Devereux, by birth the Earl of Essex, was Leicester's only hope of continuance. He knew the youthful lord would tempt the Queen, and angling hard, he dangled him before her.

She took the bait, and Kat was there as witness. Leicester presented the youth at court, and the Queen gladly granted him an interview. At the first scent of royal excitement the wily Earl snatched his brave lad back again. Leicester made ready for war in the Low Countries; the Council would not have the Dutch cow milked by papist Spaniards, and the Queen must send her troops. Essex was thus presented still in bud: the sun of court favour and the rain of foreign war were the very weathers to bring him to manly bloom.

Kat did not wait, but settled for the budding. The Queen simpered, tickling long fingers inside the youthful collar. Maids of honour swooned; matrons meted in their heads their daughters' dowries. Kat watched the long legs buckling, the fine head, easily turned, the beardless cheeks still boy enough to blush. Then she pounced.

If Essex liked to be fondled by the most powerful woman in Christendom, he might also care for a frolick with one of the most brazen. When the interview concluded, Kat was quick to speak. She flirted with Leicester as if naught were ever amiss between them, and whispered gentle poison to his charge. A gesture of the hand could easily turn Essex aside; he was a finely placed young lord, she noted to him, and a pretty one. He was very near a man, save for the boyishness that a woman of wit could easily discern. She had seen, she declared, the sweet longing looks of the Queen's and Ladies' maids. Kat pitied them all, she said – for was he not yet a maid himself?

Little more was needed to lure so arrogant a youth, and Essex proved over-hasty for a challenge. Thus he met the Queen and bedded Kat that day; the last traces of his innocence thoroughly soiled and trampled. He little knew I saw the half of it, and copied the rest in the panel he commissioned.

He thinks all lords should have their likeness made, Kat declared that night. *He wishes to be preserved for his future worshippers. God's Soul, he is a childish bore.* She sighed. *For a young and well-made body he was quickly done with sporting.*

He was long in your chamber, I countered.

Aye, regaling me all afternoon with tales of bravery. He has scarce set foot beyond his mother's garden! He told Leicester he had an appointment with an armourer to make escape with me. Silly boy.

When will he sit? I asked.

Tomorrow. He goes to the Low Countries and they will sail with the tide, he says.

He fancies himself the hero of hawkers' ballads.

She giggled. *He speaks like a stage clown in some comedy, and knows not that all are laughing. Yet he may do well. War may shake the foolishness from him.*

War may give him cause for vainglory, I said. *I will make but a small panel if he leaves so soon.*

Essex came next day to my workshop and sat pouting for his likeness. He had fitted himself in his most costly doublet and wore a brooch of the Queen's head pinned at his breast. He held a gauntlet in his hand as a girl would hold her gloves, thinking it made him seem warrior-like. I smiled as I rendered, seeing him yet unbreeched and in some infant rage, his mouth a small and perfect trembling *O*, his tiny teeth unsteady as he wailed. If he liked not his panel, I mused, it would be as he liked not his dinner, and he would stamp his feet and stammer into tears.

He liked not his panel, yet he did not weep. The piece was too small, he exclaimed: it must be small for one such sitting only, I countered. His black eyes narrowed at the panel.

My hair is not so, he snapped, tossing his head. *My hair is dark.*

My lord, I parried, *your hair is a noble colour. It is seeming dark, yet has traces of a Tudor fire.*

He glowered. *You make me look a boy.*

Your youthfulness surprises all, I replied. *So young, and yet so grave.*

Grave? He studied the peevish lips.

Aye, my lord, I smiled. I pointed to his furrowed brow, gathered as in a childish temper. *See how I have writ your brooding thoughts? Any might read your fabled prodigy in this.*

I am a soldier! he snapped. He pointed to the plump hands, cradling the gauntlet.

A soldier poet, I answered, *like your Sidney kinsman.*

Pa! he barked. *I do not waste my hours prating in verse. That is idle practice.* He stepped back and glared at the board afresh. *I like it not*, he declared. *It is not grand.*

My lord, I sighed, *it is a modest rendering of your likeness.*

It is not grand. A likeness of a lord should seem grand.

My lord has not yet seen battle, I said mildly. *If you were to sit for me on your return from war—*

I will do no such thing! he squeaked. *I have wasted time enough for this little picture, I will take my purse elsewhere when I return!*

And may you prosper for it, I said. *Yet you would have this piece and must take your purse out now.*

Essex jumped as if stung, his eyes wide upon me in disbelief. *You mean me to – pay – you?* he stammered. I smiled and nodded. *Christ's Wounds, your impertinence!*

I shrugged. *My lord has been given what he asked for and must pay like any other man.*

Essex snarled. *I will have you in the stocks for speaking so! How dare you direct me? Do you know who I am?*

Indeed so, sir, I answered, *and any man in your position would do well to honour his debts.*

I am kin to the highest Earl in England! Essex roared. *I have the ear of the Queen! I will have you driven from the Dover cliffs with stones and clubs, you insolent wretch!*

Have you ever been to Dover, my lord? I said. *I hear that the cliffs are very steep, and Mistress Joyce tells me that you are easily winded.* Essex raged and whirled about to strike me, his long unpractised arm easily dodged. I laughed. *She also says that Leicester hands you on a platter to the Queen.* He lunged again and I held up my hands to still him. *The Queen much dislikes a man who dallies with wenches, whether they be gentlewomen or serving maids. She is over-hard on the indiscretions of her favourites.*

The young lord's brow knitted with a frown. *What are you about, painter? Do you threaten me?*

I shrugged. *I merely repeat, my lord,* I smoothed, *that a man in your position would do well to pay his debts.*

Essex paid me overwell for his hated panel, sailing to the Low Countries a good purse lighter than he had minded to. Kat laughed much as I repeated his threats and oaths. We purchased a cask of malmsey and a butt of claret with his coin, toasting his safe passage to war and manhood as we drank. We both had little thought for how great such a foolish and pouting youth might yet become.

With Leicester gone, Raleigh strengthened his claim for chiefest cockerel. Raleigh was a watery Devon man like Drake, though prettier and neater of body by far, and had likewise been honoured as a knight. The Queen dubbed Lord Walter her *Water*, and salt oceans were wrung from maidens' eyes on his account.

The Queen doted on her Water; her courtiers hated him. His

cloaks were too gorgeous, his doublets too swaggering. His tongue was sharp and honeyed, his wit keen and subtle. He danced well, ventured daringly, smiled sweetly and laughed mockingly. He wrote fine verses and had a love of music. He beat them at cards and flirted with their wives. In every way he was as all men wish to be, and few can ever hope for: in consequence he had few friends, but Hillyarde was one.

I met Lord Water at the Goldsmith's house, for we were yet friends, thanks to Master Gower. Gower said little of my rising fame, yet ever sought to treat me with much kindness. He had moved to a grand new place in the parish of St Clement's and entertained there, spreading out pastries and sweet wine in celebration. Hillyarde would not be outstripped, but offered his own small supper at the Maidenhead. He would have some great patron to impress us with, and Raleigh was the choicest of the day.

Water was beautiful indeed, languid of look and limb, yet bright and attentive in his conversation. I smiled to picture Kat amongst us, her quick eyes flying from Hillyarde to Raleigh, knowing not where to light. She had cursed me for not begging her a place at table, yet I was glad we would have no woman-ish distractions; I noted how Hillyarde kept his yellow-haired Alice from temptation, sending her to sup with the children by the fire.

We talked much of court and of the wars abroad, and other such things as men will chew upon at table. We drained a flask, and Raleigh turned to deeper talk. He had a will to write, he said, upon antique subjects, yet he entertained some thought for the new arts, and gave much time to the study of geography.

It is plain to me, he said frankly, *that the world of thought is very far from what it was in Harry's day. I speak not only of spiritual matters, and our breaking off from Rome, but of the very way we tread upon the ground.* He looked about us; we gravely nodded assent. *We have seen*, he went on, *how men might study the surface of the earth and cross the seas entire.*

It is true that our instruments of measurement are very fine, said Gower. *I have made some study of astronomical devices, and we may now make such calculations as would have seemed impossible but fifty years since.*

Raleigh raised his cup to Gower and drank. *Master Gower is in the right*, he said, his lips smacking. *Those things which once seemed vast as to be beyond our knowing can now be drawn on parchment. We can delineate the world – can we not charter other, unknown things?*

I smiled. *And what things would you have us measure, my lord?*

He shrugged. *We navigate the oceans; in time we might likewise sail through the skies. We might then draw maps of Heaven, might we not?*

Or of men's souls? I added. *We think them unfathomable.*

Hillyarde laughed. *Forgive our friend, my lord. Rob thinks he can already map men's souls.*

I know I may draw a soul upon a page, I said.

You know this? said Raleigh. He smiled. *It sounds like to witchcraft.*

I do not speak of witchcraft, I said, *nor the practices of alchemists or physicians. I believe I may paint the truth of a man, his hidden soul.*

Gower shook his head. *You have a fine eye for likeness, Rob, but you are not God.*

I heard the Goat's words. *I am not*, I agreed, *yet I may be his messenger.*

A hiss sounded round the table. Gower rubbed his beard in agitation. *That is at best foolishness*, he muttered, *and at worst heresy.*

Raleigh offered me the new-broached flask. *What do your sitters make of this claim?* he asked.

I held out my cup for wine and Water poured. *I do not make such claims to them*, I said, *though they often say I render them too clearly. Some men do not wish for such truthful likenesses.*

And those men will be the least honest, Raleigh said. I nodded. He looked to Gower and Hillyarde. *Has he made such images of you?* he asked dryly. *I would gladly see your souls revealed!*

He has not, said Gower, *nor would I have him make such a panel of me.*

You are your own mirror, Master Gower, I proclaimed. *The panel that you painted of yourself is a true likeness. Your soul is clearly writ.*

I see you are good friends, laughed Raleigh, *and will not take the bait. Yet tell me, Master Rob; are there none I might pry into?*

But a month since I rendered a small panel of the young Earl of Essex, I offered. *The piece was small, but the soul was most apparent.*

Essex! snorted Raleigh. *Is that puppy old enough to have a soul? There is some thought that the soul grows with the body; though he be long of limb he is very short of wit.*

I smiled. *He liked not the one I showed him.*

Raleigh roared and drank again. *I little wonder! Idle, boastful boy. Leicester thinks to groom him for his place, yet he lacks the old Earl's wit. What wit is that? He could not climb up to the Queen's throne, but lets the Lowlanders carry him about on litters and adore him as the King he always hoped to be.* He shook his head and clapped my shoulder. *Pity you have no likenesses of Leicester!* he laughed. *Well, I shall not brood: this painting of souls could make for a good sport. Come soul-painter, will you draw such a map for me?*

Thus came the making of my second fateful panel; Raleigh would arrive for his sitting within the sevennight. Kat was like to burst from the seams of her gown when I told her, so great was her excitement.

He truly comes here? she asked breathlessly. *He will truly sit for you?*

Twice truly, I assured her.

I must make preparation! she declared, pacing about the room. *When does he come?*

Tomorrow, or the day after. Surely by the week's end.

You do not know? she exclaimed. *How can I be ready if you do not know the day? You did not enquire?*

He will send word ere he come, I said, *so still yourself. All will be ready.*

She grasped my shoulders and shone me a look of great

approval. *This is marvellous well*, she said, kissing me heartily. *It will be a great thing for us.*

You mean it to be a great conquest for you, I baited.

She smiled and shook her head. *I fear this one to be beyond my reach.*

She feared aright. Though Raleigh had much appetite for women-folk, he looked long ere devouring. He came to the Strand with a hasty clattering of horses, his coachman raining filth upon those who failed to quit the street before them. He was clad in fine black and silver, his cloak a rich gift from the Queen, sewn about with love-knots. He grinned and held his hand to me.

Well met, painter of souls, he said. He looked up to the house and whistled softly. *This is a fine good house for a base maker of likenesses.*

Too fine for me indeed, sir, I said. *I will show you the reason for our seeming splendour.*

Our? he laughed. *I like this well! It smacks of some cosy goodwife.*

My lord is mistook. I bowed. *Come within and you will be undeceived.*

Kat met us in the parlour, anxiously smoothing her skirts, her eyes wide and wondering as some new maid at court. She bobbed with great poise, lowering her eyes; modestly she rose and looked to Raleigh, her cheeks polished with a perfect blush. I hid my smiles; she was truly a master of this woman's art.

Ho! Raleigh exclaimed. *What angel is this?*

Mistress Joyce, I offered, *my dear friend and patroness.*

Raleigh kissed Kat's hand and held it overlong. *I have seen you before, sweet mistress.*

I am much at court, my lord, Kat breathed.

The court is an over-brazen place for such perfection, Raleigh flattered. Kat prettily demurred with a gesture of her hand; Raleigh clutched it to his chest. *I am in need of a physick*, he said suddenly; *I feel such a racing heat within I am like to die of it.* He winked at me. *A kiss from an angel is certain the sole cure.*

Kat laughed girlishly and placed a hasty kiss on Water's cheek.

He shook his head. *Nay, mistress*, he said lowly, *does my beard so offend you?*

Your beard is most handsome, my lord, Kat assured him.

It is sweetly perfumed, he enticed, *and there is a place in its centre that yearns for your kind attention.* He pouted longingly.

Kat feigned a sweet reluctance, then nodded gently. Raleigh pounced and drew her in a fast embrace, pressing hard against her skirts. I stepped back from the room and waited; a deal of silken rustling followed, and much sighing from Kat, ere Raleigh appeared again in the hall.

Shall we to work? he asked merrily. I nodded and showed him to the stair. He turned at the top and grinned broadly. *Fine patroness, your Mistress Joyce*, he growled. *I have heard a good deal of her at court.*

She has much favour there, I said politely.

She has much else beside, he laughed. *Would I had time to add my name to that list; there are noble titles on it.* He winked again. *You do not take offence?*

Nay, my lord, I said flatly. *I make no answer for the lady's doings.*

That is well, he nodded. *She is a fine piece, though.*

Raleigh talked much as I rendered him, huffing restlessly and shifting often from his pose. His eyes roamed about the workshop, taking in all: the unfinished boards, the new hangings, the tawdry arras. Kat brought in a flask of the Essex malmsey, and he looked thirstily upon her as she poured. His mind would not still, and thus I painted it: ambitious, ruthless, restive and impatient.

You speak bravely of what many men would not, Raleigh noted. *And Gower tells me that you paint in the same way. How comes this?*

I merely paint true, my lord, and am not afeared to say so.

He smiled thinly; I caught the fine coiling of his beard. He took a sip of malmsey. *I wonder at what truth is*, he said frankly. *Is it as the Archbishops tell us? Is it what the Queen's father said we should believe? Or is it the sharp policy of a Cecil? I know not.* He drank again and dabbed his whiskers with his thumb. *I would* discuss such matters with others; I have given much thought to a gathering of minds. Not the rhetoric of speechmongers, you understand, but to give voice to and refute wise arguments.

I know little of these things, my lord, I said. I know only of my craft.

Pfu! Raleigh snorted. Do not take me for a fool. I have asked at court about you; I know you well thought of now, and in good company. It was not always so.

All men have a past, my lord, I noted dryly.

Aye, he nodded, much is the same for me. Yet I knew how to work the Queen, and you did not. I made to object, but Raleigh raised his hands. You are deeper in mind than you show, and you have strange acquaintance.

Your pose, my lord? I said. It is near complete.

Nay, he shrugged, I cannot linger thus. He stepped down from his place and came to the board. How do you have me?

In outline only, my lord; I will fill the panel if you wish me to complete it.

He laughed. You have my eye, he said, yet I know not if you have my soul.

That comes with colour, I answered.

He clapped my shoulder and handed me a cup. I would see that, he declared, yet I warrant that I must endure more standing.

For the face and hands only, if you wish it, my lord. For the silks, I might copy your costume on a manikin.

You will not have my soul from a manikin. Nay, he said, stretching, I'll stand it, if for naught else but a mumbled moment with the malmsey-bearer.

Thus Water departed, promising to return in the same suit of silks ere the week was ended. Kat bobbed a curtsey at the door, and fell against it when he rode from view.

God's Soul, she cried, I must have him or die of it!

None ever died for lust before, I said. I warrant you'll recover.

Nay, she sighed. He is man perfected.

Ha – then he is the medley of Hillyarde and Drake that you so longed for.

With such eyes, she breathed. *And such hands!*

And such honeyed words and knavish fumblings, I added. *He knows of you.*

He told you so? she piped. I nodded. *Well, so, what matter? He knew me well enough to make advances.*

Advances? I thought he would swive you on the spot and have no thought if I watched or no.

I would have let him. She sighed and gripped my arm. *Let us to the workshop.*

We climbed the stair and Kat went to the easel. She studied Raleigh's outline and traced it with a finger.

Do not rub it, I warned, *the chalks are soft.*

I will not spoil it, she said, sinking to the boards. Her skirts billowed out around her. *Have you readied paints?*

I will mix more silver for the doublet trim, I answered. *I have some black prepared.*

Paint me in his colours, Rob, she urged. She commenced unlacing. *Give me a taste of your new paints.*

I shook my head. *Not those.*

Why not? She kicked away her slippers and unrolled her stockings. *They are too precious to you.*

They may be unhealthful, I said.

You think them too costly, Kat pouted. She removed her skirts and sleeves, folding them neatly and piling them on the chair. *Do not be mean-spirited*, she said. *I have ever given you all that you desired*. She took off her bodice and breathed out deeply. *I have paid dearly for those paints, Rob*, she said abruptly. *Now I want my portion.*

I granted her wish, though I liked it not. In some part, Kat was in the right; I was loath to spend those precious colours upon her skin, when common pigments would suffice. Yet I was also afeared; I knew not what substance the Goat's phial contained, nor what it might do to a body.

Kat insisted, as she had good cause to, and I clad her entire with black and precious silver. She moaned greatly, calling at last for the boar bristles; she writhed and cried out with demands and harsh directions. At length she waxed frenzied and seized the brush herself; I could not do enough to quench her thirst for Water.

The second Raleigh visit brought a like result. I filled out his likeness with colour and he talked obliquely of the secret arts. He toyed much with Kat and left her in a fury; she smothered her skin with his flesh tones, then lay spent and peevish upon the workshop floor.

You are grown too desirous of him, I said at last. *It will poison you.*

I have suffered worse, she said flatly.

You weep, I persisted. *You never wept for a man before.*

I wept for you, she snapped. *You cared naught then.*

I took her hand, now much besmirched with paint. *We are greatly changed since then.*

Kat withdrew her hand and commenced stroking her skin. *It burns,* she whispered.

That is ardour; it will pass.

She gave a dull laugh. *Not Raleigh, fool,* she said. *The new paint burns.*

I sat up quickly. *You must wash it off at once,* I urged. *It may do you some ill.*

Nay, she said, stretching out her legs. *I like it well.*

You like it, I exclaimed, *though it burns you! That is strange pleasure.*

Pleasure is strange, she said. She ran her hands along her thighs and sighed. *Your paint pleasures me better than a man.* She rolled towards me and smiled bitterly. *Raleigh would be but a fleshly disappointment after such delights.*

I do not understand you, Kat, I sighed.

I speak of pleasure, she crabbed. *Of course you do not understand.*

I feared much for Kat's mind and was glad to finish Raleigh's panel. He came for a final sitting, and I made certain that Kat was not at home.

Raleigh was well pleased with his likeness, and sent his page to the tavern to fetch us brandy. He sat upon my carved chair and stroked his beard, his eyes upon the panel. I feared that he dallied in the hope of Kat's return, but he made no mention of her.

The boy returned with a flask and I filled beakers. Raleigh raised a toast. *To the painting of souls*, he declared, and drank.

I am glad to see you satisfied, my lord, I answered.

He smiled, his mouth hissing after the hot liquor. *I never thought to care for paintings*, he said, *yet I find I have a fondness for my likeness. I warrant that makes me a very vain man indeed.*

Your lordship has much to be proud of, I said smoothly.

Raleigh laughed. *Don't give me your courtly bombast, painter*, he said. *I like you well enough; I like you better when honest.*

My lord, I bowed.

He stood back and viewed the panel afresh. *You have my stance well*, he noted, *I have ever stood overswaggeringly. My look is mocking, is it not?*

I think of it as shrewd, my lord, I answered.

Shrewd! He laughed again, then dropped his smile and looked frankly upon me. *There is a deal of difference between your manner and that of other painters*, he said. *You paint what you see of a man, and you see much. Yet most paint what men would only wish to see.*

Many great men think overwell of themselves, I ventured. *They do not always wish to see what others do.*

You are in the right, Raleigh declared. *Leicester is such a one; he ever looks for some false flattery.* He huffed and waved his hand.

You think thus of My Lord Leicester?

Raleigh blinked. *Of course! See how he has himself figured! He poses as King of the Nethermen. And look to how he would have the Queen's image painted! It is all base politicking, it has naught to do with how the woman looks.*

I know this for myself, I said quietly, *and Master Gower warned me of it. The Queen was not pleased with my rendering of her; it caused me much strife after.*

Raleigh poured more brandy: I had scarce tasted mine. *I know something of your interview with the Queen*, he said. I nodded and hung my head. *It shows you a man of principle, though it bring much disadvantage. Are you not imprudent?*

I must be honest to my calling, I said, *though I may not always be honest with myself.*

Men fear those who speak impolitick truths, said Raleigh gravely. *A man feared makes many enemies; the court is dark, and it is unwise to deal too plainly there.*

I nodded humbly. *I will be mindful of it, my lord.*

Would that I had been so: I had yet to render the final panel of this triptych.

Twenty-five

ILL RUMOUR IS LIKE to an unruly mob, swarming and swelling in strength as it moves. Though it be never wholly governed, yet every mob must have its captain. When rumour grows so bold as to muddy the petticoats of Queens, those who command it must rank as governors.

What manner of man keeps such a rule? I held my brushes to his features, the better to show him to the World. Though each of my three great panels would hold some danger, that third was most perfidious, for within it sat the master of all spies and assassins, the governor of ill proofs and rumour-mongery, the brand that lit a hundred heretic fires. I rendered the Secretary of State, the great intriguer Francis Walsingham.

Master Gower won the piece for me. He had some business with the Walsinghams and had rendered Lady Ursula, My Lord Secretary's second wife. She was a cold piece of womanhood, pale of face and slight of movement, and Gower had little joy of painting her. When she sent command for a matching panel of her husband, Gower feigned sickness and passed the commission to me. I bound my paints in a trunk and took horse to Surrey, putting up in an inn close to the house of Barn Elms.

Winter approached, ushering in that Dark Year, unheralded and unforeseen by all but the man I was to render. My Lord Secretary had endured an evil season, and he was not a man to be alone in his suffering. His health was in great decline, his organs swelling with disease, causing him to stoop when he rose or walked a distance. The World and all its creatures sickened him, and he shook his heavy head at them without pity.

That Summer Walsingham had triumphed greatly. His plots against the Scots Queen had borne fruit: ever the origin of such designs, he had sowed great intrigues ere he cropped success. His harvest had come in the persons of two fond and foolish papists:

Babington and Ballard, enamoured and enthralled by the Scots Queen, and clamouring to hazard all in her service. Scenting them both, Walsingham set on his hounds and soon sniffed out a wider band of conspirators. The tide of treachery rose, and traitorous missives floated to and fro in a brewer's barrel. Mary Stuart read with great delight of Rome's planned salvation, the usurping Tudor's death and her own promised place upon the throne; My Lord Secretary, mournfully deciphering, copied her words in his careful, even hand. His spy Gifford, masking as a Romish priest, uncorked and then stoppered the brewer's ransacked secrets. Ere long, Ballard and Babington had long forked tongues and stretched upon iron beds deep in the Tower.

The plotters had bargained the life of one Queen for another, and all then stood in forfeit. A brace of brutal quarterings had followed, and papers were drawn up against Romish Mary. The scaffold dripped and groaned with the weight of papists, and our pure Sovereign shuddered in her righteous, royal relief. My Lord Secretary's forgers had cunningly kept the crown, yet many murmured that his shadow had sprouted horns.

Walsingham had paid for his bloody season. The butchery had scarce been washed from the Holborn streets when Sir Philip Sidney took the shower from a musket in his leg. Sir Pip, fêted defender of Puritans, grew feverish and rotted away in the Low Countries. He left Walsingham's daughter a widow, and with her much debt, no family of his own being placed to settle the monies. In the fire of battle the popish Spaniards had shattered Sir Pip's knee bones – and fair destroyed My Lord Secretary's purse.

Barn Elms was as inhospitable as its master. The dour servants studied the ground before them and looked not up. The walls of the rooms were bare but for the dark drapes of mourning; the ale was well watered and laced with stale hops. Walsingham suffered most cruelly, as many prayed he would. He stood for his likeness, his back straight as he might hold it, pressed in discomfort to the cold wall of the parlour. I shivered as I worked, for though the pay be fair, the fire was frugal and the air steamed damp with thrift.

Walsingham was by habit an upright man, tall and angular, his head large and over-lengthened in his face by a pointed beard and the hillocks of a protracted nose. His hair receded to the crown, covered with a close black cap, a barbed lock upon his brow as a downward arrow signalling the enormity of his features. His eyes were hooded and weary, the lids weighted with sorrow at the wickedness of men. His hands were calloused and scored with inky creases; I wondered at the warrants that had stained them.

You tremble, Walsingham said suddenly. His eyes fixed upon my knees; my right leg jolted at great speed.

It is nothing, my lord.

Cease trembling, he snapped. *You will not paint well.*

I braced my feet together and continued rendering. Walsingham stared unblinkingly before him. The great clock in the hall sounded the dinner hour, yet none stirred about us or clattered beyond with dishes. My nose dripped with chill. I gripped my palette; my knuckles were rimmed with blue.

You sniff, Walsingham rapped out, his head still unmoving.

Forgive me, my lord, I bowed. I wiped my nose on a cloth.

You have taken a chill, he accused. *You bring fever hither.*

Nay, my lord, I protested gently. *I am a little cold, no more; I am not unwell.*

I am glad of it, Walsingham said. I nodded thanks. *We have no need of sickness here*, he added. *Nor have we need to burn more fuel.*

I rendered as well as I might with a trembling brush, and ventured to complete the piece in my workshop. There I thought to make better report of what I had seen, and to add the signs of what I might yet hear.

Walsingham assented approval and broke his pose. He turned stiffly towards me and held his hands behind his back. I stood, shuddering hard, and wiped off my brushes.

You are a nervous man, Master Painter, Walsingham mused. *You are all atremble. It is well for you that we meet thus, and not in the Star Chamber.* He rose and fell on his heels. *We have not met in the Star Chamber previously, have we?*

No, my lord, I laughed. *I have had no cause to be there, God be thanked.*

Why thank God for it? he asked flatly. I shrugged. *Has he hidden some wrong of yours? Or do you believe yourself to be protected by Him?*

As all Christian men do, my lord.

Walsingham's eyes, grey and brittle, now shone wetly. *There are men that believe God commands them in all things*, he went on. *They will venture great deeds for this belief. Do you not feel thus?*

I shook my head. *I warrant that God has no great plans for me.*

You think yourself forsaken, then? he pursued. *Overlooked by God? Such a man might grow desperate.*

I am but a painter of likenesses, I said carefully. *There are many men far more meet for greatness than I.*

Then to paint is not great? I wonder that you think so. I hear of painters who think painting a very great matter. They believe it to be a liberal art. They say it is a pursuit meet for gentlemen, not for simple artisans.

I have heard this said also, I assented.

You do not believe these men? He paused a moment and rocked up and down again. *George Gower is one of them.*

Master Gower is a gentleman by birth, I said quickly.

Master Hillyarde is one of them also. You are acquainted with Nicholas Hillyarde?

He is the Queen's Goldsmith and limner, I answered.

He is your friend, said Walsingham. *George Gower is your friend also.* He watched as I fumblingly stoppered the paints. *Hillyarde has many friends at court. Sir Francis Drake is godfather to his son.*

Sir Francis does him great honour, I said warily.

Sir Walter Raleigh is also a friend to Hillyarde, Walsingham pressed. *They have been known to sup together.*

That is likewise an honour, my lord. They are all of Devon, I believe.

You are of Norfolk, he said plainly. I nodded. *You have met Sir Walter?*

I covered my palette and turned aside. *I had the honour of painting his likeness, my lord*, I said.

That is great favour from such a courtier, is it not?

No greater than the honour you yourself give me, My Lord Secretary.

He nodded and smiled in shrewd acknowledgement. *You have dealings with great men*, he declared. *You do not believe some of this greatness may pass to you?*

I demurred. *As I said, my lord, I am but a painter of likenesses, no more.*

Walsingham's nostrils widened and quivered. *Yet you believe yourself protected by Divine Will, Master Painter. How might these attitudes be married?*

I know not, my lord. I rolled my brushes into a bundle and bowed deeply to him. *Your lordship's talk is too sharp and learned for my simple understanding*, I said, and smiled.

Then it is well indeed that we do not meet in the Star Chamber, he huffed, and turned to leave. *Give you good day.*

I was thankful indeed to quit Barn Elms and follow the city road again. Though the frost lay sharp about, the Heavens could not conjure such a chill as Walsingham. I sent my panel on by cart with a boy from the village, paying him overwell and studying him hard for signs of My Lord Secretary's service. I passed him as he ambled on the road, reaching the Strand before Winter darkness descended.

Kat lay on a settle by the fire, much bolstered by cushions, her eyes dark and sunken. She sat up uneasily as I entered, her hand pressed to her stomach.

What ails, Kat? I cried. *Do you suffer some ill?*

Naught but the menses, she groaned. *It is the cold.*

I poked at the fire and she eased back against the cushions. *It is a fine good fire*, I said, warming my hands. *You have not seen the empty grates of Barn Elms.*

Walsingham should be hot enough with all his fires, Kat scoffed.

He does not burn, he butchers. I lifted Kat's stockinged feet and sat on the settle beside her. *His tongue cuts likewise.*

Did he show you his thumbscrews?

Nay, he had no need. He played inquisitor while I cleaned my brushes; that was fearsome enough.

Kat laughed, yet wincingly. I pressed my hand to her belly and she turned aside. *Do not touch,* she said sadly.

God's Soul, Kat – you are not with child, are you? I held her face that she might look at me. *Come, speak plainly.*

She laughed again and shook her head. *Nay, no such trouble, Rob; that would be a seeming miracle. Tell me more of Walsingham. You have the panel?*

It follows by cart; I will complete it here. I had hoped you might have some news to help me.

Kat had news indeed, for she had spoken with Hillyarde. The Goldsmith had made enquiries about Walsingham's health, his dwindling monies and his service. All this I knew, yet he made discovery of another token in My Lord Secretary's purse: his favoured painter of likenesses, John de Critz.

He is a Netherlander, Kat said, *brought hither as a babe. He is now of Holborn. He paints for Walsingham and has done so these four years past.*

Why then the commission? I asked. *What of this de Critz now?*

Kat smiled. *He is about Walsingham's business in France. He often travels thither, and likewise to Italy.*

A painter's tour, I nodded. *He is fortunate.*

An agent's dealings, Kat corrected. *He is deep in Walsingham's service.*

I understand this ill, I said, and commenced chafing Kat's feet. *You do not say all.*

What needs be said? Kat chirped. *De Critz is across the sea, thus the Secretary called for another.*

I shook my head. *He might wait for a panel, there is no call for haste. And yet, it was his wife that gave Gower the commission.*

Yet you made the likeness, Kat pressed. *Why Gower, and not some other?*

He had painted the lady before.

Aye, yet some time since. Kat wagged her toes at me. *You are uncommonly slow today. Hilly tells me that the Secretary sniffs about you three as a dog in a graveyard, and knows not where to dig.*

Hilly! I laughed. *So you have swived the Goldsmith at last?*

Nay, Kat pouted, *and hold little hope for the endeavour. He grows anxious and watches much about him, and all the court acts likewise. Did Walsingham make enquiry of him?*

He asked much, and spoke of Gower and Hillyarde both. Yet I deem it was news of Raleigh he fished for.

Aha, breathed Kat. *Then we know why Gower was sent for, and why you served as a fit replacement.*

Kat's theory sufficed, and we stayed quiet that season, keeping to our own small company. By Nativity I had the Walsingham panel complete and delivered it to My Lord Secretary's office in the city. His deputy, a little man with crabbed features and few teeth in his head, took the piece and placed it by the wall. He handed me coin and stood long before the painting, gummily grinning and nodding. Walsingham glowered back, his stony eyes aglitter with schemes and intrigues. His lip curled with scarcely hid disdain at the World; the thin smoke of death and sickness tickled his nostrils. *You have him!* the little man whistled. He opened the chamber door and waved me out. *I'll see you again,* he nodded, *I'll warrant it.*

Thus Kat and I entered the New Year, our purses grown swollen and our days idle. The court proved a poor place for Kat's pickings, and she devoted herself entire to her loving players. Theatre men and scribblers came and went, soiling the fine cloths and table-rugs, and griming the cushions with their dirty jerkins. I figured their faces in chalk and watched their drunken sporting from the arras. Kat grew more modest in her play and scarce unrobed, yet she called often for paints upon her back and feet. She hid her pains behind a tightened stomacher, lacing herself stiffly in the bodice. That Spring she dismissed her waiting-maid and took to dressing herself, claiming that the woman had stolen some jewelled pin and that none might now be trusted. She took to the sudden wearing of periwigs, the Queen's new fashion, and sought a woman to preen and pile her hair. Ere long this maid too disappeared, for she pinched and pulled with the combs, Kat grumbled, and did her work with dirty fingernails.

We saw little of our Salisbury Goat, though he was frequent with the sending of his parcels. Word came that he had much trouble with the courts and suffered litigations. I was comforted for Kat, for she dreaded Forman's visits – yet she was ever pleased when a phial arrived for the making of more paints.

We dined richly and drank expensively. I filled panels and prospered from my work. No further word came of Walsingham, and I had the coin to prove him well pleased with his panel. I saw much of Master Gower, who made more flatteries of the Queen and was well esteemed at court. The Goldsmith flourished likewise, though he complained as ever of a want of coin.

Thus we played, untouched, as Walsingham's acts unravelled. The war against Spain was but an aside for My Lord Secretary's secret battle. Seizing on a sudden moment of Tudor pique, he had secured the royal flourish and stamped the Great Seal into a puddle of yellow wax. With a hasty carillon he had waved the warrant for Romish Mary's death; the church bells had rung, the people danced, and the Scots Queen's crown was hacked off at the nape.

When Mary's head fell, the city was a blaze of bonfires. The treasonous witch was dead, and the Puritans loudly rejoiced. Behind their hands, native recusants spoke in hushed voices of rash unlawful deeds, and claimed the death a royal martyrdom. Walsingham burned the Scots Queen's bloody robes; thus charging the gunpowder hid in papist cellars.

The war in the Low Countries rumbled on apace: Drake raided and robbed, and Leicester came back that Winter a bent and broken reed. Essex returned a soldier, sharpened by war and the death of his friend Sir Pip. He preened himself the Queen's undoubted favourite; Raleigh bristled, yet dared not bite, for none could outshine the sun of arrogant youth.

The old Queen crabbed at Leicester, and cruelly favoured his boy, appointing him her horsemaster as Leicester once had been. Essex gave and received rich gifts and set himself up as a great new patron. Hillyarde took the young lord's coin and begged Raleigh's pardon, figuring the long Essex limbs in a locket full of roses. None could but turn towards this bright new light: I was glad indeed to be free of that lord's favour.

The court shifted with the winds that blew across the Channel. The lords bickered as children in a yard, and Philip of Spain stamped his feet and shook his little fists. The Queen quailed and jumped at shadows in the night, fearing a knife in her back and poison in every cup. I painted and Kat toyed, and though we made many gains, I suffered one great loss. At the year's end, I had desperate word from Oxford: Petty's family had fled to France as recusants, and my friend was rotting in the Southwark Clink.

Twenty-six

THE CLINK STANK HIGHLY, the kennels about it bogged and broken by hard rain. I was thankful that I had no need to venture past its walls. Two heavy purses passed through the jailers' hands ere they gave me word that I might stand as bail. I waited long against the gates, fending off cries for alms and scraps of food. At length a turnkey appeared and held out his hand. I pressed it with coin.

He comes, the turnkey said, nodding behind him.

I thank you. I strained on my toes to look for Petty's approach. *He is in health?*

Reasonable, he sniffed. *There are rooms for the better sort. It's not Newgate, you know.*

Indeed, I reasoned. I thought of my friend's quick appetite. *He has been amply fed?*

Well enough if he has the white for it.

I nodded. I knew well that Petty would have little coin of any colour. At last a shuffling sounded behind the turnkey and he stepped aside: a man, loose-limbed in greasened shirt and hose, drew close towards us; he stopped and looked at me with reddened eyes.

Petty! God's Soul, I cried, *you are a bag of bones.*

Petty shrugged. The turnkey handed him through the gate and passed him a bundle of papers. *Be heedful of the warrant*, he warned. He nodded to me and closed the gate behind us.

I embraced my friend and noted sadly the pointing of his ribs. He shrugged me off shiveringly; I unclasped my cloak and wrapped it about his shoulders.

The streets are foul, I said, grasping his elbow, *we will call for horse.*

I would sooner not, Petty said flatly.

As you wish, I said, *then we must get fast to the Strand and you may wash. Kat is readying water, and you will need a flask of brandy, I'll warrant, and a roast goose.* I waved to his belly. *A flock of geese! We will feed you well again and you may tell us all of this sorry tale.*

You would fain hear me talk, then? Petty said darkly.

I pulled him along the street. *In good time, my friend. First we must look to your comfort.*

You are comfortable, Petty said. He flicked at my cloak. *This is fine good stuff, and costly.*

Aye, I said, *I have found good patronage of late. You will see it in the house; we are grown very grand since your travels!*

I doubt it not, Petty scoffed. *You painted the great lord Walsingham, did you not?*

You know of this? Naught escapes you, my friend.

He paid you well?

Aye, I laughed, *and questioned me hard for it! Would you had been there with me to make reply.*

Pfu! Petty snorted. *I am the last man you would stand by, before Walsingham. I warrant that your feet are well beneath his table.*

I stopped him with a hand. *What mean you by this, my friend? I came here for your good, yet you seek to quarrel with me.*

You can do me no good! he snapped. *I am even deeper in mistrust now, for your unwanted interference.*

I stood amazed. *Petty – God's Soul – do you mean this honestly? What were you about in that place?*

Come, you know right well, he jeered. *I am a papist, I carried messages, I consorted with Jesuit priests from Douai. You yourself had word from me there, did you not?*

I had a few lines from your travels only, I assured him. *I had no knowledge of the charge against you. Yet I know it to be false, and so it rests.* I tugged at his sleeve again. *Come, walk briskly, you will take cold in these streets.*

Petty smiled bitterly. *You think to draw some confidence from me. The spymaster has trained you well.*

Spymaster? I bleated. *Why do you treat me thus? I am abused.*

You would ever do all you could to forward yourself, he scorned. *You are yet ambitious.*

I took fire then. *You do me great wrong!* I cried. *I came on word from a neighbour of your kin; I gave all I might to buy you swift release. The jailers called for garnish and I gave them a banquet! I stood bail for you and risked my name for yours; Kat also, for she too loves you well. We would have sold all to see you safe again!*

Petty shook his head. *If you are not his spy, then you are sure his fool.*

How so? I snapped. *Explain yourself!*

You are a proud man, Rob, he said sadly. *How you tremble for fear that you might look the gull.*

I am not the man shivering in a borrowed cloak, I baited.

Petty laughed and, unclasping, threw the cloak to me. *I would rather shiver in my shirt than be beholden to you.*

No, I roared, thrusting the cloak at him, *you will not treat us so!*

And why not? he hissed. *You cannot undo your wrongs by petting me like a dog.*

I do not understand you! I cried. *We were ever friendly; what has befallen you?*

It is oft times safe to be slow in comprehending. He shook his head again. *You are too dangerous, Rob, and I cannot bear further scrutiny.*

I? Dangerous? I laughed. *But, Petty, you are greatly misinformed! I see now, there has been some deception, some plan to brew enmity between us. Whatever you have heard in that place, it is not true! You know me, Petty; I am no dangerous man.*

Nay, he declared, *though there has been deception, I will not be taken in it. Farewell, Rob: I will keep from your company. This is no time for us to be friendly.*

I held out my hand to him, but he stepped away. It was then I severed our amity entire. I rounded on him. *It is true, then,* I spat. *You are a Jesuit.* He turned and crossed the filthy street. I shook my cloak at him and felt a violence rising in my gorge. *Rot then, Petty!* I bawled behind him. *You will regret this! Ungrateful bastard! Papist dog!*

Walsingham had not forgot me. I weepingly sought Kat, who used her players to make enquiry in the taverns and amongst those who had dealings with the service. We learned how My Lord Secretary had taken little liking of his panel, thinking me over-honest for a painter. Such brutal truth, he had feared, might be put to ill advantage. He had intelligence that I supped with Raleigh and thought me closer to Lord Water than I showed. I had flouted the bait of entering his service; thus he thought to hook me through my friends. Petty's family, Kat learned, had been hiding Jesuits since Campion's time, suffering great penalties for keeping to the Mass. Petty himself, a mild recusant, was falsely suspected of aiding heresy. The charges were grave, though they showed all wind and lies: without witness or proof, or the ballast of my friendship, the claims against Petty were left to drift and sink. Petty had walked away from me, and My Lord Secretary had let him go.

Twenty-seven

THUS WE ROUNDED TO another year, one blown by tempests and beset by threatening shades. Little Philip the Spaniard stuck out his chin and got his beard well scorched for his troubles: Drake sailed home from Cadiz an even greater hero, and the subject of many ballads. The stout lord was now a man much marvelled at, with a fine new wife and a fondness for dice and gaming. He and Raleigh stayed friendly to Hillyarde, though the Goldsmith had wormed far into the Essex keeping. I saw naught of Petty, and the wrath of our parting soured in my belly. I had word come Spring that he had set up shop as a tailor and merchant of cloth, his love of rare drapery now cheapened to the selling of rags. Kat pressed me often to seek him and beg his pardon, yet soon found it safer never to speak his name.

Kat herself grew chary and ill of temper. The aches in her belly gave her frequent pains, and though I urged her to see a physician, she laughed and claimed that too much physick was the very cause of her ills. She scarce bedded any that season, keeping alone in her chamber, yet she pomaded and played the wanton in looks and words. When I made enquiry of the court she groaned and rolled her eyes: the Queen wore naught but black and silver, she said, and the courtiers had grown dark and steely likewise.

They are all of factions and crabbing circles, she complained, *each pecking and scowling at the next. They scrabble for favours and would think it no shame to kick and punch in the scuffle.* She huffed. *And for all this they grow bitter, and no longer have the wit to please themselves.*

There must be some that would sport with you, I reasoned. *They are not all grown womanish.*

She sighed. *Those that might, dare not, for fear of the Queen's disfavour. She watches them like virgins in a temple. And those who would dare to are little worth the catching. Nay*, she groaned, *even our entertainments are now keen-edged with malice. I dare not seem other than I am for fear of enquiry, yet I dare not dance too hard for fear of tripping.*

Do not look for Walsingham's traps, I assured, *he has little to gain from me now. What more might he cost us? He would do better to put Gower – or your Hillyarde – on the rack.*

Hilly is safe while he limns for Essex, Kat said, *and Master Gower is much favoured by the Queen.* She shook her head. *Never underestimate that assassin, Rob; his look could strike a crow dead in the sky.*

Come Summer, our lengthy dread of Spain's attack broke forth on the horizon. The Queen brazened her way towards battle, claiming to have no fear; as all men knew, God wore the Tudor colours. A great fleet was sighted from the coast; Effingham and Drake, made gallant by boasts and games of chance, routed the papists and spread them wide with fire. The lordly Spaniards fled, their skirts all ablaze; the storms of Providence scattered their remains. Great rejoicing followed, and the Puritan lords swaggered in new cloaks and caps to match their vast conceit.

While the clamour of victory raged in the streets, I met with Master Gower. We took to an alehouse, for he wished to quit his rooms and must walk some little distance. His spirits were at an ebb, and though he had news of a great commission to mark the Spanish defeat, he cared little for the note such work would bring.

It all crumbles about us, my friend, he said sadly, waving his hands about him. *We were a brave nation, and this city the flower of all. Yet what is come of our glories? This is an empty conquest; it brings naught but vain superbity.*

A nation thrives by thieving, not by honesty, I said. *We sailed and plundered, did we not? Our greatest men are pirates.*

They were our greatest men, said Gower, *now they stand in a usurper's shadow. The court is much changed by that youth Essex's bullish presence, and the Good Queen likewise.*

I hear this from Kat also, I agreed.

Ah! Mistress Joyce. She too has grown much altered.

I nodded. *She has a fear of scrutiny, and now she seeks quiet routes to profit.*

As do we all. Yet look to our good friend Nicholas; never did I think to see him so debased. He must scrape to a man he despises, and all for fear of lordly abuse and the threats of moneylenders. Gower looked sharp about him and drew close to my ear. *Essex is a brazen youth, and debauched as his mother; some yet whisper that he is truly Leicester's bastard.*

Do not say so loudly, I warned him. *He would have you in a noose for less.*

Sorry times, Gower sighed, *sorry times indeed. Do you recall young Isaac, the Huguenot?*

Too well, I laughed, *we parried hotly once.*

I do recall it. The youth is released from his papers and limns for his own profit now. He has some patronage and is in the business of establishing rooms. I hear that he too will be an Essex man. Gower clasped my elbow and eyed me sorrowfully. *Ah, my friend, I grow old and the world moves on apace, yet our Regent believes that time stands still for her. God forgive me for saying it of my anointed Sovereign, but I fear she is grown a fond and foolish woman.* He stooped resignedly. *She would have me figure her as a Springtime maiden, and for my peace I must do her bidding; yet it gives me great shame to use my talents thus.*

Such is the way of Princes, I assured him.

He smiled sadly. *Well, so,* he said. *That is so indeed.*

With Kat's want of courtiers, and great love of theatre men, it was not long ere she persuaded me to share a flask with some players. She was much taken of late with one youthful scribbler who, she claimed, was barbed and cruel of wit, and had no cause to take fear of any, so sharp was his pen and so swaggering his style. So eager was she to bring us to one place, and so sweetened by the hope of it, that I found myself persuaded to meet with him in a favoured Southwark tavern. Kat quit the house in time to sup with the company, I following on to meet them presently.

Be clement at this meeting, Kat smoothed, brushing at my collar. *This man is strange of manner, yet very large of thought, and he will prosper, certain. He has been in Walsingham's keep and made enquiry for us. He may speak as though he wished to make some quarrel, yet he will please you, Rob.* She smiled more merrily than I had seen in three long seasons.

I will do all you wish if it please you so well, I said, and kissed her hand.

Dear Master Painter, she sighed. *You would do well to render this one, if he will sit.*

The tavern was as stinking a hole as any might think to find conspiracy in. It was dark and dank, with floor, benches and long tables all of the same grimed wood painted with pitch, the easier to hide the filth in. I heard them well before I saw them, Kat seated in the centre of two rough and dribbling wretches. The one who spoke loudest and first, calling down a host of blasphemies against Our Lady's untouched grace, had rows of limp fair curls tight as moss against his skull, and a great red nose upon him that seemed to swell with the strength of his curses. The second pouted silently, and his pretty poke of a beard, wisping thin and sand-like about his chin, did naught to hide the indulgence of his lips. From where I stood I could not discern the third man's features, yet as I neared I saw by the cut of his clothes that they had once belonged to another, taller one than he.

Ah, my Master Painter is come! cried Kat.

I heard you – I flicked my glance at the rednose – *speaking treasons, from the far side of the place. All others make celebration of our conquest; if treason be your subject, you would do well to speak it lower.*

We spoke not of victory but of virginity, lisped the bearded fellow. *O, the sacred state of it! Virginity is a high matter, is it not? And a subject worthy to give good voice to.*

It brings to mind, said the rednose, *through our humble discourse, what a chaste gathering we all do make! For by my word – and if I understand the word in question, as we use it in the English of our good Queen and Sovereign – we are all of us virgins here.*

Pray, Kat put in swiftly, *let us call all things by their right names*. Her arm swung loosely across the table. *Here is seated my Master Crowhurst* (the rednose nodded), *my Master Farley* (here the thin beard assented) *and here one I have spoken much of, my Master—*

The silent one, who had hid his face deep in his goblet, lifted heavy eyes and lips.

Kit, he hissed, *and as I am Master of neither my Mistress Joyce here, nor any other, the rest can be let be.*

I trust, Crowhurst burbled at me, his mouth wet and slack, *now we have traded titles, that you will join our school of learned virgins?*

Kat snorted. *I can vouch for our painter's purity.*

Well you might, madam, said the one named Farley, showing her the tip of his tongue. *So might you vouch for many here.*

You misconstrue, Kat cried, and barbed a cruel glance at me. *He is delicate and pure indeed, and not one of the flesh.*

A saint then? quipped the nose. *An immaculate?*

He is sworn to chastity, said Kat with mock solemnity, her hands crossed at her breast. *Chastity is the price of his art. He can be tempted by no woman.*

The quiet Kit smiled. *There are others here that share the boast*, he murmured.

Ah, Kit, brayed the nose, *you would capitulate, were you forced to forgo copulation completely.*

Be not so alliterative, Crowhurst, Kit sneered, *I beg you.* He took another deep draught and I caught the sound of his innards shifting about with drink. *Hark!* he started, and held my eye. *Even my very guts rumble against the torment of your tin pan chiming.*

So, I said, keeping Kit's eyes with my stare, *here is one at least who does not play Kit to your Kat.*

No! cried Farley. *No, by no means! Master Kit is not the mouse for such a hole.*

My claws cannot catch him, Kat assented, *and more the pity.*

Kit likes not the Kat, said Crowhurst, taking up the game. *This cat's might lies elsewhere.*

Kit broke my look angrily. *Cease your puerile punning*, he

snapped. He drank again, and addressed the grimy metal rim at his mouth. *Master Painter, be you so called, you are likely to hear me called a great many things.*

A catamite! spurred Crowley.

A heretic, Kat whispered.

A spy, breathed Farley.

I know not which is worst, I yielded.

Indeed, said Kit mildly, *I have a trinity of sins to shoulder, a three-branched cross to bear. I am, in all senses, drawn to the shortened cloak and the hidden dagger. And you?* he goaded. *You, who are not tempted by woman, do you not share my point, right to the very hilt?*

Kit's eyes were limpid, drunken, and swimming with pointless lust. *In no wise*, I answered, evenly and finally as I might.

Naught counts but his ambition, said Kat unkindly. *Ambition and likeness are the World and Heavens to him.*

And so he whores himself with brushes, Crowhurst pouted.

You have sold your soul, Kit belched angrily, his chin quivering with pique. *You pact with the red-haired she-devil!* He fell to ranting, his eyes rolling and knocking at the socket corners. *You would sell your innocence for thirty pieces of silver. Such men as you, denying woman, denying man – your manhood is gelded, and you would spend all for seven years of Satan's plenty!*

Hush! hissed Farley. *Harp not on that vein again, Kit, for the love of your neck and guts, or we'll see both broken in the marketplace.*

And ours with them, Crowhurst muttered, and spat at the floor.

Kat tutted at us all and shook her head. *Leave be*, she said quietly. *Kit is deep in his cups.*

Peace! Kit bellowed, thus drawing more eyes than with any of his speeches. He swayed to his feet and rapped at the tabletop. *Make way, madam* – he motioned at Kat – *for my cup, now so full with me, runneth over – and my gorge is set to do likewise.*

He inched along the table length, Kat moving her skirts from his path. In a stride he was at the doorframe, scarce reaching beyond it ere the cries of his vomiting reached us.

What pleasant company, madam, I grimaced, and offered Kat my arm. *Let us retire.*

To bed! Kat chirped. *Ever to bed!*

We nodded our partings and I steered Kat from the tavern. As we stepped to the street she shuddered and leaned hard against me. I saw that the high colour of wine had drained from her cheeks, and with a sudden rush she pressed forward with quick and even steps.

You are soon recovered, I remarked coldly. *You were so full of spite I thought you far in your cups.*

I am less merry than you know, she said sullenly. *Take me home swiftly, Rob. I long for your attentions and your brush again.*

You do? I thought myself too delicate and pure.

Do not bait me, she spat. *I lack the patience.*

We made silently to the workshop, I in some wonder at Kat's sharp-shifting mood, and smarting at her cruel reproaches. I had a bladder of rich green new mixed that day, and I thought to try it on her. She sat stiffly on the cushions, unrolling her stockings and unlacing her skirts, yet she clung to her petticoats and bodice, keeping all but her collar and sleeves.

You do not unrobe? I asked. *Where would you have me work?*

I do not care to, she said flatly. *The air is chill.*

It is Summer yet, I said, *but I can kindle some heat.* I poked at the hearth and the remains of the fire there, adding lengths of wood to coax a flame. Kat shuffled restlessly behind me.

Where is this paint? she crabbed. *I tire of waiting.*

You are evil of spirits, I retorted, reaching for my palette. I sought the green paint and set it on my stool. The weight of the bladder seemed slight and, when unstoppered, showed to be very near dry. *This is strange,* I said, *I thought I had here a new mix of green, yet there is scarce a drop.*

Make haste, Kat snapped. *Find some other paint.*

I chose a yolkish tone and mixed it with scarlet, spreading a rich amber paste upon the palette. Kat groaned as I settled before her with my brushes. *I trust the colour pleases madam. Where would you have it?*

She gestured to her calves and I dappled them gently, brushing pools of colour and linking them as suns and shields across her shins. I raised Kat's petticoats a little, the better to reach her knees: she stiffened, and with a low moan, firmly pushed my hand away.

What ails? I said. *I wish only to please you.*

She sat up awkwardly. *I am not in the vein for your wanton tricks*, she snapped and, turning from me, fell to heavy weeping.

You are sorrowful, Kat, I said gently, *you lack diversion.* Her shoulders trembled with the force of her misery. *That Kit is not meet company for you*, I said. *It is the play you want, not those rough players.*

O Rob, she sobbed, *that is the sorry truth!* She threw her arms about me and pressed wetly against my neck. *The times are too dark for play*, she wept. *Now even the players are grown too dark for me.*

Part the Fifth

Twenty-eight

TIDES EBB AND FLOW, and the currents of Fortune are ever-shifting. Though the Queen, in her Sovereign might, thought herself ruler of oceans and harrier of all that swam or sank therein, there were yet forces that escaped her government. Our Supreme Head directed the waves and called up tempests, wrecking Spanish ships upon her shores: yet all men need safe harbour in a storm, and they swam to Essex as the sole raft in that sea.

Great victories are followed by hard falls. While Eliza paraded triumphant through the city, the handsome bear of her youth rotted away in a hunting lodge. Leicester's stomach, once so great and barrelled about with gout, grew poisoned and shrivelled as a pea blackened in the pod. Ere Autumn he succumbed and quit the World, a proud Earl without a penny of his own and no heir left to carry forth his name. He died far steeped in debt, the very farthings that weighted down his eyes but borrowed from the Queen. That Loving Monarch wept bitterly into her lace kerchiefs, draping herself in mourning and making great shows of grief; her sole comfort was to hunt and feast and dance, and to fondle her doting Essex in his stead.

All the favour the Queen had given Leicester was buried in a Warwick tomb, and the rest might only be regained by the selling of his goods. This the Queen set to swiftly, taking much joy in stripping the widowed Lettice of all wealth. The grieving lady had borne the loss with grace, and she mourned so long and deep that she waited a whole season ere wedding her boyish lover, the young friend of her son.

With Leicester removed, Essex claimed inheritance, taking the Earl's apartments at court and the highest place of favour. He danced hard, sighed and simpered for the Queen, and, in the great chase for power, galloped past all others. Even the great

Lord Water must now stand aside for Essex, and while Raleigh simmered and soured with jealousy, the youth swaggered and brandished his sword at any who defied him. He duelled and bravoed, and in his petulance the Queen petted him for a pretty, spoiled child. Thus Essex paddled coquettishly upon the Royal palms, and secured his hold upon the Royal ear.

Kat was much disgusted by this turn at court. Essex had proved but a milky youth to her, and she knew him unfit for such hard-won attention. She swooned yet for Water, though he be but second place at court, and while the Queen shined on Essex, many thought to make a catch of the pirate. Yet Raleigh, though ever mannish in his ways, grew crabbed and angered, and could not be ensnared.

Master Gower completed his commission for the Queen, though he loathed it much and grumbled all the while. He called me to his workshop, for he wished to speak with one who shared his discontent. I made to St Clement's to see the panel and learn more of the court's new patronage, for Gower saw much, and understood men well.

Gower seemed of a sudden grey and stooping, his brow deeply ploughed with furrows. He greeted me silently, taking my elbow and steering me through his workshop. I saw that he had taken on Prentices, for his wide rooms, scarce home to any but he, were scattered with desks and easels. I gestured to these and asked how the students fared, but he gravely shook his head and kept his tongue. We came to a cleared space where a vast panel leaned, turned about to the wall. He nodded to it.

Forgive me, my dear friend, Gower said, his voice atremble. *What I must show you gives me sorry pains, yet it is the Queen's will, and we are ever subject to it.*

Come, I smiled, *it is but a panel. It cannot be so grave.*

Gower sighed and, bending stiffly, turned the piece about. *I am sorrier for the making of this than I can speak of, Rob. I wonder that I make so bold as to stand with you before it.*

We stood away, the better to survey the piece. It was strangely wrought indeed, the manner of its composition cut about and muddled to the eye. In the centre was rendered the figure of the Queen, though she be but a doll cut from paper and pieced upon it. I knew not whether she stood, or was stiffly sitting, for her vast farthingale seemed perched upon the corner of a throne. This seat was of such odd proportions and diverse angles as to be seen from two sides at once, and seemed far from the table the Queen advanced towards. There she stretched out to finger a flat globe, while her elbow jostled a crown on the dais behind her. Beyond were two windows cut to show the battle: on one side the Spanish ships approaching, on the other the dark storm of their defeat.

I frowned and pondered. Gower looked to me anxiously, reading the rubbing of my chin and pursing of my lips. At length he drew up a stool and sat down heavily upon it, his shoulders rounded with defeat.

It is a travesty, I own it, he moaned. *I hate myself for the making of such a thing.*

Speak not so, I soothed. *It is a puzzle of an image, is it not? Each piece has meaning and serves its purpose, as in a church work.*

It is monstrous, he wailed, *and I have lost my art! O, I am a foolish old man to be forced to such a place, I who have rendered great men and women with all the honesty of Nature!*

Peace, I said, *calm yourself, my friend. Let us consider it.* I squinted at the panel, seeking some merit there. *You have the pearls well*, I urged. *Hillyarde would think them real.*

Gower rocked to and fro on his stool. *They are Leicester's pearls*, he sighed, and shook his head afresh. *They laugh at court, and claim none mourn him but the Queen, yet I would gladly wish him here again. He might temper that upstart Essex boy, the knavish fop—*

The ships are marvellous well wrought, I put in, *and the drapes about them likewise.*

Think you so? he said, lifting up his chin. *The drapes are not so ill, I warrant, yet the ships seem childish toys.* He sighed anew. *I must make confession, Rob, for I did not render the whole of the panel with my hand. I have taken on Prentice boys and used them for much of the figuring, for in truth I could not bear to make this piece entire.*

That answers much, I reasoned. *Which is your hand?*

He waved at the Queen's face and heavy jewels. *Those parts, and the crown, and some other things beside; yet not the throne nor the dais. They are amiss, I own it, yet I have not the strength nor will to make correction. And behold you the Queen's face,* he said, his own much drawn in anguish. *What manner of mask is that? Yet I could not render her as she is, God knows, for she would have me struck from the guild and hounded from the city.*

As she would with any, I nodded. *Did she sit?*

Aye, and watched me hard the while. I dared nothing, and so I have nothing of her. He shrugged. *I made but one rendering of her in truth, in fine metalpoint, and kept it well hid beneath my pages.*

You have it yet?

Aye, though it counts for naught. He stood and bent over his table, much cluttered with papers, and picked about between them. *I was never so undainty with matters before,* he murmured, *yet it seems I have little care for neatness of late.* He turned over a pile of pages. *Ah,* he exclaimed, *I have it here,* and he handed to me a small square of lightly silvered paper.

I turned it about in my hands. Here was a true likeness of the Queen, and such as might see him in the stocks were it discovered. It showed the face in profile, the nose hooked and haughty, the flesh about it scant and sagging. The dome of the brow was fierce and shaved far beyond Nature, the eyes staring in the sockets, the mouth and chin drawn in a bitter smile. I laughed.

You have not lost your art, my friend, I said. *Look how you render! This is from life and there is life yet in it.*

Yet it cannot be used, Gower grumbled. *Such is the way of court.*

I nodded, and looked to the panel again. I studied the face of the Queen, waxen as a death mask, then to the paper likeness in my hand. *'Tis a pity indeed that this cannot be used,* I declared, *it would make a worthy panel.*

Aye, Gower moaned, *in place of this unworthy one. There is naught but some further piece of foolish allegory to be added, for the Queen wishes a siren or mermaiden in it, to make allusion to dangers of the sea.*

The mermaid is a whore's badge, I laughed. *She does not think on that. Where will you have it?*

He shrugged. *It does not fit the piece, and I can find no place for it. I thought to figure it as an emblem or a jewel, I know not which.*

I looked to the panel again. *Permit me*, I said, *and pray forgive me for it; the throne is the least worthy part of the whole and could be overpainted.*

Nay, Gower huffed, *she must have her throne, it is decreed. I cannot take it out.*

Then could not the mermaid cover part of it? As a piece of patterning upon a cloth?

Gower leaned towards the work and rubbed his brow. *It might be best rendered as a carved figurehead, such as are placed upon the prows of ships.*

As part of the throne's design, I said. I looked to the paper likeness of the Queen. *And here*, I laughed, *is the face to give your mermaid; you will have some truth in your commission then.*

Master Gower was much diverted by the mermaid, spending his final hours on the work with glee, his beard awag with mischief. His finished gift to the Queen showed her true features carved atop a whorish, scaled sea-devil; yet he had no fear that any might spy the trick, for the panel at large was so far from natural truth that none sought a likeness in it. Gower summoned me for the presenting of the piece, that he might have one at hand to share his hidden mirth.

Thanksgiving for the great Spanish defeat had heightened to a frenzy. Come November there were such pageants and displays as all grew sick of splendour. Kat grumbled of her stomach, claiming that the rich feasts of the court would give her dropsy, and declined to follow another royal Progress. The court took up nearby in Somerset Place, and for want of apartments, the courtiers fought and grudged. Kat could little dare to go, for the house was not so discreet as vaster places. She was glad of it, taking early to her chamber and lying long abed into the morning.

Gower sent for a carriage and we rode from his house to Somerset Place, for though it was but a step, he feared the mud of the Strand on his fine new stockings. I was much taken with the thought of court again, for though I had oft stood in the margins, I had not spoken with the Queen since my shameful Greenwich interview. Gower smiled and winked often, noting how greatly we were altered since our first court meeting.

The court is soured these several years, he said, *and overmuch itself; it would do well to learn a lesson from us, Rob.*

I nodded and watched as the walls of Somerset's house grew tall and close about us, my innards skipping and bubbling with each jolt.

Somerset Place was in grand Italian style, such a palace as Petty would have fashioned in stone from his fond imaginings. I smiled bitterly that I should still recall my friend and wonder how he fared; stranger yet was my wish to have him there beside me. I stepped from the carriage and smoothed out my cloak, shaking off all thought with the pleasing touch of the cloth. No longer forced to borrowed finery, I had cause to strut in as good velvet as any there that day.

Gower hastened to bring me within. He had sent the panel forward some days before, a trusted yeoman of the house setting it in an alcove that it might not be uncovered by chance. The place was abustle with servants and gentlemen, and we gave our names and intentions twice ere we were given leave to walk about unchecked. The court was not expected for some hours, and I had a great yearning to see the gardens of the place, for Kat had spoken of its designs and wondrous ornaments. Yet Gower would not still, wishing to lead me straightway to the panel, and we ranged through the web of parlours and halls 'til we found the alcove.

Soon it will be delivered from my sight, he said, waving to the piece. He nodded winkingly as he drew back the drapes to check the varnish; the panel was unspoiled, the rendering yet a muddle and the mermaiden hideous as before. *'Tis ill*, Gower whispered, his eyes asparkle, *yet they will gasp and sigh for astonished delight when they see it.*

Poor fools to know no better way, I said.

We carried the panel to the Great Rooms, where the Queen would view and receive it. The Master of the Wardrobe had left strict instruction for the curtaining of the piece, which was to hang draped with blue cloth until the appointed time. We set the panel down amid the clamouring servants, who were hard at sweeping and polishing the flags, and laying fresh carpets upon them. Two burly grooms hoisted the panel in place, and a maid busied herself with the draping of the cloth. I saw her eye flick shrewdly across the Queen's face and figure, though she bobbed a mild enough curtsey, and said naught of her thinking.

There was little to be done but wait 'til the Queen arrived. The rooms began to swell with lesser gentry and other hopeful folk, sniffing out preferment. We stepped aside and seated ourselves on a cushioned settle, the better to talk and keep a watch about us. Gower nodded to many and whispered names to me, and for my part I acted the natural courtier, deigning to give attention to those who earned it. The crowd thickened, and through the press of cloth and jewel we noted Hillyarde, bowing his way towards us.

Nicholas is come! Gower cried, and stood to beckon him. He turned and bid me stand with the pressing of my elbow. *Be soft with him, my friend*, he whispered, *he is deeply troubled of late*.

Hillyarde approached and embraced us heartily. He too seemed swiftly aged, I noted, though his hair and beard were finely groomed, and his face not a whit less handsome.

'Tis long ere we met last, Rob, he said. *What a gathering is this! They are all come to view your celebrated panel, George, I'll warrant*.

Speak not of it, said Gower, *I am mortified to think on it*.

Have no fear, I said, *they come to hold out their hands, not offer praise*.

You are of the same wit as ever, Hillyarde noted, his voice hard through his smile. *Yet you are in the right*.

Gower studied the Goldsmith's face with apt concern. *You have good work of late? I hope that the sea victory has gone well with your workshop, Nicholas*.

Hillyarde nodded. *I had a fine commission for a great jewel, and all men crave lockets of the Queen. My Prentices work from tracings, for such demand requires a speedy harvest.*

Your coffers are set to be replenished, then, Gower said with satisfaction.

Hillyarde shrugged. *So it would be, if men paid meet prices for the work.*

I had heard this tune before. *How fares your old Prentice?* I asked. *Master Gower tells me he is released.*

The excellent boy Rowland? exclaimed Hillyarde. *He is a fine limner indeed and will prosper, surely. I have great hopes for him, and he is a courteous youth; his father is beside himself with pride.*

I am glad to hear it, I said, *yet it was the Huguenot I spoke of.*

Hillyarde's face fell thunderous, and Gower poked me stiffly in the ribs. The Goldsmith set his shoulders firmly, yet looked quickly about him.

Isaac is faring well indeed, he said, scarce veiling his sourness. *He has much skill and is taken into the same circles of patronage as I. He is wed, lately, also.*

How the time moves apace! Gower exclaimed, and shot a foul look at me. He turned about and hailed a passing page. *We would have some ale, if any be at hand,* he called.

The page bowed and pointed to the doors. *Ale is served in the passage beyond, if you wish it, sirs,* he piped, and ran on his way again.

So, Gower huffed, *a gentleman must fetch his own ale here. What times are these?*

Hillyarde bowed and backed away. *I will fetch us each a cup,* he said, and strode into the swarm of bodies.

Gower turned to me, a deep dismay scoring his brows. *Pray do not speak of Isaac Oliver,* he warned, *for Nicholas is much wounded by the youth's present demeanour.*

How so? I said. *Does he speak ill of him? I warned him the lad was a cuckoo.*

Indeed so, Gower nodded, *yet it is not always well or pleasing to be in the right.* He felt for the settle behind him and crumpled back upon its cushions. *The Prentice rivals the Master, and takes commissions in his stead. Ere long we may see the youth in Nicholas' place entire, and that will be a sorry day indeed.*

We dallied and talked, taking Hillyarde's ale and looking to those in the crowd. At length Isaac Oliver himself appeared, standing far to the back in his dark Frenchish garb. Hillyarde turned artfully about to close our little circle. Gower muttered under his breath and smoothed at his collar, his fingers of a sudden grown impatient.

At length She came, the trumpets sounding in the passage long ere She entered. All bent and scraped before Her, a Canopy of State held above Her, a train of nobles following. She was fabulously attired in a gauzy silver robe, Her face white as a corpse and little more alive, Her skin violently leaden against the bright scarlet of Her wig, Her vast stiff ruff a web of pearls and lacing.

God's Soul, I whispered to Gower, *how She does look!*

Peace! he hissed back. *Look upon Her as you would upon an angel.*

This commandment puzzled, yet I had much cause to wonder at the woman who rustled solemnly towards us. Though Her face seemed ravaged, yet Her body was tall and graceful, Her waist yet dainty and slight, and Her movements finely polished. Though there was every proof of Her greatly tarnished beauty, none could gainsay Her lasting Majesty.

The Queen climbed to the dais and stood before the assembly, Her grooms swiftly draping Her canopy about the throne. She made some lengthy speech, discoursing tiresomely on the battle against Spain. I little heard Her, following instead the sharp lines of Her mouth and the strangeness of Her garb. At last She desisted and, calling Her nobles and Privy Councillors to the dais, commenced receiving gifts. My Lord Treasurer Burghley and his crookbacked son Robert Cecil stood to one side of the Queen's throne, while all others engaged in a childish jostling for precedence. Essex and Raleigh locked dark looks and the youth stepped swiftly to the Queen's side, taking the favoured place and tossing his curls girlishly. Raleigh stood beside him and glowered. I spotted the long face of Walsingham lurking at the rear.

Gower hemmed and shuffled beside me, muttering the while. I felt his quickening unease and my belly rumbled in sympathy. Though he had long been subject to such an audience, the Sovereign temper was a capricious beast; we had cause to fear its sudden, heated rising.

Burghley called attention to each gift for the Queen, and She took them in turn, marvelling greatly at some priceless toy, then passing on to the next. Hillyarde bowed gracefully at the presenting of each limning and jewel, for many gifts were of his devising, or else his workshop's. In a hushed and stilted moment a gentleman offered a locket by Oliver; the Queen courteously asked for the limner's name and bid the Huguenot kiss Her hand. Hillyarde smiled the while, yet I saw the nails of his fingers slowly riveting his palms.

Gower's moment came, and with much flourishing and pomp the blue drapes were pulled from his panel. The Queen feigned great surprise, showing none that She had commanded the piece and detailed each part within it. She stepped towards it, nodding thoughtfully, the great red pile of Her wig aglitter as She moved. Gower wrung his hands behind his back as She waved Hers in practised grace across the panel. All those about Her nodded with like amazement, pondering the meaning of the parts and gazing at the whole. They showed not a whit of understanding at the mermaid, though Raleigh smilingly sought and held my eyes awhile.

The Queen turned imperiously to where we stood and held Her hand to Gower. *My thanks to my loyal Serjeant Painter*, She thundered; all nodded and murmured assent.

Gower stepped forth to kiss the royal hand and offer his humble service. *I am glad that it so please Your Majesty*, he said softly, bending his knees with unexpected grace.

Essex, quick at his Sovereign's side, gestured to the panel. *It will serve as a fit remembrance*, he bellowed ponderously, *of Your Majesty's noble conquest, and Your true defeat of the devilish Spanish foe*.

The Queen patted Essex's arm and murmured gently to him. She turned Her black eyes back to Gower and bid him rise.

Your Majesty needs no explanation of the allegory here writ, Gower said, *yet I would gladly speak of it, should Your Good Grace wish it so.*

It is well, the Queen said, *though I wonder at the placing of the mermaid. You have it wrought as the figurehead of a ship, and set it about my throne.*

Gower bowed again. *Your Majesty has dominion over all dangers of the sea; Your Sovereign Power, figured in Your Grace's very throne, ploughs through all perils as the prow cuts through the waters.*

Well spoken, said the Queen gravely; a muttered echo of approval sounded about Her. *You have chosen meetly.* She held out Her hand to dismiss him, but Gower remained and bowed again.

Permit me to make so bold, Your Majesty, he said, *yet I must direct Your Grace's kind praise to another.* He turned to me and smiled. *This young man did make suggestion, Your Majesty, that the mermaid be treated thus; he is Your humble servant, and a painter of much skill.*

Much murmuring broke out and the Queen nodded to me.

Step forth, She commanded. I bid my legs obey.

I approached the dais, my mouth of a sudden sour and dry. Essex glowered at me as I neared, though I kept my eyes well lowered. A rushing sounded in my ears as I knelt before Her, glad of the sinking carpet beneath my knees; as I lifted my head I felt the dread of Her recognition and held my breath. She peered hard at me.

I have some notion that we have met before, painter, She declared.

Your Majesty does me great honour, I hedged, and bowed again.

My thanks for your assistance to my Serjeant, She said carefully. *He must hold you in esteem.*

Your Majesty, I intoned, *Master Gower does me great honour with his acquaintance.*

It would seem, said the Queen archly, *that there is a surfeit of great honour to be had.*

The courtiers laughed daintily; my palms grew damp and cold.

Essex leaned towards the Queen and whispered. She smiled and nodded, turning brightly back to me.

My Lord the Earl of Essex claims to know something of you, She said. *Pray acquit us of this fancy.*

Your Majesty, I said humbly, *I once rendered the Earl's likeness when first he came to court.*

Indeed? said She, amazed. *I would fain see the piece.*

I bowed. *My grateful thanks, Your Majesty; the piece is in My Lord Essex's keeping.*

I will seek it there, She said. *Pray tell me, painter*, She quipped, stroking the tender Essex cheeks, *how came you to make such a rare and dainty likeness?*

I smiled at the Queen and at the haughty, stooping Earl. *My Sovereign*, I said plainly, *My Lord Essex had some acquaintance with a lady of the court who kindly made our introduction.*

The murmur of a laugh sounded amongst the nobles; the Queen arched Her shaved and over-painted brows. *A lady of the court?* She said pettishly, tapping Essex on the thigh with Her fan. *And who is she? Is she here today?*

Essex scowled at me, yet simpered to the Queen. *There is none here but Your Majesty*, he cringed, kissing Her bony fingertips with such a hunger as to make them seem confection.

The Queen's eyes narrowed, then lifted as Essex played whorishly upon Her. She barbed a look at me and bid me rise with Her hand. *Keep your lady at home where she belongs, Master Painter*, She said lowly; then, raising Her voice, declared that I may withdraw.

Thus I passed my second interview with the Queen as poorly as the first; though I bade my tongue be still, I could not but rile such foolish men as Essex.

The Queen retired for dinner with a few words to the assembly, thanking us for our loyal attendance and assuring us of Her Loving Thoughts. She swept through the Presence Chamber doors to dine with Her chosen party; all bowed Her out, then stood about uncertain, not knowing whether to remain or no. Gower's shoulders sank with relief; Hillyarde breathed deeply and looked shrewdly to me.

Well, my friends, he declared, *shall we to a tavern? I warrant you are both in need of sustenance.*

And liquor, I sighed.

Gower shrugged. *It was an uncommon audience, yet the panel was accepted.*

My thanks for your introduction, I said; *I am sorry for it if I caused you much disquiet.*

Peace, said Gower, clasping my arm. *You acquitted yourself with much wit when forced to a dangerous place.*

It was well, said Hillyarde. *You have earned your flask of claret.*

We turned to leave and, in the press of men, drew level with Isaac Oliver. The Huguenot nodded to us, his lip thrust forth and his hand held swaggering at his belt. I felt Hillyarde's sudden halt behind me; Gower commenced prattling to deliver some distraction. Oliver was joined by an elder man, a lean-faced and greying fellow; he held his hand to Oliver's shoulder and spoke into his ear. Behind them followed a younger man, somewhere of my years, gauntly featured and tall of stature. Both looked as strangers, garbed in dark attire with flat Dutch collars. Hillyarde pressed forward through the mass and gained the doorway; Gower and I were pushed far back by the swell. I gestured to Oliver's party.

What men are those? I asked my friend.

Gower rose on his toes, the better to survey them. *One is the son of a Netherlandish engraver who also has some good skill in small oils. The father is growing aged, his name is Gerts or some such. I do not know the son.* He gestured to the older fellow. *The other, with the grey beard, is a painter of much skill, also a Netherlander. His name is de Critz.*

De Critz? I marvelled. *I know of him; he is Walsingham's man.*

Then God spare us his master's looks, Gower hissed, *for see, he comes towards us.*

The greying fellow pushed a passage through the room and stepped before us. He bowed reverently to Gower and nodded then to me.

Serjeant Painter, he said, his voice all strangely tuneful. *Your work is highly praised.*

My thanks, Gower nodded. *You have not met my friend of Thetford?*

De Critz shook his head and bowed to me. *I have word of you before*, he chimed. *You made a good meeting with the Queen today.*

I likewise hear word of you, I said. *I had the honour of rendering your Master Walsingham, when you were about his business across the sea.*

I travel with My Lord Secretary's leave, de Critz said singingly.

You have seen the panel? Gower asked.

I saw it, he said, his *aw* overlong and his mouth working hard around it. *I have painted many of mine own in that time.*

I warrant it, I said. I looked past his shoulder; the man Gerts, subtly stepping, picked his way towards us. De Critz turned and the men spoke a few odd words in their dragging tongue.

This is Marcus Gheeraerts, de Critz chanted, *son of the Master Gheeraerts of Bruges.*

I bowed stiffly; the younger man held my look with a searching stare. His eyes were sharp and oval, and within them I saw an ill-veiled conceit that I little liked. His nose was likewise sharp and pointed, and though it lacked the flesh of Lovett's great beak, he put me in mind of that man. I felt a heated dislike of the stranger, and heartily wished to be rid of them both at once.

Master Guts! I exclaimed. Gower stifled a noise in his throat and feigned to clear it with a cough. *I am glad to make your acquaintance*, I bowed, fixing my smile as sweetly as I might.

Gerts bowed in his turn. *And I yours*, he pealed, his voice as strange and ringing as his friend's.

I understand that your father has much craft, I said politely.

Gerts stiffened. *It is so*, he said lowly. *I have learned much art from him.*

We must be schooled by those who would teach us, I said. *If you follow your father, you may fare well in time.*

I have my own style, Gerts snapped. De Critz spoke lowly aside in his tongue and Gerts hissed back. *I have my own style*, he said again, *Master Painter. I paint in large.*

I have not seen this, I said, waving a hand. *Have you seen the work, Master Gower?* Gower shook his head and inclined it in gracious sympathy. *I am sorry, Master Guts*, I said amiably, *we are not acquainted with your style.*

His lips chewed sourly. *You will soon see much of it*, he said, the tune of his voice now quite discordant.

I laughed. *I will keep a close watch for it*, I said, *for fear I miss it.* I bowed. *Give you both good day.*

We nodded and I steered the quivering Gower to the door. He laughed lowly in his beard and held my arm for steadiness, shaking in his mirth. He leaned close against me. *Guts!* he squawked. *Guts! Ah, Rob, God save us from these damnèd foreign upstarts!*

'Tis a pity, I said, *that these Netherlanders paint so well. I warrant we will see something more of him.*

Hillyarde hovered beyond the doors, his eyes wilfully diverted from the company. Gower nudged me gently. *Do not speak of those men to Nicholas*, he said. *They are friends to Oliver; let us spare his pride.*

Twenty-nine

JUBILATION IS THE BLAST of a trumpet: lofty and piercing, it rings hollow and empty, and, of a sudden, is dead. Naught is left but the aching of heads and ears. Thus the bright and noisy pageants of Victory ended, and while she looked away a moment, Disenchantment cunningly stole her seat. The Winter whipped and tattered the 'broidered pennants, the fine silk shoes of the court were soiled with mud, and the liquor of conquest soured in our bellies. The nobles digested and found they had feasted too well, their gout much increased and their teeth arot from sweet marchpane and comfits. The rain fell chill and unending; the Queen learnt to Her Royal Chagrin that she did not govern clouds.

Hillyarde was much occupied with the labours of the season, for though he had made lockets and limnings for the Armada and Accession, the Queen would still look for her accustomed Twelfth Night gifts. My hands might not rest, for the demands on my brushes were likewise great. My audience at Somerset Place had brought me no preferment, yet those with a loathing of Essex held me as champion of the day. While newcomers flocked to the glittering Essex standard, seasoned courtiers swore behind their hands and stuck out their feet to trip him. Many of these came to me for likenesses, and I filled a clutch of small panels with frowning brows and pursing lips. Much could be read in men's faces of those days, and I did not miss a line.

Gower prospered also, producing copies of his victory panel and tracings of the Queen. He retained his Prentices, the speedier to fill in colour and bulk out cloth, and begged me unburden him of some copy work. Kat took to court for the Nativity celebrations; for the masque I painted silver stars upon her brow and chains of hearts about her wrists and ankles. Twelfth Night came swiftly, the courtiers gorged again, and thus we limped our way to another year, and a Spring heavy with thunder.

Little Philip of Spain, indignant and shamefaced, pouted and stamped, then built himself more ships. Drake and Raleigh were sent to sniff him out and burn the fleet. They sailed for Lisbon and set to lining their purses; Essex, not to be outstripped, stole off to join the looting. The Queen raged and sulked at the loss of her favourite, her jaw swollen with toothache, her temper as quick as a hound in the bearpit. Hatton and Heneage danced attendance and did all they might to divert her, yet she was bored with the World and all men in it, longing only for Essex. *She is like to a child with none but broken toys*, Kat complained, *and her favourite plaything missing.*

When at length the Earl returned, the Queen's joy was so great that she forgave him all at once. Her Sovereign fire was spent on Drake instead, for he had quit his post to pursue a treasure fleet and, by misfortune, lost the floating prize. Raleigh's fighting won him a new-struck medal, but Drake's greed won him a spell far out of favour, and he took himself to Devon awhile to brood.

At Maytide, Gower and I took to the Maidenhead to sup with the Goldsmith. He showed us about his workshop, now tight with Prentice desks and stocked with fine provisions. The buttery Alice bounced another babe upon her knees, and her swelling litter crawled and ran about us. Hillyarde smiled proudly, though he yet complained of the cost of their food and raising. We had scarce breached a flask when the nursemaid announced that a Fine Lord was below and would speak with the Master at once: we stood as Raleigh broke noisily upon us.

My lord, Hillyarde bowed, *an unexpected honour.*

Well met, said Raleigh sternly, nodding curtly at us. *I did not think to find so many here.*

Gower bowed humbly. *We are honoured to see your lordship, as always.*

Aye, Raleigh huffed. He turned briskly to our host. *I will not dissemble*, he barked, *for your company is friendly and all here know me well enough. To the point, Master Hillyarde: you must henceforth decline to work for the Earl of Essex and his circle.*

Hillyarde let out a startled laugh. *My dear friend*, he said bluffly, *were your face not so thunderous I would say you speak in jest.*

You know me, Goldsmith, Raleigh growled. *This is no jest.*

Hillyarde frowned. *I know well that you dislike the Earl*, he said frankly, *and I have ever sought to honour your friendship to me. Yet you must understand, my lord, I cannot refuse his patronage.*

You can, Water thundered, *and you must. There is no debate.*

The Goldsmith looked to us for some assistance. Master Gower cleared his throat as if to speak.

Peace, Serjeant Painter! snapped Raleigh. *I know what you would say.*

My lord, Gower said firmly, *I would not seek to reprove you.*

Your look does so, Water said.

Master Hillyarde must work, I put in. *Essex, though he be vile, is heavy of purse, and our limner here is not.*

Raleigh rounded on me, the point of his beard atremble. *I sought not your opinion, painter!* he bawled. *Do not dare to contradict me!*

His cheeks purpled and I knew him to be in earnest. I made to speak again but Gower stayed me with his hand. All looked to Hillyarde.

My dear Walter, he said smoothly, *I understand well your loathing of Essex and his unworthy rebukes to your honour. I know also that you blame him for the late treatment of Sir Francis. I have ever been grateful of your amity and your many kindnesses; likewise I do not forget the honour of our noble countryman. Yet, I beg of you, think on my dilemma: a man must make monies, and I am yet deep in debt.*

Raleigh shook his head. *God knows I hate Essex, let us speak plainly of it; yet there is more to my commandment than courtly politicking.* He pulled at the ring in his ear as though it might unlock his tongue. *Essex and his sister, the Lady Rich, are drawn in some dark matter.* He nodded gravely. *I fear they mean to draw you to it likewise.*

What matter? exclaimed Hillyarde. *What does the Earl attempt?*

He writes in cipher to the King of Scots; his sister passes his thoughts on in her letters. He seeks to marry off all those in line to the throne and place the Scots King upon it. Raleigh drew up his brows in a deeply disdainful frown. *He proclaims the Queen a foolish woman and longs for a change of monarch.*

Gower hissed revulsion; Hillyarde puffed out his cheeks and whistled. I shook my head. *You have some proof of this, my lord?* I asked mildly.

Raleigh waved me off in irritation. *Burghley has the cipher,* he snapped, *he has seen the letters.*

And you have seen them also? I pursued.

Nay, what needs that? he barked. *Burghley is a man of trust.*

My lord, I reasoned, *Burghley is a man of policy.*

What mean you by that? Raleigh huffed. *He is the greatest man of this State.*

I do not doubt, I smoothed, *that My Lord Treasurer Burghley is wise and has much statecraft. It is because of this that I wonder at his purpose.*

Raleigh pulled at his ear again. *What is your claim?* he said sourly. *Do you think me to be duped into some base conspiracy, painter?*

I would never presume it, I bowed. *Yet Burghley wishes to see his son Robert take his place, does he not? And Robert Cecil and the Earl of Essex are ever divided.*

Surely you do not think, put in Gower, *that Burghley would discredit himself in such a way?*

I think, I said softly, *that he might wish My Lord Raleigh to whisper some Essex treason to the Queen. Such a step would discredit an unpopular favourite, and aid Robert Cecil's assent to the Privy Council.*

Fie! Raleigh sneered. *Your grasp of courtly politicks amazes! I thought you a painter of souls, not an ambassador of gossip.*

I bowed again. *My lord, I only wish for your safety. I would advise you to allow Burghley to speak to the Queen of this, and not to be led to some rash accusation of Essex. If it be true, Walsingham will likewise know of it; he misses naught.*

You would advise? Raleigh exclaimed. *You would presume to advise me?*

I would, my lord, I smiled. *You are a great man, and great men do not ignore the counsel of their supporters, however humbly placed.*

Gower drew breath sharply, Hillyarde fell open-mouthed and staring. Raleigh's eyes narrowed, then slowly rounded into mirth. His lips twitched beneath his beard and his teeth flashed with a sudden smile. He came to the table and clapped his hand heavily upon my shoulder. *God's Soul!* he growled. *You are a forthright creature! I have a mind to put you in the stocks.*

You are all kindness, I sweetened.

Raleigh laughed. He looked to Hillyarde and shook a finger at him. *Keep from limning Essex,* he warned, though now smilingly. *I am yet in earnest.*

My lord, I said, *if Hillyarde does not limn the Earl, then his Huguenot Prentice will. Do you wish such indignity upon our friend?*

Raleigh looked shrewdly at me and mused awhile, tapping his gloves upon the table. He picked an apple from the dish and rolled it in his palm. At length he looked at the Goldsmith and nodded curtly. *Very well,* he allowed, *but keep from him all you can. Do not render the Lady Rich, and above all, make no limnings of the Stuart clan.* He tossed the apple high and caught it neatly. *Any of them.*

I will do all you say, Hillyarde assented. *I thank you for the warning.*

Thank your friend here, Raleigh said, pinching my sleeve.

Well, so, said Gower shakily, gesturing to the spread table. *Will you sup, my lord, or take some ale?*

Nay, Raleigh laughed, *though my thanks for it. I cannot stomach advice and ale together. I will leave you to sup.* He bowed to leave and pressed the apple in my hand. *Come,* he said lowly, *a word apart with me.*

All bid farewell and I followed him to the stair. He rounded upon me and caught fast my collar.

You have not learned to hold your tongue, painter of souls, he hissed. *You would do well to follow the advice that I once gave to you.*

If I speak rashly, yet I mean no ill, my lord.

I know it well. Raleigh loosened his grip and smoothed out my collar gently. *I tested your mind once upon the subject of a school for thinkers,* he said quietly. *I have some men readied for assembly and look to hold a meeting soon. You will come?* He sought my eye impatiently. *It will be a company of great interest and even-tempered debate,* he pressed; *you would do well in it, and I much desire you to join us.*

I demurred. *You honour me, my lord, yet I have too little wit to offer such a gathering.*

We will have men from all paths of learning, he insisted, scholars and astronomers, *some schooled in alchemistry, some in divinity, some in music. A master of images, and one so clear of speech, would add much to our gathering.*

I thank you, I assured, *yet I feel myself too little schooled. It would shame me to speak to such a company.*

Raleigh nodded ruefully. *I doubt this the reason,* he said, *yet I will not press you further. Come to me when your mind is altered; you will be ever welcome.* He looked to grasp my hand and saw that I yet clutched his apple; he held out his hand for it. *Would that you were so quick to share your knowledge,* he said, and fiercely bit the fruit.

I returned to the table. Hillyarde smiled and bid me eat well, for I had greatly earned my supper. Gower looked to me as a man pardoned on the gallows.

Take better care of your tongue, my friend, he said gravely. *I fear that one day soon it may lead you to strife.*

His brushes will do that sooner, Hillyarde laughed.

I shared my fears with Kat. She was likewise suspicious of Burghley, though she flatly proclaimed Essex for a broiler of treasons.

You have not seen him of late, she said frowningly. *He is ever telling the Queen how greatly he adores her, how she is yet youthful and beautiful as a girl, how she has his heart entire.* She rolled her eyes. *All know too well that he thinks her a weathered crone. She is grown suspicious of change, and jealous of all who are young.*

I do not doubt that Essex may falter yet, I said. *I fear that in this, however, Raleigh may fare the worst.*

Let it happen as it will, Rob, Kat said softly. *What matter is it to you how they fight and bravo?*

None, I said, though with very small conviction.

Kat sat up and pressed her hands to mine. *What do you fear?* she urged. *Have you some other hand in this?*

Nay, I assured her, *I only see the long shadow of Walsingham upon it. Raleigh seeks to draw me close to him, and enjoin me in his school of tobacco and dissent.* I sniffed. *I fear that I may yet reek of conspiracy, and Walsingham has a long nose.*

I need not have feared long. Within the twelvemonth Walsingham's nose was cold as marble, safe sealed in a tomb.

Thirty

THE SPYMASTER TOOK UP his sulphurous new lodgings, and many prayed for his eternal repose upon Satan's rack and wheel. While the Late Secretary burned and screamed below, those yet above devoured his goods and vied for his seat at the bounteous Council table.

Essex was quick to covet, swiftly weaving his own web of assassins. He begged the Queen and bribed the court, and, in hope of taking Walsingham's place, secretly wed his daughter. Frances, widow of the noble Pip Sidney, was a plain piece of womanhood far past her youthful prime, yet her price was cheap, her value high, and Essex was rarely obliged to visit home.

In spite of her favourite's hopes and pleas, the Queen dallied and shifted, refusing to name the Spymaster's replacement. While the youth raged and entreated, old Burghley leaned upon his long white staff and whispered softly into the royal ear. His son Robert, he murmured, was a very able Secretary. His son Robert, he urged, was a thoughtful and temperate body. His son Robert, he advised, was a meet choice for preferment. The Queen listened and lingered, and in her great indecision, let the little crookbacked Cecil take up his pen and commence scribbling upon State Paper. Ere long, her little Elf was the Leader of the Commons; his father Burghley presided at the Lords.

Essex and Cecil came straightway to blows, and while the Earl brandished his sword, the Elf fought back with words. Essex cried for war with Spain: Cecil drew up treaties. Essex sneered at his rival's stunted form: Cecil barbed back with quick and shapely wit. Each gathered men and sought intelligence against the other; the court was cleft, and the two factions snarled and circled like hounds in the marketplace.

Divisive natures teem and breed: their offspring is Discord. Essex and Cecil set the fashion, and all men grew divided. The painters and limners of London city had ever rivalled and jostled, the schools of natives and those of strangers fighting for the same small fortune. Now we English painters looked about us and saw ourselves invaded, for the novel strangers of Puritan lands had grown overfamiliar, and taken up much of our trade.

One afternoon that Summer Gower appeared, unannounced and unbidden, at the Strand. He was flushed and short of breath, the sweat standing out upon his brows, his courtly clothes much crumpled and askew. Kat bid him enter and he fell into a chair, pulling at his collars and swallowing gaspingly.

Forgive me, my friends, he wheezed, *for paying such a hasty and unbecoming visit*. Kat poured him a cup and he straightway emptied it, setting it down with a clatter. *I have come from court at Greenwich; I took oars at once, for I have tidings of import.*

Speak then, I beg you, I urged. *What is amiss?*

Gower shook his head. *Grave matters. Nicholas was called to attend the Queen today, for she has some notion to renew the Great Seal and wished to speak of its design. I accompanied him, for I had some matters to settle with the Treasury.*

You are not in difficulty? I exclaimed.

Nay, he said hastily, *it is but a trifle. We were admitted to the Presence Chamber and there saw the painter de Critz. Do you recall the man?*

Kat looked up quickly; I nodded. *He was with Oliver's party at Somerset House*, I said. *He spoke with us.*

Indeed, Gower said. *I asked how he fared; he answered that he fared very well indeed, for he is now much in demand and renders for both the Earl of Essex and Robert Cecil.*

Ever the Spymaster's pupil, I scoffed, *with a hand at each table.*

That is not all, said Gower wincingly. *We waited upon the Queen, he told me, for she was within, being rendered by a limner.*

I whistled. *Isaac Oliver?*

The very man, Gower sighed. *Nicholas was much shaken, as you may suppose, though he acted as graciously as ever. Oliver himself appeared and was most discourteous. The Earl of Essex*

*had sought the Queen's limning by him; he has made clear his
support of the foreign painters, and proclaims them the height
of fashion.*

Poor Hilly, sighed Kat, sinking upon a cushion.

Oliver will never outstrip his Master, I said, *have no fear.
The Queen does not want such likenesses as his; they are too
honest.*

He is an ambitious youth, said Gower, *he will render in
whatever manner the court commands.* He shook his head.
*Soon a painter in large will look to challenge me, and there
will be no English Serjeant, nor Master Limner, at court. When
the Queen is gone – God preserve Her! – who may tell what
manner of Sovereign we will have?*

A Scots one, sneered Kat, *if Essex has his way.*

My position counts for naught with these strangers, Gower
muttered. *I have no advantage over them; though the Queen
may wish me to be mindful of her image, I cannot prevent Essex
from letting these foreigners in.* He shook his head sadly. *There
are no guild rules to govern this.*

Cannot the Painters-Stainers bring some challenge? I asked. *I
thought them quick to ensure monopolies; they are hasty enough
to dispute with Englishmen.*

I fear they will do naught, he sighed. *You recall Marcus
Gerts?*

I laughed. *The Guts? Overwell.*

*He looks to intrude himself upon the court, and he is well
placed to do so. Though he is yet kept firm beneath his
father's will, he quickly garners favour. He is now close-tied
in a Netherlandish circle, for his father is wed to one sister of
de Critz, and he to another.*

He has wed his aunt? I baulked.

Nay, Gower laughed, *he has wed the sister of his father's
second bride.*

'Tis close enough, Kat declared, clapping her hands with mirth.
*Are they like as twins? What sport that would be for two
matrons!*

It is all one, I said, *and smacks incestuous to me. I am loath
to think on it.*

I also, Gower mumbled, *though not for the bedding of an aunt. I fear that they are grouping, Rob; they mean to eat our bread.*

Then we must send them off, I declared, *we must challenge them.*

We are painters, not brawlers, Gower said.

You are so at least, Master Gower, laughed Kat.

Gower rubbed his beard. *We must hold some manner of Council, the better to settle our disputes and divide our patronage. We would do well to make no enemies, for you see how that fares with Nicholas and his Prentice.*

Councils engender discontent, I averred, *they solve nothing. See how it goes at court, one Councillor ever ranged against another?*

We will see, Gower muttered. *I am purposed of today; I will herald the Painters-Stainers' and Goldsmiths' guilds, and we will call an assembly. It will clear the matter entire.*

My much increased patronage drained my stock of paint: I wrote to the Salisbury Goat and bid him send me phials. A fortnight later my message was returned; Doctor Forman was no longer of Salisbury, I was informed, but had settled into lodgings in the city, and could be found in his Stone House practice at Billingsgate.

I took the note to Kat. She had been little at court of late, her disdain for Essex keeping her much at home. Nor had she bid any visitors come for sport; these many months past I had forgone the arras, for naught might be viewed but Kat abed in her shift, restlessly turning. I feared her anger at finding Forman near, for though he had not sought us, he might yet wish to pay Kat a hard visit.

Kat was seated on cushions by her open casement, a scribbled mess of pages in her hand, her mouth silently working as she read. I stole upon her and kissed her brow, but she waved me off and held her finger to the page.

What script is this? I asked, bending to the papers. The inky sprawl was ill writ indeed, and spaced in the manner of an interview.

A play, Kat said, her eyes fixed upon it. *A marvellous well-turned play.*

It is play I must speak of with you, I said, and turned her face to me. *Come, put down the papers, I need a moment only.*

Very well, she huffed, laying down the script and picking up her cup. *What manner of play?*

I flourished the note before her. *I am sorry for this, dear Kat, yet it must needs be done. I sent word to Forman in Salisbury for more phials, and I find he is in London.*

Kat paled. *He comes to visit?*

Nay, worse, he resides here now. He has set up practice in Billingsgate.

God's Soul, Kat breathed, and drank deep from her cup.

I know how loath you are to see the Goat again, I pressed, *yet I am in urgent need of the liquid for my paints. I have mixed much of late, for I filled many panels. I also fear that the liquid's power fades with time, for though I mix whole bladders of paint, they are greatly diminished when I open them.*

How so? asked Kat archly.

I know not; I reason that the vapours of the air must cause it to disperse.

Kat blinked urgently. *What stock do you have?*

Some little for these few days: I thought to have more, yet I find there is much missing.

She swallowed hard. *Go to him, Rob,* she directed, *I will bear the cost.*

I am greatly sorry for it, Kat, I humbled. *I will do all I might to divert him, and pay him in coin if he will take it in your place.*

We must have the paint, she urged. *Go to him at once.*

Dear Kat, I said, and stroked her cheek. *I thank you.*

Kat picked up her script again and fell to reading. I kissed her hand and withdrew to the door. There I halted, for by the light of the casement I saw how greatly she had thinned of late, and how sunken were her features. The beauty of her dark locks was fading, and the curls about her face and beneath her caul were thickened with false hair. She held the pages close to her face, the papers aflutter and rustling in her hands. I wondered if I might not seek some physick of Forman, and bid her tell me more about her pains. She looked up sharply.

Do you yet tarry? she piped. *Go and see the physician, Master Painter. Fetch your phials!*

Billingsgate was thick with trade, and I marvelled at how the commerce had swelled since I first came to the city. The waters of the Thames were high and, beneath strong sun, smelling mightily of sea and filth. The stalls were awash with fish tails, guts and blood, the gulls and kites screaming above and picking beneath for scraps. I came slippingly to the Stone House, hard by the port, and looked amongst the signs there for the physician's name. Here he grandly announced himself for practice: DOCTOR SIMON FORMAN, PHYSICIAN, ASTROLOGER AND CASTER, PURVEYOR OF HEALTHFUL ELIXIRS, SALVES, POTIONS AND MEDICAMENTS, TRADING IN THE CLEANSING OF SORES AND BINDING OF WOUNDS, HEALING AND SETTING, CONSULTATIONS ON ALL MATTERS OF BODILY ILLS AND THE DRAWING UP OF HOROSCOPES.

I found him occupied, stroking the brow of a young woman great with child. He looked not up as I entered, but barkingly bid me wait without, for might I not see that he had business? I stood beyond the door, studying knots in the wood, and felt the contents of my purse. I might easily pay him in silver, I mused, to keep him from Kat's bed, for I had such good fortune of late that the money would not be missed. I had sent a large bill of paper to Thetford as a Twelfth Night gift, the better to preserve my family; I had given gloves and some silks to Kat that season, and had dined twice in some splendour with Gower and Hillyarde, carrying the cost for all. Yet I had a pot of coin stowed fast in my workshop, and would gladly pay much for some remedy for Kat.

The door opened and the swollen-bellied goodwife stepped without. She passed slowly by, her feet two tiny points beneath the great bulk of her skirts. Forman's bushy head appeared and he narrowed his eyes at me.

Come within, he barked. I followed as he trotted to his desk, closing the door behind me.

The room within was ranged about with jars and bottles holding diverse coloured liquids and dried preparations. Shelves reached to the very roof, littered with books and pamphlets, bound volumes and unpolished points of rock. Forman sat beneath a chart of scribbled symbols; about the wall behind him were pinned signs and papers writ with notes, and ill-wrought renderings of human heads and limbs. At the casement hung a length of silver chain, with what seemed a piece of spiralled horn swinging from it. Forman followed my look.

Unicorn, he growled.

Indeed?

He held his head aside, his eyes round and searching. *What ails you? You look in health. Do you fear buboes? Have you some carbuncle to lance? Or is it the virga virilis?*

I coughed. *Nay, I am well, Master Forman; I come seeking further phials for my paint.*

Ah! he exclaimed, leaning forward. *You have used all I lately sent?*

I have had much work, I said, *and use much paint.*

You do not waste the liquid? he enquired, peering closely. *It needs but a drop.*

I am ever careful of it; yet I wonder if the liquid does not disperse with time.

Disperse? he snapped. *What mean you, disperse?*

Only that my paints seem to keep for fewer days each time I blend them.

Do you bleed them, thin them?

Nay, I reasoned, *I ever use the same measure. Yet they are lessened when I unstopper them, as though they were vanished into air.*

Find fitter seals, then, he grumbled. *It cannot be the potion.* He stood stiffly and pulled a leather flask from a shelf. *Take this*, he said. I reached for the flask but he swiftly set out two beakers and, uncorking, poured out ale. I laughed. *What humours you?* he barked.

I gestured to the flask. *I thought— nay, no matter.* I took the beaker and raised it to him. *Your practice fares well in London?*

Well indeed, though I am ever short of purse. The rent is high.

It is well placed for business, I offered.

It is. He drank and wiped his beard. *The ale is good.* I sipped and nodded, though the drink was over-warm and savoured sweatily of leather. *How fares Mistress Joyce?*

Well, I answered, then thought the better of it. *In truth*, I said, *she is ailing greatly, though I know not the cause of it.*

Women's matters? he sniffed.

I think not. She has long complained of pains in her belly. Now she grows thin and sallow, and lacks her wonted spirit.

The dropsy? he mused. *She is still wanton?*

I laughed. *That is direct, sir: yet in truth she is not. She has not entertained a man these many months.*

He nodded. *It will be some venal ill.*

The pox? I cried. *Kat knows better than to leave such a matter untended.*

She may have the pox, he nodded. *She may well have the gonorrhoea passio. It has taken me in the yard these seasons past. I may have taken it first from her.*

I caught my breath. *You have it?*

Aye. Yet I am a physician. I may heal myself.

I pressed him forward, impatient to be gone. *What will you take for two phials of the liquid?* I urged.

He rubbed his furred and ink-stained hands together. *Two sovereigns*, he said, and artfully licked his lips.

Agreed, I said, rising hastily. I took out my purse and shook the coin into my hand. *I will take them now, if I might.*

He frowned. *I do not have the mixture readied. I will send it on.*

Very well, I said. I rolled the sovereigns in my palm. *Pray tell me*, I said mildly, *what is in the liquid?*

Pa! he spat. *I bade you never question me.*

Is it in any manner dangerous? I persisted.

He raised the great thatch of his brows. *You see what it does to pigment. You know well not to drink it.*

Would it harm a body, were it spilt upon the skin?

Enough of this baiting! he snarled. *Do not bathe in it unless you be a fool. It may burn but can be soothed with water. Do not dip your hands in it overlong: I cannot tell what may befall you.*

I nodded. *Here*, I offered, *a sovereign now, and one to follow when you send the phials.* I threw the coin upon the desk; he grasped the piece and hastily bit the edge. *It is true*, I said, *I avow it.*

He spat and smiled thinly. *I will send the phials tomorrow. I have no leisure to pay a visit.*

I turned to leave. *Pray*, I added, *do not think to swive Kat again, for her body will not stand it.*

I have no thought for court whores at present, he crabbed. He stood and drained his cup. *I know what it is to father a son. I got one upon a wench in Salisbury. Now I look to wive.*

A wise pronouncement! I cried, very much relieved. *I wish you well in it.*

I have had much trial and woe of late, he growled. *Yet I have learned to scry and conjure.* He puffed out his chest. *I mean to make my fortune in this city. I possess the good favour of one at court.*

I doubt not your success, I bowed. *Give you good day.*

I made straightway home, my feet light and my spirits much lifted. Kat was yet by the casement, the papers scattered about her, her head anod with sleep. I knelt by her chair and gently took her hand. She stretched and yawningly opened her eyes.

What is the clock? she sighed.

Not yet supper, I said. *I have seen the Goat.*

May he rot, she gasped, and sat up wincingly. *When does he come?*

He does not! I trumpeted. *He is content with coin.*

How much coin?

A good deal, I laughed, *but a better price than you would pay.*

Jesu, I am thankful! How does he fare?

Saturnine as ever, I said, *and grown important. He boasted to have a bastard son in Salisbury and now he seeks a wife.*

Kat laughed. *He is a poor offering for a maid.*

He has a poor wedding gift for her also, I said carefully. *He has the clap.*

Clap? she cried. *That is meet for him. And he a physician!*

He says he may cure himself. Dear Kat, I urged, *are you certain that there be no similar ill with you?*

Rob! she squealed, and merrily pinched my cheek. *I have danced too hard and bedded too often, that is all. I have no clap. Do you have the liquid?*

It will follow.

She sighed. *Have you any for me now? I would delight in a little decoration.*

I think it unwise, I said gently. *Forman will not tell what is within it, yet I fear his liquid may prolong your sickness.*

Nay, she said firmly. *We have said all on this matter.* She stood and held out her hand. *Come, let us sit at your easel.*

I followed her within and she made straightway to my table. I set to mixing a paint of simple oil and clay, a reddish ochre of unsullied, natural pigment. Kat unlaced her sleeves and bodice and rolled down her shift; her breastbone and ribs showed clear and pointed through her pale skin, blotched reddish in places.

I would like a little chain of colour here, she said, tracing her fingers along her throat and breast. She turned to my palette and wrinkled up her nose. *I am no fool*, she sighed, *do not think to trick me. Take up another.*

Dear Kat, I dare not—

Here, she snapped, thrusting a bladder of ultramarine into my hand. *This was ever my chosen hue.*

I know it. I unstoppered the bladder and squeezed out a drop. *Kat*, I honeyed, *you no longer take much pleasure from our life. Why do you not give me up and wed?*

I cannot wed, she said. She reached for my pot of brushes and pulled out a thin sable. *There is none that would love me so well as you.*

Forman looks to wive, I teased.

I wed the Goat? she cried. *Pfu!* She sat at the easel, rolled back her neck and handed me the sable. *Were I to wed, it would be to a man with no hope of heirs*. She closed her eyes and I dipped the sable into the ochre mix. *If only you could seed*, she sighed, *and I bear fruit, what children we might have had!*

What monsters, I said, dappling the paint upon her chest.

What beautiful monsters, she corrected. She opened her eyes and looked down at the earthen dabs above her breasts. *Fie*, she said wearily, *that is a muddy hue*.

There are many men that would wed you, I persisted.

Sweet Rob! she groaned. *As you will no sooner wive me than swive me, for pity's sake give me the paint!* I circled again at the base of her throat with the ochre; she caught my wrist and looked pleadingly up to me. *The blue*, she said, *the brilliant blue, I beg of you*. She smiled weakly. *It is the only pleasure left me, is it not?*

Thirty-one

THE SUMMER PASSED IN a damp and florid haste, and I made preparation for the coming season of commissions. The Nativity past had paid me some several sovereigns in copy work alone, and I relished the prospect of encroaching Winter, herald of coin and plenty. As Kat no longer bedded nobles she had little hope of gaining gifts or monies; thus, at last, it was I who carried our fortune and kept us in meat and ale. It pleased me much to make such provision for Kat, as it proved me in some wise mannish enough to offer her succour.

Master Gower had not forgot his planned assembly of limners and painters, and from the hard lesson of Oliver and Hillyarde, sought to lose no commissions of his own. He had sent announcement to the guilds, bidding them make invitation to all there subscribed; he likewise sent word to the many schools and workshops of strangers, calling them to attendance. As the appointed day approached, Gower waxed determined; Hillyarde grew green-gilled at the notion of sitting at table with the Huguenot, and for myself, I looked to the council as the rumble of a stormcloud hastening towards us. For all our doubts, Gower was resolved that the moot would bring our several selves together, all amity restored: a pretty picture of kinship, and one that would yet prove horribly awry.

That no favour might be shown, the meeting place agreed was the private room of a tavern, a clean and well-appointed inn beside the Fleet. The landlord was noted for the moderate strength of his ale, and his two sturdy sons for their strong-armed intolerance of dispute. The chosen hour was eight of the evening, that all might put their works aside and sup ere they arrived; thus full of belly, they might also prove better inclined to plain, judicious speech. Gower made to the tavern early, supposing to ensure a cordial reception for all, and make preparation for lanterns and linkboys, should the evening run so late. Hillyarde and I determined to enter together, and I met with the Goldsmith for a strengthening dish in a chophouse close at hand.

I found Hillyarde already at the board, a jug of ale frothing beside him. I sat and took a cup with him, and as we were in haste to sup, we called for broth. The tapster declared with much apology that none might be had; Hillyarde sighed gloomily, muttering that it boded ill for us, broth being a necessary part of his good humour. The landlord's girl, a dainty and quick-fingered creature, commenced setting out spoons and trenchers; she bobbed and whispered to me that we might take a heartier supper, if we willed it, for there was much yet in the kitchen. I answered that we would take what we could, and she swiftly returned with a deep dish of stew the colour and savour of claret. I broke the surface, aswim with bobbing roots; beneath lay a rich loam of gamey flesh amply doused with gravy. Hillyarde smiled.

This is a better omen than broth, is it not? I offered.

He nodded and held out his cup. *Ale seems poor company for such a dish*, he said. *Shall we call for Burgundy?*

It takes little wit to reason what might follow; come the hour of assembly, the Goldsmith and I were fair seasoned in our cups, and sat picking our teeth with deliberate satisfaction.

We made to the meeting place, Hillyarde pausing on the stair to call for a flask to follow directly. As I neared the door I heard many voices within and, opening, broke into a swell of noise. The room was long and low, a vast chain of ill-matched tables dividing the centre. To either side of these ranged all manner and ages of men; some known to me by name, others by sight, and a number of them strangers. Master Gower was seated at the head, his back towards me; he turned and shot me a look of profound relief. At the far end of the tables I spied the nodding curls and whiskered lip of Oliver; about him were the Netherlanders, among them de Critz and the sour-faced Guts, and an older man sporting a wide Dutch collar and round black cap. I bowed and, searching the faces, lit suddenly upon the smooth features of Ambrose Leggatt.

Ambrose stood and bid me welcome. The man seated by him

looked me over seekingly. He was round of face, his beard an acreage of oiled and short-sheared whiskers. He seemed much puffed out, being over-swathed in velvets, the trimmings of which thinned shabbily with use. He stood arduously, unfolding laps of cloth, and noisily cleared his throat.

May I present Master Segar, said Ambrose readily, *a most distinguished painter of the court, and herald to Her Majesty.*

Well met, Master Segar, I bowed. He nodded, the vast badge in his cap shifting perilously. *This looks to be a rare evening, does it not, sir?*

You were of the same school? asked Segar archly.

Indeed, I nodded, *though not oft of the same mind.*

Ambrose smiled coolly. *I am glad to see you prosper,* he said levelly, his eyes upon my doublet. *I see it has mattered little that you did not gain your Prentice papers.*

So it would seem, I said, flicking a speck from my sleeve. *And you prosper likewise?*

I share a workshop with Master Segar, he replied. *I learn much from him.*

Segar nodded complacently. *I have painted the Queen and nobles these many years.*

Indeed? I ventured. *I wonder that I have not heard of you before.*

Segar's nostrils flared like a colt's. Ambrose looked over my shoulder. *One beckons you,* he said lightly.

I turned; Gower waved me to him. *Forgive me, Master Leggatt, Master Segar,* I declared, *my friend the Serjeant bids me sit with him.*

I made back to Gower and sank upon the chair beside him. He looked to me frowningly.

I thought myself altogether abandoned, he hissed. *Who is the white-faced man with the herald?*

An old playmate, I huffed. *I little like that new toy of his.*

Gower sniffed. *You have been taverning, Rob,* he chided, *and Nicholas is not yet here; I knew him ill disposed to this meeting.*

Fear not, he comes, I whispered.

The door swung forth with a kick and Hillyarde entered

clumsily, a flask already breached in one hand, a brace of cups clutched to his chest with the other. He sat to Gower's left and, with much clattering, poured wine and passed a cup along to me.

We were not to take liquor tonight, Gower scolded softly.

My apologies! Hillyarde piped, a little loudly. *I have forgot your cup, George.* He picked up Gower's beaker of small beer and swilled about the contents. *If you drain this slurry from it I will pour for you.*

Desist, Nicholas! Gower hushed. *The whole assembly awaited you, and now I see that you have been taverning with Rob.* He shook his head frowningly. *I can scent the claret on you both.*

It was a fine Burgundy, Hillyarde smiled, a stained line of the grape tarnishing his inner lip. *It was the gamey stew that swam in claret.*

For shame, Gower sighed, *and you say you can scarce feed Alice and the babes.*

I settled the reckoning, I put in.

Confound your supper, Gower puffed, *I have a council to order!* He took his cup from Hillyarde and set it on the table. *Keep your heads, my dear friends, and all will be well.* He drew his breath in deeply and stood, rapping heavily upon the tabletop. *Gentlemen!* he called, *good gentlemen and fellow-painters all! Pray be seated, that we may begin.*

Much scraping of chairs and murmuring followed as all settled into their families and factions. To the left of the tables gathered a lean and ragged host: men of middling years with deep-scored parchment skins, their cheap-dyed cloth the certain badge that they were painters in large, and lacking papers. Beside them the smooth-cheeked Prentices bullied and bravoed, some of their number buoyed with the pride of recent release. At great distance to the right, as though mediocrity were a contagion, the Masters of the Painters-Stainers swelled and blustered, amongst them Ambrose and his bulbous herald. The Goldsmiths, quick eyes and guild badges aglitter, ranged beyond them. At the far end of the room, between these English flanks, the strangers of the city met in Puritan congregation; amid their black jerkins and sombre cloaks the youth Oliver rocked lazily on his tilted seat, his arms crossly folded. I looked back to Hillyarde, who drained his cup smackingly.

Gower commenced the meeting, intoning gravely how disputes had arisen amongst our number, and that he wished to see all matters settled affably. *There are gentlemen here*, he went on, *that have come from other lands, and are thus not of the guilds; this has led to difficulty. Yet we are all of one trade, and there is patronage enough for us all.*

There may be for you, piped a voice from the Prentice corner, *you're the Serjeant Painter. It is not so for others.*

Many nodded and murmured agreement. A greying fellow to the left tapped his cup upon the table. *I have no quarrel with the Serjeant*, he croaked, *yet I am moved to agree with the youth there, though he speak over-hastily to his betters.* He grunted and shifted in his seat. *Our trade is much diminished, and the fault of it lies with these strangers.* He waved a trembling hand towards the dark circle of Netherlanders. *It is for their good that we suffer!*

A roar of ayes and yays sounded about me; the Nethermen shook their heads and muttered. Gower called for order.

There are many workshops here established from other lands, he averred, *yet this has ever been so.*

Burn them! cried a voice; more roaring answered.

A broad-featured youth rose from amongst the Goldsmiths and looked timidly to Gower. *If I may speak, Serjeant Painter*, he said shyly, *I would say something of this matter as a limner.*

Gower smiled. *Master Lockey*, he waved, *I beg you speak.*

The youth nodded and reddened. *I have been honoured enough to serve as Prentice to Master Nicholas Hillyarde*, he said, *who is known to all. I learned from him to follow the style of limning practised by Master Holbean, who was no Englishman. Likewise I worked with Prentices of other lands and we were all of a trade.* He nodded to Oliver and swallowed gulpingly. *What I mean from this is that, whether we be Englishmen or no, we may all learn, the one from the other.* He looked about the room and sat down hastily.

Hillyarde clapped noisily. *Well said, young Rowland*, he

bawled, and swung a fierce look to Oliver. *I am glad to have formed one Prentice to be made thus proud of.*

Nicholas! Gower hissed aside. Hillyarde dragged the flask to his cup and poured, then shook the wine at me. I made to pass my cup but Gower broke between us.

I am glad to see our youthful painters thus readily reconciled, he said diplomatically. *We may all learn from this.*

Segar the herald rustled a velvet arm and thumped it upon the wood. *It is not the foreign painters only that take all work,* he puffed. *You look to monopolise the Queen's image, Gower, do you not? And you sit there and preach and mind us to be friendly.*

Gower sniffed and leaned forward to the board; Hillyarde handed the flask to me behind his back.

It is Her Majesty's desire that I foster some control upon her public image, Gower said, his eyes flicking to my cup as I poured. *I am not placed to question our Graceful Sovereign's command.*

Ha! Segar spat. *Nor would you. What are you doing as Serjeant, Gower? You scarce paint any more. What is that castle of folly you are planning now?*

Gower's lip quivered with ire; he placed his palms squarely upon the table. *I render Her Majesty when she bids it; I make designs for her decorations. This has ever been the role of Serjeant Painter. At present I am planning a fountain for Her Majesty.*

A fountain! Segar snorted.

No doubt it has many devices upon it, I said cheerily. *That should please you, Master Segar, being a herald.* I laid a finger on the neat 'broidered trim of Gower's sleeve. *We might yet persuade Master Gower to design you some new costume of livery.*

Many laughed lowly; Gower swallowed his mirth, dipping his nose into his beaker and biting upon it. I met Ambrose Leggatt's eye. Segar stood quakingly.

Who are you to mock me? he howled. *I am a herald to Her Majesty!*

You spoke ill of my friend the Serjeant, I smiled. *He is the better of us all here, and he is meetly dressed.*

Get a new doublet, herald! a voice jeered.

Segar spun about, his eyes hard and piggish. *I wear the colours of Her Majesty's heralds!* he piped. *It is noble garb, and English. It is better wear than this* – he pointed shakingly to the Netherlanders – *these black Dutch crows!*

More jeering ensued; Gower banged the table. Several of the strangers jumped up and argued singingly.

There is no call to slander the Nethermen's clothes! I cried.

Ambrose stretched tactfully along the table. *You were once called Netherman, I recall*, he mouthed.

The man in the black cap, seated by Oliver, drew proudly to his feet. *Master Gower*, he called, his voice thick and chiming, *I thank you for your invitation.*

Master Gerts, Gower urged, rising to his feet, *I pray you, do not think to leave of such a sudden.*

I looked to the man Guts, whose squirming features left no doubt that the black-capped speaker was his father.

This was to be a sober meeting, the older Gerts said, *I will not sit to such discourtesy.* He nodded to his son, mumbling some order in his Nether-tongue. The Guts bowed his head, but, with a nudge from de Critz, rose unsteadily.

Good fellow, Master Guts, I called, *you must do as your father bids you.*

Guts flushed scarlet, his eyes flicking swiftly about to see if any mocked him. His father barked again and waved him from his seat. They made towards us, the elder man leading and gaining the door. Gower fussed about them; on all sides men rose and commenced disputing. Hillyarde smiled to me and leaned back in his chair, blocking Gerts' path to the door.

Your father fears for your maiden manners, the Goldsmith said smilingly. *He thinks we Englishmen a poor example.*

So you are, the Guts pouted. *You are drunken.*

Drunken! Hillyarde crowed. *Fie on my drunkenness! I could limn better in my cups than you could sign your name sober, you Dutch puppy!*

And such a name, I baited. *Your father awaits you without, Master Guts; he whistles, and you must come to heel.*

Peace, I pray you! Gower hushed.

You do all that your father bids, I'll warrant, I went on. *Even unto the swiving of your aunt.*

Guts hissed and drew his hands up into fists; I laughed, for his little wrists seemed ill-made pivots for such a bunch of fingers. De Critz loomed silently behind his countryman, his cold eyes quick and sharp between us.

Do not make quarrel, he said flatly. He spoke aside again to Guts, who waved his arms in sudden irritation.

Your brother tells you to make peace, I said. *Or is he your uncle? I am confused.*

Hillyarde let out a snort.

Do not laugh, old man! Guts piped. *You are but a faded trumperer, a mere socket maker!*

Hillyarde hooted – I near choked with mirth. *Socket maker!* Hillyarde squealed. *Did you hear that, Rob? Socket maker! Challenge him, my friend, my honour lies in tatters!*

I think he meant locket, I laughed, *though I cannot be certain. Yet faded trumperer – that is a grave affront.*

Guts growled and tugged at my collar. *Stand when I pronounce!* he cried. *I will not take insult from a man who is sitting at table.*

Very well, I answered, rocking to my feet. *I will insult you thus, Master Guts.*

Do not disgrace your profession, gentlemen, Gower pleaded. *Pray, be seated, we must debate in even tempers.*

This is no gentleman, Guts said, flicking my collar.

Do you dare comment on my breeding? I scoffed. *That is meet from a man who beds his own kin. How will you address your own daughters, as cousins or bedfellows?*

I would know how to address your beddingfellow, he sneered. *She is a sorry court whore. Not even the grooms will now have her.*

I roared and blindly snatched for his collar. He pulled back, and in the tangle of chair and cloak we fell together by the table, landing on the boards as one piece of felling. I set to him then, pinioning him with knees on chest and elbows, and made much clamour with the drumming of his cheeks. Gower yelled behind me and I felt one hauling back my shoulders,

my fists yet flailing, the blows scraping the air above Guts'
face.

I stood kickingly and found my arms braced to my sides,
two stout and red-faced tapsters holding me fast. Guts groped
about and, with his arm upon de Critz's shoulder, stood and
turned to me.

I had made a lively palette of his face, his nose well twisted
and bloodied. He wiped it in horror on his sleeve, his mouth
a frenzied working of silent Nether-speak, a foretooth raggedly
swinging from his gum.

He spat bloodily. *I knew you a brawler!* he gurgled. *I know
of your schooling!* He turned to de Critz. *What was that man,
Johann?* he whimpered. *His brawler friend?*

The tailor? asked de Critz mildly. *Patton, I think it, or Petty.*

The papist! Guts sputtered, his mouth afoam with crimson.
*He was a painter once. Any Englishman can be a painter, is it
not so? Even a Jesuit; even a Jesuit spy.* I made for him again
but the brawny ale-hands held me fast. Guts sneered then and
leaned towards me, his mouth close to my ear, his bloodied cheek
brushing mine. *My friend Johann here did help to dispossess the
papist*, he hissed wetly, *the better for us all. Look if you are not
soon to follow him.* He flicked his eyes to mine, agleam with
malice. I smiled toothily then and, with a sudden plunging, sunk
my jaw into his beard.

A scream sounded from what seemed afar: with a dull clatter
and a sharp scattering of light behind my eyes, I dropped down
into a thick, enveloping pit.

Thirty-two

I AWAKENED TO FIND myself stretched out upon my own Strand bed, my ears aroar and my bolster mightily soaked and bloodied. I had taken a violent crack upon the skull, and was sweetly tended by Kat, who soaked rags and parted the stiffened roots of my hair, the better to wash the wound. She would not suffer me to speak, and while she chided me frowningly for brawling, I saw that her brows were drawn in tender concern. I could do naught but lie upon my belly like a babe while she nursed me: I moaned and gurgled, and vomited a hogshead of wine-sickness at the chamber pot.

Hillyarde came next day with a meek countenance and sat in the chair by my bed, rubbing at his belly and begging Kat for salep. He stayed long, green of face and nauseous, complaining that he may not lie abed for the wrath of Alice, nor toil in his workshop for the trembling of his hands. Kat fussed about us both, pecking and scolding, and took great pleasure in stroking Hillyarde's brow. Though she was anxious to know the cause of my quarrel with Guts, we kept his base affront between us. I said naught to any of Petty, nor did I speak of the Netherlander's whispered threat.

Though my head smarted exceedingly from the blow, worse yet was the severing of Master Gower's amity. The Serjeant took my use of fists very ill, and though he blamed and crabbed at Hillyarde bitterly, yet he kept wholly from my company. He sent me grave words of condemnation and I replied, earnestly begging his forgiveness; my letter was returned at once, the seal intact. When at length I was well enough to go abroad I sought him at St Clement's – his wilful maid Lucy barred the door and stopped her ears to me.

I remained that season in exile at the Strand, with naught but a handful of commissions to occupy me, each one of which I suspected to be of Hillyarde's procuring. The Goldsmith did all he might to repair my loss, feeling himself a large part of the mischief, and thus we grew thick together, bound by a loathing of Oliver and his crows.

Nativity Eve brought reconciliation. After much dogged persuasion, Gower supped at the Maidenhead. Alice cunningly fed affection with her feast of warming pies and hearty puddings; Gower was firmly set of jaw ere I coaxed him into smiles. He revealed how Guts had made a great show of the beating, thinking to sue me for it, yet had been dissuaded by his careful intercession. *Be thankful*, he pronounced, *that Marcus the elder is a sober man, with a great dislike of slander and litigation.* I noted that it was the father who ruled the matter, yet I bit my tongue. Gower was worth the swallowing of pride.

The year turned, with tidings in Raleigh's hand arriving from Durham House. He urged me again to join his School of the Night, for there was to be another great meeting of enquiring minds, with many new persons attending. I declined, arguing that I had had my fill of assemblies. Raleigh penned a swift reply, bidding me pay him a visit. *Come when first you might,* he wrote, *yet leave your fists and quarrels at the door, for I too hear gossip and know you a brawler and the scourge of Dutchmen. There is here a matter I would have you see that much concerns you. I trust that your head be well mended enough for thinking.*

I delayed and tarried, for though I well enough liked Lord Water, I scented danger upon him: I wondered likewise at his courting of me and his knowledge of my doings. Kat baited me daily, cursing me for a fool to keep such a man waiting, and urged me to the visit. Though Walsingham be dead, I warned her, spying and intrigue flourished, and Raleigh would yet be under the Essex watch and, certain, Cecil's also. His house, Kat countered, stood very near at hand: I might come and go, see none, and be unseen. Thus we contended 'til Kat swayed me to her course. On the next fair day without snow I dressed finely yet plainly as I might, pulling a hat low to my eyes and a cloak highly about my chin, and rapped softly upon the doors of Durham House.

Raleigh received me in his study room, a chamber lined with learning and a layer of grey ash. He drew hard upon a long-handled pipe, the smoke of it hanging in blue and fetid clouds about him. He nodded as I entered; I bowed low and, rising, broke into choking coughs.

How fares your battle wound? he cried. *I trust it does not grieve you.*

I rubbed my head. *It is slow to heal, my lord, yet it will mend.*

I will cauterise it. He made to pass the stinking tube to me but I waved it away. He laughed and set the bowl of it crackling. *I have tidings of one who is known to you and little liked,* he puffed. *I thought you would fain hear me.*

You may speak of many, my lord.

I speak of the very one you bravoed with. He has made a likeness of my countryman Francis. His name is Gheeraerts – it was he, was it not, whose nose you pulped?

I laughed at the pulping, yet dryly. *Are you certain of the man, my lord? His work is scarce known: it is more like to be the father.*

Nay, said Raleigh, chewing upon the pipe. *It is the second Marcus, a man of about your years.*

I cannot but wonder at the little Guts painting My Lord Drake, I said. *I had not known that he might pick up a brush without his father's hand to guide it.*

Raleigh smiled. *His father ails, I believe.*

He will be little grieved of it. Yet the family is like to a warren, with much sharing of sisters; he will be ever buried in it. I warrant that the spy de Critz won him the commission.

Come, said Water peaceably, *the young Marcus has some reputation.* He arched his brows. *I hear word that he commences work for Essex and his mob.*

Indeed, I scoffed, *and who does not!*

You do not.

Nor do I have a wish to, my lord.

He nodded approval. *Though Francis bid the panel be done, he little likes the piece. There is something altogether – how might I say? – squashed about it. Though he be a compact body, he does not stand thus rooted.* Water rubbed his beard. *Francis meant it for a gift to the Queen, for he has suffered her displeasure overlong. Now I fancy that he will not give it to her; it does not show him well.* He grinned and tapped the tip of his pipe on his teeth. *You would care to see it? He has left the panel with me, for he knows not whether to keep it in the city or drag it down to Devon.*

I would much care to see it, if you have it here, my lord.

Raleigh stood and knocked his pipe into a dish. *Why else would I bid you come hither? I will leave the pipe, for I see it makes you green.* I made to object but he held up his hand to stay me. I bowed. *And desist from this lordliness,* he said bluntly. *We are not at court here.*

I followed Water to a small side parlour. The casements here were draped with heavy cloth and he commenced tugging at it, calling me to aid him. At length we brought down the cloth, the cold light streaming in harsh upon our faces. Raleigh waved for me to turn and look behind us.

Upon the plain wall hung a three-quarter panel of a man, hand upon hip, with a globe and a crest floating beside him. I narrowed my eyes at the likeness, the better to see the features, for the touch of the brush upon the face was smooth as to seem foggy. Though I little wished to own it, the countenance was Drake's indeed, though frail and much aged since I saw him. I studied the body, which was well wrought enough for cloth, yet stood strangely leaning and half stunted.

What say you to this? asked Raleigh.

I stepped closer and felt the panel. Though it was taut with paint, yet it yielded to the touch. *This is not wood,* I said. *It is painted upon cloth.*

The man claims this his genius, Water laughed. *He told Francis that such cloth would soon replace English wood.*

I wonder at that, I breathed. *It is much used elsewhere, though I have never seen it done.* I ran my fingers across the cloth again; the casing of paint upon it was smooth as marble, though it be not rigid.

What of the rendering? Water prompted.

I looked again. *The face looks to be made of powder, it is so weak of line and hazily done; it is like to a whore in her pastes and lotions.* Raleigh snorted. *There is something greatly awry in the body,* I added, stepping back. *It is stretched about sideways. See how the arms and hands do not match the shoulders! He is shrunken on his right side, and swollen on his left.* I sighed. *Also the globe upon this table was added later – for certain it was not stood in the same room as Sir Francis.*

You are in the right, Water mused, tilting his head and smiling. *I have spent some minutes together standing before this piece, puzzling out the line of it. Then it came to me that Francis is shaped like to the curvature of the globe, and that the globe here is upon another plane entire.* He straightened. *To see him aright, we must step aside.* He came forward and, taking me squarely by the shoulders, walked me several paces to the right. *Now look to it again. Do you not see him?*

I studied Sir Francis anew: Water was right. Of a sudden the body pivoted into shape, the gloved hand fitting the wrist and arm whence it came, the stretching chest thinned to naught but a swaggering stance. Limbs were of their right proportion, the jewelled pendant hung in the centre of its chain, and though the face was yet misted, the figure was clearly writ.

I laughed. *Did any watch Guts as he painted?*

Aye, said Raleigh, *Drake's wife and maid were there.*

Then his vanity has undone his work! I crowed. *This is the angle of his easel, certain: he moved it thus, that he may be watched while painting. He painted Drake from the side, and knew not how he twisted!*

Raleigh peered and rocked back and forth upon his heels. At length he gave a hoot and clapped his hands. *I have seen such a thing in the Queen's keeping,* he cried, *a panel of her brother. It was so stretched as to be impossible to view – I had to stand square to the side of it to see the face.*

A marvellous well-wrought piece of artistry, if it be done by design, I smiled. I looked to the panel again. *A marvellous piece of vanity when it be done in error.*

Sir Francis blushed down girlishly upon us, his face wrapt in cloud. I flicked my eye across the neat trim of his doublet, the precise folds of his ruff, the rounded silver of his pommel. The jewel at his waist hung brightly down; even thus painted I knew it to be Hillyarde's work, the carved likeness of the Queen within it cunningly copied. Though I laughed, I heard the hollow ring of it: the Guts was a bombast and a fool to misview his panel, yet when he learned to stand aright, he may well prove no jesting matter.

The seasons that followed blossomed with quarrels and intrigues; with the greening of the trees all men grew restive and vexatious. Essex fell to blows with the Earl of Kildare and was bound by the forfeit of vast monies to keep his peace. A rash of pamphlets and poetising spread through the city, one bawdy tale being passed amongst the Queen's maids, the better to teach them corruption. Puritan protesters proclaimed and preached sedition, the iron doors of the Fleet silencing their sermons. In France the new King of Navarre was besieged by papist rebels, the Spanish might be sighted off the coast of Cornwall at least twice before breakfast, and the Queen heard ill rumours of poisoned poniards and darts blown through pipes from high towers. Come Maytide the Elfin Secretary Cecil won his knighthood, and the brooding Essex glowered and festered further. In the city streets a madman proclaimed himself Christ on Earth and King of Europe, his ravings gathering a crushing crowd. Come the week's end he drew the greatest flock of all, for many came to see his divine flesh defiantly rent on the Cheapeside scaffold.

A great Progress was planned that Summer, and both Gower and Hillyarde looked to follow it. The Goldsmith greatly needed patronage, for he was afflicted with debt and weathered dire storms. Alice, rent with grief, mourned her lately lost father: she soon had cause to thunder through her tears. The lamented Brandon had been Master when Hillyarde was but his Prentice, a man of some substance and wealth: when the will was read, all learned in what wise he held his former pupil. Brandon denounced Hillyarde for a poor husband, an unfeeling father and a luckless debtor to boot: he left Alice naught, for fear that her husband lose all. This was a sore wound for my friend, for Alice chided him hard and bemoaned her marriage to a limner who had given her naught but woes, a quickened womb and seven mouths that ever cried for supper.

Thus pressed, Hillyarde sought work and made to keep close watch upon Oliver, the better to thwart his ambitions. Gower was likewise afeared to remain at home, lest the Queen allow some other to covet his place in his absence. Both men thought it unwise for me to follow, for fear I find the Guts and seek to spill more of him. Thus my friends departed for the little towns of Sussex, and I sought to pass a quiet season in the Strand with Kat, my purse saved from the strains of travelling.

We stayed much within doors, for the Plague came hard that season and held many streets. The Strand was little trod by man or horse, those who dwelt about us being well placed enough to quit the city or follow the Progress. Kat and I played at cards and drank good wines; I painted upon her toes as she read to me from some new-scribbled play. She knew many whose words had lately thundered from the painted boards of the Rose, her sly Kit making much noise with his brutish speeches sprinkled with Latin, the better to confound. Now Kat's theatre men had quit the town and were about the country, the playhouses closed to contagion. With none to note it, we idled our days in mild occupation, chewing lazily upon cold meats. Kat stretched upon my workshop cushions in her shift; I stayed in my painting garb, and toyed with layering paint upon cloth.

Thus we were found one afternoon, the hour of dinner long past. The air was heavy with heat, Kat lay drowsily upon the cool boards in her smock, and I worked upon a study of her hands in chalk. A clattering of horses sounded along the street and halted beneath us; Kat sat up stiffly and bid me look below. I rose and peered from the casement at the carriage as the horseman jumped down and rapped upon our door. Kat gasped and drew her smock about her neck.

Who is it? she hissed.

I peered at the livery. *Someone of the court*, I whispered, *though I cannot tell whom*. The knocking sounded again and a man unfurled from the carriage. I drew my head back quickly. *It is Raleigh!* I cried.

Raleigh? Kat piped, her eyes round with terror. *Go! Go down to him!*

Dress quickly then, I said, *I will bid him come in.*

O Rob! she wailed, clutching at her cloth. *Do not let him up! Do not let him see me thus!*

Put a frock on and come down, I urged. *He was not expected.*

The knocking sounded furiously. Kat commenced weeping and pulled at her undressed hair.

You cannot think I would let him see me now? Look at me, Rob! Look how I am altered! She shook her head angrily. *It takes an hour and more to look myself now. Tell him I am gone away!*

I stared at Kat's face, drained of health and drawn with fear; her hair hung limp and thin about her ears, the skin of her neck was ashen.

Stay in your chamber then, I bid her. *I will say nothing.*

I went swiftly below and opened to My Lord Water. He bowed and cleared his throat.

Forgive me my rash appearance, he rumbled, *I am in some difficulty and would speak with you.*

You honour me, my lord, I said, waving him in. *You will take some wine?*

Aye, the strongest you have.

I led him to the parlour and bid him wait while I drew some malmsey from the cellar; I returned to find him standing in the pantry, rubbing at his beard. We made back to the parlour with our flask and cups, a scuffling and rustling sounding at the stair top as we passed.

How fares Mistress Joyce? Raleigh said, rolling his eyes to the ceiling. *We do not see her at court of late.*

She likes not the courtly air at present, I said bluffly. *She is grown melancholic.*

He nodded. *It is the humour of the times.* He studied his cup and drained it noisily. *A fine good malmsey*, he declared, holding forth for more.

I poured again. *How may I aid you, my lord?*

I seek your counsel, you have proved quick to advise me. You flatter, my lord.

Do not be lordly with me; I am but Walter. He weighed me with hard shining eyes. *I am not beloved of men, I own it; I have ever been more the ladies' favourite. That has been my undoing. There are few that I trust yet you are one of them.* I bowed. *Also I believe you a man who sees much and understands his fellows.*

I will aid you if I might.

I have ever dallied with the maids at court, he said; *they are vain and easily plucked. I took one against a tree last Summer, poor fool knew not what I did 'til I unknotted her.* He smiled bitterly. *These two months past I have been plucked myself, for I have swived Bess Throgmorton and she is quick with child.*

It is the pay of such sport, I said frankly.

I had hoped you might assist me, he rejoined. *To my understanding Mistress Joyce has never taken thus. How do you remedy it?*

I drank deep, the wine a balm for my words. *I do not swive Kat,* I said unsteadily, *thus we have no difficulty. Nor can she ever take with child. It is no matter of potions and sticks, but a matter of Nature.*

Raleigh sighed deeply, his shoulders rounding. *I had looked for some other answer,* he grumbled. *Bess commands me to give her a ring. You have never wed, painter – I would know the secret of it.*

I near wed a Bess once, I corrected. *The lady died.*

I am sorry for it, he growled. *I was mistook.*

It was long since. Would you not willingly wed this Bess?

Though she be a goddess in raiments of the sun, he cried, *I would not willingly be put to it. I have ever sworn to be my own master: I have been tricked and lured, for she is forceful of temper and will have all she wants. I fear she will prove a termagant.*

Never more so than the mistress you now serve, I smiled.

Raleigh laughed. *Do not say so abroad! Yet that mistress will take these tidings ill indeed. I will lose my titles.*

I can scarce think it, I reasoned. *Essex was soon forgiven for wedding Walsingham's daughter.*

Aye, Water sneered, *for he claimed it was for the getting of lawful heirs; it was not for the too hasty getting of a bastard one. Bess is a beauty. Frances Walsingham has the face of a gaping trout. The Queen knew well that Essex did not wed for love or lust. That is the sole reason she forgave him.*

I laughed and filled our cups again. *Do not be heavy-hearted*, I encouraged. *If you truly seek my counsel, marry the lady. If she will not keep her tongue, better to seem to the Queen a courteous husband, and not some dishonourable ravisher.*

Water held his cup to me. *Bitter medicine*, he said lowly, *yet I thank you for it.*

The Summer ripened and fell, and we heard some tidings of courtly doings in our exile. The threat of the French papists rumbled apace, for the Catholic rebels had allied with Spain and looked to overthrow their King. Word reached us from Hillyarde that Essex had pleaded release and, with the Queen's reluctant assent, rode off to do battle against the popish hordes. He proved proud and inept, spending more in hawking and hunting than fighting and besieging, and caused grave talk by knighting an army of his partisans. The Queen raged at his absence and threatened to recall him, though all suspected it was for love of him, and not for rage at his failings.

That Autumn another emblem of the Queen's youth vanished, for her Mutton Hatton died a broken man, his coffers empty and his kidneys rotted away. The Queen stormed and wept, and would suffer no mention of age or Death, so closely did she feel the sweep of His scythe. When Essex's brother was shot in the head in battle, she raged at tempestuous youth for spending itself so hotly; when one bid her look to the succession, she clapped him in close chains for daring to utter treasons.

Essex returned that Winter a conceited, bitter man, his ruined captaincy dimpling no dint in the armour of his vainglory. He and Raleigh grappled and quarrelled greatly, Bess Throgmorton swelled, and Water looked to scape censure with some swift quitting of the court. At length he was sent out against the

Spanish, his fleet slipping beyond reach as his son slipped secretly from Bess' heaving belly.

Ere long the deed was proclaimed, the betrothal an infamous whisper and the Queen a tempest of Royal Wrath. She straightway called her wretched Water home, dragging him from the sanctuary of Panama. He returned shamefaced and humbled; she berated him for a traitor and sent him, his spoiled maid of no honour and their brat to fast rooms in the Tower.

Essex danced in triumph, for the fall of Water was a trumpet of victory to him: all those about the Earl rained hearty congratulations upon him. Kat wept for her pirate, in part for his shame, yet more for his undoing by some other woman's hand, and not her own. Hillyarde and I choked on our friend's disgrace and mourned him bitterly. Though we be not shunned, all knew us for Raleigh's men, and many snide words were said aloud that we might hear them.

Gower, now mended to me, broke more ill tidings. In his loathing of me, and his sniffing and rooting about for the Essex favour, the Guts had made a panelled satire of Raleigh's fall.

I fear that the young Marcus seeks to stir more trouble, Gower told me, his hands wringing. *He has overpainted a portrait piece with Raleigh's face, and behind him shows the Queen, her back turned in pique upon him.*

Where is this thing? I cried. *Surely it is not known beyond the schools?*

Gower shrugged and bent his head. *He has gifted it to Essex*, he sighed. *No doubt he seeks some preferment from it.*

I roared and smacked my fists together. *I will teach that crow better manners*, I snarled. *Where does he hide? Does he yet tremble behind his father's cloak?*

Gower caught my arm. *The elder Marcus is shortly like to die*, he said sternly. *Do not speak ill of him.*

I have no quarrel with the father, I snapped.

Nor will you make one with the son, Gower retorted. *Take care, Rob*, he warned, *and keep your peace, for it is not wise to make enemies of these men.*

Too late, I rejoined. *This is no time for peace.*

Thirty-three

AS THE YEAR WAXED the Plague swelled violently, harsher yet than ever I had seen it. Some parishes within the walls grew more like to slaughterhouses than city streets. All in health kept to their homes or fled to the villages; the court kept apart, flocking from one pastoral palace to the next, the Queen in a delirium of fear lest the harvest reap her.

In August a scurrilous pamphlet of Jesuit lies spread through the city, each word writ upon it a slander against some person of the court. Sir Walter proved the eye of this calumnious target, though the darts of scorn pointed not to his ravishing of Bess Throgmorton, but more fearfully, to his gatherings of liberal thinkers. The paper denounced Water's School of the Night for a ferment of atheism and corruption, crying in popish outrage that Raleigh and his Wizard Lord Percy conjured demons with tobacco and laughed at the divinity of Christ. Hillyarde sent word from court, bidding me assure him I had tended no such meetings, for Essex had stirred up the Council and sought to sniff out atheism and treason amongst Water's friends. Kat grew fearful and jumped at each creak of the boards; she cursed herself for bidding me be friendly to Raleigh, who, though sweet of looks, had proved dangerous indeed. Yet the bold pirate was soon loosed, sent South by the Queen to restore order amongst his sailors. His men had fallen to looting their prize, a great Spanish Carrack moored in at Dartmouth, and only Water could halt them from carrying off its gems. I reasoned to Kat that this showed much favour from the Queen; yet Raleigh, though he be useful to her, remained banished from the court, and his bride was yet kept in the Tower.

The elder Marcus truly proved not long for this World, his firm grip upon the son thinning to the vain clutching of boxed air. The Guts scented liberty and, like the weasel from the hole, darted forth and fell to snapping. He oiled and curled his whiskers, preening himself for the prime place of painting fashion; in pursuit of the court he made to Windsor, flattering and wheedling with his brushes. Through Essex he won the favour of Sir Henry Lee, retired Champion of the Queen. That aged knight had naught but a mistress to spend his money on, and he threw his coin amongst painters much that year.

Lee had spent long years in diverting and entertaining his Sovereign Lady. He had planned each Progress, plotted each pageant and devised distraction for each Holy Day and courtly celebration. Retired from his post, he had little to amuse him but the ordering of his country seat and the preening of his gardens. He longed to become the pivot of court again, and thus planned to receive the Queen on her lengthy Progress, designing much lavish folly for her visit.

Lee had a fancy for things allegorical, and contrived a great pageant for the Queen's arrival. His royal visitor was to enter by passing through a magical forest; there she would find Lee himself asleep, wrapt in a spellbound slumber, and with her Sovereign touch wake him from the bonds of enchantment. Lee styled himself custodian of the Fairy Queen's pictures, a gallery of flattering panels through which the Queen would pass: thus he threw out commissions to many, for he would have a great tunnel of paint to receive her. Though the Guts and his flock had taken some part of the work, Gower was yet heralded chief painter of the court, and was charged to produce some panels. He bid me assist in the composing of the works, for though he had the tracings of the Queen to place within them, he had little mind to wreathe fey parables about her.

Lee chose the themes that we must treat: Gower winced at the painting of them. Elizabeth must be shown as a Vestal Virgin; Elizabeth must be crowned as the Goddess Diana. Elizabeth, though fast approaching her three-score years, was truly a Spring nymph; she was Flora, she was Cynthia, she was all things youthful and fair. Thus we traced the Queen's mask from Gower's Armada piece and wreathed her in flowers, showered her with moonbeams and dressed her in gauzy veils. We littered her gowns with roses and eglantine; we set her in bowers of green and draped foolish mottoes about her. When we had her complete, we wrapped the dried panels in cloth and stowed them in a cart. Glad to quit the contagion of the city, Gower and I took horse and escorted the cart to Ditchley, following it by road and river to Oxfordshire.

For fear of buboes, none from London were permitted within two miles of the Progress. Thus we made straight to Ditchley a twelvenight ahead of the Queen, who yet dallied on her way in Oxford city. I had not before seen the round hills and fair villages of that country, once the cradle of my lost friends Petty and the golden Benson; I had a longing to see the famed centre of scholarship, and to walk among some ancient stones we passed. Yet we may not tarry, for Gower would have us set up the panels in the primest place; he also had a mind to stay at Ditchley 'til the court arrived, for after such time we would prove past fear of contagion. *I have not been at leisure to follow thus far*, he reasoned. *I will not quit ere the Queen comes and views the work, for others will certain be in attendance to take their praises*.

Ditchley was a fair place, neatly ordered in design and richly set amongst fields and parkland. Lee had set a horde of servants to work in preparation; we were led from maid to groom and on again 'til we found one who might assist us. The gardens were aswarm with groundsmen; trees and bushes were clipped and shaped, trellises wreathed with vines, and bowers woven from flowers made of silk. The paths were swept and strewn with chalk, the meadows transformed to a city of 'broidered tents. The weather held fair for the season, though Autumn's approach could be seen in the golding and falling of some leaves. Lee would have Spring in October, setting false branches of May in great arches and scattering crafted violets about the pathways. The house itself was hung with swags of green, the false forest planted as an avenue to the entrance. I gaped at all like a gull at a country fair, Gower tugging at me and bidding me keep my jaw from dragging.

We passed through much inquisition ere we might enter the house, seeking one to direct us on where to place the panels. A troupe of actors clustered in the hallway, reciting to the air and quarrelling over speeches; we pressed through them and I saw one I knew from watching at Kat's arras. He nodded to me and I bowed, yet I had no wish to parley with the theatre men. Gower beckoned a page and asked that we be taken to Lee; the page shrugged and claimed that his master was busy and would see none. Thus we searched and wrangled with servants, 'til at length an usher appeared and steered us to a parlour. He waved at a panelled door beyond and bid us place our pieces there.

Fetch stableboys to help you move the works, he said, *the men are all put to task in the gardens.*

Surely the panels will not be closed up in a room? Gower piped. *They were made to be viewed on the Queen's arrival.*

The usher rolled his eyes. *You painters*, he sighed, *no thought for machinations. The pictures will be hung on the trees, 'til then they stay in here out of the way.*

Panels on trees? I exclaimed. *And what if it rains?*

The usher raised a brow. *It will not rain*, he crabbed. *Rain has not been arranged.*

For want of a better-reasoned plan we did as we were bid, pressing small coin amongst the stablelads and unloading the cart of panels. The boys knocked the corners of the frames and walked into walls, yet, once unwrapped, the pieces proved unhurt. We draped them in clean cloths to keep off the dust and leaned them to the wall. Gower tucked the cloth about and straightened stiffly.

I see there are many pieces here before us, he said, waving to the corners. *Shall we view them? There may be fine works hid here.*

I nodded assent and we commenced unwrapping the rival panels. Some half-dozen pieces of small scale were bound together, each depicting a beast or bird of strange design. Gower shrugged and replaced them, pulling forth a larger piece. This proved to be a poor picture of Lee himself, clad in green costume and clutching a rope of keys.

We have naught to fear from this one, I said. *Those legs are like to a cockerel's.*

Gower snorted and wrapped the panel up again. We searched

through several more and found none of merit, for each served as naught but decoration, with mottoes and whimsies pieced together from flowers and dancing elf folk. A set of six pieces showed nymphs and water sprites; yet more were crude allegories of the Seasons and the Graces.

Gower shook his head. *Pitiful pieces of folly*, he sighed. *I had hoped for one thing of merit. Let us go below and enquire of lodgings; I am in need of a rest for my bones after such a journey.*

As we made to leave a pair of grooms staggered in, shouldering a vast draped bundle. They groaned as they bent their knees to set it down: Gower and I sprang to aid them.

I thank you, sirs, one said wheezingly. *'Tis a heavy burden.*

What is within? Gower asked. *It looks to be a panel.*

Aye, grunted the groom, *one of the Queen, so the master said.*

Indeed? Gower sniffed. *One of the Queen?* He barbed a look at me.

I would fain see it, I said pleasantly. *Is it well?*

The second groom shrugged. *Wouldn't know*, he puffed, his face crimson and shining. *Take a look. We've more work to do.*

The grooms nodded and quit the room. Gower pursed his lips. *So*, he said archly, *a panel of the Queen? We will see.*

He commenced unfastening and tugging at the bundle. I stayed his hand and we pushed it to the wall, the better to steady it. The frame was heavy indeed, and high to reach: I sought about and found a box to stand upon, unhooking the wrapping from the high back of the panel. With much heaving and wrenching I loosed the cloth and let it fall forward; Gower seized it and pulled it to the ground.

God's Soul! he murmured. *Well, well, indeed.*

What is it? I cried, ill balanced on my perch.

He shook his head and pulled hard at his beard. *Well, so*, he muttered. *Indeed.*

You say nothing, I grumbled, stepping down from the box.

I turned and, turning, caught my breath. The Queen, bedazzling in jewelled white and pearl, rose imperious before us. Her small black eyes pierced from a waxen face, her hair a pile of gems flanked by great gauzy wings. She trod with tiny slippered feet upon the world, her frame impossibly wrought from silk and lace, her waist but the span of a hand across, the wheel of her farthingale ludicrously fashioned. Behind her head to one side raged a storm; before her the clouds parted with the sun. I commenced choking.

Gower leaned forward and peered at the ground by her feet. *'Tis a map of England*, he marvelled, *and she stands upon Oxfordshire.*

It is a monstrous thing, I whispered.

Read the doggerel, Gower said shakily, pointing to some words writ upon the panel.

I cannot, I breathed, my hand across my mouth. *I fear that I might yet vomit. Behold the face! Where did such a mask come from? For certain it is no tracing of yours.*

I know well who has made it, Gower sighed, his shoulders stooping. *It is the younger Gerts.*

What! I cried. *That dog! How can it be? Surely she has not sat to him, the bastard?*

Nay, Gower mused, tugging again at his beard. *The face is none of mine, but it is like to that of Oliver's. I know also the manner in which the Queen stands thus, with gloves and fan; it is from the pattern of his father.*

Doubtful as Thomas, I prodded at the piece: it was painted upon cloth. *Curse him for a bag of Guts!* I raged, near sobbing. *It's a grotesque!* I sank heavily upon the floor before it, my legs weak and folding as straw. As I gazed, my belly flooded with waterish envy: it was vile, yet it stirred me with the wonder of a holy altarpiece. I knew not whether to weep for pity or kneel in worship: I hated the thing, I loathed its maker, and my pride capsized in a roaring tide of spite.

I am undone, Gower said, querulous. *This is the beginning of my eclipse, my friend.*

Nay, I groaned. *Nay, it cannot be.* I gripped my hands to fists and thumped the boards. *Christ's Soul!* I bawled. *I will not leave this unanswered!*

Gower could not stay me: I rode straightway back to the city. My brain burned with a fury that would not still 'til I deal an answering wound to the bastard Guts. I drove my horse hard and covered great distances at speed, cursing the drawing of nights and the country pathways. When at length I gained the city and quit my horse, I saw none of the horrors wrought by the grip of Plague, my eyes blind to all but the work I had set myself.

I burst upon Kat in her chamber. Though it was scarce dark she already lay abed, sheets and blankets heaped and tucked about her. I called her name and made towards her – she let out a cry and sat up in sudden terror. Her eyes were wide and staring, sunk deep in the sockets, her cheeks drawn as to seem starved. Though she was clothed in bedcap and jacket, yet she shivered violently.

God's Soul, Kat, I cried, *what has befallen you?*

What do you here? she groaned, her teeth aclatter.

I have work to do. I made to stroke her brow but she hissed and pulled away.

Leave me be, she croaked, *I am unwell.*

Christ, Kat, have you the Sweat?

She shook her head. *'Tis but a sore sickness.*

Have you some cure for it? I urged. *Shall I fetch a physician?*

Peace! she sighed wearily. *Have you no eyes? The whole city is dying. A physician is like to bring the Plague.* She shivered and lay back upon the bolster, her cheekbones pointing painfully beneath the skin. *One came for you, Rob, an ill-looking man. He pressed me with questions.* She swallowed dryly and fell to coughing.

What manner of questions?

The manner that leads to the Tower, she choked. *He asked of Raleigh.*

There is no answer to that. I took hold of Kat's hands and pressed them upon the covers: she flinched, her brows furrowing deeply. *Do your hands pain you?*

Press not so upon my belly! she winced. I released her hands and she drew the cloth about her face. *They are watching you, Rob*, she whispered. *They think you one of Raleigh's atheists.*

I laughed and rose, smoothing the covers down again. *You have a fever, Kat*, I said, *you fall to ranting. You will become as a piece of your theatre, all assassins and the sniffing of poisoned flowers.*

She cackled feverishly. *You would know of poisoned flowers!*

You begin already, I said, smiling. *It is a good omen, for the fever will soon pass through you. I will let you rest – I am in some haste to do this work.*

Thirty-four

THE IMAGE OF GUTS' Ditchley idolatry was fixed to my eye,
a piece meetly made for corruption. I set to my panel at once,
refashioning Guts' work with all the mockery and scorn I could
summon for its creator. Where the map of Her Proud Kingdom
had stood I wrought a dunghill, a squalid heap of matter so clearly
writ that the very air of the workshop stank with it. Where the
Queen had stood, so daintily silk-shod, two bare, gnarled claws
of feet trod in the mire, fetid filth rising between the monstrous
toes. Above them rose no farthingale and bodice of white, but
a tattered bundle of blackened rags, bejewelled with blood and
grime. Where the pale mask of the pretended Queen had been
there now glowered forth an ancient Tudor crone, her nose a
great hooked beak, her black teeth agape, her skin thick-spread
with white lead. Where the sun had shone, now hard black rain
fell, muddying the wretched rat's nest of her hair; her wings were
no gauze of lace but the weave of cobweb, stuck with flies. She
wore yet her pearls, though they be threaded alongside severed
papist heads. Her left hand clutched not at gloves but at a sack of
sovereigns; her right held no fan on a girdle-rope of red, but a rein
as of a horse's bridle, the Earl of Essex chomping at the bit.

I worked tirelessly. Within three days I had it all but done,
lacking only a doggerel verse to float upon it. Kat stirred not from
her chamber that long time, and though her fever abated, yet she
seemed greatly afeared of some nameless peril. She would take
no food and scarce drank – yet she fell to long bouts of pitiful
vomiting.

As I neared completion I painted through the night, quitting
at last with the dim fleckings of sunrise. My workshop grew
chill, the fire but a scattering of grey embers. The house shifted
and settled: through the dawn noises I made out the creaking of
boards in Kat's room, and the muffled sounds of sobbing.

I made straightway to Kat's chamber and found the door bolted. I called to her but she would make no answer, save for the whimperings of grief. I fell to the boards and pleaded long through the crack beneath the door, begging her to open. At length I returned to my rooms and made to the arras, drawing back the cloth. My spy-hole had been shuttered, for Kat had closed the hatch and sealed it fast. I pressed my mouth to the stoppered grille.

Do not weep, Kat, I begged. *Do not shut me out.*

The sobbing rose and fell, drawing closer; a wet sniffing sounded on the far side of the grille. Kat's breath was drawn in broken gasps.

I know you to be there, Kat, I said softly, *I can hear you. Why do you grieve so? Will you not tell me?*

Kat sniffed again. *I cannot*, she choked.

Ah! You speak at last, I urged, *now say some more. Why do you shut me out?*

I would not have you see me thus, she moaned.

Open the grille, sweet Kat, I entreated. *I may yet help you. When it is fully light I will fetch a physick.*

Kat laughed, yet sobbingly. *O Rob*, she sighed, *no physick can cure such a surfeit of sorrow.*

Yet you were ever merry, I implored. *Let me cheer you. I have finished the panel I worked upon; it is an answer to the vile piece that Guts made for the Ditchley pageant.* I laughed lowly. *I will call it my Ditchwater. It will divert you, Kat – come out and see it.*

Nay, she whispered. *Leave me be, Rob, go to bed. I will come and look at it when you wake again.*

The day began to brighten as I lay upon my bed, yet breeched and booted and in my painting shirt. I slept fitfully, dreaming ill scenes of Kat's distress. Sleeping, I heard a voice crying curses upon me: I woke with a sudden jolt into broad light, a screeching and crashing sounding in the workshop beyond.

I leapt from the bed and rushed upon the scene. My worktable lay in broken strips upon the floor, the bladders of paint rent and bleeding colour into the boards. Kat stood wailing and sobbing at my easel, her hand working with furious flashes upon the panel. I ran to her and wrenched back her fist – she clutched a blade, and with it she had scored deep gashes upon the piece.

What do you! I screamed, wresting the knife from her and waving it in her face. *What madness is this?*

Treason! she shrieked. *Treason! You will hang!*

I stared at her in horror – she seemed maddened, her eyes rolling wildly. Her shift was soiled and besmirched with streaks of crimson and blue, her skin yellowed and damply glazed with fever. *Kat!* I cried. *What has become of you? You are as one possessed!*

She glowered at me as a beast in a trap. *Do you wish to follow Raleigh, fool?* she spat. *They will not give you such apartments in the Tower!*

It is but a satire, I bawled, *and you have ruined it!*

It will ruin you if I do not! she cried.

Fie, Kat! I shouted. *Enough! You are grown crazed. You must take physick or you will find yourself within a Bedlam cell.*

Bedlam! she cried, laughing shrilly. *Come, threaten me, painter, use your knife on me!* She hissed, baring her lips over gums raw and strangely blackened. *Finish what you have begun!*

You have lost all reason, I groaned. I looked to my panel, smeared and spoiled with scratches. *You have destroyed it.*

You have destroyed me! Kat wailed, clinging upon my arm. She leered towards me, her hair unravelling in limp threads from her greasened caul. *Look what you have rendered with your poison! Look at me!*

What poison? I cried. *Only your mind is poisoned.*

She threw the easel to the floor and fell gasping upon it. *This is poison!* she wept. *This!*

You rave, I sighed, sinking to the floor beside her.

Kat stretched across the boards and grabbed at a bladder of paint. *Poison,* she cried, waving it at my face. She dropped the bladder and dipped her hands into the crimson pool that seeped from it, smearing reddened fingers across her cheeks.

Sweet Kat! I groaned. *I never thought to see you thus.*

Kat crawled forward and fell into my lap, her crimsoned face rubbing at my hands. *O Rob,* she sobbed, *I have loved you and your paints too well, and now I will die of it.*

I shuddered, for her voice seemed of a sudden clear. *Why do you say so, Kat?* I tipped her face to mine; she was not wild but calm of features again, though daubed with paint, her eyes swollen with sorrow.

It is your paint I sicken of, she cried. *I wanted but you and your brushes, yet I caught a poisonous hunger from your paint.* She breathed rapidly, her chest rising and dipping. *I will die of it, Rob; it was an appetite I fed in secret. When you would not give me the paint freely, I came and took it.*

I shook my head. *Nay*, I urged, *you cannot die of wanting paint.*

I have had too much of it, she wept. *See what it has done!*

She stood tremblingly and, with her eyes fixed upon my face, lifted the fabric of her shift. Her thighs were bereft of flesh and blackened with blisters, between them rose a great red wound; she raised the cloth yet higher, her belly a heap of scars and ulcers.

My gorge rose – my head swam with fear. I cried out and fell upon Kat's feet, whimpering and begging her mercy. She bent above me and gently stroked my hair. *O Kat!* I wailed. *Why did you not stop me? Why did you not tell me what I did?*

Dear Rob, she whispered, *I loved you too well to have you stop. I cared not for anything but you and your brushes, though they be poison to me.*

Forman! I yelled, jumping to my feet. *It was his potion, his poison!* I grasped Kat's shoulders. *He knows what is in it, he will know how to unlock it!*

Kat stroked my cheek mournfully. *It is too late, Rob. Do not go to Forman, I beg you. I would have none know of your hand in this.*

Nay, I cried, *I will not hear that!* I snatched up the jerkin that hung upon my chair and wrestled my arms into it. *I will go to him now and bring him hither.* I grasped Kat and pressed a kiss upon her brow. *The Goat will cure you!* I cried and, running, quit the house.

I raced along the Strand to the city wall, thrusting aside one who made to stop me at the gate. The air was thick with the stench of sickness and death, the streets barren save for a woman who ventured weepingly, a red wand of contagion held out before her. I cared for naught but reaching Billingsgate, certain that the Goat could find some remedy for Kat. As I neared the river I heard the bell of the charnel cart tolling close by; I rounded a corner to see it crake towards me, its load of corpses veiled in a cloak of flies. I ran past a row of houses whose every door was crossed and nailed fast, the cries of those yet within more terrible than Judgement.

I came at last to the Stone House and threw myself pounding upon the door.

Forman! I shouted. *Forman, open at once! Mistress Joyce is ailing!*

A casement above creaked open and a woman leaned out, a cloth over her mouth.

Get you gone! she called. *There's none trading here.*

I must see the physician Simon Forman, I called, *it is most urgent!*

The woman's head disappeared: a pot of slops splashed noisome at my feet. She leaned out again and waved a fist. *Now get gone,* she squawked, *don't bring more sickness here!*

I am not sick! I cried. *I but need to speak with the physician Forman.*

He can't help you, she bawled. *He's abed with buboes.*

She slammed the casement: I fell hammering upon the door and tried in vain to force the lock. *Forman!* I screamed. *Forman, you dog! Get up!* None stirred within. *You bastard, Forman!* I wailed. *You murderous poisoning bastard! Plague on you – I will kill you if you live! Get up!*

I rattled and battered, and fell hopelessly against the Stone House door. Where might I go? Who might aid me? I knew of no other physician in the city that would have a key to Kat's wounds. Only one who knew the properties of poison could aid me – or, I grasped, one who knew of paint. I raged and beat my head with fists. Hillyarde was with the Progress, his workshop closed and Alice fled to the country. Gower was yet at Ditchley where I had quit him. I knew no other that understood paint so well as these. Who might listen, I raved, who might aid me, give me some counsel? I staggered from the

Stone House and stared fitfully about me. Who else? Only one I knew of.

I sought him in his tailor shop. Though I had never dared to find him, yet I knew well where he lodged. My blood raged with fear for Kat – yet when I saw the place a shudder of remembered shame crept chill upon my skin.

I made to the boarded shutters, my breath racked and heaving with the labour of running. I steadied myself against the heavy door and hammered hard upon it. The knocking sounded hollow in the street behind me; I knocked again. A sound came of one moving about within.

Who is there? a girlish voice cried. *We make no trade.*

My business is with Master Petty, I called. *I must speak with him.*

We have no contagion, the girl replied, *we wish none to enter.*

I sighed. *I beg you – I have no contagion. Kindly bid Master Petty come to speak with me.*

A shuffling came from behind the door. I waited, my ear pressed anxiously to the wood. Steps thumped towards it.

Who is there? said a man's voice. It was he.

Petty! I cried. *God be thanked! I must speak with you.*

I heard a bitter laugh. *So*, he said, *do you bring me a gift of Plague at last? You wished it upon me.*

Petty, I implored, *I beg you open. I am not sick. I was foolish – I was crazed with pride. I never truly wished you ill.*

I have naught to say to you, he intoned. *Leave my door.*

Take pity, I beg you, I urged. *Let me speak. I must make confession to you.*

He laughed again. *I was a papist dog, now you bid me act reverend priest? I am but a man of cloth. Go find a church.*

Petty, I pleaded, *Kat is dying. There is none I may tell the truth of it to but you.*

I heard the drawing of his breath, then the rattling of the lock. He opened a crack: I near fell upon him in relief.

Petty, Petty, dear friend! I cried, reaching for him.

He drew back as if scorched. *I am no friend to you*, he said flatly. He opened wider and stood before me. His face was much aged, the lines about his mouth deep and scourging. He looked me over slowly, his eyes lifting to mine as if he had prophesied that, one day, he would be bound to stand just so, and behold me grovelling.

Kat is dying, I said again. *May I not step within?*

He shook his head. *This is well enough. She has Plague then? You carry it.*

Nay, I said. I grasped his hand, though he tried to wrench it from me. *Petty, I have poisoned her.*

Let go your hold on me, or I will cry for help.

You will not, I countered, *for none will come. The streets are empty.*

I will rouse the watch and shout that you mean to rob me.

Christ! I cried. *Listen to me – there is none here! The city is a heap of bones.* I loosed his hand and he pulled back savagely. *Hear me, Petty – I have poisoned her!*

I always knew you to be dangerous, he said. *I had no mind that you would turn murderer. It must profit you somehow, as your spying did.*

God's Soul, I wailed, *you are a stubborn man! I was never a spy, nor did I threaten you. I have not poisoned Kat by design but by misfortune, for she has taken in too much of my paint.*

Paint? he baulked. *You painted on her?*

Aye, I said, *as I know you had likewise done. Yet this is no natural pigment, but a preparation of alchemistry; she is sore wounded from it, and I know not how to mend it.*

Petty frowned. *Fool*, he said. *I know nothing of these matters. You need a physick.*

I can find none, and he who made the paint is abed with Plague.

What would you have me do? he hissed. *I cannot aid you.*

You are the only man I might trust, I insisted. *Kat will not speak of what ails her, nor will she seek physick. If she die, I will certain hang for it.*

And so! he said, his eyes hard. *I care not what you do, save that you keep from me.*

I beg you, I implored, *I will do all I can to save her – yet if I fail you are the one man who knows how well I loved her, that I meant her no harm.*

I know nothing of your love for Kat, Petty said sourly. *I cannot help you. I do not know you.*

My shoulders weakened and I held a trembling hand to him. *God's Soul,* I said despondently. *You know not how greatly I have missed you, my friend.*

Humility sits ill upon you, he rejoined. He held the door and closed it slowly upon me, his mouth pressed to the crack. *Go back to her, Rob,* he said, *come not here again.* The door closed fast and he drew the bolt behind it.

Petty, I groaned. *Petty, I beg you, say something more!*

Very well, he mumbled. *Go away.*

I staggered back through the city, my thoughts muddied, all reason or purpose crushed. I scarce knew what I did or where I walked, yet I found myself approaching the Strand again, my feet dragging. A beam of clarity broke upon me then: I would take Kat to Whitehall and throw myself upon the mercy of the palace. Though the court be on Progress elsewhere, I reasoned, yet still there would be some who would seek officers of law to aid me. I would take Kat, yet living, and make confession of all; thus one might be found amongst the remaining court physicians that could treat her sores. I would be in the Counter or Clink for certain, yet what mattered that? If I confessed and she died, I might yet hang for it – but what hope was there if I did not? What mattered that, if Kat's life may yet be spared? I laughed aloud and rapped my brows for their folly. I could yet save her! I broke into a gallop and made straightway to the house.

Too late, too late: *semper absens.* I had left Kat distraught and, ever the strongest of purpose, she had sought her own remedy. A dull whirling of smoke and ash coiled above the fine Strand rooftops: a faint screaming sounded, and the clattering of bells. As I rounded St Mary's church I saw the flames, not the bright licking of a hearth fire or of blazing crops, but the yellowish glow as of a lamp, the wick dampened. My running slowed, for I could govern neither legs nor feet. I reached the house just as the roof collapsed, splintering in shards of ember and sparking alight the roof beside it.

Those to either side threw their possessions into the street: I knew this, yet I saw none of it. Nor did I see those who hastened to throw water upon the pyre, though certain many did. I stood insensible, rooted and dumb. I felt naught, I said naught, my eye fixed upon the shattered casement of Kat's chamber and the blackened shape that – I well knew – lay heaped and charred within it. At length the rooms of my workshop fed the flames: only then did the heart of the fire burst forth, bright and greedy.

Epilogue

SO PERISHED MY MUSE, my shame – and all my glories with them. What greater sorrow than the greyness of ash after the bitter brilliance of fire? All of worth was lost to me, for Hope too had been razed and ruined. I fled the city, not for fear of reprisal, but as one disgraced welcomes the muffled cloak of obscurity.

There have been worse fires; there will be worse to come. I have heard tell of a man who sought to overthrow Crown and Parliament with fire. His heart was cut out and burned on the coals before him; his eyes saw the embers ere they clouded and set staring. He saw what man was never wrought to see – his own heart roasting.

Though I mourned Kat deeply, Thetford wrapped green folds of comfort about me, and at length I found some solace in the long black manes of my father's mares. Stock and stone are passed to my keeping now, though I be ill placed to tend them – my mother proved in the right, for few fit helpmates may be found here for small coin. I may keep no such grand manner as I once did in the city, nor look for so sweet a companion to abide with.

Heads roll and dynasties fall. Even thus placed I heard tell of courtly doings: the meet fall of Essex, the passing of the Queen. The new King is squat and ugly, they say, and thus sees no beauty in the truth of things. He despises his likeness. The players prosper, for now all is costume and pose. Gower faded as he feared; Hillyarde stepped aside. I hear word of the heroes of these ruined times and curse that shrew, Fame. Oliver grows rich, de Critz a Serjeant Painter, Guts a fine gentleman.

No candle or lantern can bring back the brightness to my eyes; daily, and with cruel measuring, the shadows deepen. The circle of my vision narrows to a point: ere long my orbs' eclipse will be full. Pale malicious discs spread across my pupils, growing and widening, floating before my sight 'til all becomes misted and foggy. The Norfolk air is cold and sharp, a sweet sting upon these jellied spheres, slowly weathering as marble.

Eyes that see what is hid are fruit to be plucked out. Unhappy eyes! You have seen too much.

Lines grow feathered and flattened, edges soft; the colours of this World blur and swim, the palette washing light and weak. Skin stretches thinly, for Man is frail and fragile, and the city he builds about him likewise. Such is the fashioned likeness of the age. I give thanks that I am not there to see it.

P.S.

Ideas,
interviews
& features ...

About the author

About the book

Read on

The One Brilliant Hand

Hephzibah Anderson talks to
Sonia Overall

What inspired you?
I wanted to write a story of an artist who was
actually better than the person who was
supposed to be teaching him, so I started with
the character of Rob. I didn't know when best
to set this, but then I visited Penshurst Place,
a big house in West Kent with an amazing
array of Elizabethan works. A lot were by
anonymous artists, and every now and then
you'd spot the one brilliant hand. I realized
that this could be it and started researching.

Did you enjoy the research?
Yes, and I fell madly in love with Walter
Raleigh. He's the perfect man, really. He's
bold, a poet, a philosopher – an absolute rake.
I also became quite obsessed with the
Elizabethan underworld and learnt amazing
things about streetwalkers and the language
of the underworld. I spent a couple of
excellent days walking around London,
scribbling all over maps and trying to glimpse
the old city.

Do you have an art history background?
No, but my husband is a painter and gave me
a crash course.

**And you weren't tempted to pick up a brush
yourself?**
I did push some paint around just to feel what
it would be like but I was absolutely hopeless.
It was great fun experimenting with colour,
though. I've also sat for my husband and had

the experience of being a life model, which was interesting when I came to write Kat's part.

Did you note any similarity between prose and paint portraits?
When I'm depicting a character in words I tend to start with the details and work outwards, whereas when you're painting a portrait you get the outline and the surroundings in place first. But with both, you have to find something in a character that's unique to make him or her real.

You write very lushly about surface details.
What we surround ourselves with says much about us, so I think it's important to look at how people set themselves in the world. I'm more interested in the way someone plays with their glasses or their coffee cup when they're talking than in what they're actually saying. Body language and the way we present ourselves can say so much more.

Can you talk a bit about how you went about creating Rob?
I wanted him to be somebody you didn't particularly like but who you were curious to see succeed, or to get through it at least. If he'd been more likeable, it would have been hard for him to have done so badly. He had to have the prowess but not necessarily the personality to go with it. I think he'd have been very frustrated in today's art scene. ▶

**Do you have any
writing rituals or
superstitions?**
Not really – just the coffee.
On good days it sits next
to me and goes cold.

**Which living writer do
you most admire?**
Milan Kundera –
philosophical, political,
but never preachy. His
humour is deliciously dry.
Sadly, I have read
everything of his available
in translation.

**What or who inspires
you?**
Reading, walking,
overheard snippets of
conversation, places,
people, history, chance
discoveries . . .

**What's your guilty
reading pleasure?**
Favourite trashy read? I've
got a cheap copy of Jane
Austen's complete works
that I frequently re-read in
the bath. Austen is my
comfort read – but there's
nothing trashy about
her. ■

◀ **Did he do anything that surprised you?**
He never slept with Kat! I thought: will he,
won't he? And then at one point, oh maybe
they should just consummate this. But that
would have been too easy. It would have
spoilt everything.

And what about his ambition?
Rob is ambition gone awry. He has no
balance, nothing to keep him in check and,
without that, ambition corrupts. I'm sure
there were plenty of people who were in
Court for all the right reasons, but anyone
who goes into power ends up in a faction of
some sort and it's a slippery slope wherever
you are, whenever you are. We only have to
look at Blair and Brown – I mean, they're
Elizabeth and Essex if ever they were.

**When did you first realize you wanted to
become a writer?**
I was always an avid reader as a child and I
wanted to be a literary critic until I went to
university. It was there that it first occurred to
me that I could just write literature instead.

**This is your first published novel. Have you
a drawer full of half-finished others?**
I have a drawer full of bad poetry and some
stories that didn't really go anywhere, plus a
couple of short novella-type things. I did a
creative writing course as part of my
undergraduate degree that included a
dissertation in fiction – absolute rubbish
when I look back over it, but fun at the time
and all useful experimentation.

Have you found your voice writing historical fiction?
I don't think I'm an historical novelist, it's more a case of having found a story and having to set it in that time. But it's interesting that I say this because my second book, which I've just finished, is also set in the past – in the 1830s. I had to completely change my style after writing *A Likeness*. It had got to the point where I'd pick up the phone and automatically say something quite florid. I'd started sounding like my characters, and it just wasn't suitable for the nineteenth century, let alone the twenty-first. The book I'm writing at the moment is contemporary, although it is connected to the past.

Who are your favourite writers?
Milan Kundera, Graham Greene, Hemingway in his earlier years. The writers I love are all quite sparse and dry, their novels short and bittersweet, which isn't really the way I write. Maybe one day.

Had you read much historical fiction before you wrote *A Likeness*?
No, I was a real snob about it. I like Peter Ackroyd because he has such a light touch. And Beryl Bainbridge is someone who gets away with writing historical fiction without anyone noticing because she's so good. While I was researching I read as much historical fiction as I could and so much of it is simply history lessons with a parade of costumes. ▶

> ❝ I don't think I'm an historical novelist, it's more a case of having found a story and having to set it in that time. ❞

5

BORN

Ely, Cambridgeshire, 1973

EDUCATED

Ely Community College; Cambridge Regional College and Anglia HEC; University of Kent at Canterbury (BA and MA).

CAREER

Served time behind the counter as a bookseller, then as a reviewer. Took a part-time job as an admin assistant in a local art college while writing *A Likeness*, to pay the rent and get close to the daily mess of oil paint and artists' gossip. Secret life as a puppeteer's assistant (see below).

FAMILY

Father and brother are musicians, mother an artist. Married to a painter, art lecturer and puppet-maker.

6

The One Brilliant Hand *(continued)*

◄ **Why do you suppose historical fiction is so popular today?**
I think it's partly because the world we live in now is so transparent. We know everything there is to know about the present, whereas if you read something that's set in the past it's immediately escapist because everything has a different texture – there are different ways of speaking, behaving, dressing, eating. Everything is familiar and yet it's removed. Also, I certainly come from a generation where we didn't get taught the juicy stuff in history. We learnt who invented the spinning jenny when what we really wanted to know was who was sleeping with whom, who killed whom . . . Social history has its place, but we're rediscovering how much fun the other stuff is, and historical fiction plays to that lost knowledge. ■

Painting in Elizabeth's England

by Sonia Overall

ART AND THE REFORMATION
The iconoclasm of Henry VIII has a lot to answer for. Not only did it destroy pivotal centres of learning and the arts through the dissolution of the monasteries and ransacking of churches and cathedrals, it also transformed the lives of fine artists and the course of their work in England.

In Catholic countries, painters could still seek out a range of rich patrons from Court and Church. In Protestant England, the only source of income was the Court itself. No more lavish commissions for altarpieces or sacred paintings: the God of England liked a plain church. It was the King of England who wanted to be glorified in paint. We can instantly summon up an image of Henry VIII because he loved to be painted, and he ensured that his image was everywhere: imposing, daunting and, above all, memorable.

With the waning of sacred art came a new secular trend: portraiture. Artists transposed their treatment of divine figures to human ones. In place of Christ in his heavenly majesty, they depicted the King in his very worldly one. Instead of popes and bishops they painted earls and lords. And so it continued, save for the blip of Catholic Mary, to the reign of Elizabeth I.

PAINTING ELIZABETH'S IMAGE
Elizabeth's image was a vital part of her public persona. At the beginning of her ▶

Painting in Elizabeth's England *(continued)*

◀ reign much emphasis was put upon her youth and beauty. Her looks were integral to her popularity – she was spring, rebirth, a hopeful, peace-bringing maiden. This optimism was a refreshing breath of air after the horrors of Reformation and anti-Reformation, of a sickly boy king and a barren Catholic queen. The Protestant cult of Elizabeth, Virgin Queen, quickly replaced the Catholic worship of Mary, Virgin Mother.

Elizabeth was an evident mix of her parents. She had the dark eyes and slight frame of Anne Boleyn, and the fiery red hair and steady gaze of Henry. Much was made of her Tudor ancestry, and early portraits drew deliberate attention to similarities with her father. But as she aged, and her chances of marriage and childbearing dwindled, so her popularity waned. What good was a single woman on the throne? People feared that her reign would end without an heir, and that turmoil would follow. England could not stomach another War of the Roses.

Age and barrenness were symptoms of Elizabeth's decline, and she wrestled with them tirelessly. Her desperation is evident from accounts of her wardrobe – she offset sallow features with increasingly extravagant attire, and plastered the cracks of her face with leaden cosmetics. She cultivated her image of the eternal maiden through elaborate pageantry (such as that given by Sir Henry Lee at Ditchley) and everyday courtly etiquette (surrounding herself with beautiful young 'suitors', like Raleigh and Essex).

In her portraits, Elizabeth maintained the smooth mask of youth. She posed as Flora, goddess of spring, as a nymph, as a peer of the Three Graces. She surrounded herself with emblems of pious modesty. She played up to her early reputation as a great beauty, and insisted that her court did likewise. And to placate the masses, she made certain that every image of her, every public print, painting, miniature and design, showed her to her best advantage. Elizabeth managed this by keeping a steely grip on the production of her likeness, to the great detriment of painters and limners alike. Only a limited number of artists – including George Gower and the miniaturists Hilliard and Oliver – were permitted to reproduce her image. By the end of her reign, the Queen's portrait was no more than a cut-and-paste collage of head, hands, clothes and symbols. She had become an icon. Like her father, she had used the art of painting to great political advantage.

SWIFT AND HIS STUDIO

Because the Queen set the trend, courtly Elizabethan portraiture was not concerned with realism. A likeness was admired if it showed the sitter in a good light. If the face was handsome, realism was called for – if not, it was better to improve upon nature with paint. The portrait was a record for posterity, a statement of wealth and power as much as a depiction of character. It was emblematic. Little wonder that artists were expected to turn their hands to all manner of work, including shield painting and furniture design. Unlike the goldsmiths who practised the delicate art of limning, fine artists 'in ▶

TEN FAVOURITE
**ELIZABETHAN
AND TUDOR
BOOKS** *(continued)*

**ART HISTORY AND
ICONOGRAPHY**

The Cult of Elizabeth – Sir Roy Strong (courtly images and Elizabethan propaganda)

Hilliard & Oliver – Mary Edmund (lives and works of the great miniaturists)

◄ large' were no better than painters and decorators, as their guild status indicated.

We know very little about how the English portrait schools worked, but they were almost certainly modelled on those of the Italian Renaissance. A Master – such as the fictional Swift – would receive commissions, which would then be painted by a number of his apprentices. He would then add the finishing 'master strokes'. Portraits attributed to the anonymous 'English School' are often patchworks of several hands – the head by one artist, the clothes by another, the background by a third. Sometimes the hands seem to be painted by two different people. The result is a cacophony of styles, with the occasional note of excellence ringing through the mediocre jumble. It is hard to imagine how some of these works could be prized by their owners; yet, if what mattered to the sitters was not the quality of the likeness but the mere possession of it, we can begin to grasp how Swift and his like might have got away with it.

MASTERS GUTS AND DE CRITZ
Capturing a true likeness, warts and all, was the province of 'Netherlandish' painting. Honesty would have found no place in Elizabeth's court. Yet the candour of Dutch portraiture did find an outlet in the sixteenth-century nouveau riche. Less influenced by courtly ways, the new wave of wealthy merchants and tradesmen provided a much needed source of patronage for painters. And as patronage was thin, squabbles ensued.

6 Elizabeth's image was a vital part of her public persona. Her looks were integral to her popularity – she was spring, rebirth, a hopeful, peace-bringing maiden. 9

The merchant class and lesser nobility were the bread-and-butter employers of English portrait studios. As the taste for Dutch candour developed, so native painters became increasingly resentful of foreign artists. Calls were made to oust foreign painting schools, and violence, particularly amongst apprentices, was not uncommon.

Towards the end of Elizabeth's reign, all eyes turned to her successor. Political factions developed, with characters such as the Earl of Essex at the helm. A new style of leadership was looked for, and a new style of painting wanted to reflect it. It was in this atmosphere that painters such as Marcus Gheeraerts II and John De Critz came to the notice of the courts. The iconic painting of Elizabeth's heyday was replaced by the foreign frankness of a new, cosmopolitan generation. By the time James I got to the throne, the age of the polite English likeness was over. ∎

❛ She made certain that every image of her showed her to her best advantage. Elizabeth managed this by keeping a steely grip on the production of her likeness. ❜

A Note on the Artists

by Sonia Overall
Historical artists that appear in
A Likeness:

George Gower (1540–1596), Sergeant Painter to Elizabeth I. A hugely fashionable portrait painter in the 1570s and 1580s. His work typifies the Elizabethan icon. Renowned for exquisite treatment of jewellery and court dress. Famous paintings include *Armada Portrait* of Elizabeth I, *Elizabeth Knollys Lady Layton* and a pair of early portraits of Sir Thomas and Lady Margaret Kytson.

Nicholas Hilliard (1547–1619), limner, painter and goldsmith to Elizabeth I. Trained under royal goldsmith Robert Brandon and married Brandon's daughter, Alice. Ran flourishing studio of apprentices. Son Lawrence also a limner. Famous works include numerous portraits, medals, coins and miniatures of Elizabeth I, *Young Man Against Flames* and *Young Man Amongst Roses* (possibly a portrait of Essex).

Isaac Oliver (*c.*1556–1617), limner and painter. Born in France, trained in London under Nicholas Hilliard. Married Marcus Gheeraerts II's sister. Work typifies the late Elizabethan and Jacobean portrait miniature – melancholic and dark. Strongly influenced by Flemish painting. Son Peter also a limner. Famous works include miniatures of James I's court, a canvas of *Henry, Prince of Wales* on horseback (attributed) and a striking *Self-portrait c.*1595.

❛ Courtly Elizabethan portraiture was not concerned with realism. A likeness was admired if it showed the sitter in a good light. ❜

Rowland Lockey (*c*.1565–1616), limner and painter. Apprenticed to Nicholas Hilliard and worked alongside Isaac Oliver. Trained his brother Nicholas in limning. Many works attributed to Hilliard's workshop could be Lockey's. Famous reworking of Holbein's lost painting *The Family of Sir Thomas More*.

Marcus Gheeraerts the Elder (*c*.1520–91), painter. Born in Netherlands, escaped religious oppression of Protestants with son (below), settling in London. Remarried into the De Critz family. Famous *Olive Branch* portrait of Elizabeth I from 1580s, strikingly similar to son's *Ditchley Portrait*.

Marcus Gheeraerts the Younger (*c*.1561–1636), painter, son of above. Trained alongside other Flemish exiles in London. Also married a De Critz. Along with Isaac Oliver, moved popular style of portraiture towards melancholy. Fantastical, dream-style, allegorical portraiture. Famous works include *Ditchley Portrait of Elizabeth I*, *Captain Thomas Lee* and *Barbara Gamage Lady Sidney and her Children*, a family group.

John De Critz (*c*.1551–1642), painter. Part of the Gheeraerts group of Flemish painters in London. Renowned for his remarkably frank likenesses of statesmen. Dark and haunting. Famous works include portraits of his ▶

6 Towards the end of Elizabeth's reign, all eyes turned to her successor. A new style of leadership was looked for, and a new style of painting wanted to reflect it. 9

A Note on the Artists *(continued)*

◀ patron Sir Francis Walsingham, *Robert Cecil* and *James I.*

William Segar (d. 1633), painter. A herald, eventually knighted by James I. Worked in later years of Elizabeth's reign. Heavily stylized, flat portraiture of great detail. Famous works include portrait of *Earl of Essex* (*c.*1590) and the *Ermine Portrait* of Elizabeth (attributed).

ALSO MENTIONED

Hans Holbein (*c.*1497–1543), Court painter to Henry VIII. Worked in England from 1526, living in London. Died there of the plague. A master of realism and a major influence on portraiture and limning. Famous works include portraits of Henry VIII and the ill-fated likeness of *Anne of Cleves*.

Master John (flourished 1540s), anonymous Court painter. Achieved a wonderful balance of character and delicate stylization. Famous work includes portrait of Mary Tudor. ■

If You Loved This,
You Might Like . . .

OTHER HISTORICAL FICTION

Orlando *by Virginia Woolf*
In this romp from Elizabethan England to
the twentieth century, Woolf confronts the
boundaries of genre and generation.

An Instance of the Fingerpost *by Iain Pears*
A seventeenth-century thriller, set in Oxford,
the story revolves around the mysterious
death of Dr Robert Grove, who is presumed
poisoned. Four different characters narrate
their versions of what happened.

The Queen's Fool, The Virgin's Lover and
The Other Boleyn Girl *by Philippa Gregory*
In *The Virgin's Lover*, Gregory tells the story
of Elizabeth I's relationship with her oldest
friend Robert Dudley. The pressure on her to
marry mounts but Robert, the ideal choice, is
already married, so their match seems
impossible. Then, curiously, his wife Amy
dies. In *The Queen's Fool*, Robert Dudley
resurfaces as the employer of Hannah, a
young woman on the run from the
Inquisition who is sent to spy on the Princess
Mary Tudor. Hannah is torn between her
duty to Dudley and the Queen, and her desire
to help Mary. Finally *The Other Boleyn Girl*
tells the story of the rivalry between Mary
and Anne Boleyn. Mary preceded her sister in
Henry's affections but, once Anne displaces
her, she is sidelined. Then she is offered an
escape from Court if she is brave enough to
take it. ▶

If You Loved This, You Might Like . . .
(continued)

OTHER PAINTERLY NOVELS

The Painter *by Will Davenport*
In the seventeenth century a broke
Rembrandt stows away on a ship to England
and in order to pay his passage agrees, in a
deal brokered by another passenger, Andrew
Marvell, to paint the Captain and his
beautiful wife, Amelia. But the poet
challenges him to a duel between words and
paint: which is better suited to capture
Amelia's beauty?

Girl with a Pearl Earring *by Tracey Chevalier*
Still in the seventeenth century but now it's
Vermeer's turn: a young female servant,
Griet, arrives in the painter's household and
their relationship, and the tension between
them, develops as she moves from domestic
to artistic duties, much to the chagrin of his
wife. Chevalier's tale of the girl in the
Vermeer portrait has now been made into a
film starring Colin Firth and Scarlet
Johansson.

The Passion of Artemisia *by Susan Vreeland*
The story of Artemisia Gentileschi, one of
Italy's most famous women artists, who led
an incredibly dramatic life: her patrons were
the Medicis, Galileo was her friend, she was
tortured by the Inquisition and longed for
acceptance by the artistic establishment. ∎

Find Out More
To see portraiture of the period, including pieces mentioned in the book

VISIT

The National Portrait Gallery
St Martin's Place
London WC2H 0HE
Search the collections online at
www.npg.org.uk

Tate Britain
Millbank
London SW1P 4RG
Search the collections online at
www.tate.org.uk/britain

**AND VIEW THE PRIVATE
COLLECTIONS AT**

Windsor Castle
Berkshire SL4 1NJ
Visit it online at
www.windsor.gov.uk/attractions/castle.htm

Penshurst Place, Kent – ancestral home of the
Sidneys
Penshurst
Kent TN11 8DG
Visit it online at www.penshurstplace.com

**SEE PORTRAIT MINIATURES BY HILLIARD
AND HIS CONTEMPORARIES AT**

The Victoria & Albert Museum
Cromwell Road
London SW7 2RL
www.vam.ac.uk ▶

17

Find Out More (continued)

◄ or The Fitzwilliam Museum,
Trumpington Street
Cambridge
www.fitzmuseum.cam.ac.uk

**EXPERIENCE ELIZABETHAN THEATRE,
ATTEND A LECTURE OR VISIT THE
EXHIBITION AT**

Shakespeare's Globe
Bankside
London
www.shakespeares-globe.org

or The Royal Shakespeare Company
Stratford-upon-Avon
Warwickshire
www.rsc.org.uk

LISTEN TO

The Triumphs of Oriana compiled by Thomas
Morley (1601). Recorded by 'I Fagiolini' with
David Miller on lute (Chandos Records, CD
0682).

WATCH

Rosencrantz and Guildenstern are Dead by
Tom Stoppard, an ingenious play (1966) and
film (1990) following two Shakespearean
characters who wander in and out of
Hamlet. ■